THEY CARVED
A SAVAGE
AND FULFILLED A
TO EXPAND WESTWARD

OWEN KILLEFER—Barely more than a boy, he set out for the Chickamauga country to avenge a bloody crime. Instead he found a life that both tried and strengthened him, heightening his stature as a man and as a fighter.

EMALINE KILLEFER—Torn from her family in a bloody raid by a redcoat deserter and taken to live among the Chickamauga as the unwilling wife of her kidnapper, sixteen-year-old Emaline would climb from the depths of fear and despair to become a courageous woman.

JOSHUA COLTER—He had made a life amid the perils of America's frontier, but once the Tennessee wilderness had been tamed, a deep restlessness stirred his adventurer's heart.

JOHN SEVIER—A frontiersman and leader of raids against the Indians, he was named governor of a would-be state, one the federal government never recognized. This proud man's struggle for power over disputed territory would divide a fragile young country . . . and bring him arrest on a charge of high treason.

ANDREW JACKSON—A brash young lawyer with a fiery temper, he first met Joshua Colter as an opponent in a brawl; but Joshua soon found a strong ally and loyal friend in a man who would one day govern the United States.

Bantam Books by Cameron Judd
Ask your bookseller for the books you have missed

THE
CANEBRAKE
MEN

A NOVEL OF THE TENNESSEE FRONTIER: 1785–1800

CAMERON JUDD

BANTAM BOOKS
NEW YORK • TORONTO • LONDON • SYDNEY • AUCKLAND

THE CANEBRAKE MEN
A Bantam Book / July 1993

ISBN 0-553-56277-0

Published simultaneously in the United States and Canada

Bantam Books are published by Bantam Books, a division of Bantam Doubleday
Dell Publishing Group, Inc. Its trademark, consisting of the words "Bantam Books"
and the portrayal of a rooster, is Registered in U.S. Patent and Trademark Office
and in other countries. Marca Registrada. Bantam Books, 1540 Broadway, New
York, New York 10036.

PRINTED IN THE UNITED STATES OF AMERICA

OPM   0 9 8 7 6 5 4 3 2 1

For the Housers:
Kirk, Melissa, Seth, and Rebecca

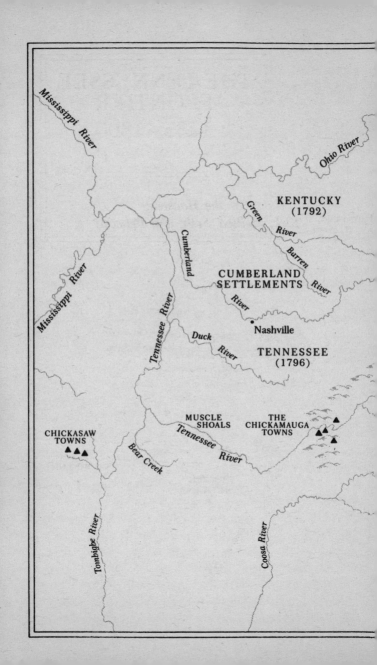

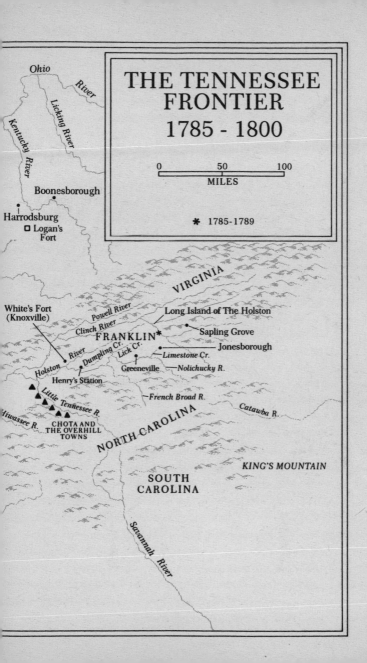

THE TENNESSEE FRONTIER
1785 - 1800

0   50   100
MILES

*   1785-1789

Ohio River

Licking River

Kentucky River

Boonesborough

Harrodsburg
□ Logan's Fort

VIRGINIA

White's Fort (Knoxville)

Powell River

Clinch River

Long Island of The Holston

FRANKLIN *

Sapling Grove

Dumpling Cr.

Lick Cr.

Jonesborough

Holston River

Limestone Cr.

Henry's Station

Greeneville

Nolichucky R.

Little Tennessee R.

French Broad R.

Catawba R.

Hiwassee R.

CHOTA AND THE OVERHILL TOWNS

NORTH CAROLINA

KING'S MOUNTAIN

SOUTH CAROLINA

Savannah River

PROLOGUE

Snow had fallen for hours now, damp and clinging. Sodden flakes descended heavily through branches already sagging under a white burden. Every twig carried a shimmering load, so that even the smallest branches were made stark. Cold crawled across the forest floor, not the clean, piercing chill of the sunny winter days the travelers had enjoyed up until the day before, but a moist, permeating cold that ate into the joints and marrow and made even the young feel old.

At the lead of the party, Aaron Killefer stopped and scanned the forest. He was a thin but strong man, standing six inches taller than five feet, dressed in a buckskin coat, a homespun shirt woven from wool and linen, and a brimless cap of beaver hide. He had made the cap himself; it reflected no standard design and evidenced no particular skill on the part of its maker. As Killefer's brown eyes scanned the white forestland all around, which at this spot was hilly and rough, he lifted first one foot, then the other, and gingerly rubbed each. His moccasins were old, very soaked from the snow, and the dried leaves he had stuffed around his feet for warmth were helping very little. He would have put on other moccasins, but he had none. He was a poor man, owning little worth the having except his family, rifle, and now, by fortune's kind hand and the death of an heirless uncle, a piece of good land and a stout little cabin, as yet unseen by him. Claiming that inheritance, the only he had ever received, was the purpose of this journey in the harsh month of February in the year 1785.

A long morning of striding had left Killefer breathless, so he waited until his lungs ceased straining and his heart slackened its pounding. His family was grateful for the break in travel; all had been wishing for a rest, but were unwilling to ask for it for fear that Aaron Killefer would chide them as weak.

There were five others: Aaron's wife Doanie, a short woman whose eternally somber face reflected the stresses of life with a difficult husband; Nash Winston, Doanie's older brother, who limped from a wound received many years before at the Alamance fight; Emaline Killefer, sixteen-year-old daughter of Aaron and Doanie; Owen Killefer, Emaline's soft-spoken fifteen-year-old brother, whose thin, almost frail look and tendency to silence belied a strong constitution; and Joseph Killefer, aging widower father of Aaron. All were afoot but the latter, who was stiff in the joints from age and rode a horse almost as crippled as he was. The old man's coat was very old and made of buffalo hide. His hat was a tricorn, warped and shiny from handling.

Aaron Killefer reached beneath his coat and pulled out a small bottle, from which he took a swig that he swished about in his mouth before swallowing. Young Owen Killefer smelled a familiar alcoholic scent as he approached his father.

"I saw a man yonder," he said softly.

Killefer looked down at his son, frowning. "What?"

"I saw a man yonder."

"What in thunder are you talking about? What man?"

"Over there." Owen pointed through the swirling white, toward the west. "There was a man. I saw him, just for a moment. He was looking at us."

Killefer squinted. "There ain't nobody there."

"No. He's gone now."

"He was never there. You saw the wind making shapes of the snow, that's all."

Owen said nothing. He hadn't expected his father to believe him. Aaron Killefer was like that. Owen wondered why he had even bothered to speak.

"It's getting colder, Aaron," Doanie said. She was standing close against one of the packhorses for warmth. She shivered violently; her lips were edged in blue.

"We'll move on, then," Aaron replied. "It's not far now. We should find sign of settlement soon. We'll find someone to lodge us for the night."

The group shook off the cold, brushed away the snow that clung to their clothing, and advanced on numbed feet. Owen was the last to move. He stood, looking toward the place he had seen the lone figure.

His father's disbelief stirred no self-doubt; Owen knew what he had seen. The man had been there, watching them, and Owen was sure it was the same lone man he had seen in the forest the previous day. Owen had said nothing of that sighting to the others, figuring the man was merely a passing hunter. He might as well have said nothing today, considering his father's reaction.

Owen's uncle Nash turned. "You coming, Owen, or are

you aiming to claim cabin rights here on the spot?" He laughed; Nash always laughed at his own unclever jests, never seeming to notice that no one else ever did.

"I'm coming," Owen said. Hefting up the old musket his father had given him the year before, he fell in behind. As he traveled he glanced continually at the forest. It was apparent that the man, whoever he was, was following them, and equally apparent that he didn't want to be seen.

They didn't reach the settlements by nightfall. Owen had believed all along that they wouldn't, for he had been mentally estimating their travel distance. This was an instinctive woodsman's skill he possessed. It certainly wasn't inherited; Aaron Killefer completely lacked any good sense of either time or distance, as his erroneous prediction once again had demonstrated.

Owen built the fire, being more skilled than the others at that as well. The heat was delightful, though the gusting wind sent it swirling out in varying directions, so that it was necessary to shift positions constantly to keep warm. At least the snow had stopped. Owen's grandfather, very sensitive to cold, sat so close to the blaze that his face was reddening, but he would not retreat despite Doanie's admonishment to do so. Nash Winston, meanwhile, was having his usual stomach trouble, and made wry faces as he belched and rubbed his belly.

Owen sat with his back to the fire, keeping its light out of his eyes so he could see better into the darkness. Above, the sky was clearing and the moon shining through, so that bit by bit the forest was lightening.

"Still looking for your man in the woods, Owen?"

Aaron Killefer asked. His tone was condescending, but not harsh like before.

Owen said nothing.

Aaron stood and took another swallow from his bottle. His father grunted and said, "Let me have a taste of that."

Killefer reluctantly handed the bottle to the old man. "Don't waste it," he said. "I've got little left."

"By grabs, what I drink may seem wasted to you, but not to me," Joseph Killefer replied with a cackle. He turned up the bottle and let the last of its contents gurgle down his throat.

Owen stood. "He's out there."

"Who?" Emaline asked.

"There's a man out there. He's been following us for two days."

Emaline came to her feet. "It's an Indian! Oh, God!" Emaline had been fearing Indian attack almost since the family had crossed the crest of the mountains.

"I don't think so," Owen replied. "It looked like a white man when I saw him today."

"You saw him? Why didn't you say something?" Doanie Killefer said.

"I told Father," Owen replied, truthfully enough.

Killefer, who had been glaring angrily at his own father as his precious whiskey was usurped, now turned his wrath on Owen, whose comment marked him as negligent. "There's nobody out there—never has been," he said. "You got no bloody call to go stirring up the women, boy!"

Nash Winston stood abruptly. "Aaron ..." He picked up his rifle, staring into the woods. Owen, musket in hand, edged closer to his uncle.

The figure, advancing gradually into the light, gave the

impression of a materializing ghost. He came only close enough to allow himself to be visible. Even Aaron Killefer couldn't deny he was there now. Snatching up his rifle, he lifted it to waist level and backstepped closer to the fire.

"Who you be, friend? You an Indian?"

"No Indian," the man said. Owen noted with surprise that the man's accent was strongly British. "I'm a white man, friendly."

"Why do you come to our camp?"

"I'm cold, and hungry."

Silence followed. Owen edged over to his father and whispered, "Don't let him come. He'll hurt us." Owen couldn't have given a good reason for this conviction. It was entirely intuitive.

Normally Aaron Killefer would have chided his son for daring to advise him. This time, however, he seemed to listen. Swallowing and lifting his rifle to his shoulder, he called back, "How do we know we can trust you?"

The man spoke in a calm, level voice. "In this country, white men help white men. They don't treat them like savages."

Silence followed. Doanie came to her husband's side and whispered, "Maybe we should let him come."

"I don't know . . ."

"If we turn him away, he might plague us from the dark. That would be too much to bear. Better to have him in our sight."

"She's right, Aaron," Nash Winston said. "And maybe he's someone who can help us along in some way."

Aaron Killefer thought it over, lowered the rifle a few inches and called, "Come in, then, and warm yourself. My name is Aaron Killefer, from North Carolina."

"I'm grateful for your kindness, Mr. Killefer," the man

said. He advanced. "My name is Turndale. Thomas Turndale."

Owen Killefer watched as Turndale drew near. He was clad in furs, and wore a hat with the brim clamped down over his ears by a long rag tied under his chin. His face was ruddy and lean, his eyes deep-set. What little could be seen of his hair by firelight looked white, perhaps gray. He had no beard. His visible weapons were a rifle and a fearsomely long knife, the latter tucked into the sash of his coat. As he passed Owen, Turndale looked down at him and smiled, and then his eyes swept around the group until they settled on Emaline, and there they stayed for too many moments.

Doanie, seeing this, deliberately stepped between the man and her daughter. "May I get you some food, Mr. Turndale?"

"Indeed, my good lady. I'll thankfully accept whatever you are kind enough to share."

He smiled; his gaze shifted to Owen again. The boy stared back into his face, and as their gazes locked and held a couple of seconds, Owen felt unaccountable revulsion rising. Who was this Thomas Turndale? And what? Owen wished he had not come to their camp.

Doanie moved from her position to fetch Turndale's meal. As soon as her intervening form was out of the way, Turndale immediately looked toward Emaline again, staring so openly at the nubile girl that she shifted to the far side of the fire and huddled beneath a fur blanket.

As Turndale ate, Aaron Killefer made attempts to stir conversation, but the efforts faltered. Turndale, though smiling and outwardly cordial, clearly had no interest in saying much about himself. Owen's distrust grew.

Tonight, he decided, he would not sleep. Not with this stranger in the camp. He would keep one eye open all night, and not for one moment take it off of Thomas Turndale.

But he did sleep, for he was exhausted. And it was while Owen slept that Thomas Turndale silently rose and drew out his long knife.

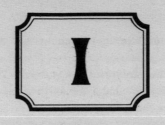

KILLEFER

KILMER

I

It was morning, and snowing again. The frontiersman stood motionless in the gentle precipitation, sniffing the cold air. The scent he had detected was so subtle that even his experienced senses could easily have missed it. He turned his head, sniffed again, and confirmed his suspicion.

His posture was slumped and unstrained, his manner easy. He seemed unaware of the cold. Topping and completely hiding his linen shirt was a rifleman's coat made of deerskin. The shirt was caped and fringed, and bound closed around his narrow middle by a heavy leather belt, upon which hung a scabbard with a knife. From straps slung over his shoulder hung an ornate powder horn and a rifle bag his wife had decorated with beads. His hat was made of heavy felt and sat softly and comfortably on his rather shaggy head. He wore woolen trousers, leggins, and moccasins.

He tied his horse to a branch and checked his rifle's priming before he advanced, following the vague scent. He had been on the lee side of the hill that rose beside him, and when he moved into the wind, the subtle scent became much stronger. There was no questioning it now. The scent was that of blood.

11

He rounded the hill and looked about. A dark object in the snowy clearing ahead caught his eye. Lifting his rifle, he went toward it. Three steps farther he stopped and looked more closely.

It was a corpse. A woman's corpse, half buried in new snow.

The frontiersman lifted his brows, took a deep breath, and went forward. He had lived on the bloody border country for many years, but such things as this still set his nerves on ragged edge.

There, a few yards beyond the woman's body, was another, that of a man. He lay in his blankets beside the smoldering remnant of a fire. It appeared his throat had been slashed while he slept. Looking farther, the frontiersman saw a third corpse. An old man, this one had been. He was halfway out of his blankets, and it appeared he had been fatally stabbed in the chest while trying to rise.

The frontiersman shook his head in disgust and astonishment. It was evident this massacre had occurred hours ago. The odd thing was, it didn't seem to be the work of Indians. No bodies were mangled, no scalps missing. The horses hadn't been taken, and there was no sign that the travelers' packs had been rifled.

The frontiersman took another step, then stopped abruptly, tilting his head. There—he heard it again. A man's voice, moaning as if in great pain . . .

Following the sound, he moved through the forest for about a hundred feet. He scanned the woodlands ahead until he saw a small, makeshift shelter, made of branches and evergreen boughs. He heard another moan.

"Hello!" he called. "Don't be afraid in there—I'm coming in to help you."

He approached the shelter carefully. Whoever was inside might be injured, but he also might be armed. When he was satisfied there was in fact no such danger, the frontiersman crouched at the open end of the shelter.

The man inside was in a bad way, his chest bloodied, his hands mangled as if from turning aside the blade that must have inflicted his injuries. The pitiful fellow moved and groaned again. The frontiersman wasn't sure his presence had even been detected by the wounded wretch.

"My name is Cooper Haverly," the frontiersman said. "I don't know what's happened here, but I'll lend whatever aid I can."

The man coughed and cried out. He groped the air, blinding clawing down some of the protective branches above him.

"Who built this shelter for you, friend?" Cooper asked, not really expecting an answer. "Is there somebody else still about?"

"Don't move, or I'll shoot you dead."

The voice came from behind. It was the voice of a young boy on the fringe of maturity. Even so, there was iron in it.

"I won't move," Cooper said. "And don't you shoot. I'm here to help."

"Who are you? Where did you come from?"

"My name is Haverly. I was hunting and I walked in on all this by accident. Now you tell me who you are."

"I'm Owen Killefer. That's my father in there. His name is Aaron."

"Was it you who built this shelter for him?"

"Yes."

"I want to turn around and see you, Owen. Can I do that without you killing me on the spot?"

A time of silence, then: "Yes. Move slow, and slide that rifle out first."

Cooper complied, then pivoted with some difficulty on the balls of his feet. He was still crouched, and feeling rather foolish to have been surprised by a mere youth.

The boy he saw looked smaller and more frail than he had anticipated. He didn't look nearly as authoritative and strong as his voice had sounded. His face was pale, and he trembled badly, making the end of the muzzle of the musket he held waver in an irregular circle. Cooper swept his gaze up and down the slender form, noting clotting blood on the boy's left leg.

"Boy, what happened here?" Cooper asked.

Owen Killefer gave no answer. The musket drooped downward as if it had suddenly become too heavy for him to hold. The young white face became even whiter, and the boy fell forward in a dead faint, landing atop his own weapon.

Inside the shelter, Aaron Killefer groaned and thrashed again, tearing down more of the branches above him and dumping snow onto his own face.

The weather had broken before daybreak, and the sun rose in a clear sky, warming the air and turning the snow to dripping slush. The road that led two riders to the door of the Pinnock Inn was an expanse of mud that splattered beneath them, clung to their Chickasaw horses from hooves to underbellies and speckled the riders' legs to the knee. Both men rode with long rifles in their left hands.

Joshua Colter and Cooper Haverly dismounted together, while to the inn door came the stoop-shouldered form of Salem Pinnock, clad in elkskin breeches that reached to just below his knees, wool stockings, buckled shoes, and a loose linen shirt beneath a wool waistcoat and very dirty apron. Pinnock swept his big hand across his sheened pate and through what remained of his hair, and nodded greetings to the new arrivals.

"How are they faring, Salem?" Joshua asked as he strode forward. He was a tall man in his mid-thirties, muscular and fine-featured. Dressed, like Cooper, in the simple garb of a frontier hunter, Joshua Colter was graceful of motion and authoritative in bearing. His dark hair was swept back and queued at the crest of his neck, around which hung an ancient coin on a thong—an old Roman coin, a boyhood gift from his departed father-by-blood, the late Indian trader Jack Byrum. Byrum had fathered Cooper Haverly as well, in the physical sense if in no other way. Both Joshua and his brother had been abandoned by their father, adopted and raised by others, accounting for their differing surnames.

Salem Pinnock shook his head. "The boy is hardly hurt at all. The man is a different tale altogether. I fear for his survival."

Pinnock stepped aside to let the pair enter, then followed them to the rough staircase leading to the second floor. The frontiersmen stood their rifles against the wall at the base of the stairs. Pinnock led them up the stairs, opened the door to one of the two upper rooms and waved Joshua and Cooper inside.

Aaron Killefer was on the corn-shuck bed closest to the fireplace. The trundle bed on the far side from the fire had been occupied by Owen Killefer, but at the moment the boy was seated at his father's bedside, his face white and grim of expression.

"Hello, son," Joshua said. "My name is Colter. You must be Owen."

A quick nod. The boy's eyes were wide, making him look scared and small.

Joshua reached down, patted Owen's shoulder and felt the boy tense at his touch. He turned his attention to Aaron Killefer. Apart from the labored movement of his chest and an occasional twitch of his tightly shut eyelids, Killefer gave the impression of a laid-out corpse.

"Any rifle balls in him?" Joshua asked Pinnock.

"No. Knife wounds. Deep ones. Young Owen here was the only one of his party to be shot, and to his good fortune the ball plowed its way clean through and didn't lodge."

Joshua leaned close to Aaron Killefer and studied his face. When he straightened, he nodded. "Owen, your father is in a bad way, but I see life in him. With Mr. Pinnock's care he may live. Mr. Pinnock is a fine bleeder, and a good healer of the wounded as well. Cooper was wise to bring you and your father to him."

"Thank you," the boy murmured. He fidgeted and scooted his three-legged stool a couple of inches closer to his father's bed.

"I'm told this was done by a white man," Joshua said.

"Yes," Owen replied. His voice was so soft, Joshua could hardly hear him. "He told us his name was Thomas Turndale."

Joshua's brows rose and he spun to face Cooper, who stood near the fireplace, hands extended to the blaze. "Turndale! Why didn't you tell me that, Cooper?"

"I didn't know it," Cooper replied. "Owen didn't tell me that before. Turndale . . . is that who I think it is?"

"Aye. Tom Turndale. I'll be jiggered! Mad Tom himself!"

"Who is this Tom Turndale?" Pinnock asked. His deep voice resonated in the little room.

"I can answer that," Cooper said. "A British defector from the war years. Supposedly he was wounded, abandoned his commission, and remained among the Cherokees. It was my understanding he lives near the Overhill towns."

"Not anymore," Joshua replied. "He's been among the Chickamaugas for the last two years or so, somewhere about the Five Lower Towns. I had no idea he had ranged up this far."

"No? Well, I'm not surprised," Cooper said. "I was told by Jim Squire that Mad Tom was seen as far up as the upper Holston not a year ago. They say he's quite a case. Very dangerous and hard to predict. Most think it was that head wound that did it to him. Others declare he was mean long before that, and brags of men he killed in London as a young fellow."

Joshua knelt and looked into Owen's face. "Tom Turndale took your sister—is that right?"

"Yes."

"Did he hurt her?"

"No. I don't think so."

"Did you see which way he went?"

"No."

Joshua stood and rubbed his stubbly beard. "Tom Turndale! I never would have thought it."

"Why would he take the girl?" Pinnock asked.

"If I had to guess, I'd say he's taken her to wife."

"He's said to live with a squaw already," Cooper said. "What need would he have of another female?"

"Who can say? Maybe his woman threw him out. Maybe she died. There's no way to know."

Owen's eyes were beginning to grow red and wet. His voice trembled when he spoke. "Will he kill Emaline?"

Joshua probed his mind desperately for some reassur-

ance to give the boy, and could find none. As unpredict-
able a man as Thomas Turndale indeed might kill the
girl, if he tired of her, or she resisted him. "We'll hope
not, Owen," he said. "I suppose that if he wanted to kill
her, he would have done it at the same time he killed the
others." He put his hand on the boy's knee. "How many
of your people did you lose?"

"My mother, my uncle. And my grandfather."

"I'm mighty sorry. I've lost close kin myself. God bless
you, son, I know how it feels."

Owen turned his face away and wiped his forearm
over his eyes. Not wanting to embarrass him, Joshua
stood and joined Cooper beside the fire.

"Where are the dead ones?" he asked in a low voice.

"Outside, in Salem's stable. Now that the snow has
quit, maybe we can get them buried."

"It'll be a hard job in this cold ground, but it'll have to
be done. Salem, you can see to it, yes?"

"Aye, indeed."

"Did the boy say what brought them here this time of
year?"

"Mr. Killefer yonder is nephew to old Ben Simms. Ben
left his land to him, and they were coming to claim it in
time to get in early spring crops. They're a poor family."

"I'd heard Ben speak of a nephew a time or two,"
Joshua said. "Lord a'mighty, what a sad thing to happen,
especially to a poor man! When a poor man loses his
people, he's lost all the treasure he's likely to ever have."

"Do you really think Killefer will live?" Cooper asked.

"There's a look of strength left in his face. I've not
seen a man die yet with that look still about him. With
Salem's care and providence, I'm hopeful Owen will escape being orphaned."

Pinnock drew up close and thumbed subtly toward

Owen, who was still valiantly trying to avoid crying in front of the men. "Let's go back down and give the boy some privacy," he whispered. "Not all our talk needs hearing by his ears."

In the lower portion of the inn, where Pinnock ran his tavern, selling the product of his partner and distiller Matthew Barton at six pence a half pint, Joshua filled one of Pinnock's churchwarden pipes. Cooper took a flaring twig from the fire and held it out so Joshua could light with it. Rich tobacco smoke rose toward the ceiling, which was merely the underside of the second-level, hand-riven floorboards. They creaked above the men's heads as Owen limped around his father's bed.

"Should we gather the rangers and go after Turndale?" Cooper asked.

Joshua blew out a thick white cloud and thought it over a few seconds. "I think we owe it to the boy to give it a try. But I don't think we'll do much good. Turndale is a canny man."

"How could a madman be canny?"

"Why, sometimes a madman is the canniest kind there is, Cooper. Mad like a fox is mad, you know. Turndale has been too long among the Indians not to know how to cover his tracks. He's been chased before, and no one has ever even caught wind of him."

"Where will he take the girl?" Pinnock asked.

"To the Five Lower Towns or thereabouts, more than likely, if that's still his roost."

"He came a long way just to find a woman, if that's truly his motive," Cooper said.

"He's a far-ranging man, as you yourself said. He'd be clever enough not to steal a female too close to his own range. That would make it too easy to track her down and get her back, you see."

Cooper sighed wearily. "Salem, have you any food to spare? If I'm to be out fetching rangers and chasing madmen, I don't want to do it on an empty belly."

Pinnock fed them cold beef, bread, and boiled beans. They ate quickly, with no talk. When they were filled, they stood.

"I'll go with you, if you think I can help," the innkeeper said.

Joshua Colter smiled his thanks but declined. "You've got enough to do with caring for Killefer. Besides, Salem, you're too fat and slow for what we'll be doing."

Salem Pinnock smiled. Joshua Colter's words were always frank, but never carried any intent of insult. "You're right, as always, my good captain. Now be off with you, and Godspeed. Find that Turndale—and be sure you take a rope with you. I can think of a good use you could make of it with this Mad Tom."

They took their rifles, left the inn, mounted, and rode off down the muddy road. Pinnock watched them until they were out of sight, then closed the door. Gathering a plate of food for Owen, he climbed back up the stairs.

Joshua's skepticism was quickly vindicated. He, Cooper, and seven other capable woodsmen rode the mountains and found no trackable sign of Tom Turndale and Emaline Killefer. The renegade Englishman had covered most of his tracks, and the melting snow did the rest. To attempt tracking him was so futile that Joshua soon ordered the men home.

Returning to the Pinnock Inn, Joshua found Salem Pinnock with quill in hand, writing in the great volume in which he kept an ongoing journal of life and events in the region he typically called the "Land of the Rifle and the Canebrake." Pinnock, after the death of his wife back in his home city of Wilmington, North Carolina, had come with Matthew Barton to the Tennessee country less than a year before, in the summer of 1784. The inn he built between Limestone and Little Limestone creeks was so new that the popular logs comprising the building still put out a strong but pleasant fresh-timber scent. He had purchased the land from Joshua himself.

Joshua stood in some awe of Pinnock, for the man was remarkably knowledgeable, though he had never enjoyed the privilege of formal schooling. All he knew he had taught himself. Pinnock was fluent in Latin and Spanish, spoke some French, had a small but excellent library of classical volumes, and expounded political views heavily influenced by Thomas Paine. Joshua appreciated Pinnock, not only for his self-discipline and learning, but also for the fact the portly tavern keeper didn't feel superior to his generally uneducated Overmountain neighbors. Indeed, Pinnock often expressed sincere admiration of those around him, whom in his journal he had declared a "civilizing army of the self-reliant, bowing the knee to no tyrant and standing unflinching before the dire threat of the savage." That was from one of the few entries Pinnock had allowed Joshua to read; normally he guarded the volume closely, considering it private and too frank in some of its commentary to be viewed by other eyes. Someday, Pinnock told Joshua, the journal would provide the basis for a history of the region that he proposed to write and publish.

Joshua had thought occasionally it was regrettable that his old clergyman friend, Israel Coffman, had migrated off to Kentucky before Pinnock had come here. Coffman and Pinnock would have shared many interests. On the other hand, the two would have also differed on much.

Coffman, though gentle and unabrasive with all, was a staunch and persuasive Presbyterian; under Coffman's influence, Joshua and his late adoptive father, Alphus, had adopted that same confession back in the 1770s. Pinnock, on the other hand, declared himself a "rational Deist," believing in a rather abstract, distant deity that set the world into motion and then left it to run itself, like "an intricate, perpetual clock," as Pinnock explained it.

Pinnock's Deism was a scandal to the region's leading clergyman, the well-educated Reverend Samuel Doak, at whose Salem Church the Abingdon Presbytery had been created the prior year, and who several years before that had established a full-fledged academy on what was still a wild frontier. Joshua and his family had joined the Salem congregation late the prior year, even though distance kept him from attending very often. Doak initially had encouraged Joshua to break off his association with "the infidel Pinnock," to which Joshua had gently replied to Doak that he himself was a good friend of John Sevier and many others who professed no religious affiliations. Besides, Joshua noted, Jesus himself had spent most of his time among sinners.

Doak had seemed impressed with Joshua's arguments, and actually changed his approach to the matter of Salem Pinnock. He began to occasionally visit the inn to argue philosophical and theological issues with Pinnock. Though each struggled valiantly to purify the thinking of the other, Joshua had detected no shift on the part of either, both of whom were about evenly matched in intellect.

"Tell me, Mr. Pinnock," Doak had once challenged the Deist in Joshua's presence, "in this 'clockwork' world of yours, do you hold your opinions because of the free exercise of reason, or because you, as merely one more piece of the clockwork, are compelled by the determination of blind forces to believe whatever you do, whether it be true or false?" To which Pinnock had replied: "I will answer that, my dear reverend, when you tell me whether you believe in your religion because you have freely reasoned your way to a comprehension of its truth, or merely because your sovereign God has predestined you to believe it, whether it possesses good grounds or whether it does not?" So went the typical arguments between Doak and Pinnock, flying like arrows over Joshua's head and drawing blood from each combatant, but without moving either one inch off his prior position. At least it was entertaining, even if unpenetrable to the uneducated inn patrons who were audience to it.

Pinnock put down his quill as Joshua entered the inn. Joshua had come alone, Cooper and the others having already gone home, and there was no one but Pinnock in the lower level of the inn. "Well?" he asked.

Joshua shook his head. "Just as I had thought. No sign left to follow. Mad Tom is long gone, and the girl."

Pinnock exhaled loudly. "Then I'll so inform young Owen."

"How is Aaron Killefer?"

"Looking a mite stronger, I think. I'm more hopeful now than before."

"Go on with your writing; I'll go up and tell Owen," Joshua said. "Since I'm the one who has failed to find his sister, it seems more my duty than yours."

Owen stood when Joshua entered the room, his expression asking his unspoken question. Joshua's own expression must have answered it, because the boy lowered his face and slumped back to his seat.

"Don't be discouraged, Owen," Joshua said. "I didn't expect to succeed, though we were obliged to try. The thing for you to do now is to give your attention to your father. Get him well, and worry only about what you have the power to control. All other worry is wasted."

Owen looked up into Joshua's face, his lip trembling but his eyes fiery despite their sheen of tears. "I'll go get her myself, if I have to. She's my sister."

Joshua smiled. Hearing the boy propose such an impossibility was touching. "You've got the right spirit about you, son. That will do well to get you through this time of trouble. Tell me, has your father stirred much at all?"

"A little. But it hurts him."

"It will hurt him for some time to come. But you watch him for the next several days, and you'll see him getting stronger."

"When he's well, he'll go with me and get Emaline back."

Joshua stepped forward and put his hand on Owen's shoulder. "I like you, Owen. There's strength in you." Joshua turned to go. At the door, which was so low he had to stoop to get through it, he stopped and looked back. "In a day or so, I want to take you to my house. Let you meet my family and share a meal with us. Will you do it?"

"I can't leave my father."

"When he's better, then."

Joshua went out the door and down the stairs. Salem Pinnock was scribing in his journal again, the quill making a steady, pleasant scratch as it applied polkberry ink to paper. Joshua said his farewell, pledged to return within a couple of days to check further on Killefer's progress, then left the inn and began the ride back to his stockaded home on Limestone Creek.

2

As he neared Jonesborough, Owen Killefer noted a marked increase in human and equine traffic, and began to understand what Joshua Colter had meant when he said the day was to be a big one in the little frontier town. In the approximate month since his traumatic journey to the Tennessee country, this was Owen's first trip to Jonesborough. Though the town wasn't much as towns go—a smattering of cabins, taverns, stables, stores, and so on, and one small log courthouse—the crowds entering it today for the most important political event it had yet hosted lent it an exciting atmosphere and made it seem bigger than it was.

"Where will the meeting be, Joshua?" Owen asked.

"Yonder, in the courthouse," Joshua replied, pointing out the two-story building of square-hewn logs.

"Will I be able to see it?"

"No. No room in the courthouse for many. Salem Pinnock will be sitting in, I hear, taking down what happens for that journal of his."

"I wish I could see it."

"It won't be interesting for long to a boy your age, Owen. If I was you, I'd get out and stretch my legs. Look

25

around. Get some fresh air. You've been cooped up too long."

Owen had to agree. It seemed forever since he had done much except sit by his father's bed, feed the man his food, help Salem Pinnock change his dressings and clean his slowly healing wounds, and tote and empty Aaron Killefer's slop bucket. And frequently he had brought his father the liquor he demanded with increasing frequency. Owen had done the tasks without complaining, even without a sense of imposition. Aaron Killefer was his father. It was his duty to tend him when he was hurt.

In the last week, however, Owen had received some welcome respite, thanks to Joshua Colter and his family. Aaron Killefer, though far from fully healed, was sufficiently better to allow Owen some freedom, and the boy had gladly accepted a long-standing invitation from Joshua's wife, Darcy, to visit the Colter home for some meals, rest, and recreation in the form of a little squirrel hunting with Joshua, his son Will, and Cooper Haverly, who lived nearby with his own family.

The time with the Colters was the happiest Owen had known in a long while. Not only was it a reprieve from his recent duties for his wounded father, but also from a life that in general had been somber and worrisome. And it helped quell the grief and loneliness resulting from the murder of his other kin, and the abduction of his sister.

Joshua Colter had come by the Pinnock Inn two days before to check again on Aaron Killefer's progress. Conversation had turned to the coming political gathering—a state-making effort—and when Joshua invited Owen to come along for the day, he had quickly accepted, though only after Matthew Barton said he would take over the job of tending to Aaron in Owen's absence.

The entire Colter family was here; Darcy, with little daughter Hester, rode in the center of the party, alongside Hannah Haverly, whose small son, Ben, rode behind her, his arms around her waist. Will Colter, Joshua's handsome son of about eight years of age, rode behind Owen on the same horse. Zachariah Colter, who had lived with Joshua's family since the death of his mother, Sina, and his stepfather, Alphus, brought up the rear.

The party rode to a nearby cabin on the edge of town, where Joshua greeted the man of the house and turned the horses into the stock pen. Owen watched the smiling man greet Joshua Colter and saw the admiration in his eyes. Owen had already noticed how much Joshua was appreciated by his peers. He felt a flush of pride at being in the man's company.

The streets were filled with people. Owen strode beside Joshua, looking around with great interest. Jonesborough was an entirely log-construction town. Its streets were of dirt rutted by Conestoga wheels and pounded to powder by human and equine traffic. In many places the traffic had to make its way around stumps not yet removed from the streets. Today almost every available place was taken up by horses, carts, wagons, drays. Here and there he saw sledges loaded with fresh-cut logs that would soon comprise new buildings. Jonesborough was a growing little hamlet, a town with its eye on the future and its hopes pinned on the political effort taking a big step forward today.

Owen didn't fully understand all that was going on. Politics were beyond his experience. All he knew was that the easternmost Overmountain settlements, long a part of North Carolina, were in the midst of an effort to form themselves into an independent state, to be named Franklin in honor of the great American statesman, Benjamin Franklin. The event that had such numbers gathering in Jonesborough today was the first session of the elected Franklin assemblymen. This session, which would certainly go on for many days, would deal with such matters as electing a governor, passing basic laws, and creating counties within the proposed Franklin boundaries.

Cooper Haverly was in a bright, unfettered mood. "It'll be 'Chucky Jack as governor before the day's out," he said. "You wait and see, Joshua."

"There's no argument on that point," Joshua replied.

"Who's 'Chucky Jack?" Owen asked.

"Why, John Sevier, of course!" Cooper replied. "There ain't no other like him, without a doubt."

Owen had never heard of Sevier, and wondered what about him could be so grand as to obtain the admiration of one such as Cooper Haverly, who seemed grand himself to Owen. Only one man, in fact, loomed larger in Owen's sight, and that was Joshua Colter.

A great whoop and holler arose from the clump of humanity at the opposite end of the street. Owen looked to see what was causing the excitement. It appeared the crowd was responding to the arrival of a lone rider who was rounding the corner of a log building. Owen's initial impression was of a military man—it was something in the man's stance and bearing that came across even from this distance.

Owen was wondering who the man was when Cooper startled him by letting out a loud, Indian-style yell, meanwhile tearing his wide-brimmed hat from his head and tossing it skyward. " 'Chucky Jack himself, by heaven!" he exulted.

"Calm yourself, Coop. It's not like you've never laid eyes on the man before."

"Huh! You sound purely jealous, Joshua. That man yonder is the future of the new state, and you know it."

Cooper retrieved his hat, which had fallen, unfortunately, into a puddle. He put it back on without sufficiently shaking it out, making water run visibly down the back of his neck. Joshua grinned at Cooper as he trotted around the people just ahead in order to get closer to Sevier.

"John Sevier has got his enemies and he's got his devoted friends, and Cooper Haverly is sure as shooting one of the latter," Joshua said to Owen. "So am I—though I ain't yet felt the need of hollering every time he comes around."

Owen wondered if maybe Joshua really was jealous of John Sevier. He decided not; the way he had spoken had more observation than envy in it.

Sevier's horse was being put away in a nearby stable by several boys obviously eager for the task, and Sevier himself made his way through the crowd into the courthouse. He had a big smile on his rather lean face. Sevier's eyes were blue, his nose straight and chiseled, his hair and skin fair. He struck Owen as tall, like Joshua Colter was, until a quick comparison with others around Sevier revealed him to be of average height. He was a handsome fellow all in all, confident but not haughty in his airs, and Owen hoped that when he was a man, he would be as fine-looking as John Sevier.

"Will he really be governor of the state?" Owen asked Joshua.

"Yes, barring the intervention of God Himself," Joshua replied. "Nothing less could stop it."

"What is so good about him?" Owen asked, but Joshua had no chance to answer. Some friend in the crowd grabbed his shoulder and pulled him aside to talk.

Darcy Colter stooped and spoke into Owen's ear. "Owen, run free if you wish, and have a look around, but keep yourself out of trouble. If you need me, I'll be mostly about the courthouse."

Owen nodded. Glad for freedom on such a bustling, exciting day, and enjoying being in a town after too long away from one, he veered off through the throng, looking for whatever he could find, limping a little on the leg that Tom Turndale had injured. He realized a few moments later that Will Colter had followed him. Owen would as soon have been alone, but he grinned at the younger boy, gestured with a toss of his head for Will to join him, and the youths set off together to explore Jonesborough while the assorted Franklin assemblymen arrived and entered the courthouse.

Owen's excitement lessened as the day passed. The Franklin assembly was well under way now, and the news that came to the meandering crowd from a caller who stood in the door of the courthouse wasn't understandable to Owen. He enjoyed eating the food Darcy Colter and Hannah Haverly had packed along, but after that his spirits began a slow decline.

It happened after he glanced across the street and caught a glimpse of a girl who, from his angle of view, looked exactly like Emaline. For a moment his breath caught in his throat. Could it be? Might Tom Turndale have released her? Then she turned and he saw it wasn't Emaline, and he began to brood.

With the brooding came a sense of guilt. How could he roam idly through this town, seeking his own enjoyment and diversion, while his sister was in the clutches of a man everyone said was insane and dangerous? Owen

felt he was the only hope for rescue Emaline had. Their
father was injured, their kin were dead, and there were
no others who could fairly be asked to intervene, not
with lives and families of their own to be considered.
Who else but him could go after her?

He had no idea of how absurd a notion it was—a
fifteen-year-old boy heading alone into a wilderness he
had never seen, to rescue a sister held by a madman who
lived among the most dangerous of the region's native inhabitants, in a river country about which relatively little
was even yet known, even though several flatboat voy-
ages had been made through it. Despite an affinity for
the wilderness and a natural skill in the woods, Owen
Killefer was by experience more a Carolina farm boy
than anything else. He was still far from being a man,
and what he had in mind would require more than a man
to accomplish.

But grief and immaturity blinded him, and a desperate
feeling of urgency swept him there on the Jonesborough
street. He feared he would cry publicly, so he headed
into a broad alley beside a tavern, sat down, and stared
at the log wall as he attempted to regain his composure.
He remained just objective enough to realize how remarkable it was that the mere sight of a girl resembling
Emaline had stirred him. It let him know just how much
Emaline's kidnapping had wounded him.

A horseman rode to the front of the tavern and dismounted, tethering his mount to a post. Owen lifted his
head and looked at the man. He was a remarkable sight.
Hulking and muscled, he had a large gut that made the
front of his rifleman's coat pooch outward. He wore moccasins and baggy trousers topped with a breechcloth that
hung to his knees, front and back. Owen couldn't figure
out the need for the breechcloth, unless it counted in this

man's mind as adornment. His hat was made of coonskin, with the face intact on the front and the tail hanging down the rear. So much dirt was ground deep into the man's skin that Owen couldn't tell where beard stopped and flesh began. He watched the man step toward the tavern door and out of sight. Then Owen's eye drifted to the horse.

From the corner of a buckskin saddle pouch he saw the butt of a pistol protruding, marked with the initials P.T., and instantly a vivid picture flashed through his mind: him holding that pistol, aiming it at the head of Tom Turndale, and sending a ball hurtling through the hated kidnapper's skull. So vivid was the scene that Owen couldn't have seen its details more clearly had it been played out before him.

He stood, eyes on the protruding pistol butt. He wanted that pistol. Owen's mother had been a superstitious woman, believing strongly in signs and wonders, and had implanted similar ideas in her children. To Owen, the mental image of shooting Tom Turndale therefore naturally seemed an omen that this pistol was the weapon that could end Tom Turndale's life. Breathing rapidly now, glancing about, Owen headed straight for the horse, reached out toward the pistol, felt its cold firmness against his hand . . . then stopped.

What am I doing? he thought. They'll put me in the stocks for this!

He withdrew his hand and turned, just in time to feel a callused, hard palm jam itself flat into his face, pushing him back against the horse, which nickered and stepped to the side. Owen slid to the ground, light exploding inside his head. His nose throbbed and burned from being jammed back against his skull. He let out a grunt and then a shout.

Immediately he was pulled upward. He stared straight into the dirty, bearded face of the big frontiersman who owned the horse. His feet left the ground. The man clenched what teeth he had remaining and said, "What are you doing at my pack, you thieving little sod?"

Owen tried to speak. The man's knuckles squeezed against his throat and he could find no voice.

"I'll teach you to go thieving from an honest man, whore's brood!" At those words, the man lifted Owen straight up, so that his feet swung a yard off the ground, and threw him back. Owen sailed backward through the air, groping as he flew, and landed flat on his back, the breath jolting out of him and leaving him unable even to gasp.

Men had emerged from the tavern. Owen heard several coarse laughs, and, "That's the way to do it, Parnell!" He struggled to get up, but could not move quickly enough. The abusive frontiersman advanced and put his right foot onto Owen's chest, pushing down hard so there was no chance at all for the boy to regain his breath.

"Wonder how long it takes a thieving scoundrel to die from the want of breathing, eh?"

Owen's vision began to go white. He struggled like a bug on a pin, closing his hands around the thick ankle of his tormentor, vainly trying to push the foot away. Panic overwhelmed him. Would this man actually kill him, right here on the streets of Jonesborough in front of dozens of witnesses? Would no one help him?

"Mr. Tulley!" a nervous-sounding voice said. "Mr. Tulley, you must stop this straight away!"

The pressure against Owen's chest lightened, just a little.

"Stay out of this, Alexander Carney," Parnell Tulley said. "This here boy was trying to steal my pistol."

"It doesn't matter, Mr. Tulley. If you keep this up, you might kill him, and there'll be no helping you then."

Tulley was silent a minute, then he cursed, gave one final, painful push of his foot into Owen's chest, and pulled off. Owen struggled to suck in air, but couldn't.

The man who had intervened for him knelt beside him and lifted him to a sitting position. "Relax, young fellow. Let the air come on its own."

Owen felt he might faint. Relaxing was impossible. He tried to force his breath, failed again, and then tried once more. This time he was able to draw in air. After that it was like a great block of ice in his chest melted and broke up. He breathed in great, painful gulps.

"That's good, young fellow. That's good." Then the man stood and faced Parnell Tulley. Even though he was clearly cowed by the big frontiersman, he spoke up boldly, if somewhat shakily. "Mr. Tulley, I've represented you twice now in our court of law and served you well when you couldn't control your temper. I am obliged to tell you, however, that if you persist in this sort of behavior, you'll not find me so ready to take on any future cases you might face."

Another person knelt beside Owen. A soft hand touched his shoulder. At first he thought it was Darcy Colter. When he turned to speak to her, he saw it wasn't Darcy at all, but a young woman, perhaps sixteen years old. Her face was freckled and fair-skinned, her hair a deep auburn, her eyes wide and very brown. Owen was looking at a girl more beautiful than he had ever seen, a girl whose expression was gentle and sympathetic and kind. Owen's eyes widened. Suddenly it was hard to breathe again.

"Oh, poor boy, are you hurt?" Her voice was as smooth as fresh cream, and very soft.

Owen could do nothing but stare at her. He was embarrassed by the sudden realization that his chin was covered with drool that had flowed out as soon as his breath had returned. He turned away from the angelic face and swiped the dampness away, blushing profusely.

The man who had saved him was still trying to reason with Parnell Tulley, who was cursing furiously in response. At length the man gave up trying and came back to Owen. He knelt beside the young lady, and Owen noticed a similarity in their looks.

"My name is Alexander Carney, young man," he said. "I'm an attorney in this county. The man who bothered you is Parnell Tulley. I've had the *pleasure*"—he put ironic emphasis on that word—"of representing him in our county court as the result of other incidents of this nature. As his legal representative I apologize for what has happened here."

Owen could think of nothing to say. His eyes flicked toward the girl's face again—just a glance, for he couldn't hold her gaze. He was very conscious of her hand on his shoulder.

Carney continued, "Are you in town alone?"

Owen said, "No. I came with Joshua Colter." His voice squeaked, embarrassing him.

"Ah! Well, I see Darcy Colter coming right now. We'll turn you over to her. How's that?"

Owen nodded. The girl and Carney stood; Carney held out his hand and helped Owen pull himself to his feet. By now Parnell Tulley was back inside the tavern with his friends.

Darcy reached them. "Owen, what happened here?"

"An unfortunate bit of trouble with Parnell Tulley," Carney said. "I don't think any lasting harm has been done."

"I thought he'd kill this poor boy," the girl said.

"Owen, are you injured?" Darcy asked.

"No."

"What in heavens name did you do to turn Parnell Tulley on you?"

"He can explain all that later," Carney said. "At the moment I suggest going elsewhere, before Mr. Tulley imbibes too much. He might return and cause more trouble if he gets drunk. Young man, your name is Owen?"

"Owen Killefer."

"Killefer! I see—you must be son of the poor man being tended at the Pinnock Inn."

"Yes."

"Our part of the country has given you more than your just share of troubles. Again, I apologize that Mr. Tulley has added to them."

Owen grunted, and stole another glance at the girl.

"Come, Owen," Darcy said. "I see Joshua coming out of the courthouse. Mr. Carney, Nell, thank you for your help."

Owen, humiliated by the public spectacle of his victimization, kept his head down as he walked beside Darcy back toward the courthouse. When he looked up, Joshua was drawing close, his expression indicating he could see something was wrong.

Darcy explained what had occurred. Joshua's face reddened in anger. "Parnell Tulley is a blight on this country," he said. "I wish the old devil would pack up and head somewhere else." He paused. "Of course, he is the best gunsmith I've known, short of Callum McSwain."

Cooper Haverly emerged from the crowd, came up, and inquired what was going on. Owen flinched inwardly as again the incident was described.

"What turned Tulley on you, Owen?" Cooper asked.

Owen lowered his head. "He thought I was going to steal a pistol from his saddle pouch."

"Were you?"

"At first, yes."

Joshua frowned. "Why, Owen?"

"I was going to take it and use it when I went to get Emaline."

Joshua was silent a moment, and his frown grew darker. "Owen, you're going to have to face up to the truth about your sister. There's nothing you can do for her. It's not in your hands. At the beginning I was pleased by the spirit you showed when you declared you'd go find her. It showed me you had the grit to make it through the difficulties that had come upon you. But in truth, there's no possibility of a boy your age heading into the Chickamauga country and taking back a captured female from a madman. If she's ever found and brought back, it will be through war, or prisoner trade, or treaty. There's naught you can do about it, sad to say as it is."

Owen felt like he had been kicked in the stomach. He wished he hadn't come with the Colters today. His earlier pleasure at being in Jonesborough had given way to humiliation, and now to wrenching disappointment.

"I want to go to my father," Owen said.

"I'll take you to him, Owen," Darcy said. "I need to be heading home myself. Joshua, are you coming?"

"I can't, Darcy. It appears I'll be spending the night here."

"Why?"

"I'm being considered for appointment as sheriff."

"Will you accept it?"

"I don't know . . . it might be my duty, my part of supporting the new state. In any case, I feel bound to stay until the matter is settled." He turned to Cooper. "And by the way, Cooper, John Sevier is now officially the governor of the great state of Franklin."

Cooper Haverly grinned. "In that case, brother, let me host the likely next county sheriff for a drink to our new governor in yonder tavern."

Good-byes were said, and all but Joshua and Cooper left the town and began the journey home. It would be dark before they arrived, and cold. Hannah Haverly sang softly as she rode. Her son Ben was tired and very irritable, fussing all the way.

Owen was silent until they reached the Pinnock Inn. At the door he dismounted. Looking up at Darcy, he said, "I'm sorry for the trouble I caused."

"It's forgotten, Owen. All ended with no one hurt."

"Missus Colter, the girl you called Nell—who is she?"

"Nell Carney. The younger sister of Alexander Carney."

"Oh. How old is she?"

"Fifteen, I think. No, sixteen. Fresh turned."

Owen frowned.

"What's wrong?"

"She called me a boy. But I'm nigh as old as she is."

"You have a boyish look. You are small of bone."

"But I'm not a child. Even if she thinks I am. Even if Joshua thinks—" He cut off, remembering to whom he was speaking.

Darcy smiled. "Good evening, Owen."

"Good evening, ma'am. And you too, Missus Haverly."

Owen entered the inn and headed up the stairs to join his father. Outside, the horses plodded on, carrying the Colter and Haverly women and children westward toward Limestone Creek and home.

*   *   *

The day's session had been long and trying, so it was no surprise that by night the tavern was crowded with thirsty Franklin assemblymen. Joshua Colter, though not part of that delegation, was in the midst of them, seated beside Cooper on a long bench against one wall, secretly feeling relieved that he hadn't received the sheriff's appointment after all. The atmosphere in the tavern was markedly boisterous. Jokes and banter flew as freely as the amber dollops of tobacco spittle that arced with regularity to the filthy puncheon floor, and spirits rose with pipe smoke toward the roofboards. The evening had cooled, so the tavern keeper built up a big blaze in the fireplace.

Salem Pinnock, enjoying the unusual luxury of a tavern's pleasures instead of its duties, sat comfortably on a stool across from Joshua, talking in his deep, authoritative voice to a newcomer who had asked just what the state of Franklin movement was all about. Pinnock was happy to educate him.

"The seaboarders of Carolina have always feared the expense of defending us. They say we pay too few taxes, that we serve as a refuge for criminals and debtors and the ignorant of the earth. In April last, the North Carolina legislature ceded our region to the federal government. The westerners were suddenly thrown on to their own resources, with no Carolinian support. The only option, obviously, was for the western frontier to take its future in its own hands—where it had substantially always been, in any case—and begin the process of state formation on its own.

"That was the very thing that was done, with a convention meeting here in August. But at the same time, North

Carolina was having second thoughts about the cession, and in October backwatered the entire thing, taking us again into their fold. But they were too late. The Franklin effort was already too far along—and news travels slowly. It wasn't until after we had officially declared ourselves free of North Carolina, and adopted a temporary constititution, that word of North Carolina's change of mind came to us. By then any hope of reversing our course was past."

Joshua cut in, "Now, Salem, that's not really true. Sevier himself was ready to stop the Franklin movement then and there and go back to the way things were. Carolina had offered him the post of brigadier general over all the western counties. It was Bill Cocke and you and all the other Franklin firebrands that changed his mind to stick with Franklin."

"A mere momentary diversion, of course, that's all it was," Pinnock said, looking irritated at having been interrupted. "Once the Franklin river began flowing, there was no stopping it."

"Don't know that that's fully true, Salem," Joshua said.

Cooper snorted. "Of course it is, Josh!"

"Well, either way it's all settled now," Pinnock's student said.

"Settled? Far from it! In the eyes of the former mother state, we are in civil rebellion. Our new state, they say, is illegal. Illegal! Better our 'illegality' than their ingratitude and scoff! Who was it who came to the eastern folks' aid so often during the war? Who was it who crossed the mountains to do in Ferguson on King's Mountain?" Pinnock was getting full of steam, and stood, cup held aloft and voice rising. He began addressing the tavern patrons as a group. "Who was it, I ask you, who wrested this country from the Indians? Who was it who moved into an empty wilderness and established the Watauga Association to let the people govern themselves, as it should be? Who is it who has answered the call time and again to neighbors in Carolina, in Kentucky, in Virginia, who have been plagued by the savage foe? Was it the perfumed and peruked membership of the North Carolina assembly? Was it the high governor Alexander Martin? Eh, was it?"

"No!" thundered a chorus of voices.

"I'll tell you who it was!" Pinnock declared. "It was the men of over-the-mountain, the men of the wild borderland, the tomahawk men, the men of the land of the rifle and canebrake! It was you, my fine citizens! The new state men! You who will henceforth be known by the name of Franklinite!"

Cooper, swept away by the emotion of Pinnock's impromptu speech, leaped atop the bench and raised his cup.

"Gentlemen of this new state, I give you Franklin!" he shouted. "And I give you the health of our new governor, John Sevier!"

"By the eternal, Cooper Haverly, I appreciate that sentiment quite a lot," came an unexpected voice from the doorway. Everyone recognized the voice, and every eye turned. John Sevier, newly named governor of the state of Franklin, stood grinning in the doorway, having slipped in just as Cooper was offering his toast.

The sight of Sevier brought every man in the place to his feet, and an ear-ringing roar of welcome and pride exploded. Cups touched lips, Sevier's health was toasted, and then the man was engulfed by his devotees and swept into the tavern amid a babel of greetings and a flurry of handshakes.

Joshua watched the tumult, grinning to himself. If

pride and love of leadership was enough to build a new state, it would appear that the state of Franklin had a bright future indeed.

"I'll have no lip from you, boy!" Aaron Killefer said in a sharp whisper. "You're my son, and you'll do what I tell you!"

"It's stealing. That whiskey belongs to Mr. Pinnock and Mr. Barton."

"Don't go turning all righteous on me over a little swallow or two of whiskey, boy. And it ain't stealing. Mr. Pinnock has took me in out of the kindness of his heart, and has give me whatever I need. He won't care for me having a little of his whiskey to cut my pain."

"If it ain't stealing, why do you send me sneaking in the middle of the night?"

Killefer's face was hidden by the darkness of the room, but Owen could easily picture what his expression was. He had seen that angry glare many times lately. "Enough talk out of you, Owen! Get down there and get me some whiskey!"

Owen let out a slow breath. "Very well, then." He took up the momentarily empty crockery bottle that his father kept hidden in the bed.

He descended to the lower floor without benefit of candle or lamp, taking care to make as little noise as possible. Away from the immediate presence of his impatient and liquor-hungry father, his defensiveness gave way to sadness over the man. It was odd: His father was different than he had been before, but different by being more himself than ever. The harsh and nettling characteristics that had always made up the personality of Aaron Killefer had not been reversed or softened by the Killefer family tragedy, but intensified. Where he had been irritable before, now he was bitter. Where he had been mildly self-distracted, he now was thoroughly self-centered.

Owen crept through the sleeping inn to the corner cabinet where Pinnock stored jugs of Matthew Barton's whiskey. He slid the little latch bar away and swung it open. Quietly he took down a jug, removed its stopper, and poured the crockery bottle full. He stoppered both containers and put the whiskey jug back in its place on the shelf, then closed and latched the door.

He was on his way back to the staircase when Salem Pinnock appeared before him, clad only in trousers and looking much like a great white ghost in the darkness. "Owen, is that you stirring about?"

Owen put the bottle behind him and gaped at the dimly visible, broad face. "Aye, yes, it's me. I was just—" He broke off.

A moment of silence, seeming much longer to Owen than it really was. "Up and about," Pinnock said, completing the youth's sentence for him. "Up and about at night. There's always something to stir one from his bed, eh?" He reached out and patted Owen's shoulder. "Well, if all is well, it's back to my own bed for me."

"Yes, sir. Me too."

Pinnock turned away, and at that moment the bottle slipped from Owen's fingers and clunked loudly against the floor. Pinnock reacted slightly and began to turn— then did not. "Good night," he said again, and went on into the darkness.

Owen picked up the bottle and climbed the stairs. He handed it to his eager father without a word.

Aaron Killefer opened it and took a swallow with the eagerness of a thirsty man drinking water. He swiped his hand over his mouth. "I heard Pinnock. Did he catch you at the whiskey?"

"No."

"Good, good." He took another drink, stoppered the bottle, and lay back down. Abruptly, he sobbed out loud—an emotional explosion that would have completely taken aback any observer other than Owen, who had grown used to these warningless bursts of grief. "Oh, Doanie, Doanie, I miss you, woman! Oh, Doanie! Come back to me, please! I need you with me, Doanie!"

Owen made no attempt to offer comfort, not because he wasn't moved by his father's sorrow, but because there was absolutely nothing he could do about it. Doanie Killefer was dead. She would never return.

He lay awake until his father's weeping subsided into silence, then snores. All the while a hot knot of anger burned the inside of Owen's belly. Salem Pinnock *had* caught him; he had known he was taking whiskey, had clearly heard the clump of the bottle on the floor—and had not turned. He had pretended not to hear, simply because he was a good and generous person. Like Matthew Barton, like Cooper Haverly, like Joshua and Darcy Colter.

And in contrast to these bighearted ones, the self-obsessed Aaron Killefer only seemed that much pettier, lower, smaller. For the first time in his life Owen Killefer was beginning to feel shame at bearing his family name. Apart from the grief of his bereavement, it was the worst feeling he had ever known.

3

On Friday, June 10, 1785, Joshua Colter stood at Henry's Station at the mouth of Dumplin Creek, a tributary of the French Broad River, seventy or so miles southwest of his home on Limestone Creek. He watched the conclusion of treaty negotiations that had been under way here for three days, and felt a sense of detachment from it all, even though he had been an integral part of the proceedings.

Joshua's feelings stemmed largely from simple weariness. He and several fellow Franklinites had been here the entire three days as Sevier treated with an Indian leader named Ancoo, from the Overhill Cherokees' sacred city of Chota, and Joshua had been called into such frequent service as an interpreter that his throat was sore from talking. Having grown up as the son of a trader in the heart of the Overhill towns, Joshua had excellent command of the Cherokee language—but he was a taciturn man, unaccustomed to long discourse of the sort typical in treaty-making. He had hardly any voice left.

There were strains beyond the physical at work on him too. These talks went on in an atmosphere of lingering Cherokee anger over a violent incident that had occurred the prior autumn: the killing by a white man of a half-

breed Cherokee named Noonday, but commonly called
Butler, a principal warrior of the town of Settico. Little
had been directly said about the killing during these
talks, but Joshua saw the thought of it behind every dark
Cherokee eye, and detected its silent presence like a
stench in the air. These Indians knew what he also knew:
that James Hubbert, the man who had killed the Settico
warrior, was a known Indian hater. His act had created
dangerous hard feelings, and while these had made this
treaty all the more diplomatically important, they had
also added tremendously to its difficulty.

This was on Joshua's mind as the Franklinite and
Cherokee officials gathered for the actual signing of what
would be known as the Treaty of Dumplin Creek. Because of his hoarseness, Joshua had been replaced now
by a different interpreter, giving him the chance to stand
aside and observe the situation from some distance.

He had his doubts about this treaty. The whole founda-
tion of it was too unstable on both the white and Cherokee sides. This was the first effort at treaty-making on
Franklin's authority, and that authority was uncertain. As
of yet, Franklin wasn't federally recognized as a state.
William Cocke, a man Joshua admired for his woodsman
abilities as well as his leadership skills, had recently pled
Franklin's case before Congress. North Carolina's congressional delegation had opposed Cocke's efforts and,
through legislative maneuvering, forced an early vote
that fell short of the nine-state approval needed for
Franklin's admittance as a state. So for now Franklin remained an entity existing in limbo, defiantly governing a
region over which North Carolina still claimed legal
sway.

Joshua filled his pipe and tamped in the tobacco, then
knocked the weed back into his pouch again when he re-

alized his throat was too raw for him to smoke. As an alternative, he borrowed a chew of tobacco from another of the Franklin delegation and settled it against his jaw until it sat comfortably.

He watched the Indians and listened to their voices, letting the sight and sound take him back to boyhood days in the Overhill towns. Most of these Cherokees looked much the same as those he had known as a child, the main difference being that more of them wore articles of white man's clothing with their native garb. Along with the traditional breechcloths, leggins, gorgets, beads, ear ornaments, and head wrappings, were plenty of frontiersmen's trousers, hunting shirts, and even a few tricorn hats. One unintentionally amusing warrior sported a gentleman's peruke that he had obtained from heaven knew where. Further, Joshua noted several faces among the Indians that revealed evidence of white ancestry along with Cherokee. Time was changing more than the land of these people. It was changing the people themselves.

Joshua watched Ancoo putting his mark on the treaty document, and was struck anew by a notable absence he had detected from the outset of the talks. Where was Old Tassel, successor to the late chief Oconostota, whom Joshua had helped lay to rest in Chota on a spring day many months ago? Joshua wondered if a treaty struck without Old Tassel's imprimatur would hold any real force among the Cherokees.

In fact, might not that very issue be at the heart of what the Cherokees were doing here? Perhaps Ancoo's plan was to hear Sevier's words, sign his paper—and then walk away from Dumplin Creek the richer in payment goods, with Sevier holding nothing but a document signed without sufficient authority.

Joshua had broached these thoughts to Sevier in a private moment at the outset of the talks. Sevier had listened and nodded, but changed none of his intentions. Quietly he explained his reasoning to Joshua.

"My friend, such a question is worth the asking. But the truth is, we cannot wait for greater authority on either side before we make this treaty. Should we wait for Congress, who as of yet doesn't even recognize us? I think not. And there is an argument to be made in our favor. Here in the West we're in much the same situation as our states were in their colonial days, and almost every colony forged treaties when circumstances required it. And if ever anyone faced such circumstances, we do now. We are doing nothing more than what has been done by others in the past.

"And consider this: In this spring alone, Joshua, we've had thousands upon thousands of people migrating over those mountains to settle on western lands. What are we to do? Leave them to see their homes burned and their wives and children scalped while we wait on easterners to decide our fate? Better the wrath of our larger government than the wrath of the Indians. If Ancoo is willing to sign, then he'll be allowed to do so, with or without Old Tassel, just as I'll sign with or without official statehood, with or without North Carolina, and with or without congressional approval."

Joshua understood. Sevier might be portrayed as impulsive by his detractors, but Joshua's experience he always had reasons for what he did, reasons that seemed sound to him, even if others sometimes disagreed.

At the end of his discourse, Sevier had slapped Joshua good-naturedly on the shoulder. "By gum, Joshua Colter, I think I'll name you minister of fretfulness for our new state. You're always looking for what might go wrong."

"Only to keep it from doing so, John."

"I know, I know. And I respect your caution, believe me. But sometimes a man's hand is forced. He goes ahead because he must. I want a document in hand before we have another problem like the Hubbert incident."

The Hubbert incident. Even the mention of it was distressing to Joshua. By now the circumstances of the incident were well-known. It was a sad story of old enemies, unfortunate chance, and hot tempers.

Major James Hubbert was nothing if not an interesting man. The frontier people knew of his skill as a woodsman, of his courage in battle, and that his home was always open to any weary traveler, so he was popular among his peers. He was a veteran of the battles at King's Mountain and Boyd's Creek, and on his face bore a scar left by an enemy saber that had slashed him during the Guilford Courthouse fight. He was reputed to be fearless. His personal qualities and history of battle bravery went far in his favor in the minds of his neighbors. Joshua, like John Sevier and almost everyone else he knew, couldn't help but like Hubbert.

Yet, like many borderers, Hubbert had a dark side. As a boy he had lost several family members in Virginia in a fearsome massacre by Shawnees, escaping death himself only by hiding in a chimney. Ever since, he had hated Indians with an almost unrivaled fervor. He had killed many of them without any trace of remorse. Ironically, the stockade at the very station where this treaty-making was taking place had been built because Hubbert had purportedly killed an Indian during a shooting contest, and the settlers had felt the need for a fort in case the incident brought reprisal.

Hubbert's hatreds went beyond despising Indians. He also despised the Indian agent, Joseph Martin, whom he and many others believed too often took the side of the natives over the whites, and who was in the Carolinian camp on the Franklin question. The fact that Martin had a Cherokee wife and family in addition to his white family back in Virginia did nothing to raise his merit in Hubbert's eyes. So bitter was Hubbert's malice toward the Indian agent that, one time during the prior year, he had cursed and driven from his home a Moravian missionary who stopped for hospitality and rest, and made the mistake of telling Hubbert he was bound for the Indian country and an appointment with Martin.

However, during that same year, Hubbert ironically had found himself in need of aid from the same people he hated. Food was scarce because of crop failure, but the Cherokees had corn. So Hubbert left his home on the north bank of the French Broad River and ventured with a companion to the Cherokee country in hopes of bartering for food. Driving a string of packhorses laden with trade goods along a forested trail near Settico town, they had met two other travelers. That one of them should be the half-breed called Butler was one of the most undesirable scenarios fate could have brought about.

There was already a bitter history between Hubbert and Butler. Back during the war, Butler and another half-breed Cherokee, Guwisguwi, known to the whites as John Watts, had served as guides for the white army. Hubbert and Butler had quarreled, and Hubbert had humiliated the half-breed by unseating him from his horse. Butler hadn't forgotten that embarrassment when he later came across Hubbert and his packhorses.

Faced with his old foe again, Butler demanded to know why Hubbert was in the Indian country. Hubbert replied he had come to trade for corn, and threw open a sack to display some of the clothing he and his friend had brought for trade. From the sack he also produced a bottle of whiskey, which he gave to the Indians.

Hubbert was carrying his rifle at the time, and set it against a nearby tree to show peaceful intent. Tensely, the whites and Indians sat down to share a meal of brisket and venison provided by Hubbert, and frozen dumplings carried by Butler.

Shortly into the meal, Butler's temper got the best of him, and he flung one of the dumplings at Hubbert. It struck him on the mouth and cut his lip, leaving a mark that would remain as a scar long after the wound healed.

Hubbert leaped up, and Butler went for his horse and rifle. Mounting, he moved his horse between Hubbert and his rifle and clubbed at him with his weapon, but missed. Butler then raised his rifle and fired; the ball clipped the top of Hubbert's ear, but gave him no more than a mild cut that momentarily stunned him.

Butler, now holding an empty weapon, turned his mount and began to ride away with his companion. Overcoming the stunning effect of the grazing rifle ball, Hubbert snatched up his rifle and fired a mortal shot into the fleeing half-breed from a distance of about thirty yards. Hubbert was an excellent marksman, reputed all across the border country for his skill with weapons.

Butler fell from his horse. Hubbert ordered his companion to see that the other Indian didn't escape, but escape he did, to carry word back to his peers of what had happened.

Hubbert went to see the results of his bloody work. Butler was dying. Hubbert dragged him to a tree and sat him up against it. The half-breed defiantly told the white men not to touch him, for he was "a dead man."

Hubbert replied, "Butler, you draw your breath

damned hard; the longer you breathe, the longer you'll live. Don't strike me again with a bean pone. Now tell me: are your people for peace or war?"

Butler, defiant even in pain, told him they favored war and that Hubbert would lose his scalp if he dared continue on to Settico. Hubbert, his temper flaring anew, declared that if the Indians dared attack the whites, they would be defeated. The dying Butler derided that, and taunted Hubbert so furiously that the Indian-hating man lifted his rifle and clubbed Butler to death.

When Hubbert later described the incident to others, he noted that Butler died a hard death. It was the only time he was ever known to give anything even close to a sympathetic word for any Indian he killed.

Word of the slaying spread rapidly among both Indians and whites, so that by December even the governor of North Carolina was aware of it, and had written to Sevier to demand Hubbert's incarceration and trial, as well as the removal of all settlers from Indian lands.

Sevier himself had told Joshua how he replied to the governor: Any other person who met the same degree of insult from "one of those bloody savages, who have so frequently murdered the wives and children of the people of this country for so many years," would have done nothing different than Hubbert had done.

The whole affair made Joshua Colter feel very sad, and doubtful that every puzzle of life and death and right and wrong could be solved this side of the grave.

Activity among the Cherokee and Franklin delegates brought Joshua out of his thoughts. Looking up, he saw smiles, nods, handshakes. The Treaty of Dumplin Creek had been signed.

The state of Franklin, if state it could be called, had once again demonstrated its brashness by treating, on no authority but its own, with the Indians. It was a historic day. Under the Dumplin Creek agreement, white settlement would be permitted on all lands south of the Holston and French Broad rivers, all the way to the Tennessee River. And the Cherokees, it was agreed, would in no way molest or hamper that settlement.

Joshua drew in a deep breath, then slowly exhaled. He was glad this task was complete. Not that it really would make much difference, in his opinion. Settlement would have gone on even without any legal sanction. Frontiersmen paid scant heed to words on scraps of paper.

And mostly likely the Cherokee promises of peace would make little difference as well. The Cherokees who had signed the treaty today made up only a fraction of their people, and probably had signed in the full expectation that the leading headmen would promptly recant the accord. And the Chickamaugas, who had substantially cut ties with their mother people, had taken no part in this treaty at all.

Joshua set off for home the next morning, wondering what the outcome of the last three days' work would be in the long run, and if it would be for good or for bad. Or if it would really make any difference at all in either direction.

Three days after his homecoming from Dumplin Creek, Joshua Colter's voice was healed and he was in a much brighter frame of mind. He set out with Cooper Haverly toward Jonesborough, picking up Owen Killefer along the way to help herd five fine horses to be sold to Colonel Charles Carney, the aging father of Alexander and Nell. By the standards of the time and locale, Carney was a well-off man. Joshua had traded stock with the old colonel before, and liked the prices he paid as much as Carney liked the animals he received, so Joshua was in high spirits, whistling and riding in an easy slump, and even cracking a few jokes along the way. Owen was quiet and thoughtful, but in a good humor, grinning at Joshua's banter.

Cooper, on the other hand, was as sour as old milk, and sporting a black eye to boot. He had gotten into a wrangle with a couple of newcomers to the region the day before. In Joshua's view it was Cooper's fault. Cooper had been talking politics in the Pinnock Inn with his usual pro-Franklin, pro-Sevier fervor, and he hadn't shown the good sense to let the subject drop when the pair disagreed with him and threw in a few insults against John Sevier to boot. Words turned to shouts, shouts to fisticuffs, and Cooper's healthy right eye to a swollen, black lump he could hardly pry open.

Joshua was enjoying gigging his brother about the injury. "Maybe you can tell folks you got it scrapping man-to-man with Dragging Canoe and his Chickamaugas. You could tell them you used that eye to catch a rifle ball in flight."

"Shut your yap, Joshua. I don't feel like joshing over this."

"Why, you ought to be proud! You were wounded defending the cause. You've sacrificed the welfare of your own peeper ball for the new state and the good name and honor of Franklinites everywhere."

"I said to shut your yap! I'll turn around and ride home if you don't."

"Oh, don't do that, don't do that! I'll shut up." He grinned slyly at Owen. "If I don't hush, Owen, I fear Cooper might come up and strike me unexpected in the knuckles with that one good eye he's got left."

Cooper let loose some colorful descriptions of his brother and might have actually turned back if a long black snake hadn't picked that moment to scurry across the road ahead and frighten the horses. Regrouping and calming them diverted his attention and gave his anger time to cool a little. When they resumed their journey, Joshua prudently decided it was time to leave his brother alone.

It was easiest to drive the horses directly through Jonesborough to reach Charles Carney's house. Unexpectedly, the three encountered quite a bit of activity around the courthouse.

"What's happening here?" Owen asked.

"Court in session, it seems," Joshua replied. They rode on out of town, thinking no more about it for the moment.

Colonel Carney was in the dirty yard of his log home when Joshua and Cooper arrived. Carney was a pleasant-looking man in his seventies. He was rotund and somewhat short, but proud in bearing and very self-assured, though lately he was beginning to show disturbing signs of senility.

It required some effort to make the old man understand who Owen Killifer was, but once he did, he welcomed the youth heartily. And he quickly showed that one aspect of his mind—his keen business acumen—was as able today as ever. When the transaction was done and the horses were being driven into the stock pen by Carney's slave, Titus, Mary Carney, the colonel's wife, brought out cold springwater and corn bread. She gave the largest piece to Cooper, who had once described her corn bread as the finest to be had within five hundred miles—a compliment she hadn't forgotten. To Joshua's delight, Mary Carney expressed great concern over

Cooper's swollen eye. Joshua stifled a devilish grin as Cooper fidgeted while she talked about it.

Charles Carney drained off his water, nibbled a bit of corn bread, and said, "Joshua, I'm sorry you didn't receive the sheriff's post. I can't think of a better man for the job."

The old man had made a nearly identical comment only moments before, but obviously had forgotten it. With no sign of irritation, Joshua replied as he had the first time. "Well, I'll confess to being glad things worked out as they did. I'm a private man at heart, Colonel. I make a better citizen than public officer."

"You underestimate yourself, Joshua."

"Is Alexander in court today?" Cooper asked. "There was business at the courthouse when we passed."

The colonel seemed unsure. Mary Carney answered on his behalf. "Alexander is there. It's not the best of days for him. He was called on to defend Parnell Tulley yet again. The trial was yesterday. Another theft charge— Tulley was accused of stealing a milk cow from some traveler on his way to the Dumplin Creek settlements. Alexander defended him as best he could, this time without success. Tulley is to be branded for his crime today."

Joshua was all the more glad he hadn't received the sheriff's position. One of the most unpleasant aspects of law enforcement work on the frontier was carrying out the branding, ear-cropping, and other disfigurements sometimes imposed by the courts on convicted criminals. Many was the man who went through life with part of an ear gone, or the letter T permanently burnt into his cheek or palm. For horse thieves, a double-letter brand was sometimes given: H and T, one letter on one cheek, one on the other. Harsh as the punishment was, however, a horse thief could consider himself lucky if that was his sentence. In Washington County many convicted horse thieves were simply sentenced to hang, the executions usually happening in a particular hollow outside Jonesborough, often on the day sentence was passed.

Joshua said, "It was only a matter of time for Parnell to receive some kind of punishment for his sorry ways. The man is his own worst enemy."

"Indeed he is," Mary Carney said. "I can only hope that Mr. Tulley has enough decency about him to be grateful that Alexander at least kept him out of the noose."

The group talked some more, discussing mostly politics and news of neighbors. Colonel Carney, who seemed to have lost interest in the conversation, took Owen aside and showed him the horses he had just bought, having apparently forgotten that Owen had helped drive them there to begin with. Owen had been forewarned of the old man's mental decline, and went along obligingly to avoid embarrassing him.

"How is the colonel doing, on the whole?" Joshua asked Mary Carney when her husband was out of earshot.

"Declining, I'm sorry to say. Some days are good, others not so good. I must keep a sharp eye on him almost all the time now. Alexander worries a lot about his father, and talks of moving back here to help me care for him, but it isn't necessary—not yet."

They took their leave and headed back toward home. When they reached Jonesborough again, they happened upon a somber scene. Parnell Tulley, his face dark and angry, was locked in the pillory outside the courthouse. A fire burned off to the side; into it was thrust a long iron rod. Gathered before the pillory was a crowd of about twenty, mostly men, but including women and children as well.

"It appears we've arrived at just the moment," Cooper observed.

"Aye—and look there, Cooper. There's Alexander Carney."

Joshua and Cooper dismounted and strode toward the young lawyer. Owen Killefer remained in the saddle, watching Tulley like he would watch a coiled rattler. The memory of his earlier encounter with the man was still very fresh; he had no desire to draw any closer.

Alexander Carney's face was ashen, and he stooped as if under a burden. The charge, conviction, and sentence of Parnell Tulley was being recited as they reached the man.

"Alexander, you look sick," Joshua said.

"I feel sick, Joshua. Sick to my soul. You see what's happening here."

"Yes. We've just come from your father and mother. They told us about this. Don't fret, Alex. Every attorney loses a case from time to time, and if Tulley did the crime, as he surely did, he's getting his just punishment."

"It's not the losing of the case that distresses me so much. Blast it all, I know he was guilty! The verdict was justified." Alexander Carney paused, shook his head and held out his hand. "Look at that, Joshua. Look—even though I'm not proud of what I'm showing you. My hand is shaking. Trembling like a leaf. I'm sorry to say I'm not like you. I'm a cowardly man."

Joshua found the words surprising. Not many men would say such a thing about themselves in a society in which cowardice was perhaps the worst stigma a man could face. "I don't understand, Alexander."

"It's fear that's making my hand shake, Joshua. Fear for

my own safety. I'm disappointed in myself, and I won't try to mislead you on that point. What's happening here today has made me an enemy I don't want to have."

Joshua was all the more confused, but further explanation was rendered momentarily impossible. The sheriff had just finished his recitation, and now walked over to the fire and picked up the long iron rod by its cool end. A murmur passed through the crowd as the red-hot branding end came into view. Parnell Tulley swore and wiggled about in the pillory, swearing violently. He spat toward the crowd, making those in the front step back.

"Hold still, man, and let's get this done," the sheriff said.

Tulley spat again, but quit struggling. "Get on with it, then! Get your burning done—and may you roast in a fire ten times hotter the day you go to hell!"

Alexander Carney refused to watch as two men flattened Tulley's right hand back against the stocks, exposing the callused palm. Immediately the sheriff advanced and firmly applied the hot iron to the prisoner's flesh. Tulley let out a terrible roar. Smoke rose from his hand, and the burning of the flesh made a loud hissing noise. A child in the crowd began to wail.

"Parnell Tulley, the sentence of the court has been executed," the sheriff said in a loud, ceremonial voice after the branding iron was removed. "Let the mark you carry in your palm be a reminder to you of the cost of thievery."

"Go to hell!" Tulley raged. "And let me be the man to send you!"

"Threats against an officer of the court will not be tolerated," the sheriff replied. "Any more of that kind of talk, and you'll be before the bench again. I'm turning you loose now, Parnell. Got get some salve on that hand, and keep yourself out of trouble from here on out."

Alexander Carney said, "Heaven help me."

Joshua opened his mouth to ask Carney what had him so fearful, when a great commotion at the stocks once again interrupted him. Tulley, just released, had leaped toward the crowd, grabbing a man at the front.

"Oh, Lord—what's he doing?" Carney said, stepping back rapidly.

In one deft twist, Parnell Tulley yanked a knife from a sheath on the man's belt sash. He shoved the fellow away; the man stumbled, fell on his face, then rolled to the side and jumped up. "Give me back my knife!" he yelled.

"When I'm through with it," Tulley said.

Joshua Colter had seen many remarkable things in his time, but none that caught him so by surprise as what Parnell Tulley did right then. The branded man lifted his burnt hand, exposed the seething letter mark to the crowd, and declared, "You want to know what I think about the good court of this bloody county? Do you? Then I'll show you!"

He probed the blade into the flesh around the burn, and without a flinch carved deeply around and under the brand. Blood streamed out and splattered on the ground. He gave the knife one more twist, and a piece of flesh, bearing the burnt letter, came free and arced toward the sheriff, who instinctively jumped away to avoid being hit by the repulsive thing.

"There's your pretty letter mark!" Tulley declared. Blood ran down his wrist. "You want it, you keep it—I got no use for the cursed thing."

He wiped the bloodied blade clean on his trouser leg,

walked up to the man he had taken the knife from, and handed it to him. "I'm obliged for the use of your blade."

The crowd parted as Tulley walked through the midst of it and up to Alexander Carney. Tulley held up his clenched fist, flinging blood onto Carney's face. "This here is your doing, attorney. It was your place to keep me from this. I won't forget that you failed me. You keep you eyes open, Carney. You don't know when you're going to see me, but see me you will. Yes sir, you'll be seeing Parnell Tulley again!"

Joshua thought Alexander Carney was going to faint. The man staggered and went white, but managed to keep his feet. Parnell Tulley looked at him silently, snorted in contempt, and strode off, pausing only long enough to fire a harsh stare at Owen Killefer, who gaped back, wide-eyed.

"I ain't never seen nothing like that in all my days," Cooper said.

"Neither have I, Cooper," Joshua replied. "Alexander, I see now what's got you scared."

Alexander Carney opened his mouth, but no words would come. He wheeled, staggered off to the other side of the street and vomited. Joshua started to go to him, then pulled back. He didn't know what to say to the man.

"Joshua, there's one fear-froze man," Cooper said.

"With Parnell Tulley after him, he's got cause for it. Tulley's a dangerous man."

"Do you believe he'll really harm Alexander?"

Joshua watched as the young attorney, wiping the blood from his face with his cuff, walked like a drunk man down the street, toward the stable where he kept his horse while in town. Joshua nodded. "He might, Cooper. He truly might."

The brothers watched Carney ride out of the stable

and out of town, then returned to Owen and their horses and began the ride back to Limestone Creek. Joshua's joking manner was gone now. The grim things they had witnessed had stripped away all levity.

Clouds came when they were within three miles of the Pinnock Inn, and rain when they were within two. Cooper grumbled at being soaked. His were the first words any of the three had spoken since leaving Jonesborough.

4

She saw the dark interior of her North Carolina cabin home and the face of her mother by firelight as she leaned over a steaming pot of potatoes stewing with venison Owen had brought in. She smelled the scent of her father's pipe, heard guttural sounds from the old dog as it slept by the hearth and re-lived the chases and conquests of its long-vanished youth.

Emaline Killefer opened her eyes, and peace shattered as she realized it was all just another dream.

She sat up sharply, her long-unwashed hair falling in strings across her dirty face. The corn shucks beneath the smutty blanket that was her bed rustled and crunched at her motion. Emaline stared into the darkness and felt her heartbeat quicken as a familiar, panicked feeling tight-ened her throat. Then a glance around the dark cabin in-terior revealed that *he* was not here. She closed her eyes and thanked God for that blessing, small and assuredly temporary as it was. In her circumstances, Emaline had learned to appreciate the most meager pieces of good fortune.

She reclined again. If she could go back to sleep, maybe she could return to the pleasant illusions of her dream. Soon it was evident this would not happen. She rose sadly. Walking barefoot across the packed dirt floor of the filthy log hut, she poked up the banked fire, added wood, and let the heat bathe her. A scrawny pup, one of a litter of curs born a couple of months before by one of Turndale's dogs, came through the door and nuzzled against her. She ignored it initially, then swatted it away. It yelped and ran to her bed, where it nestled in the warmth her body had left there, and began to sleep. Emaline envied it.

At last she went to the door. The first light of dawn was rising, greeted by bird song. Emaline stepped outside. The September morning was cool and misty, and the creek that ran through the woods on the far side of the path that passed the cabin was loud and musical, brimming from rains that had fallen yesterday and the day before. To her left stood a broad canebrake, its tall canes moving gently in the wind.

For a moment Emaline appreciated the beauty of her surroundings. Only for a moment. This place was evil. It sought to destroy her. She could not let herself think anything good about it. To do so would be to yield, and lose what remained of herself. There seemed less of that every day. Her surroundings, her situation, somehow they were eroding her, wearing away the life she had known before. Sometimes she had to strain just to remember the names of old friends back in Carolina, or the color of her grandfather's eyes, or the sound of her mother's voice. Only when she dreamed did such memories have clarity.

Restless, she walked out to the pathway that led west toward Black Water Town. A cramping feeling made her stop abruptly and put her hand against her abdomen. She closed her eyes and breathed thanks for the day's second blessing. The cramp indicated the approach of her monthly issue, and gave her the joyous relief of knowing that, as bad as her situation was, at least she was not yet carrying Thomas Turndale's child. Since becoming Turndale's prisoner—his *wife*, he had the brazenness to call her—she had dreaded the prospect of bearing his offspring in her body. It was horror enough to endure forced intimacy with a man whose very touch made her shudder. To bear his child would be far worse.

Turndale and his status among the Indians confused Emaline. He kept mostly to himself, but when he was among others he seemed no outsider. The Chickamaugas apparently accepted him as part of their society, though he did not participate in war-making or ceremony. His value to the Indians, Emaline surmised, lay in his skill at making medicines of forest plants and herbs. Five times since she had come here, Emaline had seen Turndale called out to treat ill or injured persons. Twice he had brought the ill ones to his cabin; other times he had gone to their own homes or sweat houses. Every time his treatments had succeeded. The conjurers, Emaline had heard, were envious.

The menstrual cramp passed, and Emaline continued walking, playing with the fantasy of simply continuing to walk until at last she was home again. Yet she knew this could not be. Where, across this vast wilderness, was home? She didn't know. Turndale had blindfolded her for two full days after taking her as prisoner, so that she could not tell where he took her. Sometimes he had deliberately led her in circles. Even if he hadn't deliberately confused her, she would have been unable to escape. Her life in Carolina had been confined mostly to the cabin and the cook fire; unlike her brother Owen, she had no natural affinity for the wilderness and no skill in finding her way in unknown places.

There was irony in the relative freedom of movement her captor allowed her. He had kept her confined only for the first week she was here; in the subsequent seven months, she had been allowed to go where she pleased. She did not attribute this to any kindness on Tom Turndale's part. It was merely that he knew she had come to understand her situation. She was in an alien place, surrounded by a wilderness that was in itself a sufficient prison for her. To leave here would mean her death. She knew that, and Turndale knew she knew it. Thus she was bound.

From time to time she had caught herself thinking that maybe death in the wilderness wouldn't be so bad, if all life had to offer was enslavement and repeated violation by Tom Turndale. When she thought that way, it scared her. Each time, she would gather up her courage, fan the flame of defiance that still burned in her, and pledge to herself that somehow and someday she would escape this nightmare.

Her mind was moving along such assertive lines when two Indians, traveling in the opposite direction, rounded a curve in the path ahead. Emaline stopped; her mouth dropped open and she took a backward step. The two men also stopped, looking as surprised as she. One of them was bearing a freshly slain doe on his shoulders. For several moments the three stood there, looking at each other. The man bearing the deer glanced at his companion, stooped and let the carcass fall to the ground behind him. With a vague grin he pointed at Emaline and said words to his partner in their own tongue. Emaline picked out only one English word: Turndale. From this she surmised she had been identified as Turndale's woman. Or his property.

The Indian who had dropped the deer approached her,

grinning more broadly. Emaline faltered uncertainly, then turned and walked hurriedly back toward the cabin, her hands clasped before her, her shoulders slightly hunched in an unconscious posture of self-protection. The other Indian chuckled. Now both were following her, and closing the gap.

They want to make me run, she thought. They're trying to frighten me.

They were succeeding. Emaline's heart trip-hammered; her pulse throbbed audibly in her ears. She glanced over her shoulder. One of the men lifted his hands like a bear raising its claws, made a face of comic fierceness, and leaped at her with a roar. Emaline, startled, stumbled and fell. The two Indians laughed and came on.

Emaline scrambled up and ran. She stumbled again and fell on her face, pounding her nose against the foot-hardened path. Fear became sheer panic. She screamed without meaning to. They weren't intending merely to frighten her. They would kill her; she was sure of it.

"Beware the Creeks," Tom Turndale had told her. "There's many of them among the Chickamaugas, and you've got much more to fear from them than from the Cherokees."

Emaline couldn't distinguish one Indian from another. Maybe these were the Creeks Turndale had warned her about.

She lay on her face, gasping, muscles rigid, expecting at any moment to be roughly grasped. Nothing happened. She rolled over and looked up to see the two men grinning broadly at her. Neither looked particularly threatening now. They had simply been toying with her, after all. They had seen a good chance to have a few moments of idle fun at the expense of Tom Turndale's female, and had taken it.

But suddenly they looked up and beyond her, and lost their smiles. Emaline sat up, turned, and saw Tom Turndale standing in the midst of the path, holding a rifle in one hand and a long string of fish in the other. For the first time ever, she was glad to see her captor.

"What is happening here, Flower?" he asked, calling her by the name he'd given her—for she had staunchly refused for all the time of her captivity to tell him her first name. It was one of the few things within her power to withhold from him.

"They're scaring me," she replied, standing.

Turndale's eyes locked on the two Indians. He spoke to them in their own language; one spoke back. Turndale's words were soft, but there was cold iron in his gaze.

The Indians turned, went up the path and retrieved their dropped deer carcass, then came back, passing Turndale and Emaline without words and with no backward glances.

"It's to your fortune they weren't mean-spirited," Turndale said. "You should watch yourself, roaming about so free. If those had been Creeks instead of Cherokees, they might have done more than try to give you a fright." He stopped talking; had Emaline been looking back into his face—something she never did—she would have seen a momentary burst of sadness. "Flower, I'd pull my own teeth if you'd just look me in the eye from time to time."

Emaline said nothing.

"I'm no beast. I'm a lonely man who's took you for his mate. I care very much for you, sweet maid. I would relish the chance to look into those pretty eyes of yours."

"You *are* a beast." As quickly as the words were said, she was amazed she had found the courage to utter them. It felt so good, she said more. "You're a murderer, a captor, a violator. Why should I look at your face when I despise the sight of it?"

Turndale's silence was heavy and lingering. After a few moments Emaline felt compelled to look at him, if only to see if she had angered him to the point of danger. She turned her head slightly and gave him the briefest of glances. He surprised her with a smile. She looked away immediately.

"There now!" Turndale said. "That didn't bring much pain, did it? All you need is time, my dear. You'll come to appreciate my feelings for you one day. Now come on—let me cook you some fish for your breakfast."

She followed him at about ten paces behind, staring at his back and hating him. And hating herself, too, for letting him believe her feelings about him were beginning to thaw.

In the cabin, Turndale cooked the fish by the fire. Though Emaline was very hungry, she ate only a few bites. Turndale ate his own portions, then hers. When he was finished, he swiped his hand over his mouth, smiled at her, rose, and approached her.

She sensed his intention and stood, clenching her fists. "No!"

Turndale stopped. His hands dangled at his sides, fingers moving like snakes. He looked angry. Without a word he turned, picked up his rifle, and walked out the door.

Emaline went to her bed, grabbed up the pup that still slept there, and flung it across the cabin. It yelped, rolled, came to its feet, and ran out the door after Turndale.

She lay down, hiding her face in the blanket. She felt like an untempered glass in a fire, struggling to endure, but knowing that if this went on much longer, she would shatter. Her will was strong, but not infinitely strong.

She longed for her family. Life in Aaron Killefer's household had been difficult, but in her current circumstances, those difficulties seemed infinitely small. She had hoped her father would have come for her, would have found some way to find her and get her away from this terrible captivity.

Day by day that hope of rescue was declining, and now she was beginning to believe that her father was dead. She had seen him stabbed by Tom Turndale—but she had also seen him writhing on the snowy ground just before Turndale had blindfolded her. Because of that, she had held out the hope of his survival. Owen, she believed, had made it through Turndale's attack without great injury. Maybe he had found help for himself and their father. Maybe . . . but probably not. She couldn't be sure that even Owen was still alive.

She wondered if there was a living soul left in the world to know, much less care, what had happened to her.

Despite Emaline's fears to the contrary, Aaron Killefer was still alive, though he hardly looked it at the moment. Salem Pinnock's partner, Matthew Barton, strong despite age, was standing in the doorway of the Killefer cabin, Aaron Killefer draped over his shoulder like a sack of dirt. Three hounds the Killefer's had obtained from Cooper Haverly at the beginning of the summer sniffed at Aaron's hands as they dangled floorward.

"Drunk again," Barton said as Owen opened the door.

Owen nodded sadly, and stepped aside for Barton to enter. The old man wheezed and grunted under the strain of carrying Killefer's dead-weight body over to the bed in the corner of the cabin. He dumped the man unceremoniously onto the pine-needle bed tick and pulled a quilt over him.

Barton, relieved of his burden, arched his back and made his spine pop audibly. "Likely he'll be sore when he wakes up," he said. "I rode him draped over the rump of my horse all the way from the inn, and he fell off once. Sorry I let it happen."

"It's no one's fault but his own," Owen replied, looking sourly at his passed-out father. "Thank you for bringing him in. I didn't know where he was."

"You can generally figure that when he ain't here, he's off drinking at the inn or somewhere else," Barton said. "He's too fond of the liquor, your father. But don't fault him too much. There ain't many who have lost as much as him who could make peace with it."

"Are you hungry, Mr. Barton? There's some salt pork and biscuit in the case yonder."

"I ain't hungry, thank you. Reckon I'll be going on now."

After Barton left, Owen stood examining his father with an expression of great distaste. Aaron Killefer had been a difficult man all Owen's days. But never had he been so bad as he had over the seven months since Tom Turndale had brought the family tragedy in the snow-filled mountains. Before that, liquor had been a mild plague on the man. Now it was a demonic pox. It humiliated Owen to know that his father had gained the reputation of drunkard and brawler. It humiliated him even more to know that people felt sorry for him, just for having to be Aaron Killefer's son.

Owen went to the fireside, sat down on a three-legged stool, put his elbows on his knees and chin on his hands and stared into the flames. He felt very sad. Seven months—and Aaron Killefer had not made the first effort toward the recovery of Emaline. Owen had waited with mounting impatience for his father to do something, anything, to indicate the time of her rescue had come. He had asked again and again, only to be rebuffed in increasingly harsh tones.

It seemed that these days, Aaron Killefer cared only for his almost daily baptism in liquor. His days were spent in silent, grudging labor in his fields, his evenings in drinking, sometimes at home, sometimes at the Pinnock Inn, sometimes in places unknown to Owen. There were times he didn't come home in the evenings at all. Once, after a day of hunting with Cooper Haverly and Zachariah and Will Colter, Owen came home to find the cabin empty. Eventually he found his father passed out in the cornfield, where he had imbibed most of the day from a jug of whiskey he had taken with him.

Worst of all to Owen, Aaron Killefer didn't even cry for his lost wife and missing daughter anymore.

Owen despised his father's self-destruction and the apathy it nurtured. He despised himself as well. After all, he had done no more than his father had toward finding Emaline, even after it began to be evident the job was going to be up to him, if anyone.

When Aaron Killefer woke up, sunlight was streaming through the cabin windows. He rolled over, groaning, and groped at his head, hiding from the beams. When he opened his eyes again ten minutes later, Owen was at his bedside, looking solemnly at him.

"You were drunk again last night," Owen said. "Matthew Barton brought you in."

Killefer was in no mood to talk. He mumbled something beneath his breath and pulled the quilt up over his ears. Owen reached over and yanked it back down.

"Whaugh! What in the—"

"I want to talk to you right now," Owen said. "I want you to tell me when you're going to be ready to go after Emaline."

"Leave me be."

"No."

Killefer glared at Owen; even the effort of frowning seemed to cause him pain. "My head's pounding like a hammer, boy. Leave me alone."

"No." Owen, who had slept hardly at all, was close to becoming tearful. "I want you to tell me if you ever intent to go after Emaline."

"Close your yap, boy, and leave a man be!"

Owen clenched his fists. "No! No! You tell me now!"

Aaron Killefer swore, grimaced, sat up in bed. "What's got you in such a state?"

"You have, you and your bloody drinking. Now you answer me: When will we go after Emaline?"

"Where would we go, boy? You think I ought to go after her, you tell me where she is!"

"She's wherever Tom Turndale is—the Chickamauga towns. That's what Joshua Colter says!"

"He don't know where Tom Turndale is no more than you do or I do. That's Indian country, boy."

"But Emaline is there. We can't just leave her!"

Aaron raised his bleary eyes and looked his son in the face. He spoke in a soft, hoarse voice. "Haven't you figured it out yet, boy? Emaline is dead."

Hearing that was like taking a kick in the groin. Owen gaped at his father. He violently shook his head. "She's not dead! Joshua Colter said Turndale took her for a wife. He wouldn't kill her!"

"Hell, boy, Joshua Colter was making his best guess, that's all. He don't know any more than nobody why Tom Turndale took her. He said his own self that Turndale's a madman. Think about it, boy. God knows I have, every cursed day. You knew your sister. She was stubborn as they come. Even if Turndale did take her for a mate, she'd never let him touch her. He'd only put up with that for so long."

Owen stammered, vainly looking for something to say. He hadn't allowed himself even to consider the possibility of Emaline's death. He didn't want to now.

"There's nothing for us to do, Owen," Aaron went on. "All we'd accomplish by going after her would be to get ourselves dead. That's all. And even if she was alive, how would anyone get her back from a place like that? You've been thinking like a boy. It's time you took to thinking like a man."

Owen had no voice. His father's shocking words had stripped the heart out of him. He pivoted, stalked to the door, flung it open and ran out of the cabin into the forest.

He roamed alone all day, thinking, pondering, sometimes crying, sometimes shouting in anger at the sky, until at last hunger and the westering sun drove him home.

He found the cabin vacant. He wasn't surprised. Probably his father was out drinking again. For once Owen was glad. What he had in mind would be best achieved without his father about.

He scrounged a supper and ate until the gnawing in his belly was gone. Then he fetched his father's flintlock rifle from the pegs above the door and cleaned it. He worked well into the night, gathering ammunition, flints, food, and the other essentials of wilderness travel. Then, to avoid the possibility of his plans being thwarted by his father's return, he left the cabin and headed for the woods again. The hounds followed him. He led them back, tied them, and disappeared into the woods with them baying after him.

He was awake long before sunrise, walking toward the Nolichucky River.

They found him before sundown. Owen was hiding behind a fallen tree when Joshua Colter and Cooper Haverly came upon him. They peered over the log and nodded a hello. Owen looked quite disappointed.

"How did you find me?"

"Son, you left enough sign behind for a blind man to have found you," Joshua replied. "And the last part of it had some blood smears. How've you hurt yourself?"

"Cane stab," Owen said, extending his left foot. He had removed the moccasin; the bottom of his foot was rusty with dried blood, and a sliver of cane that had jammed deep into the foot was still in place. "I went through the canebrake to try to cover my tracks. Reckon it was a mistake."

Joshua winced sympathetically. "I've had me some bad cane stabs of my own from time to time," he said. "But I have to say I never walked as far on one as you have on that one. Where the blazes are you trying to go, anyway?"

Owen lowered his head, knowing how foolish the truth would sound. "Just going, that's all," he mumbled.

"Running off from home?" Cooper asked.

"Aye. Yes."

"Your father is right worried about you," Joshua said.

"He came to my house this morning, thinking maybe you would be there."

Owen stood, putting his weight on his good foot. "Worried, was he? But not worried enough to come with you to look for me."

"No," Joshua admitted. "But he is worried about you. He truly is."

"I'm surprised he didn't just decide I was dead and gone, and leave it be at that." Owen spoke with undisguised bitterness.

"If I had to guess, I'd say you and your father have fell out over something," Cooper said.

Owen held his silence a few moments, then said, "Well, that's true. And you may laugh at me, but I'll tell you where it is I'm going. I'm going to the Chickamauga towns to get my sister back from Tom Turndale."

He waited for them to deride him. They didn't.

"The fact is, Owen, that's exactly what we had figured," Joshua said. "Your father told us a little about what you and him had squabbled over."

"He told me that Emaline is dead. He said there's no reason to go looking for her now."

Joshua sat down on the log. "It's likely your father is right. I know that ain't what you want to hear."

Owen looked at the frontiersman as if he had just betrayed him. "She *ain't* dead—she's alive, and I'll not leave her to rot among the Indians with the very man who murdered her kin!"

"Strong talk, coming from a sprout of a boy," Cooper said.

"I'm as much a man as a lot I know! And I'm more a man than my own father, who'd sit the rest of his days with his whiskey jug and let his daughter be forgot!"

Joshua said, "Well-spoken, Owen. You talk a man's talk, no question. But doing what you're trying to do won't help your sister or anybody else. It'll just get you killed."

"There has to be a way to get her back again."

"There are ways, but walking into the heart of the Chickamauga country alone and facing off with a madman like Tom Turndale ain't among them. When prisoners among the Indians are freed, it's generally through trade or treaty. But this is different. Tom Turndale lives among the Chickamaugas, but he's a man unto himself. He's not tied to following the Indian ways as much as a true Indian would be. Even if we had prisoners to offer in trade for your sister, there's no reason to think Turndale would go along with the bargain."

Owen was beginning to get angry, seeing his hopes again being shot down. "Well, I'm going after her. You won't stop me."

"We don't have to," Cooper said. "That cane stab has already done it. You won't go far with that thing poking into your foot."

Owen lowered his head and, to his shame, began to cry. He hated to cry, especially in front of strong men like these, who he figured probably never shed a tear over anything. When he regained control of himself and looked back at them, he was surprised to see no evidence of disapproval in their expressions.

"Owen Killefer, I have to say that I admire you," Joshua said, surprising Owen even more. "I vow, you'd walk right into hell itself if you thought it would help your sister."

"It ain't right, just turning your back on somebody like that," Owen said. "My father might declare her dead and gone, and you might too, but not me. Not me."

"Owen, let's get that cane out of your foot and get you back home," Joshua said.

"Not home," Owen replied defiantly. "I'll not go back and live with my father after this."

Joshua and Cooper exchanged glances. "Owen, that's something you and your father will have to work out between yourselves. It ain't our place to get involved in such as that." Joshua paused, then added, "But if it comes down to it and you won't go back, you've got a place at my house, if you need it."

They removed the stabbing cane with some difficulty; part of it had splintered inside and had caught in the muscle. Owen bit his lip as Joshua held his foot still and Cooper gouged out the bit of stalk with his knife. When the makeshift surgery was through, Owen could put no weight on the foot at all.

"We've got horses over the hill," Joshua said. "At least you won't have to walk, and we won't have to carry you all the way back."

In the end, Owen did go home to his father, but only after a stop at the Pinnock Inn to have his foot treated. Salem Pinnock bathed Owen's foot in liquor, eliciting a yowl of pain from the boy, then applied a salve of his own formulation that took almost all the pain away, followed by a poultice of tannin-rich oak bark held in place with a cloth bandage.

By then Owen had calmed down, and after Pinnock was finished, allowed Joshua to take him home. Aaron Killefer, half drunk, gave his son no greeting beyond a grunt, then took his rifle and examined it to make sure Owen hadn't hurt it.

When Joshua Colter was gone, Aaron Killefer walked

over to Owen, who sat on the side of the bed. "What did you do to your foot, boy?"

"Stepped on a cane stalk."

"Colter said you were trying to go after your sister."

"I was."

Aaron Killefer scratched his beard and gave Owen the coldest stare the boy had ever seen. "You're a fool, boy, and a shame to your father. If you ever do such as this again, I'll knock every tooth in your jaw down your throat." With that, he turned and staggered back to the table, where his whiskey jug awaited him. "And mind you see that foot doesn't putrefy. You wouldn't be good for nothing or nobody at all with only one peg to stand on."

Owen stayed awake late that night, thinking. Perhaps his attempt to rescue Emaline had been foolish, but he was glad he tried. Just making the effort had shown him he was capable of doing important things on his own. He was less a boy, more a man. Less Aaron Killefer's son, more his own person.

He intended to keep it that way from now on.

5

After his futile attempt to go after Emaline, Owen Killefer's life became only more trying and tumultuous. Aaron Killefer clearly resented his son for what he had done, because despite the wild foolishness of the effort, it had been a noble and touching foolishness that drew the respect of all who heard about it. In households all over the Nolichucky region, Owen's attempt to rescue his sister was discussed at length, and as Owen's name became representative of valor, Aaron Killefer's reputation further declined by comparison.

It surprised few when, less than a month after the incident, Owen Killefer left his father's house—was forced to leave, in fact. He showed up at the door of Joshua Colter's cabin with his face bruised and bloody. Aaron Killefer, nursing his rage and guilt, had beaten his son and thrown him out.

The Colters took Owen in without hesitation. Joshua Colter rode through the bright autumn countryside the next day to the Killefer cabin, and in an angry exchange warned Aaron Killefer that he was on the verge of stern discipline from the men of the community. Aaron answered angrily, accusing his son of having defied him repeatedly, refusing to work, refusing to respect him,

refusing to cease his accusations of complacency toward
the fate of Emaline. He had beaten Owen, he said, only
because the boy had pointed a loaded pistol at him,
threatening his life.

When Joshua confronted Owen with this charge, the
boy didn't deny it. But he had only been acting in self-
defense, he said. Aaron, drunk, had been coming at him
with a heavy piece of firewood in hand, and Owen had
feared for his life. Owen declared he had not threatened
his father until his father had first threatened him.

Joshua believed Owen, but because witnesses were
lacking to verify either Killefer's story, believed it would
be futile to pursue the matter further.

Joshua enjoyed having Owen about, even though
Owen was somber and brooded often about the break-
down of what little remained of his family. Joshua battled
Owen's depression by keeping him busy at farming and
hunting, and by beginning to teach him the Cherokee
language in the dialect of the Overhills. He was astonished at how quickly Owen picked up the basic structure
of the language, and a substantial vocabulary as well.

Joshua and Darcy talked over the possibility of letting
Owen live with them permanently, and were ready to extend the invitation when something happened that made
that prospect seem unwise. Matthew Barton rode out
from the Pinnock Inn to tell Joshua that Aaron Killefer
had come to the tavern, drunk, declaring he was going to
ride out to the Colter place and punish the youth for his
"devilishness."

"I filled him up with more whiskey, until he couldn't
move, much less ride out to your home," Barton said.
"But he seemed mighty stirred, and for some reason he
seems to resent in particular that Owen has abandoned
him in favor of you. If Owen remains here for long, I

think you'll see trouble on your doorstep from old Aaron."

Joshua pondered the problem and talked it over with Darcy, and the next day rode out to visit Charles Carney. Happily, he found the colonel in clearer mind than was common for him lately. He laid out the problem to Carney and his wife, and was gratified when both suggested the very solution Joshua had in mind: Owen would take up residence as a farmhand for the Carneys, living in a lean-to at the side of the main house. This would place him physically farther away from his father's house than was Joshua's residence, provide him employment, and more importantly, place him under the care of a man with sufficient connections to the courts and bodies of law—entities that Aaron Killefer held in great awe and fear, if various prior comments he had made in Joshua's presence were an indication. Colonel Carney had been active in the first phases of the Franklin movement, though he held no official seat in the assembly, and his son was a licensed attorney. The hope was that these statuses would intimidate Aaron Killefer sufficiently to discourage him from impulsively going after his son.

When presented with the proposal, Owen Killefer was reluctant, and it took much diplomacy for Joshua to convince him that he wasn't being asked to leave out of lack of welcome just where he was.

"It's strictly to avoid trouble with your father, who is nigh a neighbor to us here," Joshua argued. "Who can tell? It may be that soon matters will reach the place where you can return here, or even home, if your father should reform himself. In the meanwhile, the Carneys are offering you a fine opportunity. They are good people, Owen—the colonel, his missus, and Nell . . ."

Owen's eyes shifted slightly at mention of the last

name. He paused a couple of moments. "Well, perhaps I can give it a fair try."

"There's a good young man," Joshua said, patting Owen on the shoulder. When he turned away, he was smothering a grin. He had caught Owen's subtle reaction to the reminder of Nell Carney's presence in the colonel's household, and suspected he knew what it meant.

The year brought trouble and change to far more than the Killefer household. Salem Pinnock's pen remained busy, recording developments in the Franklin movement as they occurred.

Governor John Sevier kept his pen busy as well, corresponding with various officials and dignitaries, describing and supporting the Franklinite effort. Among the recipients of his letters was Virginia governor Patrick Henry. Correspondence with North Carolina's governor Martin ceased after the spring, with Richard Caswell, no stranger himself to the Overmountain country, succeeding Martin in office.

In October, Sevier wrote anew to Caswell, updating him on the Franklin matter and sending it by way of Captain Elijah Robertson to North Carolina. By this time, Jonesborough had ceased to be the capital of the fledgling state, the westward shift of population having led the Franklinites to change the capital to a growing little hamlet called Greene Courthouse, or Greeneville, county seat of Greene County, formed in 1783. The town and county had been named for General Nathanael Greene, the Rhode Islander who had played a prominent role in the American Revolution, and who was the first recipient of a land grant in the sprawling new county. A small log courthouse was notched together at the juncture of Greeneville's Main and First Cross streets, but the actual meeting place of the Franklin senate was the more commodious home and inn of one Robert Kerr, who had settled at the Big Spring around which Greeneville was springing up.

Franklin's leaders, while awaiting official federal recognition, busied themselves with developing laws, making appointments, setting official salaries (payable in animal skins), establishing a plan for tax payments (with skins, woolen cloth, bacon, whiskey, brandy, tobacco, linen, sugar, and other items of value acceptable in place of currency), and creating new county divisions within the state's rather loosely defined borders. Two new counties, Caswell and Sevier, were carved out of portions of Greene County. A third new county, Spencer, was made through a division of Sullivan County and part of Greene. A fourth county, Wayne, named after General Anthony Wayne, was erected out of part of North Carolina's Washington County and a piece of Wilkes County.

Then came November, and an event that brought the year to an uncertain close for the people of Franklin.

It happened at Hopewell, South Carolina, on the Keowee River, and the instigator was the Congress, which moved without consultation of the residents of Franklin or the Cumberland settlements farther west.

On November 18 representatives of the upper towns of the Cherokees met with congressional appointees for what would be a historic treaty. The atmosphere was charged with a sense of hope and anticipation on the part of the Cherokees, who saw in the meeting the best opportunity yet for fair dealings concerning their continual loss of land to white encroachment.

This was a significantly different treaty meeting than the Dumplin Creek conference that Joshua Colter had attended. For one thing, the Hopewell meeting carried the authority of Congress, rather than that of an officially unrecognized state. For another, this meeting had the approval and attendance of Old Tassel.

Old Tassel and his fellow Cherokees listened to the American representatives describe their defeat of the British, and as such were now sovereign over all the country, including that held by the Cherokees. Rest assured, Old Tassel was told, that the new government wished no harm to the Cherokee people, and desired not to encroach on their lands. Any Cherokee grievances would be gladly heard, and any wrongs already done would be corrected. Now, just which portion of the land did the Cherokees seek to be their own?

Old Tassel stood and replied in the typical Cherokee oratorical fashion that never failed to impress any who heard it. The land upon which he now stood, he declared, was the very land the Cherokees had fought for during the American struggle against Britain. The Great Man Above created it for the country's aborigines. Only for a few years had the white men known this country, while the "red men" were its first stock. It was as friends and guests that the white men lived on this land now, and as a sign of that friendship, Old Tassel presented the traditional beads to the white men.

That ceremony behind, Old Tassel's talk drove straight to the point. The North Carolinians had taken the Indian lands and used them to build their own fortunes. Richard Henderson, the Carolina judge who some years before had signed a treaty for vast amounts of lands in Kentucky and the Cumberland country, declared he had "purchased" the lands, but he, Old Tassel said, was a rogue and a liar. The late Cherokee statesman Little Carpenter had signed

Henderson's deed, but without the consent of the Cherokees. Oconostota's name was also on the deed, Old Tassel
noted, but was put there by Henderson himself.

With those stunning charges made, Old Tassel picked up
a copy of a map brought by the commissioners and indicated on it the boundaries claimed by the Cherokees, and a
small circle indicating Henderson's purchase area.

The diplomatic situation facing the commissioners was
delicate, because Old Tassel's understanding of Henderson's treaty was quite different than the conventional view.
Conferring, the commissioners gave a carefully worded answer. Colonel Henderson, Oconostota, and Little Carpenter, they noted, were all dead and could not be consulted
about Old Tassel's claims. Showing a copy of Henderson's
deed, they pointed out the signatures and noted that much
time had passed since the Henderson transaction had been
struck. The country had been settled on a good-faith assumption of the deed's validity, and it was out of the power
of any government now to void it. Therefore, Old Tassel
would have to lessen the Cherokees' claimed area on the
assumption that Henderson's deed was valid.

Reluctantly, Old Tassel acceded. "There are three
thousand white people now living in the forks of the
French Broad and Holston," the chief replied. That spot
was a favored one of his people and could not be given
up. Yet already there were settlers moving to within
twenty-five miles of the Cherokee towns—and they
would have to be removed.

The commissioners replied that the settlers had come to
the Holston and French Broad while the Cherokees were
under the protection of Britain. If they were to have been
removed, it should have been done by the king. Now the
settlers' numbers were simply too great for the new government to deal with. They could not be evicted.

Old Tassel, expressing surprise that Congress would be so weak as to not be able to deal with its own people, argued further, but in the end again downwardly revised the Cherokee claim. Thus the Hopewell Treaty boundary was set. It ran from a point forty miles above Nashborough on the Cumberland River, over to six miles south of the Nolichucky, then south to the Oconee River. Reserved as a treaty ground was the sacred Long Island of the Holston River. All previous treaties, Sevier's Dumplin Creek pact included, were now disavowed and nullified.

So went the treaty of Hopewell, and its impact on the Franklinites would be enormous. By agreeing to the Hopewell boundary line, the commissioners had officially declared that even Greeneville, Franklin's capital town, lay on Cherokee ground, and by terms of the treaty, would have to be vacated within six months.

When terms of the Hopewell Treaty were learned in the Overmountain country, more than a few Franklinites accepted the viewpoint voiced in the Pinnock Inn by a furious Cooper Haverly: "It's punishment, that's what it is. Punishment against Franklin itself for daring to exist when Mother Carolina doesn't want it to."

Even Joshua Colter, far more reserved and cautious in his views, was prone to agree. And he also had to agree in large measure with Salem Pinnock's observation: "According to that treaty, the Cherokees have the right, given by authority of our own nation, to punish any settler who doesn't vacate from beyond the line within half a year. It's as open a door for Indian raids as ever I've heard one. The Cherokees are no fools—they know those settlers can't pull up every root they've planted and just walk away. They've prodded the fool government into issuing them an official invitation to take the scalps of the very people who drove off the Tories and brought down Patrick Ferguson at King's Mountain!"

Joshua could not say whether the Cherokees' motivations were as duplicitous as Pinnock perceived them, but it hardly mattered. The end result would inevitably be exactly as Pinnock had said.

Joshua thought back on his feelings of doubt at the Dumplin Creek treaty conference, and realized they had been prophetic. As sure as the sun would rise, a time of violence was about to descend on the Overmountain frontier.

The events most immediately responsible for bringing about the troubles Joshua Colter anticipated occurred at the Great Bend region of the Tennessee River, and involved both John Sevier and his brother Valentine. Ironically, an act of the state of Georgia, which had been represented at the Hopewell Treaty, provided the tinder upon which the spark was lit.

John Sevier's political activities in 1785 had included discussions with Georgia about the settlement of the Great Bend, a rich and coveted area along the Tennessee River. Georgia's assembly moved to create a county called Houston at the Bend, and named John Sevier as a commissioner, along with others, including Indian agent Joseph Martin, and John Donelson, who had led the flatboat flotilla of settlers to the Cumberland country in the bitter winter of early 1780.

An initial settlement attempt of the area was in the works about the same time the Hopewell Treaty was struck. Valentine Sevier, leading some ninety settlers, descended by boat to the Great Bend for the purpose of building a protective stockade around which the proposed settlement would develop.

In the Five Lower Towns of the Chickamaugas, the militant chief Dragging Canoe was infuriated by the influx of settlers, and immediately moved to stop it. The isolated band of settlers and speculators, already well along the way to naming civil and military officers and erecting a protective blockhouse, was attacked by the Chickamaugas in the first of what would be an ongoing and debilitating series of raids. As the year closed, the would-be settlement builders found themselves under such severe siege that it became apparent the project could not go on. Early in 1786 they began their withdrawal, Dragging Canoe plaguing them all the way.

There were deaths in the fighting. A pair of Indian fatalities were to prove of particular import. Two sons of a warrior named Headman died in skirmishing with the retreating settlers, and Headman declared that white scalps must be taken in revenge. He hired warriors from the town of Coyatee to secure them.

In Greene County the family of a man named Ebenezer Birum paid Headman's price at the hands of the hired warriors. But the raids did not stop there. The Chickamaugas, heady at their success in driving Valentine Sevier's settlement party from the Great Bend, fanned out across the frontier, ranging far and striking isolated farmsteads and cabins. In the valley of the Powell River, where Joshua Colter had roamed as a long hunter many years before, a settler named Archie Scott was killed, along with four children. His wife became a prisoner, and made her name famous on the frontier by escaping some days after her capture, roaming through the wilderness, catching fish by hand and foraging for roots to keep herself alive. Eventually she reached Martin's Station and safety.

Ravages of the Indians spread even farther. A band of

warriors from one of the Five Lower Towns entered Kentucky and began a series of raids and horse-theft excursions. After one successful raid near Logan's Station, the Chickamaugas employed their tradition of shouting the name of their base town—in this instance, Crowtown.

Colonel John Logan, Kentuckian leader, was infuriated. With the speed characteristic of frontiersmen, he gathered riflemen and set out in pursuit of the raiders, crossing the Cumberland River and striking an Indian path that followed Walden's Ridge, following the track of the retreating raiders.

Joshua Colter waited expectantly as Cooper Haverly came rushing toward him, his rifle balanced in his left hand and a look of excitement on his face. He had been sent to investigate the cause of noise ahead, noise of the sort made by a band of traveling men.

"It's militiamen, Josh, and you'll never guess who's among them!"

"Then I won't try. Who?"

"Callum McSwain, that's who!"

Joshua was astounded. Scotland-born Callum McSwain, his old blacksmithing, gunsmithing friend from years past, had been living in Kentucky since migrating to the Logan's Station area in 1783 with the congregation of the Exodus Presbyterian Church, shepherded by the blind preacher Israel Coffman. Since that move, McSwain had married Ayasta, the Cherokee widow of slain Chickamauga militant John Hawk. Joshua had not seen McSwain for about two years.

"If Callum's with them, it must be Kentucky militia," Joshua said. "Come on—let's go meet them and see what's brought them."

Callum McSwain looked totally but pleasantly surprised to see Joshua Colter and Cooper Haverly ride into view, leading the band of Colter's Rangers, of whom he had once been a part. Joshua and Cooper dismounted, McSwain did the same, and there was much slapping of shoulders, pumping of hands, and broad grins as the men renewed acquaintance. Others who knew McSwain—most of Joshua's ranger group falling into that category—left their own saddles to join the enthusiastic greeting.

McSwain eagerly introduced Joshua to the leader of his own group, Logan. "Colonel Logan, I'm pleased to meet you," Joshua said. "Is it Indian raiding that's brought you down this far?"

"Indeed it is," Logan replied, going on to describe the raids and horse thievery his region had suffered. "The raiders are from Crowtown, that much we know. We've been hard on their track and hope to overtake them soon."

"We've had trouble aplenty of our own," Joshua said. "Me and these good rangers here have been scouting this countryside in search of war parties. We're acting under color of the state of Franklin."

Logan looked Joshua's woodsmen over. A ragtag bunch they were, but strong and clear of eye. He turned again to Joshua. "Sir, we would be honored to have the famed Colter's Rangers join us."

Without hesitation the rangers voiced their agreement to the proposal. With all the men feeling encouraged by the heightened numbers, the riders continued their search, Joshua, Cooper, and McSwain having to fight off the urge to talk freely among themselves as old friends long separated are prone to do.

*   *   *

The encounter and fight came abruptly. It was in every way typical of frontier battles. No advance bluster, no fanfare, no fifes and drums, no thundering hooves of mounted battalions, no crisply barked formal orders. Nothing but the crack of rifle fire, the rising of gun smoke, and various shouts of warning, of threat, of triumph, of pain. Then there was silence, gun smoke dispersing through the branches, and the bodies of seven dead Cherokees on the ground, their dark blood spreading slowly around them.

Joshua Colter relocated and tried to get his heart back down from his throat. He had fired only once in the brief altercation, and had missed his man. That he had missed was no accident. Joshua had recognized the Indian in his sights as his finger had triggered the shot. He had deflected his aim at the last half second—only to see the Indian he had spared struck down immediately after by a ball fired by one of the Kentuckians.

Joshua walked over to the familiar Indian's body and rolled it onto its back. His stomach knotted. "Cooper, come here," he said.

"You know him, Joshua?"

"Yes. His names escapes me, but he's a brother of the Fool Warrior." Joshua looked about at the other corpses. "And I've seen a couple of these others too."

"Chickamauga?"

"Upper town Cherokee. Lord help us, Cooper, I think we've killed the wrong ones. You heard them when we came upon them: They claimed to be peaceful. I believe they were telling the truth."

Callum McSwain had walked up in time to hear Joshua's words. "Joshua, if you're right, there will be much trouble to come of this."

Joshua felt great dismay. He turned and stalked off, angry at himself, his rangers, and especially at Logan's militia for the too-quick attack. This expedition had corrected no problems by its hasty violence. It had worsened them.

Colonel Logan, contrary to Joshua, remained sure the slain Indians were the ones who had raided in Kentucky; the issue would remain at debate for years to come. In any case, after the battle, Logan gathered his men together and began the journey home, satisfied that the militia's intent had been fulfilled.

Joshua and Cooper said their farewells to McSwain, regretting that their unexpected reunion was cut so short. As McSwain rode away with the militia, Joshua realized he had not gained much news about other friends now living in Kentucky. There hadn't been enough time for a good talk.

"I'm going to go to Kentucky one of these days," he told Cooper. "I'd pull one of my own teeth right now for the chance to set down and have a long talk with Israel Coffman." He looked back at the sight of the battle, if such it could properly be called. "Lord knows it would be good to talk to somebody who could make some sense of the fool things we get ourselves into."

The deaths of the seven Cherokees at the hands of the militiamen fueled a fire that was already too hot. Indian agent Joseph Martin sought to maintain peace by sending a messenger to the Cherokee chief Bloody Fellow, a relative of whom had been among the survivors of the fight. He and the other survivors had escaped, no doubt to bear immediately news of the killings to the Cherokee towns.

Martin pleaded with Bloody Fellow to not seek vengeance for the attack, and to ask similar restraint of the Fool Warrior, even though Cherokee tradition would have him seek recompense for the killing of his brother. Satisfaction surely could be provided by the whites in some other way.

Bloody Fellow's reply was heavy with contempt. He knew what came of patience and restraint and demands for satisfaction in peaceable ways. "I will take my own satisfaction for my brother." The Fool Warrior was equally determined, declaring he would kill the white traders among the Cherokees in retaliation.

Joshua Colter watched developments thereafter with a strong awareness of how predictable all this was. It was ever this way on the frontier: killing, more killing in response, and even more killing in response to that. The cycle was endless, kept in motion by those of both the races who competed for land and power. Joshua wondered if the wheel would ever stop turning.

Together, Bloody Fellow and Fool Warrior led warriors to the Dumplin Creek settlements. Their revenge was fierce, leaving as its mark burned cabins, stolen horses, dead cattle, and dead men. By the time the raiders' thirst for vengeance was slaked, fifteen settlers had lost their lives and scalps.

Beside the body of one of the slain was a note, left by Bloody Fellow and addressed to John Sevier, governor of Franklin.

I have now taken satisfaction for my brother and friends who were murdered. I did not wish for war, but if the white people want war, that is what they will get.

Owen Killefer raised his cocked rifle slowly and carefully sighted down its length. His finger touched the trigger, began a slow, careful squeeze—and then, against all common hunter's sense, he moved, took a slight step forward for no good reason, and in so doing made enough noise to send his target, a squirrel, scurrying around a big oak and out of sight.

Owen lowered the rifle with a sigh. What was wrong with him lately? He was making a bad job of everything he attempted. Couldn't keep his mind on what he was doing.

The truth was, he knew fully well what was wrong. With *her* around, how could he hope to keep his mind on anything else?

He put the rifle over his shoulder and turned back toward the Carney house with a sigh. He was only a half mile or so from the house, hunting in a grove of trees that was always rich with squirrels and from which he seldom failed to bring in good meat for Mary Carney's flavorful stews. Today would be different, obviously. He was too distracted by his never-ending thoughts of Nell Carney to have much hope of bringing in game this day.

It was the oddest feeling, being so wrought up over a young lady. And aggravating too, especially since this young lady seemed to think herself older than she was. Though Nell Carney was only a few months his senior, she acted as if he were a mere boy, and her a grown woman. She seemed hardly to notice him most of the time, and when she did, "spoke down" to him. Sometimes her airs were merely irritating. Most times they were downright hurtful. He might easily have come to despise her . . . but he couldn't despise Nell Carney. Not ever, no matter what she did. And that was too bad. It seemed to him it would be a devil of a lot easier to live around someone he despised than someone he loved but who refused to even notice him, much less love him in return.

He trudged on, until movement in a treetop nearby caught his attention. Freezing, he looked for the cause, and spotted a big squirrel perched on a precariously thin limb, readying itself to jump to the next treetop. Owen swung up his rifle, cocked it, and fired. The squirrel fell with a soft thud to the leafy forest floor. Owen walked over, picked it up and grinned. A good clean-killing shot, grazing right across the top of the head and damaging none of the meat.

He reloaded and moved on, feeling better for success. Now that he had one squirrel, he might as well try for three or four more. The Carneys were fond of squirrel-meat stew, and a good fresh supply would impress them. Maybe even impress Nell. If she noticed he was a good hunter, she might notice him in other ways, maybe even come to think of him as the kind of fellow a young lady like herself really needed . . .

Owen's spirits began to rise, bouyed by romanticized fantasies. He turned to his right and headed through the grove, his mind on an ancient, Indian-cleared meadow about a quarter of a mile away. Along its tree line squirrels could usually be found in abundance. With any luck, he could bag several and be home in plenty of time to skin and clean them for supper.

Nell Carney moved with deliberate, sweeping grace through the midst of the meadow, her arms spread, her head tilted, her hair hanging loose around her face. She was lost in romantic fantasies of her own, imitating in her posture a beautiful character she had once seen in a painting that hung over the mantel in the opulent home of one of her father's powerful Carolina friends back east of the mountains. She had been only a little girl when she had visited that house. Where it had been and who it had belonged to she could not remember, yet she could recall every detail of that painting above the fireplace. She had stood before it, mouth open in childish awe, staring at the remarkable beauty of the unnamed woman it depicted and thinking that all the world would be a wonderful place if she could grow up to possess that kind of feminine splendor in her own person. Thereafter, Nell Carney's concept of the summit of beauty had been wrapped up in her memory of that painting, and as the years had gone by, slowly the face in her mental picture of that painting had become her own.

She turned, pivoting delicately on bare feet and imagining that the plain and well-worn dress that adorned her was the long, white, laced gown from the portrait. Eyes closed, she spread her arms wider, turned her face toward the sky and pictured her lover emerging from the forest to greet her. His image in her mind was as precise as her own; he was Dover Hice, a longtime friend of the Carney family from North Carolina. Not *exactly* Dover Hice—her mental image of him stripped a few years and several pounds away from him. Nell had known for two years now that she would become betrothed to Hice as soon as her father deemed her of sufficient age, and hints had been strong of late that the time at last was near. She would marry Hice, move back across the mountains with him, and enter a life of bliss and comfort. She would be splendid and beautiful, and she would wear long white dresses just like that ideal woman in that ideal portrait.

And then all at once she knew she was not alone. A chill made her shiver, and she dropped her arms and opened her eyes and looked right into the face of Owen

Killefer, who stood at the edge of the meadow, gaping at her with his big, boyish eyes. He held his rifle in one hand and a dead squirrel in the other. For a few terrible moments Nell stared back at him, then humiliation washed over her, followed instantly by fury.

"You've been watching me?" she asked in a voice full of challenge. "You've been *watching* me?"

Owen's mouth dropped open. "Well, no . . . I mean, I just come to hunt squirrels, and I saw you there, and . . ."

Nell turned and ran away, toward the distant house. Her bare foot came down on a stone, and pain jolted up her left leg. She paused only a moment, then continued, running into the opposite woods with a limp until she was out of Owen's sight.

He stood there, feeling confused and sad. He realized he had caught her in a private moment and embarrassed her. He hadn't meant to do it; he had simply come out of the woods and found her there, only a moment before she had noticed him.

But she didn't know that. Clearly she believed he had been there a longer time, watching her, and now she was angry with him about it. And the worst part was, there was nothing he could say that would make her believe anything different.

Exasperation waved over him. On an angry impulse, he lifted the squirrel he had shot, swung it around his head in a big circle, and sent it flying into the trees. Let the buzzards or the dogs or the wild hogs have it! He had lost his taste for squirrel meat and squirrel hunting. Hefting up his rifle, he stomped toward the Carney house, swearing beneath his breath with every stride and knowing he would feel guilty and shamed when next he faced Nell Carney—and this even though he hadn't done one deuced thing wrong.

6

Cooper Haverly's horse was skittish today, hard to control. Cooper struggled to keep the animal still, wondering if its restlessness resulted from some inate sense of the excitement about to come. "Settle, boy, settle now," Cooper said, patting the horse gently on the back of its muscled neck. "Settle down— that's good, that's good."

"That's a spirited horse," Mark Travis said. He was a young Nolichucky farmer and friend of Cooper. "Have you ever raced him?"

"No."

"If you did, I'd wager on him. I'd like to see him run."

Cooper said, "You may see him run today, depending on how hard they resist us."

Travis, already toothless at age twenty-three, grinned, leaned over and spat tobacco juice. "They won't do nothing. Nary a thing."

Cooper looked around at the band of men. Most of them were his age or younger; all were residents of the Nolichucky settlements, and avid Franklinites. They were grouped in a forest clearing a few miles from Jonesborough, well-armed and ready to embark on an adventure of Cooper's own design. Before the day was done, they intended to show everyone on the border just how dedicated to the state of Franklin they were.

Cooper did not share Travis's optimism about likely resistance. The pro-Carolinians could be just as determined as the Franklinites, and if word had somehow reached them of today's planned action, there could be trouble, and danger. Cooper didn't worry much about that as far as he himself was concerned, but there was one member of the party he couldn't feel comfortable about exposing to possible harm.

He turned in the saddle. "Owen, come here a moment."

Owen Killefer moved his horse out of the group and to Cooper's side.

"What is it?"

Cooper braced himself for the outburst he knew his words would bring. "I don't want you to go with us."

"What? Why the devil not? Travis told me I could come if I wanted!"

"Well, I don't want you to. Too dangerous, and you're too young. If anything happened to you, Colonel Carney would have my hide."

"Too young? I'm man enough to carry my part, I reckon! Why, Governor Sevier himself was a married man when he was my age!"

"I don't doubt your ability, Owen. But I've got to trust my feelings, and my feeling is you ought not take part in this. I don't know Colonel Carney would like a boy . . . a man under his hire out busting up Carolina courts."

Owen glared at Cooper, opened his mouth to speak, then couldn't find words in his anger. He leaned over, spat on the ground, and reined his horse about. Without another comment he rode away.

Travis acted sheepish. "Sorry, Cooper. It was my doing,

having him here. He wanted to be part of it, once he knew what we were doing."

"What bothers me more than him coming along is the fact you let him know what we were planning. Who else did you tell, Mark?"

"Not a soul, not a soul. I swear it."

Cooper watched Owen ride out of sight. "Very well, then. I believe you. But next time, you talk to me before you go recruiting folk, you hear?"

"I hear."

"Got the fire?" Cooper asked one of the others. The man nodded and held up a small metal pail with a well-perforated cover. Smoke spewed from the holes.

"We're ready, then," Cooper said. He looked over the group one final time. It was a good group. Putting Owen out of his mind, he lifted his rifle above his head and said, "New state men!"

"New state men!" the others bellowed back.

They advanced, moving through the lush summer forest and out onto the road. They rode north, their destination being a house about two miles ahead, where Joshua anticipated finding, among others, one John Tipton, a man in dire need of a lesson. Cooper intended to be his educator this very day.

Cooper grew more excited the closer they came to their destination. No one but the men with him here, and a handful of others, knew what they were up to. Cooper had kept his plans from Hannah, knowing she wouldn't approve of them, and had made sure that Joshua also remained ignorant of the scheme. Cooper found Joshua's growing conservatism irritating; age was dampering Joshua Colter's firebrand spirits too much to suit him. A few years before, Joshua would have jumped at the chance to take part in this kind of adventure, which now had to be kept from him.

Joshua continued to declare his support of the Franklin movement, but in Cooper's book he showed far too little enthusiasm, especially given the growing opposition to the new state on the part of John Tipton and his faction. Cooper held a slight grudge against Joshua over the issue. Hang it all, if Franklin was worth supporting, then it was worth supporting all the way! Cooper wasn't one to back anything halfheartedly.

John Tipton, born in Maryland but a resident of Virginia through his adult life, had migrated to the Tennessee country in 1782, settling in Washington County on Sinking Creek, a different stream than the identically named one in what was now Greene County, where Joshua's adoptive father, the late Alphus Colter, had helped establish a settlement years before. Folks said from the outset that Tipton, a former member of the House of Burgesses, was a good citizen, with a distinguished military record. He had fought under General Andrew Lewis back in 1774 in Dunmore's war, and in the Revolution had recruited for the Continental Army and taken part in the committee of safety in Virginia's Shenandoah County. Tipton's brother, who had settled in the Overmountain region back in the 1770s, had fought at King's Mountain along with Cooper, Joshua, John Sevier, and many other present-day Franklinites.

Cooper had nothing all that personal against Tipton. His anger stemmed strictly from Tipton's antagonism toward the new state movement, and as a natural offshoot, toward John Sevier, whom Cooper so idolized. Over the course of the year, Tipton had become the symbolic leader of the anti-Franklin effort, just as Sevier led the new staters. Cooper resented the confusion and strife that Tipton deliberately injected into the already uncertain Franklin situation. He had to wonder why Tipton seemed so insistent on stifling every effort to create a new state. The man had even sat in on the early formative Franklin councils, but had emerged as an opponent. He voted against the formation of the new state, and refused to gracefully go along after his side lost that ballot. That angered Cooper. Why couldn't Tipton be more like John Sevier, who at one early point had been ready to drop the state effort but yielded to the public will once it was clear the majority was in favor of Franklin?

What spurred Cooper to today's action were some actions committed by Tipton earlier in the year— outrageous, infuriating actions, in Cooper's view. Late in the prior year, a constitutional convention had convened in Greeneville, seeking to replace the temporary constitution under which Franklin had operated up until then. A proposed new constitution, drawn up by a committee heavily influenced by Presbyterian clergymen and educators, had been presented, but after some of its provisions came under criticism, not adopted. The controversy had only deepened existing rifts within the new state.

Some days after that convention, Cooper had been walking beside John Sevier in Jonesborough when they happened to meet none other than John Tipton. Sevier and Tipton argued violently, until at last Sevier lifted his cane and clubbed Tipton. Tipton set in with fists, and the residents of Jonesborough were briefly treated to the sight of the leaders of both political factions going head-to-head and fist-to-fist in the dust. Cooper and others separated the two, but the trouble was not over.

When the Franklin court came into session in Jonesborough, Tipton appeared again, this time leading a group of supporters. They entered the courthouse, ripped court papers from the hands of the stunned clerk, evicted the justices, and burned the seized records. Cooper was livid when he learned of this, and only Hannah's tears and pleas had restrained him from immediately going after Tipton.

Cooper gritted his teeth. Hannah might have interceded successfully that day, but if she thought she had cooled his determination to respond to Tipton's outrages, she was wrong. Cooper had bided his time, talked to his peers, set his plans, and today was putting them in place. By heaven, John Tipton was going to learn a much-needed lesson before this day was through!

He halted his riders when they came in sight of their destination—a typical log house, with several horses hobbled or tethered to trees in the yard. Court was in session here today, under authority of North Carolina and John Tipton. Cooper studied the scene in silence for several moments, glanced around at his companions, and again lifted his rifle.

"New state men!" he roared.

"New state men!" came back the rallying cry. Then they rode down toward the makeshift courthouse, whooping and shouting, as men emerged from the door with looks of alarm and confusion on their faces, and the startled horses in the dirt yard stumbled on their hobbles or strained at their tethers. Cooper sent up an Indian-styled whoop, again echoed by his followers.

Cooper leaped off his horse before it came to a full stop, and pushed his way past three men. Someone cursed and reached out to restrain him as he entered the house. Cooper shook him off. His men poured in behind him.

John Tipton appeared, facing him down. "What is the meaning of this intrusion?"

"Step aside, you scoundrel," Cooper said. He pushed Tipton aside, advanced to the front of the room and swept up the gavel that lay on the table serving as the justice bench. He hammered the gavel against the table so hard that the head broke off and flew toward Tipton, who instinctively caught it, then stood holding it, a confused expression on his face.

"This here court is officially adjourned in the name of the good state of Franklin!" Cooper bellowed, leaping atop the table with his rifle in one hand and the broken gavel in the other. "Any having court business to tend to are advised that no North Carolina court holds sway in these parts." Then, whooping triumphantly, he kicked a stack of court papers from the table to the floor.

There was no resistance; everyone was too stunned to react. Cooper's fire-bearing companion came forward, laughing aloud, and dumped the smoldering coals from his bucket onto the papers.

They made a wonderfully hot and smoking bonfire, and as he watched them flare into ashes, with John Tipton bellowing and raging with equivalent heat in the background, Cooper Haverly thought he had never had so much fun in his life.

Owen's anger over being rejected by Cooper had degenerated to general sullenness by the time he reached the Carney house, and even that was quickly overcome by curiosity when he saw the extra horses in the pen by the stable. Visitors? He had heard of none coming—but then, he was seldom told the family's business in advance. He recognized one of the horses as Alexander Carney's. The others he didn't know.

He rode to the pen, took his own horse inside, and removed the saddle, which he took into the stable. As he emerged, he saw Colonel Carney walking across the yard toward him. At first Owen was afraid the old man was coming to scold him for his unexplained absence, but then he saw Carney's big smile.

"Owen! Good to see you!" he said. "Come inside— there's news I want you to share."

"News? Is anything wrong?"

"Oh, no, no, quite the opposite, my boy."

"I see there are visitors . . ."

"Yes. Dover Hice and some of his kin have come to see us. It's a long-awaited visit. Nell is thrilled. You know how long she's waited for all this to be worked out."

Owen was accustomed by now to the colonel's confused and confusing way of talking. Whatever Nell had been awaiting, whatever had been "worked out," was nothing Owen knew anything about.

"I don't understand what you mean, Colonel."

"Why, the engagement, my boy! You haven't heard . . . no, I suppose you haven't. The short of it is, Nell is betrothed. She and Dover Hice will be married just as soon as . . . good lands, boy, you look sick of a sudden! Are you ill?"

Owen's throat had suddenly grown so tight he could hardly speak. "I . . . yes, sir, I think maybe I am."

"Come inside, then, and have some food, something to drink. That'll put the strength in you."

"Sir, if you don't mind it, I think I'd rather go to the lean-to and lie down awhile."

"Certainly, certainly. I'll have something brought out to you."

"No thank you, sir. I don't feel like eating right now."

The old man nodded. His big grin returned. "Nell is to be married, you know," he said, his mind turning back on itself again. "To Dover Hice of North Carolina. He's come to visit us today."

"Yes, sir."

"You go lie down, then. And come in to join us as soon as you feel well enough."

"Thank you, sir. I'll do that."

Owen managed, with much difficulty, to wait until the colonel was back in his house before he turned and emptied the contents of his stomach onto the ground. He staggered across the yard and into the lean-to, where he threw himself onto his bed and felt for all the world like dying. Indeed he was sick, but not with a physical ailment.

Betrothed ... to another man. All his vain hopes and fantasies died with a jolting suddenness. She would never be his.

Cooper knew it was Joshua Colter at the door as soon as the first knock threatened to break the hinges. He scowled at his wife, for Hannah was crying loud enough that Joshua probably could hear her from the outside, and that embarrassed him.

"Cooper!" Joshua yelled. "Open this door before I kick it down!"

Cooper's attitude was far from welcoming when he answered the door, and he made no attempt to hide his feelings. And, as he had anticipated, Joshua looked plenty angry himself. Without waiting for an invitation, he pushed past Cooper and into the house.

Hannah was by the fireplace, wiping her tears. She didn't cry often, usually only when Cooper yelled at her, as had been the case tonight. Hannah had chastised Cooper so much for what he had done at Tipton's court that he had finally gotten his fill of it and shouted at her in anger. Now Cooper was beginning to feel regretful about losing his temper, but the incident was still fresh and he hadn't yet softened to the point of apology. With Joshua intruding at just this moment, in fact, it seemed unlikely he would soften any further at all. Grow angrier and harder, most probably. Joshua had a way of bringing that out in him.

Young Ben, Cooper and Hannah's son, stood clinging to his mother's skirts, clearly disturbed by all of this. The atmosphere was palpably tense. Joshua couldn't have picked a more undesirable moment to come poking his nose into matters.

He didn't waste time in getting to it. "Cooper, I want to know if it's true that—"

"Yes, yes, it's true!" Cooper cut him off. "I busted up John Tipton's court and burned his papers, and I'm hanged if I intend to apologize to you or anybody else for it!"

Joshua rolled his eyes upward. "I knew it! Soon as I heard it, I knew it had to be! Just the kind of hothead foolery I'd expect from you, brother!"

"Don't expect me to say I'm sorry!" Cooper's volume and sharp tone made little Ben start and begin to cry.

Hannah knelt and put her arm around the child. "See what you've done now, Cooper?"

"Don't be telling me how to talk in my own cabin, woman!"

Joshua said, "I don't expect you to apologize. For one thing, I know you better than to think you would. You'd rather pull your own teeth than say you were sorry for any fool thing you ever did. For another thing, I got no more love for old troublemaking Tipton than you do. It ain't on his behalf I've come."

"Then why are you here, calling me a fool and acting like you been appointed my mother of a sudden?"

Joshua laughed a mildly mocking laugh; in Cooper's jaundiced interpretation, it sounded outright derisive. "Your mother, eh? Is that how I sound to you?" Joshua said. "Blast and blazes, you could use a mother, the trouble you get yourself into!"

Cooper swore at his brother and pointed at the door. "It's still open. It'll let a wise-arse out as good as it lets him in."

Joshua appeared to catch a retort just before it could pass his lips, paused, took a deep breath and gave Cooper one of those looks that could be so aggravating, an older brother's familial look of superior wisdom and maturity, the kind that in tense times such as this made Cooper want to play Cain to Joshua's Abel. "Cooper, calm yourself. I came here because I don't want harm coming to you. What you did was mighty dangerous. Old John Tipton might have shot you, if he had taken a mind to. He may do it yet."

"Let him try."

Joshua shook his head. "You've got a bloody lot of growing up left to do. You're a man in body, but you think like a boy."

Cooper roared and lunged at Joshua, swinging his right fist. Joshua caught Cooper's forearm and twisted it, making Cooper pivot in the process, so that Joshua held him with his arm twisted painfully in the small of his back. Joshua talked directly into his brother's ear.

"You listen to me, Cooper. You're a fine brother and as good a man as I could hope to find on the border, or anywhere else. I watched you come into this world from our mother's body, and I've loved you from that first sight of you. I don't want to see you hurt—but unless you learn to cool that hot head of yours, you're sure as the devil going to get hurt. Maybe killed. I'm glad you're a new state man. I'm one too. I'm glad you support John Sevier. So do I. But I'm not willing to see my own brother get himself killed for the state of Franklin and John Sevier and pure pigheadedness. Look there at that wife of yours, and that boy. They're the ones you need to be looking out for, before you go putting your neck on the block for these high causes that have you so wrought-up lately." And with that he shoved Cooper away, dumping him on the floor. Ben sent up a renewed howling wail.

Cooper rose and shoved a finger at Joshua's nose. "Get out of my house, and don't come in here again. You're no brother of mine, not anymore. You may not think the new state and Governor Sevier are worth fighting for. I do. I'll bust up courts, burn papers, break noggins, lynch traitors, and take up arms if it comes to that. That's a man's way of thinking, Joshua. It's you who's acting the child, saying you support the new state, but doing nothing for it."

"Nothing for it? I've rode this countryside with rifle and militia, fought Indians, talked treaties—you call that nothing?"

"Get out of here."

Joshua turned and stormed out the door. Cooper followed, shouted after him: "Don't you come talking high and mighty to me again, Joshua Colter! I'll not hear no more of it!"

Cooper slammed the door closed and turned in time to see Hannah striding toward him. She looked fierce.

"Hannah, I regret you had to see—"

He cut off sharply when she slapped him. He gaped, astounded that she had done it. Then she did it again.

Cooper swore and raised his fist. Ben let out a terrible

scream. Hannah blanched, quailed, backed off. Cooper's uplifted hand began to shake, and he lowered it slowly. "God, I'm sorry. Hannah, I'm so sorry."

Hannah said nothing. She went to Ben, hefted him up, and opened the door. She walked out and across the yard. Ben laid his head on her shoulder, looking back sadly at his father in the doorway.

"Hannah!" Cooper shouted. "Hannah, come back!"

She would not turn. Cooper felt a choking sensation. "Hannah . . ." For a moment he felt very sad. But then, in the emotional caldron bubbling inside him, anger began to surface again. He knew what Hannah was doing. She was going over to Joshua and Darcy's cabin, there to join with them as they discussed what a fool and wretch was Cooper Haverly.

"Go on! Off with you, then!" he yelled after his wife. "If a man can't be respected in his own home, then to hell with it all, and to hell with everybody!"

Cooper left the cabin less than two minutes later, riding off in cyclonic fury. His intention was to go to the Pinnock Inn and down as much of Matthew Barton's whiskey as he could get into him. But no—the Pinnock Inn wouldn't do. It was too public a place, and he would be the natural center of attention, given what he and his men had done at Tipton's court. Right now he didn't want attention. Only whiskey.

He stopped, thinking, then smiled. He knew where he could go, a place where he could drink until the hurt and anger were washed away, but without making himself a public spectacle. He goaded his horse down the road, and just past a massive oak, turned north along a narrow path that ascended a timbered hillside. Despite the season, the evening was growing cool. No matter. Cooper's plan was to drink himself into such a state that he would feel no cold, no anger, no pain at the rejection of his own wife. At the moment, he couldn't think of another thing worth doing.

Cooper tried to stand and couldn't. His head was spinning, his movements out of his control. He had been drunk before, but never this drunk. He groaned and sank back onto the filthy pile of bear hides upon which he had been sitting.

A strange apparition rose before Cooper's eyes. A short, round figure clad in a long buffalo robe, topped with a mop of remarkably greasy hair. The nose was flat and wide, and crooked from some past break. The arms were fleshy and short, the hands chubby and stub-fingered.

Cooper attempted to say something, but his words came out garbled. The odd figure laughed. "Have yourself another drink, Mr. Haverly. It's doing you the service you desired, yes indeed."

Cooper reached for the crockery jug sitting at his feet and numbly picked it up. With great effort he lifted it to his lips, took another swallow, and let the half-empty jug fall. Its remaining contents began spilling out into a puddle.

The robed figure let out a high-pitched oath and grabbed the jug with his rounded little hands. "Wasteful, wasteful, Mr. Haverly! We must not waste our whiskey! It's a precious, precious commodity!"

Cooper's eyes rolled upward in his head and he fell to the side like a felled tree. His nose dug into the smelly bear hide, he tried to lift himself to a seated posture again, but only managed to roll over. One more try, and he rolled again, so that his back was toward the robed man.

A second figure joined the first. This was a dark, coppery-olive man with black hair that hung past his shoulders. He was dressed in leggins and a tattered breechcloth, topped by a hunting shirt and deer-hide vest worn inside out. His full-blooded Indian heritage marked every feature. Beyond the company he kept in the person of the rotund little man in the buffalo robe, there was nothing particularly odd about this man except for one thing: his left hand had but three fingers in addition to his thumb. This was not the result of amputations or accidents; there were no vacant places for missing digits. The man had been born this way, and it was because of this defect he went by the name of Three Fingers. What his original name was no one knew, not even his ever-present companion Saul Greentree, the man in the buffalo robe.

"I believe that Morpheus has seized our good friend Mr. Haverly," Saul Greentree said. "Our whiskey has brought him the happiness and release he sought." Greentree's voice was clean and precise, and so high of pitch that few who heard it doubted the rumor that he had been castrated as a boy. Beyond that vague tale, no one knew much about Greentree's history. He talked in a way that indicated some exposure to learning, though he seemed to possess no books and made no claim to formal education. In the three years he had lived in this remote hollow along a Nolichucky River tributary, Greentree had made no claims for himself beyond the ability to distill the strongest whiskey available west of the mountains. Yet he ran nothing that could be accurately called an inn or even a tippling house. Those who wished to partake of his product were obliged to come to the remote cabin and adjacent open-faced lean-to he occupied with his Creek-born companion with the malformed hand. Cooper was now in the lean-to.

Greentree wasn't completely correct in his assessment of Cooper's condition. Cooper was able to hear him, though as if through thick wads of cotton stuffed into his ears. He stirred, tried to talk, failed. He was beginning to feel sick, and what little part of his brain retained the ability to think and feel began to regret he had come here.

Cooper passed out for a time. The next thing he became aware of was that Greentree and Three Fingers had built a roaring fire in front of the lean-to, and were roasting rabbits on spits over the blaze. The smell of the cooking meat was sickening to Cooper in his present state. He saw figures moving on the other side of the fire, and realized others had come here. Two others, their faces hidden to him by the fire. He now was facing the open front rather than the rear of the dugout; either he had rolled over himself or, more likely, had been rolled. Greentree or Three Fingers probably had searched him for coins or anything else worth stealing.

"You going to roast that thing to ashes, Three Fingers?" one of the newcomers asked. Cooper recognized the voice of Parnell Tulley. Had he been more lucid, he would have been surprised; no one Cooper had heard of had seen Tulley since his dramatic punishment in Jonesborough. Rumor had it that Tulley had left and gone into either North or South Carolina—a rumor that had greatly cheered Alexander Carney, who took Tulley's threat against him quite seriously.

"You want it now, you take it," Three Fingers said.

"Give me mine too, and pass the jug," the other newcomer said. Cooper recognized this voice too: it was that of Aaron Killefer.

Cooper faded out again. When next he opened his eyes, the fire had died away significantly and the four men were in the midst of a serious conversation.

"You'd do it, then? You'd kill a man for money?" Parnell Tulley was asking. Cooper was a bit more sober now, sober enough to be stunned by what he had just heard.

A pause. Then Killefer's slurred voice: "Yes, I'd do it. Hell, yes! Why not? What do I care for him?"

"Then do it," Tulley said, obviously as drunk as Killefer. "You kill Alexander Carney for me, and I'll pay you good for it." He laughed, and Cooper wondered if the man was making a joke or putting forth a serious proposal.

"Why do you so despise the man?" Greentree asked. He alone sounded reasonably lucid. "It's my understanding he has defended you quite ably in the courts."

"Look at this here!" Tulley spat, thrusting out his hand to show the scarred pit from which he had gouged out the branding mark. "It was Alexander Carney who let this happen to me. I hate 'im. Hate the bloody guts of him."

"Then why don't you kill him yourself?" Three Fingers asked.

"I'd do it in a breath, except that it would be me they would blame right off. I need somebody else to do it for me."

Silence, then Killefer spoke again. "I *will* do it. I truly will."

Cooper's agitation grew. Was this just the meaningless talk of drunken men, or might Tulley truly intend to see Carney dead? If so, he was driven by bitterness rather than sense, and was an even more dangerous man than Cooper had previously thought.

Greentree stood and put wood on the fire, then came over to Cooper, who closed his eyes and pretended to still be passed out. Greentree knelt and examined him, then shuffled back around the fire to his previous place.

The men began eating, and talk declined. Cooper lay as still as death, fearing that if he moved, it might be suspected that he had overheard the previous exchange. If so, he would be in danger. He opened his eyes just a little, looking around for his rifle. It was not in sight; Greentree or someone else had moved it.

After they finished eating, the men took to the liquor again, and their conversation became increasingly garbled and hard to understand. At length the men began to succumb to the liquor, Three Fingers passing out on the ground, Greentree rising and dragging him like a bag of dirt to the cabin, where he presumably put him into whatever heap of foulness served him for a bed. Aaron Killefer, meanwhile, also passed out, and after returning to the fireside and drinking some more, Greentree did the same. The last to go down was Parnell Tulley, who stomped around for a long time after the others had faded out. He raged incoherently, his words a babble Cooper could not understand, except for picking out the name of Carney from time to time.

It was almost morning before Cooper dared to get up. He felt terrible, sick to the pit of his stomach, wobbly, weak, aching. He treaded about as lightly as he could, though his legs seemed hardly his to control, until finally he spotted his rifle leaned against the front of the cabin. He fetched it and used it as a walking stick as he went to his horse. Mounting, he rode away from the cabin and back to the road, feeling very low indeed.

He had much to think about: the offense he had
caused for his wife and brother, his abandonment of his
family the previous night, his foolishness in seeking sol-
ace in Saul Greentree's whiskey.

And most of all, the horrific thing he had heard . . . or
had he heard it? He had been terribly drunk, and in ret-
rospect it was hard to determine what was reality and
what was drunken fantasy. Had Parnell Tulley really proposed the murder of Alexander Carney? Had Aaron Killefer truly agreed to the proposition? Even if the chilling
conversation was real, would a group of drunks like the
ones still passed out in and around Greentree's place
even remember it when they came around?

Maybe not, but Cooper couldn't take what he had
heard lightly. Even apart from the outright threat, Alexander Carney deserved to know that Parnell Tulley was
back in the area again. Cooper decided to go to Alexander without delay.

Without much delay, at least. First there were some
domestic fences to be mended, and apologies made.
Cooper wished he had kept control of his anger and his
tongue. He even wished he hadn't broken up Tipton's
court. If he hadn't done that, none of the other trouble
would have followed.

Head throbbing and mind full of regrets and worry,
Cooper began riding back toward his home.

7

Cooper Haverly found he was as fortunate as the repentant biblical prodigal: he was part of a forgiving family. Hannah accepted his apology readily, even eagerly, apologized for her own overreactions, and took him in with joy.

As for Joshua, he had already forgiven Cooper. "When you've done as many fool things as I've done, brother, you learn the value of pardon right quick," he said.

There was little time to linger in the glow of restoration, however. Cooper told Joshua of what he had heard at Greentree's cabin. Joshua took the threat seriously, and together he and Cooper set off to go warn Alexander Carney. The long ride this entailed was terribly difficult to Cooper, who suffered greatly from the after-effects of his drunken spree. He kept his complaints to himself; how he felt was his own fault, and he knew it.

On the way to Alexander Carney's residence they encountered Salem Pinnock outside his inn and told him what had occurred. Pinnock agreed to keep a lookout for Aaron Killefer and informed them that Alexander Carney was not home, but at his father's house. Nell Carney had become betrothed to a North Carolinian; the entire family was preparing to go across the mountains to see her marriage performed in the old family church.

Joshua and Cooper diverted to Charles Carney's residence and found matters as Pinnock had said. Nell, looking striking and radiantly happy, was already packed for departure. After greetings and pleasantries and meeting Hice and his kin, Joshua called both Charles and Alexander Carney aside and had Cooper tell what he had heard.

Colonel Carney, enjoying one of those increasingly rare moments when his mind was fully lucid, reacted with subdued dismay. "I had hoped we had seen the last of Parnell Tulley. The threat he made earlier against Alexander has been much on our minds. I find it astounding that he still holds such an unfounded grudge."

Alexander Carney, gone pale since hearing the news, said, "I'm not surprised. I've had the misfortune of dealing with Parnell Tulley enough to know how unsensible and vengeful the man is. He thinks like an animal thinks, and in his mind it was my task to keep him from undergoing any punishment for his own offenses. I failed to do that, and therefore what happened to him is my fault, in his view." He looked over toward the loaded wagon and waiting horses. "I confess I'm glad to be going elsewhere for the present."

Joshua said, "Alexander, I give you my pledge that I'll do anything I can do on your behalf. And keep in mind that it may be there's no threat at all, just the talk of drunkards, already forgotten."

"Perhaps so. We can only hope," Alexander replied.

"We'll do more than hope. We'll dig to the bottom of this," Joshua said.

Movement nearby caught his eye. He turned to see Owen Killefer. The young man looked intensely sad, so pallid and slumped that Joshua wondered if he was ill.

Owen looked Joshua in the eye. "So my father has now become a hired murderer?"

Joshua winced. "You overheard us?"

"Yes. You said my father agreed to murder Alexander for money from Parnell Tulley."

Cooper said, "He was drunk at the time. So was Tulley. For that matter, so was I. I might have misheard."

Owen shook his head. "No. I doubt you did." He turned his head aside and tears came to his eyes. He bit his lip. "God, I hate him. I hate him for what he's turned himself into."

Charles Carney stationed himself in front of the boy. "Owen, that's not the way to talk of your own father. This isn't a matter you need concern yourself with. Leave it to us—we'll see the entire affair clarified."

Owen spun on his heels and stalked off without saying anything more.

"That young fellow is in a right poorish state," Joshua said in a low voice. "Is he ailing?"

Charles Carney told them that Owen had complained lately of not feeling well, then he wandered away to talk to Dover Hice. Alexander stepped closer to Joshua and spoke in a confidential tone. "About Owen . . . my father hasn't noticed it, but it's been evident to me for some time now that the poor boy is pretty well besotten with my sister. Her betrothal has shaken him. And Nell, bless her heart, has been blind to it all. She has no idea of his feelings for her. Hardly seems aware of his existence."

"Poor fellow," Joshua said. He watched Owen disappearing around the back of Carney's barn. "I had some inkling before that Owen was smit with Nell. Can't hardly blame him; in his situation and at his age, I'd probably have took a shining to her myself. And now she's going off to marry ... it's bound to hurt him deep. And hearing what he has about his father surely only makes him feel that much worse ... Cooper, we'd best waste no time in finding Aaron Killefer. Owen might take it in his head to go confront him about this, and nothing good could come of that." He turned again to Alexander Carney. "Alex, is Owen going to the wedding?"

"No. Father is leaving him to tend the home place while the rest of us are away. It's a good bit of trust he's placing in the boy's hands."

"I'll keep an eye out in this direction, if you wish. For your sake and the colonel's—and Owen's."

"Thank you, sir. I would be very grateful."

"Aye. We'll be off now to make a call on Aaron Killefer."

They said their good-byes, and wished Nell and her husband-to-be well in their coming marriage. Mounting, they rode away, heading toward the farm of Aaron Killefer.

It was shameful, Joshua Colter thought, the way Killefer had neglected his lands and home. His fields were filled with weeds and saplings, his cabin roof was missing two boards, and trash lay all around. Killefer's scrawny hounds, as neglected as their surroundings, barked and snarled as the riders entered the weed-shagged yard.

"Who's out there?" Aaron Killefer's voice came from behind a shuttered window. "Colter? Is that you?"

"It is. And Cooper Haverly. We'll have a word with you."

"Will you, now?" There was a brief pause, then the cabin door swung open and Aaron Killefer emerged, looking like a man in the last stages of a fatal illness. He wore only a long hunting shirt that hung to his knees. He hadn't even bothered to pull on a pair of trousers. "Why, that *is* you, Haverly! Seems that I recall seeing you last night up at the gelding's cabin in a right sorry condition."

"You're in no position to cast stones, Killefer," Cooper replied. "It's last night we've come to talk to you about."

Killefer squinted and rubbed his chin, looking suspicious. "Get down off them horses, then, and do your talking."

"Call off these dogs," Joshua said.

Swearing beneath his breath as if all this was an intolerable bother, Killefer came out and quieted his dogs. "You'd best come inside, I reckon," he said.

The cabin was dark, fly-infested, and smelled of rotted food, tobacco smoke, whiskey, sweat, even urine. Aaron Killefer lived his life, if such it could be called, in an appalling condition even by indelicate frontier standards.

"Colter, since you took my boy from me, I never figured to let you set foot in my home again. But since you've come all the way here, I'll be decent to you—for a time. What do you have to say to me?"

"It's me who's got something to say, and I'll say it straight out," Cooper stated. "I heard you agree last night to murder Alexander Carney in return for payment from Parnell Tulley."

Killefer gaped. A little trail of drool leaked from his lower lip into his beard. He didn't bother to wipe it away. "The hell! I never did no such thing!"

"My memory tells me different."

"You was drunk. Drunk as a redskin!"

"Listen to me, Killefer," Joshua said. "I didn't come here expecting you to own up to a thing. But let me tell you: make one move toward Alexander Carney, and I'll hang you with my own rope. Whatever you remember or don't remember from last night, you remember that: I'll hang you as quick as a shot. And that's not an idle threat."

Killefer's expression darkened. "What do you mean, coming into a man's cabin and threatening to murder him! I'll see the law put on you, Colter!"

"No you won't. You won't do a thing except keep to yourself and drink your life away. That's the only way you know. You keep away from Parnell Tulley. He'll bring you nothing but more sorrows than you've already brought on yourself. But most of all, you stay away from Alexander Carney. You understand me?"

"You've got a scoundrel's brass about you, Colter, talking to me like that! I ain't planning to kill nobody! I ain't even laid eyes on Parnell Tulley!"

"You said yourself that you saw me last night at Greentree's," Cooper said. "Parnell Tulley was there too. I saw you talking to him. You're caught in your own lie already."

"Get out of my house!"

"You remember what I told you," Joshua said.

"Cur! I ought to kill you!"

"Don't threaten me, Killefer. You'll have cause to regret it!"

"You're a bane to me, Colter! You've done stole my own son from me! I ain't forgot it!"

"Your son left you of his own accord, because of what you are, and I don't fault him for it. You ain't fit for nobody to live with, Killefer. You ain't fit to raise them hounds out yonder, much less a son." Joshua looked Killefer up and down with open contempt. "Look at you, man. You're no better than that white savage who stole your daughter! Likely as not she was as well off in his house as she would have been in yours."

Killefer roared in rage and reached toward his rifle, which stood against the wall. Joshua stepped forward and cut him off, shoving him back and onto the floor. He picked up the weapon and looked at it. "Hah! Not even a flint on your rifle! Too sorry even to take care of your own weapons!" He tossed the rifle to the floor. "Let's get out of this dungheap, Coop. The smell in here is about to make me heave up my breakfast."

They were halfway back home before Cooper broke the tense silence. "You spoke mighty rough to him, Joshua."

"I know it. Said too much. That's what happens when a man lets himself get too wrought up."

"Well, at least he ought to remember it, whether he remembers what he said at Greentree's or not. Speaking of that, do you think he does remember?"

"Probably not. A man who's soaked his soul in whiskey forgets a lot. But we had to assume he did remember, and meant it." Joshua paused long enough to carve out a chew of tobacco as his horse continued plodding along. He stuffed the hot weed into his cheek. "I have no high hopes for Aaron Killefer. The way he's going, he'll be dead in a year, unless something intervenes to stop it."

"What would make a man do that to himself, I wonder?"

"He's suffered a sight of loss. Saw his own wife and kin murdered, saw his daughter stole away, most likely to die far away from her own people ... some men can swallow that sort of thing and keep going. Some can't. Like poor old Aaron."

"It's a hard world some are given to live in," Cooper said.

"It is. It is indeed."

* * *

Had Owen Killefer been there to hear the brothers'
conversation, he would have agreed quite heartily. He
knew about living in a difficult world, and his at the moment seemed too difficult to endure. And not only difficult, but hollow, empty. Nell was gone. Through eyes
straining not to flood, he had watched her depart with
her family and future husband, riding out of his life for
what would surely be forever.

Owen could hardly tolerate the intensity of his own
feelings about Nell. He had never been affected this way
by another person, and his experience with the female
sex was virtually nonexistent, limited mostly to familial
life with his mother and sister back in North Carolina.
Nothing in that had prepared him for the way he had
grown to feel about Colonel Carney's younger child.

It seemed he had been able to think of nothing but
Nell lately. Not his situation, not his father, not his future
... not even Emaline. He was ashamed to admit it to
himself, but it was true. Since Nell, his thoughts of
Emaline and her captivity had substantially faded, until
now he hardly remembered her. Now he found the notion of her being dead and gone, the very idea he had
initially resisted so fiercely, to be not so intolerable after
all. For if Emaline was dead, there was no reason to
worry over her, or scheme to bring her home. He could
turn all his thoughts to Nell.

Yet now those thoughts were futile. She was gone.
Gone! Another man possessed her. Her life and home
would be elsewhere, and he would probably never see
her again.

It made him want to scream, to strike something or
someone, to vent his rage at seeing the finest part of cre-

ation he had ever met taken from him, leaving him here with nothing but empty labor, an estranged and hateful father, and the memories of a shattered family.

He looked off in the direction Nell and her fellow travelers had gone. *I wish I could go after her. For half a penny, for any reason at all, I'd do it.*

But there was no reason. So he wandered alone, lost in the misery of youthful love that appeared certain to remain forever unrequited.

Aaron Killefer hadn't been lying when he claimed to know nothing of the murderous bargain with Parnell Tulley. He hardly remembered even being at Greentree's place, mush less any clear details of what was said or done. He did recall who had been present, and the odd fact of Cooper Haverly lying drunk in Greentree's lean-to, but beyond that, all was murky.

Yet he had to ponder what he had been told. Might he really have agreed to such a thing as murder? While drunk, he might have promised anything. It was very troubling. Had whiskey really taken so much of him that even his sense of basic right and wrong was gone when he was under its influence?

He scratched his beard and looked around, and experienced an odd moment of clarity. He saw his filthy surroundings, his life, and himself, as others surely saw them. God help me, he thought, but look at the way I live my life! *What's happened to me?*

Aaron Killefer, in a burst of righteous impulse, vowed right then to change his ways. No more whiskey, no more keeping company with such scoundrels as Greentree and Three Fingers and Parnell Tulley. Such men were bad for him, pulling him down to their level. No more! He was through with whiskey and bad company.

He picked up his jug of whiskey and was about to heave it to pieces against the wall when he stopped abruptly. The jug was half full—it would be a terrible waste to get rid of such good whiskey. He did want to reform ... but surely he could do it later. There would be plenty of time to reform once this jug was empty.

Aaron Killefer put the jug back on the table and looked around again. Even if reformation was to wait, there was no reason he couldn't clean up the cabin some. He hadn't really noticed how bad the place stunk until today.

He began by putting a new flint in his rifle and loading the weapon. Then he started picking up trash from the floor, heaving or kicking anything that would burn into the stone fireplace, and putting the rest into a pile near the door. All the while he kept glancing back toward the jug on the table, until thirst and the need for alcohol overcame all other impulses, and he began to drink again. After that he forgot about any further cleaning.

Owen Killefer sat up in his bed, awakened by the barking of the dogs and agitated nickerings from the horse barn. Or had he dreamed it all? He listened, then heard it again. Something was disturbing the horses—or someone. He leaped up, pulling on his trousers. It was well-known that the Carney family was away. Owen wondered if someone had perceived their absence as a good opportunity for horse theft. It was even possible that some stray Indians might be ranging this deep into the settlements. It was known to happen sometimes.

Titus, Charles Carney's trusted slave, appeared in the

door of Owen's room. "There's someone among the horses, I believe, sir," he said.

"I heard it too," Owen replied. "Go get the rifle beside the door in yonder, and come with me." Owen fetched his own rifle too—an old weapon, but a good one, given to him by Charles Carney to replace the old musket Owen had abandoned when he left his father's home. Owen was very proud of the rifle, and had carved his name—the only words he knew how to write—into the stock.

By the time they reached the horses, whoever had been among them was gone. A quick count revealed that Belshazzar, the finest of the horses and Charles Carney's favorite pleasure mount, was gone as well.

"There—look yonder!" Titus said, pointing.

"I see it," Owen replied. What he and Titus had spotted was movement in the darkness at the edge of the forest.

"Come on—let's follow."

Together Owen and Titus crept tensely through the darkness. Owen's throat grew dry and his palms grew wet. He wondered how many horse thieves there were. Surely there was only one; if not, it seemed more horses would have been stolen.

Titus leaned closer to Owen and was about to say something when a shot blasted in the darkness ahead. The slave grunted and fell, grabbed his thigh and said, "I'm shot! I'm shot!"

Owen dropped to his belly on the ground, peering through the darkness toward the place he had seen the powder flash. Motion there, barely discernable ... he lifted his rifle, sighted down the long barrel—then held his fire, realizing that if he fired, he was more likely to hit Charles Carney's horse than the thief.

"How bad is the leg?" he asked Titus.

Titus was feeling gingerly around the wound. "I think it cut a swath, just a swath. It hurts fierce, though."

Owen pondered the situation. He was angry now, and even more unwilling to let the thief escape. "We're taking you back to the cabin," he said. "I'll come on alone after that. From where that shot came from, I'd wager he's going over the hill on the cow path."

With some difficulty, Owen managed to get Titus back to the cabin. The wound was, as Titus had suspected, merely a painful swath sliced through the flesh.

"Mr. Killefer, sir, maybe you ought not go out there again," Titus said.

"I can't let that horse be stole while I do nothing," Owen said. "I owe it to Mr. Carney to see where it's being taken. I can find that cow path in the dark, and if that's the way they've gone, I ought to be able to follow them. Get some water and wash that wound, then bind it up and wait for me to get back."

The clouds were patchy, sailing across the sky and letting the moonlight through one moment, blocking it the next. Owen easily found the place where the cattle trail that began at the edge of the meadow cut through the woodland. Rifle ready, he headed up the path.

Crossing the wooded hill, he came down the path to the meadow on the other side, then crossed that meadow to a wagon road that led northwest. Kneeling, he put his eye almost to the ground, waited for the moonlight to emerge again, and examined the road when it did. He was able to discern horse tracks, and moccasin prints as well. Indeed the thief had come this way.

He went on, and walked a long time until the clouds grew thicker and he began to be less certain. The thief might have led the horse off the road anywhere. And if he saw he was being followed, he might shoot from hiding. The thief had already proven his willingness to do violence by shooting Titus.

And so Owen became increasingly cautious as he advanced. Minutes stretched into hours. He kept going. At length the clouds broke again; light spilled out across the wagon road. Owen stopped, realizing just what spot he had reached. He had traveled a long way. A footpath led off the wagon road here. He knew the path well: It led across a long, low rise to the farm of his own father, a mile or more away.

A troubling suspicion came to mind.

Owen stepped onto the footpath and advanced a few steps. He stopped and looked at the ground. Horse droppings. Fresh.

He took a deep breath and shook his head. His suspicion was closer to confirmation. The horse thief appeared to be leading Belshazzar to the farm of Aaron Killefer.

His own father, in league with a horse thief, or thieves! Then came an even more distressing thought: Maybe Aaron Killefer *was* the horse thief!

That was enough to make Owen stand still for a full minute, not sure initially whether he even wanted to go on. But the more he thought about it, the more despair became anger. He had already been kicked in the stomach by news that Aaron Killefer had agreed to kill an innocent man for money. Now, it seemed, he might be a horse thief as well.

Owen decided the time had come to confront his father. He was tired of sensing that people around him pitied him for his paternal heritage, tired of feeling ashamed of his own father, tired of wondering just how low the man could stoop.

He went on, climbing the footpath and crossing down toward the Killefer farm.

The dogs were already baying even as Owen crept toward his father's cabin. Belshazzar was there, tied outside. What had stirred up the dogs was a loud argument under way inside. Owen recognized his father's voice, and heard another that he had heard before, but couldn't immediately identify.

The fact the dogs were already noisy allowed Owen to reach the cabin without being given away. He crawled over beneath a shuttered window and rose, peeping through the crack between the shutters. The cabin was dimly lighted. Within Owen's narrow range of vision, he saw his father, angrily facing off a big man. The man's back was turned toward Owen, and when he twisted his head just a little, Owen could see a third man too: an Indian. And as the Indian lifted a hand to sweep his long hair back off his forehead, Owen was surprised to see that the hand had but three fingers.

"I'll hide no stolen horse for you, Tulley!" Aaron Killefer shouted, causing Owen to realize that the second white man in the cabin was Parnell Tulley, the very ruffian who had terrorized him that day in Jonesborough. "You assume too much if you assume I'd do such a thing!"

Tulley made a reply that Owen couldn't hear; all he could tell was that Tulley sounded angry.

"Get that redskin out of here," Aaron Killefer said. His voice had its usual drunken slur. "I don't want his kind in my house."

Owen was beginning to figure out the scenario now. Obviously there had been two thieves, Tulley and the three-fingered Indian, and they had brought the stolen horse here for safekeeping—apparently without Aaron Killefer's consent.

The Indian moved abruptly in response to Killefer's insult, shifting position so that his back was near Owen's window, blocking his view. Tulley said something sharply, then the Indian spoke, also sounding angry, and soon Killefer and Tulley were shouting at each other at the same time, so that all their words were garbled.

Owen was about to move to another window when the Indian changed position again. As his body shifted, Aaron Killefer's face was made visible, turned toward the Indian now, and looking frightened.

"Put that down," Killefer said.

"Hell, no," the Indian said.

Then, so abruptly and unexpectedly that Owen almost yelled in reaction, a shot exploded inside the cabin. Owen saw his father spasm, saw a dark hole appear in the very center of his chest, saw him slump back against the wall and to the ground.

For a long moment all was very silent. Then the dogs erupted with even more violent barking. Parnell Tulley said, "You've killed him, Three Fingers!" The Indian cursed and then laughed. And Owen Killefer let out a violent yell.

He stood and jerked open the shutters, which had been closed but not secured. Three Fingers turned just as Owen thrust his rifle through the paneless window, let out another yell, then fired.

The rifle ball passed through Three Fingers's upper left chest. The Indian grunted and fell back, landing on his rump almost atop Aaron Killefer's form. He squirmed and pushed up on his left arm, groping at his chest with his right hand. His eyes met Owen's just as Aaron Killefer, still alive after all, came up with a knife in his hand, leaned over Three Fingers's shoulder and buried the blade in the Creek's heart.

Aaron Killefer jerked the blade free, then turned toward Parnell Tulley, who had leaned his rifle against the door upon entering and now lurched toward it. He reached the rifle, but Aaron Killefer had moved too fast, and left him no room to raise it. He shoved the bloody knife at Tulley, who deflected it from striking him in the heart, which was Killefer's obvious target, but failed to keep it from slicing his shoulder. Tulley shouted painfully, then shoved his body forward and knocked Aaron Killefer to the floor. He lifted the rifle again, aimed it point-blank at Killefer and fired.

Owen screamed, fumbled for his bullet pouch and powder horn, then felt suddenly weak. His head spun, he staggered back from the window, head spinning, and fainted to the ground.

When he came to, Tulley was gone. So was the stolen horse. Owen stood, leaned against the wall and circled around to the door.

Aaron Killefer was still alive, but barely. Owen went to him and knelt in the puddle of blood spreading around the fallen man.

"Father . . ."

Killefer's eyes opened halfway. "Owen, is that you, Owen?"

"It's me . . . I'm going to go for help."

"No help for me now. I'm dying." Blood came out of Killefer's mouth; he choked and spat.

"Don't die," Owen said, tears coming. "Don't die!"

"I love you, son. Love you so much."

"I love you too."

"Don't believe . . . all you might hear about me, Owen.

They say I was going to kill a man. It ain't true . . . if ever I said it, I was drunk . . . didn't mean it . . ."

"I know, Father. I know."

"Ain't been much . . . of a father . . ."

Killefer's body tightened; his face went taut with pain. He whispered one last word, struggled, drew in one more breath. It rattled as it left him, and when it was gone, so was his life.

Owen lowered his head and cried. It was tragedy enough that Aaron Killefer had died in so terrible a way. And the final word he had spoken only made the tragedy sting Owen all the more.

The word had been a name. "Emaline."

Joshua Colter rode to the Charles Carney farm two days later. He had been off hunting at the time of the atrocity at the Killefer place; when he returned and learned of it, he immediately saddled a fresh horse and set off to talk to Owen. He was very relieved the youth was still alive at all. According to what Owen had reportedly told the county sheriff, he had fainted away with Parnell Tulley still present. For some reason—probably sheer panic—Tulley had not taken that opportunity to kill Owen.

A search was now under way for Tulley. Joshua had his doubts it would succeed. Probably Tulley was far away, knowing that this time his punishment would be more than a branding of the palm. Tulley would hang if captured.

When Joshua rode into the yard at Carney's, Titus limped out to meet him. "If you're looking for Mr. Owen, he ain't here," the slave said. "He rode off yesterday."

"Rode off? To where?"

"He said he had to go find Mr. Carney in North Carolina, and tell him his horse was stole. I tried to get him to stay, but he was set to go and wouldn't listen. He said he couldn't wait."

"That don't make a lot of sense," Joshua said. "Charles Carney will be back here within a few days. He could've told him then."

"If I can talk free with you, Mr. Colter, I think Mr. Owen was looking for a reason to go away. I think that after all that's happened to him here, he couldn't bear to stay anymore."

Joshua thought about it. He nodded. "Likely you're right, Titus. Well, I had hoped to talk to him. It'll have to wait until he comes back with Charles."

"Mr. Colter, I don't think that Mr. Owen will come back. He told me good-bye and said he'd not be seeing me anymore. When he left, he was intending to leave for good."

Joshua looked at the empty lean-to where Owen had stayed. What a sad life the young fellow had lived so far! He regretted having missed the chance to talk to him one last time.

"Good-bye, Titus. I'll be back around again when Charles returns. Maybe Owen will come back after all."

Joshua pondered it all as he rode back home to Limestone Creek. Why was it that such a wealth of trouble had come into one life? Owen Killefer had seen kin murdered by Tom Turndale, seen his sister kidnapped and hauled off, probably to die a prisoner, watched his father decline into a drunkard and perhaps worse, then seen that same father slaughtered before his eyes. On top of all that, he had watched a young lady he had come to care for taken away to marry another.

No wonder he wanted to leave. Joshua couldn't fault him. In the same circumstances, he would have left too.

He wished the best for Owen. Lord knew that so far he had known only the worst.

It was a misty day, overcast with clouds. Far in the distance thunder rumbled. There would be rain today, probably by the afternoon. This was somber weather, matching Joshua's mood.

He prodded his Chickasaw horse forward, eager for home and the company of his family.

THE
FRANKLINITES

8

Owen dismounted in the waning light, looking wearily at the sky and knowing he could go farther, if only he felt up to it. Once off the horse, he leaned against its warm rump, head against the back of his hands, and groaned aloud. By now there was no discounting it as imagination: he felt sick and feverish.

He stripped off the saddle and gave the horse a nose bag of grain from the supply he had brought, then built a fire and cooked some jerky in tallow for his own supper. He also had a supply of dried biscuits, and gnawed on one of these while the meat simmered. By the time he had eaten, he felt so weary and dizzy that he immediately spread his blankets and put himself to bed for the night.

When he awakened the next morning, the fire was built up again and a one-eyed, white-bearded old man, short and very unkempt, was kneeling beside it, frying venison and onions in a pan. Owen pushed up on the heels of his hands, frightened and amazed, then felt the blood rush away from his face. His arms went weak and let him fall back. He came down with an audible thud, and moaned. The smell of the frying onions made him want to retch.

"Hello, young fellow," the old man said. "No need for

139

you to be afraid of me—I ain't going to hurt you. It appears to me you could use some help, matter of fact. You sick?"

"Yes," Owen rasped out. His caution toward the old man was already draining away, simply because he lacked the energy to sustain it.

"You look it. White as the belly of a dead fish in the sun. White as mortified pus. White as the ashes of a burnt-up tomcat. White as a dog wangus. White as—"

Such talk was too much for Owen. He scrambled up, stumbled to the side, fell to his hands and knees and vomited. The old man laughed, making it evident that the inspiration of vomiting was the very reason he had talked so disgustingly.

"There! You'll be feeling all purged and better now, I reckon!"

Owen didn't feel better. He swabbed his hand across his mouth and crawled back to his blankets. When he lay down, he began to shudder, his teeth rattling against each other. He pulled up his top cover and huddled into a little ball. "Them onions is making me sick," he muttered weakly.

"Well, then, I'll just have to eat 'em by myself," the old man said. "Ain't no breakfast I favor more than venison and onion. What's your name, boy?"

"Go away."

"Unfriendly, are you? Well, you're ailing, so I'll overlook it. My name's McCarthy, by the way. Frances McCarthy."

"Leave me alone."

"What's your name?"

"Killefer. Owen Killefer. Now go away."

"Killefer. Good name. Kind of name a Cherokee would like the sound of. They got certain sounds they seem to

favor saying. They never much took to 'McCarthy'—they
finally begun calling me Mah-ka-ti, which seemed to suit
them better."

Owen didn't feel like answering, but he mentally
tucked away the fact that McCarthy had lived among the
Cherokees.

He made no further attempt to rise that morning. He
truly was sick; whether he had ever been this sick before
would have been a question worth mulling, had he felt
like it. McCarthy didn't leave him, nor ignore him. He
stayed close by, forcing him to drink water even though
he didn't want it, bathing his hot brow with a cool, damp
cloth, and rolling him back into his blankets when he
rolled out. Had Owen been in condition to note it, he
would have seen that McCarthy had made himself both
guardian and nurse, even though Owen was a stranger to
him.

In mid-afternoon Owen felt a little better, enough to
comprehend McCarthy's comment that he was so sick
he'd have to perk up some to die. After that he descended even deeper into fever than before, and time,
place, and identity lost meaning.

When he came out of the worst of it a day and a half
later, McCarthy was still there. He grinned through his
bushy whiskers when Owen managed to turn his head
and look at him.

"I believe you'll live, son," he said gently. "For a time
I didn't know."

"Thirsty."

"Good. That's good." He brought him water. "You've
sweated and peed out most all the water in you. Got to
put it back in again, or you'll dry to a husk."

Owen drank as much as he could. "Why are you doing this for me?" he asked in a whisper.

McCarthy smiled. "Well, I reckon I must be a saint or something."

When Owen next awakened, it was night. McCarthy had built a big fire. This time the meat he roasted smelled good, and Owen ate. The food gave him strength, and McCarthy led him on wobbly legs to the nearby creek, where he washed the filth of sickness from his body. Back at the camp, Owen propped up against a poplar tree and covered himself with his blankets.

"There ain't no way I know of to thank you good enough for tending me here," Owen said.

"Never mind it. I had nothing better to be doing."

"Well, I won't forget it."

McCarthy grinned, but he wasn't his prior joking and jabbering self. "Boy, tell me something: When did your path ever cross Tom Turndale's?"

Hearing that name so unexpectedly was like a jolt to Owen. For a few moments he had nothing to say. Finally he asked, "Did I call the name while I was ranting?"

"You did. Called it several times. How is it you know of Turndale?"

Owen took a deep breath. "He murdered my mother and other kin. He stole away my sister. Took her to wife, or so everybody has figured."

"I ain't surprised. Turndale's a murdering whoreson."

"How do you know about him?"

"More than knowing about him, boy. I know the man hisself. I was a trader for a time among the Chickamoggy. I met Mad Tom hisself more than once. And he is mad, mad as a skunk in daytime. A dangerous man. You say he took your sister?"

"Yes."

"When?"

"First days of 'eighty-five."

McCarthy said nothing.

"They tell me he's likely killed her by now."

McCarthy eyed Owen sadly. "Well, that could be. If she ever riled him, resisted him too much."

Owen closed his eyes. Deep sadness washed through him. He felt sick again. "I want to lay down."

McCarthy helped him back to his bedroll. "Her name was Nell?"

"No. Emaline."

"Aye, Emaline. You called that name too."

They talked more the next morning. Owen described his situation more fully, though leaving out his lovesickness over Nell Carney, and discovered that McCarthy, a free-roaming man who knew Carolina and the Tennessee country equally well, knew the way to Dover Hice's house. "I'll take you there, if you like, just to make sure you don't sicken up on us again along the way."

They rode out together. Owen's strength returned almost fully, and the color to his face, but the sadness in him didn't leave. He was more sure than ever now that Emaline was dead, and all his past grief over her came alive again and wouldn't let him go. But he covered his feelings, putting on a cheerful front with McCarthy and passing the time by letting the old former trader teach him more of the Cherokee language, and talking about Joshua Colter, with whom McCarthy had once shared an adventure among the Chickamaugas. The miles fell behind, and the house of Dover Hice drew nearer.

Joshua answered the midnight hammering on his door with rifle in hand. "Who's there?" he called.

"John, John Crockett. It's my Rebecca—her time has come, and I'd appreciate the help of your missus in the birthing."

Joshua had the door open even before his caller finished speaking. "Come in, John. I'll fetch Darcy."

"No need," Darcy called from the adjacent room. "I heard. I'll be out in a moment."

The newcomer fidgeted nervously, wiping his hands on his trousers, looking this way and that, scuffing his feet on the floor. Joshua observed him, yawned, stretched, and said, "Lord have mercy, John, calm yourself. You weren't this fidgety facing off with Ferguson on King's Mountain."

"Birthing a baby puts me in a state."

"You talk like it was you doing the birthing instead of Rebecca. Anyway, I'd think you'd be used to it by now. You've already churned out a houseful of young'uns between the two of you."

"I ain't used to it, Joshua. Never will be, not when it's my wife in the travails."

Darcy appeared, dressed and ready. She had gathered up some rags and a warm blanket in a basket to take along for the birthing; Joshua was glad of her foresight. John Crockett was a respected but poor man, living in a small, crowded cabin at the juncture of the Great Limestone and Nolichucky, eking out what living he could as a farmer. It was likely there wasn't an extra bit of cloth or a spare blanket to be had in the Crockett family's hovel.

Joshua had no second thoughts about sending his wife out into the night with his neighbor. This midnight visit was not unanticipated. Crockett had come to Joshua and Darcy weeks before, asking in advance for Darcy's assistance when his wife's birthing time came.

Joshua Colter had first met Crockett in the King's

Mountain campaign, and had come to know him much better since. His cabin stood down the creek from Joshua's home, and just across the Greene County line. Crockett's cabin, small and unimpressive in itself, was in a lovely place, facing the Nolichucky where it was lined with big shady sycamores on one side and edged by a tall bluff on the other.

Joshua, now wakeful, looked across toward Cooper Haverly's cabin and sent up a silent prayer for his brother's welfare. Cooper wasn't at home with his family tonight; he was off with some two hundred fifty Franklin militiamen, bound for the Cherokee country under call of Governor Sevier. Indian troubles had continued since the spring, bringing new reports almost weekly of raids not only close by, but also into Kentucky and the Cumberland country. John Watts, the half-breed Chickamauga chief, had led raids along the lower Holston, within the boundaries of Franklin. Several were slain across the border country; among their number recently had been two men of prominence: Colonel William Christian, who died north of the Ohio River, and Colonel John Donelson, the man who had led to the Cumberland country the flatboat flotilla of settlers that had included Hannah Haverly in the days before her marriage to Cooper. Donelson had been slain on the Kentucky Road.

Joshua himself would have been part of the current campaign except for Sevier's request that he remain home, with most of his rangers, to respond to any local raids that might occur. Sevier also remained off the warpath this time, being swamped with the duties of office in a "state" that hovered close to the brink of civil war. He had placed leadership of the campaign in the hands of William Cocke, Franklin's brigadier general of militia, and Colonel Alexander Outlaw, a Greene Countian of prominence.

Joshua was privately relieved to have been excused from the current expedition. This was not the result of any cowardice, but out of his personal linkage to the Overhill Cherokees. He had been raised in the prime of his childhood among the Cherokees in and around the long-gone Fort Loudoun, and once already in his life he had faced the disturbing duty of military attack against the Overhill people who were such an intimate part of his heritage. He had watched Chota, the capital and most beloved of the Overhill towns, go up in flames in 1780. He never wanted to witness such an event again, for he loved Chota almost as dearly as any Cherokee.

Besides all that, he remained unconvinced the Overhill Cherokees were much to blame for the recent raids. Indian agent Joseph Martin had toured the towns in the spring and declared them generally oriented toward peace with the whites; Joshua suspected most of the raiders who had terrorized the border this year were affiliated with the more radical Chickamaugas. Further, the current campaign had a certain contrived, political flavor that displeased Joshua. He believed it likely that this thrust would be used in some way to attempt to overcome the problem of the Hopewell Treaty. When Cocke and Outlaw came riding home, he anticipated they would do so with some new pact in hand.

"Come home safe, and soon, Cooper," Joshua whispered into the darkness. "That's what matters to me." Now there was an odd thing about himself, Joshua noted: As most men he knew grew older, they seemed to care more and more about statesmanship, public policies, legislation, and all the other accouterments of civilization. But as he himself aged, he cared less and less about such things. Most of the affairs to which people devoted their lives and attention were but clouds skudding across the sky, here, and then blown away. It was the people themselves that mattered.

He returned to bed and awakened again before dawn. Darcy still was not home, but he was not worried. Childbirth could take a long time, even for a woman who had borne several children before. Joshua scoured up a salt pork and bread breakfast for his own brood, and was just scrubbing off the plates when Darcy came walking through the open gate of the little family stockade. He dried his hands and went outside to meet her.

From her smile he knew all had gone well. "What was it—son or daughter?"

"A son," Darcy replied. "Big and handsome and strong. They named him David, after his grandfather."

Joshua rolled the name through his mind, and nodded. "David Crockett. It's a good name. I like the ring of it."

"Yes." Darcy smiled. "Seeing him born made me want another of our own, Joshua. Our family is yet so small!"

Joshua put his arm around his wife. "If it's another child you want, then—as dear old Alphus would have said it—by Joseph, it's another child you'll have! Heaven knows I'm glad to do my part toward providing one."

Darcy scowled playfully and pushed his arm away. "Don't be getting any such notions at the moment, husband. I'm tired, and I'm hungry, and the children are all about."

Joshua chuckled and put his arm back where it had been, drawing her close so abruptly that she stumbled against him and laughed. He squeezed her, kissed her cheek. He was a happy man. He had a good wife, strong children, a home, and the ability to make a living for them all. What more could any man need? As the morning sun streamed into the yard, Joshua Colter felt as wealthy as a king.

But for all Joshua Colter's personal contentment, the bloody frontier remained the bloody frontier, and a day after the birth of little David Crockett, the Colter family received a jolting reminder of this.

Zachariah Hampton Colter, the son by her first marriage to the late Sina Colter, whom Joshua's adoptive father Alphus Colter had married late in life, was killed on the banks of the Nolichucky River by a small band of raiding Indians. Chickamaugas, in the opinion of the boatman who found Zach's body.

Joshua faced the sad task of fetching the corpse. A sorrowful sight it was: a young man still several years shy of twenty, arrow-pierced, hatcheted, stripped of his scalp, and mangled. Joshua had seen scores of bloodied corpses in his life, but looking upon the body of Zachariah was far different than seeing the remains of some unfortunate stranger. This was family. Zachariah's pale, mangled form, familiar yet now alien, gave Joshua an intensely odd sensation, a feeling of seeing himself laid out on the ground, marble-white and stone-still. It was unnatural, obscene.

Zach's death devastated Joshua's entire family. Hannah Haverly, who had never much liked Zachariah, was nevertheless the most jolted by his death. Joshua understood. She was thinking of the absent Cooper in light of this unexpected reminder of life's mutability. She wished him home again. So did Joshua.

Joshua wasn't present when they buried Zachariah. With his rangers, he was scouring the Nolichucky for the raiders who had slain the youth. These were encountered south of the river—a small band, typical of the raiding parties that had been coming from the hidden towns in the dark and mountainous Tennessee River country to the southwest, striking then retreating.

The rangers engaged the Chickamauga band with little success. The Chickamaugas fought bravely; Joshua watched with admiration as one of the Indians ran into an open area, exposing himself to fire, to pull away a wounded companion.

No rangers were killed in the fight, though two received minor injuries. Nor did any Chickamauga die, but Joshua received some grim satisfaction in seeing one of the warriors spasm as a rifle ball, fired by himself, entered his thigh. This was the very warrior who had bravely saved his wounded and exposed companion earlier in the battle. And then Joshua's satisfaction turned first to revulsion—for he saw what was unmistakably Zachariah's fresh scalp lock stretched on a small hoop dangling from the wounded Indian's rifle—then to astonishment, for suddenly he realized he knew the Indian he had wounded.

He had dealt with this warrior before. His name was Ulagu, and he was the brother of Ayasta, the Cherokee woman who had been bride of John Hawk, once Joshua's closest friend, later his most personal enemy. In a final, private battle, Joshua's own blade had found its mark in John Hawk, and made Ayasta a widow. Later, Ayasta had become a part of Joshua's own life, even his family, and now she was married to Callum McSwain and living in Kentucky.

Ayasta had assimilated into the world of the unakas, the whites—but her brother Ulagu remained a staunch Chickamauga warrior, as devoted as his mentor, Dragging Canoe, to driving out the hated race that had encroached on the native lands.

Joshua stood, awed and infuriated by the realization that Ulagu had been the very man who took the life and scalp of Zachariah Colter.

They pursued the fleeing Chickamaugas for a mile or more, then had to give it up, for the Indians had vanished like phantoms into the vast forest. Ulagu was a formidable woodsman, even with Joshua Colter's rifle ball riding in his thigh.

Cooper Haverly was weary from the exertion of military travel, but intrigued with all that had come of the Franklin militia expedition. Intrigued ... and vaguely disturbed. At the end of August the armed band had reached Chota and confronted the famed chiefs Hanging Maw and Old Tassel. Both chiefs declared firmly that they were not responsible for the killings committed by Bloody Fellow and his followers, and in fact desired peaceful relations with the whites. Cooper was familiar with Joshua Colter's belief that the Overhills were being wrongly blamed for acts committed by the Chickamaugas and Chickamauga-affiliated Creeks; hearing the chiefs so resolutely state the same had a persuasive effect.

But Cocke and Outlaw declared that the chiefs were missing the main point. They might be innocent of Bloody Fellow's killings, but Franklin's authorities were convinced they were not blameless in regard to the deaths at the Birum house in Greene County, and of the killings of Colonels Donelson and Christian.

Cooper watched and listened with great interest as Old Tassel, meeting with the invading whites, first shared ceremonial pipes of peace, then rose to speak, an interpreter at his side.

"Brothers, now I am going to speak to you," Old Tassel

said. "We have smoked the tobacco given us by the Great
Man Above to straighten our hearts. You are my brothers,
and I am glad to see you, and hold you fast by the hand.
The Great Man Above made us both, and hears us."

Old Tassel gestured at the town that spread around
him. "The people residing here are not responsible for
spilling blood. The guilty parties live at Coyatee."
Cooper knew of that town. It stood at the mouth of the
Holston, northwest of Chota and above the Warrior's
Path that led to the Overmountain settlements. "The men
of Coyatee who did these killings are not warriors, but
murderers," Old Tassel said.

Cooper believed Old Tassel, and apparently the expedition leaders did as well, for the militiamen were
promptly ordered to march to Coyatee, where two Indians were charged with the murders and killed. Then the
white army returned to Chota and talks were again taken
up.

To Cooper's surprise, the tone was even more strident
than before. Old Tassel and Hanging Maw were told in
threatening tones that the state of Franklin possessed all
Indian lands north of the river, and that if any Cherokees
tried to stop white settlement on those lands, their towns
would be put to the torch.

Cooper studied Old Tassel's face as he stood to reply.
The chief's visage was lined with weariness, like that of
a man who has been battered and harassed beyond his
endurance. Speaking quietly, he said he had never heard
of anything substantiating this new land claim. He had
even spoken to the "great men in Congress," man to
man, and none had given him any such information.

Old Tassel paused and looked around at the large force
of whites, reminding Cooper of a mouse surrounded by
hungry cats. "Now that you have told me the *truth*," he

said, giving a subtly ironic emphasis to that last word, "we hope that we may live together as brothers on the land, and keep the peace. I am sorry for any wrongs my people have done to anger you. We will sign your terms and live together hereafter. There is no need for more talk. A little talk is as good as much, and too much talk is bad."

Cooper Haverly felt depressed as he and the militiamen rode back to their homes. What he had seen at the signing of the Treaty of Coyatee, as the event would come to be called, had taken away some of the sense of assurance and righteousness he had always associated with the Franklin cause. He had watched the Overhill chiefs put their imprimatur on a pact they had no choice about. The Franklin force had been large; had Old Tassel declined the treaty, he and his people would have faced immediate dire consequences.

Yet Cooper was a headstrong fellow, and tempering his views wasn't comfortable for him. He argued with himself on the way home. Had not this excursion been done at the behest of John Sevier? Was it not proper for a state to seek the protection of its own people? Did the Cherokees really have the right to claim vast tracts of fertile land, when so many families needed them for homes and sustenance?

By the time Cooper rode back through the Colter stockade gate to be greeted by his kin, he had substantially forgotten his doubts. The effort, he told Joshua, had been successful and worthwhile, and much had been achieved toward overcoming the problem of the Hopewell Treaty.

Joshua listened, but all he said was, "I'm glad you're home, Cooper. I feared for your safety. And now I have some bitter news to share with you about Zachariah."

*   *   *

Ulagu was a very sick man well before he reached the Five Lower Towns, where he lived when he wasn't out making war or raiding. The rifle ball in his thigh had lodged against the bone, damaging it; then two days later, while feverish and weakened from his wound, he had fallen from his horse and broken the leg at the damaged spot, thrusting one splintered end of the bone out through the flesh, with the flattened rifle ball still lodged in the bone. Wolf Who Leaps, the warrior Ulagu had saved in the battle, and who himself was suffering from the painful but lesser wound he had received, plucked it out of the bone with his bare fingers.

Ulagu's companions did what they could for him, then began the long and trying journey to the Five Lower Towns. Ulagu suffered tremendously, though without complaint, and at last became unconscious. He lingered in that state most of the way back. By the time he was home, he appeared to be on the verge of death.

As Sadayi, Ulagu's new bride, hovered over him in concern, the old ones of the tribe cleaned and treated the ugly wound, and conjurers and herbalists were brought in to do what they could. Days passed, and the injury showed some signs of healing, yet Ulagu regained consciousness only intermittently. He spoke only once, saying one word: "Colter."

This mystified those around him. All knew Colter—he was the famed unaka who wore the ancient coin about his neck, the man who as a boy had lived with his trader father among the Cherokees, and who had been loved by the great departed chief, Attakullakulla, whom the whites called Little Carpenter. Ulagu had had contact with Colter from time to time—but why had he spoken that name now?

Ulagu was wasted and senseless and barely alive the day that Thomas Turndale came to Running Water Town, asking to see the wounded warrior. Among the Chickamaugas, Turndale was reputed to be a great healer whose ministrations had brought many back from the verge of death. At the request of Wolf Who Leaps, he was taken to see Ulagu. After a silent examination, Turndale stood and said that he could save the warrior, and asked that Ulagu be taken to his own house.

They placed Ulagu on a horse-drawn litter and conveyed him to Turndale's house. Turndale sent the couriers out and closed the door. After that, no one but Turndale and the white girl he called his wife were to see Ulagu for many days.

Ulagu's dreams were strange and frightening. He saw faces that were like the ghastly ceremonial masks that had terrified him as a small child, but these faces were alive and moving, and from their mouths came snakes that bit him and coiled around his body.

He knew nothing of time, had no sense of place. He didn't know even if he was alive, or if this suffering was some torment that came after death.

Then, slowly, the dreams began to change. The terrors subsided, and he seemed to be in a place of beauty, wild and delightful, where a wide, slow river rolled by. He saw himself washing in the river, and felt healing spread through his body.

And then he opened his eyes. Looking down at him was a white man. At first he did not know the man, but gradually the features began to look familiar. This was the strange unaka named Turndale, who lived among the Indians and was said to care nothing for his own race. Turndale's expression was solemn, but he nodded as if in satisfaction. "You will live, Ulagu," he said in the Cherokee tongue.

Ulagu slept after that. When he awakened, he was hungry. Boiled pumpkin was brought to him, borne by a young white woman he had never seen before. Her face was dirty, her hair stringy and tied behind her head. She wore the clothing of a squaw. There was no light in her eyes, no life in her expression. Ulagu seriously wondered if Turndale was so great a magician that he had somehow put life into a dead girl and made her his slave, for the girl reminded him of nothing so much as a corpse restored to life, yet not fully restored. But a closer look showed him this could not be true, for surely only a living woman could bear a child—and this girl's belly was swollen with pregnancy.

Ulagu ate and felt strengthened. He looked for the first time since his awakening at his injured leg, and remembered what had happened to him—and that the man who had shot him had been Joshua Colter, the coin-wearer. He smiled. He was very glad he had survived. To be killed by Colter would have been a discredit and embarrassment to his memory.

The girl came to him and took the bowl from his hands. He reached out and grasped her arm. In the Cherokee tongue he asked, "What is your name?"

Emaline Killefer looked blankly at Ulagu. She replied in a voice as lifeless as her expression: "My name is Flower." She answered Ulagu in his own language, haltingly, but correctly.

"Flower . . . you are Turndale's woman?"

Her answer was even slower to come this time. "Yes," she replied. "I am his woman."

"You are unaka."

"Yes."

"You were taken from your people."

The young woman's expression became very sad, just for a moment. Then the empty look returned, and in a tired voice she said, "I have no people, except for Tom Turndale."

9

**A**cross the frontier the story
was the same as the new year came on. Indian dangers
abounded. Governments were uncertain. Politics was
cantankerous, and in Franklin, sometimes dangerous.

Salem Pinnock was hard-pressed to keep up with his
journalizing. News traveled slowly, borne mostly by the
continual stream of emigrants from the east. Pinnock
learned of many events only long after they occurred.

Some of Pinnock's entries were of mostly personal interest; for example, the news brought by the Carney family, upon their return from east of the mountains, that
young Owen Killefer had arrived without advance notice
at the Hice home, bearing news of the horse theft and
subsequent tragedy that had taken the life of Aaron Killefer. "Of particular interest is the fact that Colonel Carney, deferring to Owen's desire not to return to the place
of his loss, has advocated with Hice to give employment
to young Owen," Pinnock scribed. "So now Owen Killefer remains in the employ of the family, though less directly than before. It is my hope the lad will find
happiness in his new North Carolina home, and put aside
the sorrows that have so beset him on the border."

Many other of Pinnock's notations dealt with reports of

Indian attack. "News has come of a terrible tragedy of the Kentucky region now many weeks past. Chickamoggies have killed more than a score of travelers, all of one party, at a spring in Kentucky. The tale is sorrowful. A young boy, one of the dead, is said to have pleaded with his father, before the fated journey, not to go to Kentucky, for he feared the Indians would there kill him. Further comes news of one woman who saved herself by hiding in the hollow of a vast tree, there travailing and giving birth to a child while in fear for her very existence. Her survival is a brightness in the midst of a story that is tragic, yet typical in these troubled days."

Winter became spring, and there came reports of troops being raised in North Carolina to be sent for the defense of the frontier, and to build a road from Clinch Mountain all the way to the Cumberland settlements. There were new Indian fights to be chronicled; many of these occurred in the Cumberland region and took weeks or months to be heard of in the Nolichucky country. "Writing this August 4, I record word that has come of three killed early in the summer in the Cumberland near the station of Greenfield." And, in an autumn entry: "Attacks have occurred throughout the summer in the region of Hendrick's Station, Cumberland, where the Chickamoggies have been fierce in killing and scalping. It is said the Spanish traders pay bounty for the scalps of whites."

Mostly Pinnock's entries dealt with political affairs going on all around him. The state of Franklin had begun to feel shifting sentiment on the part of many of its people. And even so devoted a Franklinite as Pinnock himself could not fail to understand why.

The populace of Franklin was doubly burdened by government. Two codes of laws, two competing government bureaucracies and taxing authorities, two systems of courts and justice—it was virtually impossible to live in such a perpetual dilemma. So confusing was the tax situation that many refused to pay taxes at all. Meanwhile, North Carolina, under Governor Caswell, was extending diplomatic efforts toward healing the rift between its eastern and western divisions. Early in the year, John Sevier met with his old friend, Evan Shelby, who was brigadier general for North Carolina, to seek to calm the waters. The pair made certain agreements toward that end, but no real calm resulted. The more rancorous Franklinites felt Sevier was flirting with betraying his own governmental charge, and on the other side, Tipton and his pro-Carolina faction continued to do all they could to strengthen their favored state's hold.

Tipton, in Pinnock's evaluation, was a "man of hateful brass" who went so far as to lead a force of some fifty armed men into Franklin's Spencer County to seize county records. It appeared to be one more incident of political raiding—and such had become fairly common in the region—but this time matters took an unexpected twist. Rumors spread that Tipton had taken John Sevier himself as prisoner and was ready to haul him off to North Carolina for trial and punishment.

"In the track of this rumor occurred events that show beyond question the great personal devotion so many of these Men of the Canebrake hold for their beloved governor, John Sevier," Pinnock journalized. "Upon receipt of the tale of Sevier's imprisonment, my own inn was vacated at once by its patrons. Led by Cooper Haverly, ever the supporter of Franklin and its governor, and including on this occasion even Joshua Colter, who in the usual sway of affairs is slower to take to extreme action than C. Haverly, my patrons rode toward the home of the pernicious Tipton, there to do whatever was required for the welfare of Sevier."

Pinnock's inn patrons were not alone. The same rumor had spread far, eliciting the same response from Sevier's friends all over the area. John Tipton found himself surrounded in his own home by more than two hundred armed and angry frontiersmen, with many more on the way. Only a fortuitous forest meeting between a group of Franklinites and Sevier himself averted a miscarriage of justice at Tipton's expense. Contrary to the rumor, Sevier had simply slipped off for a few days of solitary hunting, a diversion from the stress of governorship.

Pinnock's evaluation was this: "It is evident, from this extraordinary if mistaken show of protection for Governor Sevier, that the people of this great borderland hold firmly their devotion to the great State, and will in the end prevail over the Tiptonites."

Salem Pinnock's optimism certainly did seem justified by the outpouring of support for Sevier, and by the hectic activity of the Franklin assembly, in frequent session throughout the year. The new state seemed very alive.

But dissatisfaction was still mounting among much of the Franklin populace, who were weary of trying to live under two conflicting authorities. And when North Carolina's assembly shrewdly voted to forgive certain taxes imposed against the westerners a few years earlier, many borderline Franklin supporters shifted their allegiances.

Meanwhile, news of Indian raids continued to come, infuriating all and further deepening the prejudices of the many whites who had come to hate all Indians with a raging passion. Joshua Colter and others who held a more moderate view were increasingly in the minority; it was common in the Pinnock Inn and other gathering places to hear men express, in great seriousness, a desire to see the native race eliminated. Pinnock himself wrote: "There are many of my acquaintance who see the slaying of an Indian as bearing no more import than the death of a buffalo, if even as much."

In the autumn, many were cheered when James Robertson, former friend, neighbor, and leader of many of the Overmountain people, and now commander of the militia in the Cumberland settlements, led a force of about a hundred and thirty volunteers and militiamen and struck the town of Coldwater, a Creek-Chickamauga nest in the Muscle Shoals region along the Tennessee River. Almost thirty Indians, most of them Creeks, were killed, and the town was burned. When Robertson rode home, only one fatality had been recorded among his men.

The Coldwater raid, however, did not end hostilities. While Robertson was away at the end of 1787, attending the North Carolina assembly meeting, Creeks killed several Cumberlanders and wounded others. Meanwhile, the Chickamaugas beset boatloads of voyagers who passed their towns by river, and continued individual raids against the whites who built their cabins on the disputed lands.

When 1788 dawned, Salem Pinnock was writing in a new way in his journal. He would not notice it until long afterward, when he read his own writings from the perspective of time. His words, his tone, grew pregnant, anticipatory.

Changes were coming; Pinnock innately sensed it. Changes that would decide, in one way or another, the very future of the state of Franklin, and of the "Cane-brake Men" whom Pinnock so exalted and extolled.

In the fall came talk of a major campaign against the Creeks, who had been stirring up much trouble across the frontier. The state of Georgia was leading the military effort; Franklin was to assist by supplying fifteen hundred men.

Plans for the campaign stirred the blood of the frontier folk and for a time eclipsed the civil strife in the would-be state. Georgia sent young English-born Lieu-tenant Colonel George Handley to help Franklin assemble its troops, and volunteerism was high. Joshua Colter and Cooper Haverly were among those offering their ser-vices. Payment for the Franklin troops was to be in the form of lands in the rich and coveted Creek country around the Bend of the Tennessee River: a thousand two hundred acres for participating colonels, a thousand for majors, nine hundred for captains, seven hundred for noncommissioned officers, six hundred forty for privates, and so on.

The troops were formed into regiments and drilled in Jonesborough, Greeneville, and other communities. Hopes were high that a good showing by the Franklin troops would bolster the image of the new state on a na-tional level.

Then the entire expedition came to an unanticipated halt. Congress, desiring no war, had appointed commis-sioners to treat with the Creeks. Until the outcome of the diplomacy was known, no military expedition should go forth.

The troops were mustered out and sent home, all the

anticipation faded away, and Franklin's old troubles on the homefront reasserted themselves.

It was a sad thing to Joshua Colter to see the Franklin effort sullied by trouble and personal disputes. It was too bad that so many personal animosities had come to bear on the situation, too bad that what might have been a smooth, diplomatically handled transition had degenerated into virtual civil war.

Whenever he had the time, Joshua took frequent long walks into the forests, looking for the kind of peace he had known there before the Overmountain country had come under the domain of governments and courts and competing authorities. Was this civilization? If so, Joshua Colter wasn't sure he was all that eager to be civilized.

On one cold day he climbed to the top of a high hill and looked westward across the winter-browned, forested terrain, wondering how far a man would have to wander to find the kind of unsettled wilderness he had grown to love as a boy. The kind that this place had been when he was a young long hunter, roaming here in the 1760s with Alphus Colter and Levi Hampton.

He looked west as far as he could see. *Someday I might just have to go take a look out yonder. Go as far as I can go, and see for myself what's beyond. Someday.*

But not anytime soon. He was a settled man now. He had a family to raise, people to protect, stock to keep grazed, fields to plant and harvest. And that was fine, that was good. He loved his family and his life.

Still, it would be terribly interesting just to gather his rifles, hounds, horses, traps . . . and just ride off, way out there, and keep riding until he came to the end, whatever and wherever that end might be.

He looked awhile longer, fingering the old Roman coin

that hung from the thong about his neck. Then, as the sun set, he climbed down again and returned home.

Joshua Colter determined to avoid participating in the civil strife that troubled Franklin, but events that transpired in early 1788 proved too sweeping to miss him.

In the Washington County court, Tipton's faction entered an order authorizing Jonathon Pugh, sheriff under the Carolina government, to seize court records supposedly in the hands of John Sevier. The timing of the move was well-chosen; Sevier was lately spending most of his time in the lower counties, keeping an eye out for Indian raids.

The result of Tipton's action was a massive resumption of court raids, this time with a new intensity. Armed bands of Tiptonites stormed through the countryside, bringing terror to Franklinites. Even now Joshua had no desire to take part in the inevitable response, and resisted Cooper's urgings to take up arms. But when Tipton's forces physically took over Jonesborough, he relented.

Franklinites gathered at Salem Pinnock's tavern and other sites around the region, and rode in arms to Jonesborough. They repossessed the town with relative ease, but Tipton's forces regathered and, reinforced, headed back toward town two hundred and forty strong.

Joshua Colter and the more prudent and experienced of the Franklinites retreated from Jonesborough, heading west to Greeneville, the capital of Franklin and headquarters of Sevier. Cooper Haverly and a few other hotheads would not fall back, despite all urgings. "I'll not retreat before any bloody Tiptonites," he said. "You go on, Joshua. Go back home and see to the safety of our families. I'll stay, and there's nothing you can say to change my mind."

Joshua knew the futility of arguing further. He left Jonesborough, and the Tiptonite force moved in almost at his heels. The handful of Franklinite holdouts, Cooper included, were taken prisoner.

Sevier's followers soon came together again, angered by a new Tiptonite outrage. Washington County's Sheriff Pugh, carrying out a North Carolina court order, took several of Sevier's slaves as payment of an old debt, and hauled them off to Tipton's house for safekeeping.

Sevier was infuriated. The time had come to declare a halt to Tipton's arrogance once and for all, and to reassert, before it was too late, the authority of Franklin.

Joshua was at Sevier's side when the governor led a force of about a hundred and fifty men from Greeneville to Tipton's house in Washington County. Along the way others joined—and Joshua was deeply surprised when one of the joiners was none other than Cooper.

"They hauled us into court and had us pledge to do nothing else for the Franklin cause," Cooper explained. "Then they let us go."

"Did you make the pledge?"

"I did."

"Then you're here against your own word."

"The way I see it, Joshua, word given to a courtroom of snakes don't amount to a piggin of spit. It takes more than forced oaths to scour the righteous grit out of a new state man. If Nolichucky Jack Sevier is on the march, Cooper Haverly is going to be at his side."

The force rode eastward, passing the farmsteads and tiny log-house communities growing up along the creeks and through the valleys. It was late February 1788, and very cold.

*   *   *

They came within a quarter mile of John Tipton's house on the afternoon of February 27, and John Sevier sat down with quill and paper to scrawl a message to Tipton. When it was done, he read it, blew the ink dry, and handed it to Joshua Colter.

"My friend, you will have the honor of delivering this to the dear colonel in yonder house."

Joshua took the paper and read it silently.

State of Franklin, February 27th, 1788. In a Council of the Officers to secure the rights of the Citizens in this State, and from Motives to Establish Peace and Good Order:

It is our request to Colonel John Tipton that he and the party now in the house surrender themselves to the discretion of the people of Franklin within thirty minutes from the arrival of the flag of truce.

John Sevier, C. Gen'l.

Joshua folded the letter and tucked it under his coat. With a truce flag flying above him, he mounted and rode on to the Tipton farm.

He felt eyes upon him when he came into view of the farm. Joshua knew this place; he had hunted here as a young man, long before the first settlers had crossed the mountains to build their cabins on the Old Fields of the Watauga and the creek that was later named after Joshua's old friend, Daniel Boone, who had once camped in the very area. Joshua had camped here a couple of times too, near the mouth of the ancient cave that was now part of Tipton's property.

Whatever his views of Tipton as a political man, Joshua had always admired his farm. Tipton's four-year-old house was built of solid logs, piled two stories high; beside it was a small house that served as his office. What had once been an old buffalo trail circled around toward the house, passing near a little corn crib and double crib barn. The scene as it met Joshua's eye was peaceful at first glance—but a second glance revealed faces at windows, and men moving about behind the house.

Several armed men emerged from the house and came toward him. He halted his horse and held the truce flag high.

"What's your business, Colter?"

"I have a communication in hand, from Governor John Sevier."

"Hand it over."

"The message is for Colonel Tipton. I'll deliver it only to his hand."

The men whispered among themselves, then told Joshua to dismount. "Hand over the rifle," the spokesman ordered.

"I'll keep it in hand," Joshua replied.

"The hell you will—hand it over!"

Joshua let his gaze bore into the man's face. "Very well, friend. But if you so much as scratch the stock, I'll womanize you with my own knife."

The man snarled and swore at this show of defiance—but Joshua noted that when the man took the rifle, he held it very carefully.

Tipton was inside, surrounded by a small army of grim-faced men. The colonel's stare was colder than the weather.

"Colter, what have you there?"

Joshua handed over the document. Tipton opened it

and read it. When he was finished, he made a contemp-
tuous snorting sound, wadded the letter and tossed it to
the floor. "You may inform the good governor of the illegal and so-called state of Franklin that I seek no favors
from him," Tipton replied in a tone of sarcasm. "Further,
you may reverse the kind invitation he has extended to
me, and inform him that, if he should care to do his
duty of honor and surrender himself to me, bringing with
him the leaders of his rebel gaggle, I will guarantee him
all the due benefit of the laws of the state of North Carolina, the sole legal governing authority over our region.
Do you understand the message, sir?"

"I got keen ears, Colonel."

"Then be off with you, and deliver it." Tipton spoke to
the men around Joshua. "Give him back his rifle, and see
to it he isn't molested as he goes."

The man gave the rifle back quite readily. Joshua made
a deliberate show of examining the stock, up and down,
frowning and squinting when he saw a scratch. He glared
abruptly at the man who had been in charge of the
weapon. The color drained from the man's face.

"Good thing for you that it was me who put that
scratch there, a year ago or more," Joshua said.

The man's face went from white to red. He opened his
mouth to curse, then closed it. Everyone knew that when
Joshua Colter was the opponent, it sometimes wasn't
worth it to try to get the last word.

Joshua tipped his hat. "Good afternoon, gentlemen,"
he said. He walked out, mounted, and rode back toward
Sevier's camp, with John Tipton standing in the doorway
and watching him until he was out of sight.

*   *   *

John Sevier listened to Joshua Colter's report, fingered the buttons on his militia officer's uniform thoughtfully, then said, "So that was the scoundrel's only response?"

"Aye, John."

"How many men with him?"

"I had no chance for a full count, but I would make a guess at maybe forty, forty-five."

"Then we have the advantage of numbers . . ."

"At the moment. And they have the advantage of shelter while we're exposed to the cold. And he's bound to have reinforcements on the way. Our march here is well-known by now, and Tipton does have his friends."

"So does our state. And so do I."

Sevier turned away, lowering his head, putting his hand to his chin, as Joshua had often seen him do when deep in thought. At length he straightened and took a deep breath. Joshua was familiar with that gesture: It meant Sevier had made up his mind.

"There is only one course open now, though I had hoped we could avoid it. For me to withdraw, for whatever excuses, would be seen by all who observe it— Tipton included—as the new state at last bowing the knee before the old. There was a time at the beginning, Joshua, when I was ready to do that, if a peaceful solution to our problems could have been found. The Franklin effort could have died aborning, and we would have found other means to peace and protection. But I was encouraged not to do that. I was encouraged to lead the movement, accept the governorship . . . and I did. I set my course, and it has led me here. I'll not back away."

"Then there will probably be bloodshed," Joshua replied.

Sevier nodded. "Yes. Quite probably there will."

10

The crack of rifles shattered the chilly air. Powder smoke burst outward in white blossoms that dissolved and drifted toward the cloudy sky. Cooper Haverly, one of the several who had fired, lowered his rifle and examined the results of the fusillade as a cheer went up from the Franklinite riflemen who had laid it down.

"Two down, no, three," he said. "I can't tell if . . . blast it! The men are up—nothing hit but their horses!"

"Who are they?" asked Mark Travis as he ramrodded a new ball, wrapped in a patch of linen, down the long-rifled barrel of his flintlock weapon.

Denmark-born Major Augustus Christian George Elholm, adjutant and drill master of the Franklin militia, and second-in-command to Sevier, stepped up and answered the question: "It appears to be Captain Peter Parkinson and a company of Tiptonites. Coming to reinforce Colonel Tipton, almost certainly."

"Not now they ain't, Major," Cooper said with satisfaction. "We've drove them off—see them flee!"

"Aye aye. If we can succeed in keeping all such away from—zounds! What the devil . . ."

Elholm's exclamation resulted from a second blast of

170

gunfire from the opposite end of the line of riflemen. Cooper Haverly was just as startled as Elholm, and turned to find out what had sparked the gunfire.

He heard someone down the line say, "Oh, God."

The last rounds had been fired at two figures that had emerged from the house. Had the overeager riflemen paused only a second more, they would have seen that the emerging figures were women. Cooper was dismayed to see one of the women was down, grasping at her bloody shoulder. He was glad he had not been among those who fired. It appeared that these women had simply been attempting to remove themselves from a dangerous situation.

The other woman, to Cooper's relief, was unhurt, and helped her wounded companion back to the house. The ranks of Franklin riflemen raised no cheers this time. No one felt happy to have wounded a woman.

Cooper had come into this business with his usual buoyant eagerness. The wounding just witnessed, however, deflated him significantly. This was no high-spirited courtroom raid. It was a serious matter, potentially a bloody one.

He wondered how long it would be before it was over.

For the remainder of the day very little happened except moves that indicated Sevier was ready to lay in a serious and possibly extended siege of the Tipton house. He stationed men at all possible points of access to the property. Cooper Haverly was placed with a group assigned to a rocky rise to the west of the house. Among the others in that body was James Sevier, John Sevier's second son by his first wife, the late Sarah Hawkins Sevier.

James Sevier was four years younger than Cooper. The two knew each other, though not well. As the night grew colder, Cooper and James passed the time in conversation. Cooper was fascinated by James's recounting of the story of his mother's 1780 death and burial, a story brought to mind by the uncomfortable weather. Early in that year, John Sevier had been away from home, building mills on Limestone Creek. Sarah Sevier had just given birth to Nancy Sevier, who was James's youngest full sister and Sarah Sevier's tenth child. Word of an Indian threat reached John Sevier, and he fled home to take his family to a fort on the Nolichucky. The cold and inclement weather brought illness to Sarah Sevier, still weak from childbirth, and she died soon afterward.

"It wasn't thought safe to bury her by day," James recounted. "So after dark some of the men of the fort went out and dug a grave in the woods. We buried her just before midnight. Father thought it right that Mother's children see her laid to rest, and so we were all taken there, even the new baby, and even though there was the fiercest storm you ever seen going on. I'll never forget that night long as I live. We smoothed out her grave and spread brush over it so the Indians wouldn't find it and do damage to her corpse." James Sevier huddled in his coat, trying to warm himself. "Lord have mercy, what a night that was. What a night."

The talk of cold left Cooper and the others feeling all the more chilled, until finally the entire group slipped away from their post to warm themselves around a campfire some distance away. Cooper felt ill-at-ease about this abandonment of duty, but the desire for heat was stronger than his sense of obligation. Surely nothing bad would come of it.

The next morning Joshua Colter was again sent in with

a message asking Tipton's surrender. When he returned with another refusal and counterdemand from Tipton, he also brought news that brought chagrin to Cooper, James Sevier, and the others who had been supposed to guard the rise.

"Tipton has been reinforced," Joshua announced. "Sometime in the night about a dozen men from Greasy Cove slipped in. They came over the rise."

James Sevier manfully confessed that he and the others had briefly abandoned their posts, bringing reprimand from John Sevier. But what was done was done, and the matter was dropped.

The question now was how best to proceed with the siege. Major Elholm favored use of a piece of field artillery that had been brought along. He advocated construction of a movable shield that would fit over the light weapon and protect the men who would operate it. This could be pushed toward the house and used to drive out the occupants.

Sevier was doubtful about the feasibility of this odd-sounding tactic and would not approve it, irking Elholm. And so matters hovered in uncertainty for hours, and Sevier's only order was for some of his men to forage for food and supplies, using Franklin-backed promissory certificates for payment.

The day passed without action, then, about dusk, a rider named William Cox came into the camp with disturbing news. Sullivan County militiamen, he said, were taking Tipton's part in this dispute, and were gathering to come to his assistance. That night, Cox said, they expected to reach Dungan's Mill, about six miles away, and cross the Watauga River.

This intelligence created an uproar and inserted more uncertainty into an already confused situation. Could Cox be trusted? Some suspected him of treachery and believed his claim could be discounted.

Sevier concluded the dispute by ordering Captain Joseph Hardin, Joshua Colter, and his own son, John Sevier Junior, to ride to the Watauga River ford and face off with any Tiptonite reinforcements they encountered.

Joshua believed Sevier's cautionary move was prudent. The body of the troops, however, believed differently, and within a mile of the ford simply stopped, complaining of the bitter weather and refusing to go a pace farther. Hardin and the junior Sevier barked orders and made threats, and Joshua pleaded the case for seeing the reconnoiter through. It availed nothing. Frontiersmen could be a stubborn lot, and these were convinced to the man that Cox's talk of reinforcements was all falsehood. At last the entire body turned and rode back to Tipton's, their mission not even attempted, much less accomplished.

By now it was even colder, and snow began to fall. Joshua watched Sevier rage at yet another shirking of duty on the part of men sworn to follow him, and thought how all of this was falling out, in miniature, along the same pattern of the state of Franklin's larger history. What had started with broad support and strong will was degenerating into squabbling and self-service. This whole effort was beginning to take on a farcical quality. As he shivered in the snow, Joshua wondered if he had been wise to make himself part of it.

Owen Killefer pulled the bearskin more closely around him, huddled lower against the warm mound of earth-covered hickory coals beneath him, and thought about how pleasant it would be to slam his fist as hard as he could into the face of Dover Hice. He imagined the satisfaction of the hard swing, the give of bone and cartilage, the grunt of pain as Hice fell backward. He closed his eyes against the sting of the cold and pictured Hice gaping up at him, fresh blood bright and flowing. He would lean over his humiliated employer, aim his finger into his face, and say, "You bring another tear to Nell's eye, you speak another hard word to her, and you'll get worse than what I just gave you, Hice! You understand me? You even look cross at her again, and you'll be buried before sundown the same day."

Smiling, he opened his eyes again and gazed out through the Carolina snow. The fantasy faded, and so did his smile. As satisfying as it was to dream of being Nell's champion against a husband who had turned out to be tyrannical and cold and sometimes cruel, such a thing couldn't really happen in Owen Killefer's world, no matter how much he wanted it to.

Owen slipped a chew of tobacco into his mouth, working it into a soft cud that settled nicely against his jaw. He heard movement in a snowy thicket nearby and held still, hoping it was a buck. It wasn't—only a rabbit. Owen sighed and shifted again.

What am I doing here? Why am I lingering around, working for Dover Hice, when there isn't a thing for me to gain? Why didn't I just ride on with McCarthy when he left, and seek whatever life I could find for myself somewhere else?

Well, he knew why. He had stayed on all this time because he still loved Nell. He had tried to change his feelings, but had failed miserably.

It was a shameful failure, because he didn't believe she was any longer an appropriate object for his affection. He had firm standards; his mother had done her best to instill a strong sense of morality in her children. Even Aaron Killefer, despite his weakness for liquor and general lack of moral fervor for much of anything, had been a righteous-minded man where marriage was concerned. Everything in Owen's background told him he should put Nell out of his mind, even avoid being around her. That would be the right thing. He had learned that lesson long ago.

But lately he had also learned something else: Knowing the right thing and doing it were two very different matters. As a thoroughly infatuated young man, Owen coddled his feelings toward Nell, even though, against the background of his raising, they scared him, made him feel guilty.

Sometimes he would lie awake at night in his roughly enclosed little room in the loft of Dover Hice's barn, where he slept, and think about Nell, his feelings alternating between his familiar bittersweet, lovesick longing for her, and fears of divine punishment for the sure sinfulness of that longing. Owen was not schooled religiously and possessed only a vague notion of heaven, but a much less vague notion of hell. That was the place where bad things were paid back in punishment, he had been told. And surely, loving Nell when she was married to another was a bad thing. For his own welfare, he should go ... but his attraction to Nell kept him here.

As did another thing: the obvious fact that Dover Hice so obviously wanted him to be gone. Owen knew that the only reason Hice had given him work and lodging at all was that Charles Carney had told him to, and Hice hadn't been ready to buck the will of his new father-in-law. Almost from the day Owen had ridden onto the grounds of Hice's farm with McCarthy, it had been clear that Dover Hice wasn't pleased with his intrusion. Even then, perhaps, he had sensed the young man's feelings toward his new bride.

And now the situation had an even more compelling twist, one Hice had surely noticed, just as Owen had: As Nell's marriage grew more difficult as months passed, she seemed to be growing uncommonly interested in the young farmhand who slept in the loft. In light of Nell's past coldness toward Owen, her newfound attentions to him seemed terribly ironic.

Nell was always giving some new attention to him, either through conversation or slipping Owen an extra slice of pie or a loaf of the fine bread she baked. Whenever such things happened, his will to do the right thing and depart was washed away. Her attention to him, though always exhibited in innocent fashion, was so flattering, so craved by him, that it overcame all contrary impulses.

Owen couldn't honestly be sure Nell's attitude toward him was romantic in the usual sense. It might be merely a reflection of her regret at entering a bad marriage and her homesickness for her family. Owen, having been attached to the Carney household, surely served her as a reminder of her former, happier home. He was a living memento of a longed-for past. Was that enough to explain why Nell was so tender to him? Or did her affection go deeper?

Owen didn't know. And it really didn't matter. Nell had made her choice when she married Dover Hice, and she—and Owen—would have to live with it, whatever feelings he or she had toward each other. And there the situation stood: Owen attracted to a young woman who had overlooked him when it would have been possible for their relationship to find some fulfillment, but who now, far too late, seemed to finally think him worth at least some kind of affection. It was so ironic that sometimes Owen had to laugh. But it was laughter without joy.

Another creature stirred in the brush, and this one was a buck. Owen waited for his chance, then raised his rifle and felled the beast. He stood, reloaded, and advanced to field dress his kill. For a winter buck, this was a fat one. It would provide venison for the Hice family for many days. Nell would be pleased; she liked good venison. Of course, Dover Hice would complain the meat was tough—he always found fault with the game Owen brought in. Owen didn't really care. As far as he was concerned, he thought wryly, Dover Hice could choke on the meat. It would open up a new world for Owen Killefer and Nell Hice if he did.

William Cox had been no liar after all. In the darkness, the Tiptonite reinforcements gathered at Dungan's Mill, huddling in their heavy coats, and rode through the driving snow toward the besieged Tipton house.

The snow fell heavier than ever as they took position near the house, careful to keep themselves out of view of Sevier's increasingly restless guards.

As the sun rose unseen behind the shroud of gray covering the sky, James Sevier and the junior John Sevier set out with about thirty scouts, including Cooper Haverly and Joshua Colter at the rear, and moved out along a road in front of Tipton's house. The snow was so thick now they could scarcely make out the boundaries of the road.

Without warning, rifles cracked and balls passed through the ranks of the scouts and slammed into the fence near them. The volley scattered the men, but none were hurt. Horses whinnied in fear as the scouts urged them forward at full gallop. Joshua and Cooper, at the end of the column, were more exposed than any of the others, and were obliged to seek cover or be shot out of their saddles.

"Cooper, I believe it's about to start in earnest," Joshua said to his brother as they rode into the closest available cover.

Cooper was about to reply when a second volley sent concussive waves of sound and a hail of lead above them, shearing off leafless small branches and dropping shards of wood and snow onto them. A babble of voices rose in a coarse war cry, and Sevier's men realized how foolish their earlier carelessness had been. There *were* reinforcements for Tipton after all, and now they were here.

"We should never have turned back from Dungan's Mill," Joshua said to Cooper as they dismounted and dropped behind a log. "That's bound to be where they came over."

"Look,, Joshua! The house!"

Tipton's men were pouring out of the house, advancing to join the attack of their reinforcing party. From somewhere in the white and gray murk, Joshua heard Elholm's voice, ordering retreat. "Come on, Cooper," Joshua said. "Let's join them before we're cut off out here."

They mounted and made a dangerous dash toward the main body of Franklinites, which was now breaking up and heading toward a nearby knoll, leaving behind much equipment, including the small field artillery piece. Shots popped flatly in the air, fired both by the advancing Tiptonites and the retreating Franklinites, many of whom were on foot. Joshua heard a rifle ball whiz about a foot above his head. He ducked lower and moved into the midst of the Franklinites. A man near him raised his rifle and fired into the oncoming Tiptonites. One of them yelled, flung up his hands and fell back onto the snow, where he writhed only a few moments before expiring.

Joshua and Cooper reached the top of the knoll and dismounted. Seeking cover, Joshua dropped behind a boulder and began looking for a target.

But his heart wasn't in this. He had fought many times before, from Point Pleasant to Haverly Fort to King's Mountain, and scores of lesser skirmishes and Indian fights besides. In one of those fights had he felt so ambivalent about what he was doing. What was this battle really about? The future of the new state . . . or the bitterness of two antagonists, Tipton and Sevier? The former was worth fighting for. The latter was not, at least not in Joshua Colter's way of thinking. And yet here he was, kneeling in the snow with his rifle in hand, looking for human targets to wound or kill.

Someone came to his side; it was John Sevier himself. His expression was somber and dull. He looked straight ahead, not even acknowledging Joshua's presence. Joshua was surprised. He had seen Sevier in battle before; always he had been full of vigor and life, barking orders and guiding his men with assurance. But today it looked as if Elholm and others were more in charge than was Sevier.

And then the Tiptonites were upon them, and Joshua had no more time to think of such things. The skirmish was hot but brief, and the Tiptonites prevailed. Sevier's forces were driven off the rise. The snow spewed down all the harder, making it impossible to know the size and exact location of the opposing force.

And so the retreat continued, Sevier's men heading for Jonesborough, where they would regroup and reassess.

Joshua Colter felt disgusted. He had no business being here. Furthermore, he was growing sure that the state of Franklin was nearing its end. This civil squabble was being fed by the last flutterings of Franklin's heart.

Sevier's force reached snow-filled Jonesborough. Joshua looked around for Cooper, and at last found him tending to a minor wound in his left arm.

"You shot, Cooper?"

"No. I ran against the end of a broken branch riding out from Tipton's. Poked me pretty good—must have gone in an inch."

Joshua was silent. Cooper looked at him inquiringly. "You got something on your mind, Josh." It was an observation, not a question.

"Aye . . ." Joshua ran his palm down his snow-dampened beard. "Cooper, I'm not staying on. I'm through with this fight. I've done my share. I'm going home to Darcy."

Cooper said nothing, but his expression told much. He lowered his face and resumed cleaning his arm wound.

"You think I'm playing Judas, don't you!" Joshua said.

"It's you saying that, not me."

"It's what you're thinking. And you're wrong. I'm betraying no one."

"No one but John Sevier. No one but the new state."

"There'll be no new state. It's over. All that really remains of the state of Franklin is John Sevier himself. Him, and a few hotheads like yourself."

"I'm a loyal man. I don't back out on my duties."

"Nor do I, Cooper. As far as I see it, I've done my duty. I've stood by Franklin, I've stood by Sevier. But in my day I've learned a few things from the Cherokees. One of them is that there's little worth in fighting on after the battle's lost. And this battle's lost."

"Lost? We withdrew, but we'll be back in the fight as soon as we pull together again."

"I'm not talking about this little turkey shoot. I'm talking about the new state. The whole effort. It's done with. What began as a good thing has become a squabble that it ain't worth nobody dying for. This all will do no good that I can see. And don't think the Indians are blind to this. The more we fight among ourselves, the more they'll believe we're divided and weak. That will only lead to more raids, more killings, more scalpings—and all in the name of preserving a state that isn't yet really a state at all, never has been, and likely never will be."

Cooper's expression remained stony. "Sevier won't appreciate you running out on him, Joshua."

"Likely he won't. But I saw him in the fight, Cooper. He wasn't the John Sevier I saw at King's Mountain. I think that in his heart he knows the same things I've said to you here. He might not have admitted it to himself yet, but he knows. He knows."

Cooper pulled down his sleeve and slipped his coat back over his shoulders. "I can't go along with you this time, Joshua. I'm with 'Chucky Jack to the end." His tone was snappish, defensive.

"Then be careful, brother. Look out for yourself."

Cooper nodded curtly. Joshua watched him walk away through the driving snow, then, with a heavy heart, he mounted and began riding back toward Limestone Creek, shivering in the slicing wind.

When Joshua Colter later heard what happened after his departure, he found nothing to be surprised about. It all fell out substantially as he had thought it would.

Despite the pretense that the retreat to Jonesborough

was only a temporary withdrawal, it in fact marked the end of the fight. Tipton and his men followed the Franklinites toward Jonesborough, but were not far along the way before they were met with an emissary from Sevier who asked for time to consider terms.

The request had a certain pathos in it. After reaching Jonesborough, Sevier had learned that his sons, James and John, along with a cousin, had been captured by Tipton and were to be hanged. Those close to Sevier saw how deeply shaken he was by the news.

Tipton returned to his farm, still determined to carry out the executions. But an odd thing had happened. Just as the battle at Tipton's farm had cleared the last clouds from Joshua Colter's eyes, the prospect of hanging two sons of one of the region's leading citizens greatly sobered those around Tipton. Several of those closest to him began to counsel restraint, urging him to consider how he would perceive the situation if it were his sons in the hands of John Sevier, and their executions that were pending.

Their pleas actually succeeded in touching the heart of the fiery pro-Carolinian. With tears on his face, Tipton waved his hand and ordered that the Seviers be released.

Joshua learned of this from Cooper, who came riding into the Colter family stockade shortly after the release of the prisoners. Joshua expected Cooper to still be angry over his departure from Jonesborough, but Cooper wasn't. He had been thinking about what Joshua had said, and watching Sevier. The logic of the former, and the visible sorrow and tension of the latter, had worked together in Cooper's mind to bring him to a realization of the truth. The new state effort, for all its good intention and support, as doomed, just as Joshua had said.

As Cooper walked slowly back to his cabin, where

Hannah awaited him in the doorway, Joshua smiled privately. Cooper had been headstrong all his life, often too headstrong for his own good. Rarely did he believe himself in error about much of anything, and when he did, he was slow to admit it. That he had done so today, and on such a close-to-heart matter as the Franklinite effort and John Sevier, was remarkable. Might it be that at last Cooper Haverly was beginning to gain some benefit from the passing years? Joshua hoped so.

The fight at the Tipton house made for big news all across the region, and for weeks thereafter Joshua heard it continually discussed in every public setting he walked into. The Pinnock Inn, as usual, was the center of most such talk in Joshua's area, and there he learned of the ironic outcomes of the confrontation.

John Sevier had lost the fight in the short term. He had failed to silence or capture Tipton, and had scarcely escaped losing two of his own sons. His term as Franklin governor had expired the very day after the Tipton battle, and thereafter that position would remain technically unfilled, even though Sevier would occasionally continue to refer to himself in correspondence as "governor," and would hold out vain hope for Franklin's future for some time to come.

For John Tipton, his perceived victory over Sevier would cost much. Correspondence highly critical of his handling of the dispute over Franklin would soon begin arriving from sources ranging from the new North Carolina governor, Samuel Johnston, to North Carolina militia brigadier general Joseph Martin, who happened also to be the Indian agent. With every passing day, Tipton would become an increasingly rebuked man, even though he, like Sevier, continued to have many devoted adherents.

Before long, however, a new and more pressing concern apprehended the attention of the Overmountain people, and particularly John Sevier. As Joshua had predicted to Cooper, the Indians had kept an eye on the Franklin strife, which was still continuing in the form of personal and family feuds here and there. Within mere days of the fight at Tipton's, war parties began appearing in the lower settlement areas. Families fled their farmsteads and forted for safety in the rugged stockades. Disturbing communications came from the militia leaders in the outlying areas and from the Indian agents and traders.

"Have talked at length to many today," Salem Pinnock wrote in his journal early in April. "From all quarters the same fears are presented. Rumors of war with the Savages abound to the distress of the people. I fear that before the summer is past, great suffering will come to us in the form of the arrow and the scalping knife. A cruel season is soon to descend upon us." Then a scored line, and beneath it one of the personal afterthoughts that motivated Pinnock to keep all eyes but his own off the pages of his journal: "If there be, as so many would seek to persuade me, a Diety who hears the prayers of men and at times moves the workings of this world in accordance, then of a surety now is the time to make those prayers, and swiftly."

BLACK WATER TOWN

II

Ulagu had always felt a tribal superiority over the Shawnees of the north, but today, as he rode back toward Running Water Town at the side of one particular Shawnee warrior who had come around the first of the year to aid Dragging Canoe, he had to admit he was impressed. This Shawnee, about two decades old, was different from any he had ever met. He possessed an inner power that seemed to radiate from him and generate trust, and his cunning and battle prowess was undeniable. In the presence of the Shawnee named Tecumseh, Ulagu knew intuitively that he was keeping company with greatness.

Ulagu felt the wind against his brow, and a burst of exhilaration surged inside him and forced a smile onto his usually placid face. For the past six days, he had ridden with Tecumseh and a band of Shawnee and Chickamauga raiders. They had struck two isolated farmsteads, and three scalps tied to Ulagu's saddle pack gave evidence of their success. Their return to Running Water Town would be marked by celebration, and Ulagu looked forward to it. Judging from Tecumseh's keen expression, he looked forward to it as well.

As pleasant as Tecumseh's time among the Chickamaugas had been for Ulagu, Tecumseh himself had suffered a great tragedy since his arrival in the Tennessee country. He had arrived early in the year with his brother, Chiksika, to visit his mother, Methotasa, a Cherokee who had moved north to live among the Shawnees after she married Pucksinwah, a chief of that tribe. In 1774 Pucksinwah was slain in the Point Pleasant battle on the Kanawha River, and the widowed Methotasa moved south to rejoin her native people.

Initially, Tecumseh and Chiksika had greatly enjoyed their visit with their mother and the Chickamaugas. Ulagu knew from conversation with Tecumseh that both he and his brother had found Dragging Canoe an inspiring, impressive man, whose talk of the need for unity among the Indians against the common white foe had closely matched concepts forming in Tecumseh's own mind.

When the Chickamaugas attacked one of the Cumberland stations, both Tecumseh and Chiksika participated, as did Ulagu. The station was forted, the space between a double log cabin serving as the entrance. Early in the morning, while the children of the station were loudly singing under the direction of their schoolmaster, the Chickamaugas crept to the stockade and used the musical distraction to cover their noise as they knocked out some of the chinking between two logs. One of the raiders thrust a rifle through the hole and shot at the singing schoolmaster, striking him in the chin.

Pandemonium erupted. The children inside scrambled for safety as the Indians hacked open a window shutter with an axe. In a fateful move, one of the boys inside grabbed a rifle, ran to the window, and fired into the Indians outside.

The shot struck Chiksika. The Indians, shocked by the

Shawnee's fall, grabbed him and dragged him away, abandoning their siege.

Chiksika, employing a mysterious and prophetic fore-knowledge that often made itself known in Tecumseh's family, had predicted that he would die in such a way. Even so, Tecumseh was shaken by the death of his beloved brother, and vowed revenge. Ulagu was glad to aid him in obtaining it, and though he was saddened by Chiksika's death, felt glad at least that it would result in Tecumseh remaining longer among the Chickamaugas to lead retaliatory raids such as the ones just completed. He was a capable man, the sort of ally Ulagu was happy to have at his side in battle.

At Running Water Town boys ran out to greet the returning warriors, whooping triumphantly at the sight of the scalps they bore. Ulagu sat up straighter in his saddle, riding into town with a look of great satisfaction on his face as cheers and war songs rose around him.

The celebration lasted long into the night. Ulagu was eager to return to his own home near Black Water Town and rejoin his bride Sadayi—but not eager enough to miss such a festivity as this. As the people of Running Water Town danced and rejoiced at the successful raid, Ulagu joined Tecumseh for a long overdue meal. The Shawnee, though obviously pleased with the success his band had enjoyed, seemed pensive and quiet. Ulagu knew he was surely thinking of his lost brother.

Two figures passed before Ulagu and Tecumseh, and caught the latter's eye. "Who are these?" he asked Ulagu.

"That is a man named Thomas Turndale, an Englishman who fought the Americans and then stayed among our people," Ulagu answered. "The young woman is his squaw. She is called Flower. She was taken from her people by Turndale, after his Cherokee wife died."

"Do they live in this town?"

"No. Turndale's house is off the road past Black Water Town. I do not know why he is here—it is likely he has been called to give medicine to someone sick or hurt. He is skilled as a healer. That is one reason he has never been molested." Ulagu reached down and massaged the scarred place on his thigh where the broken bone had come through. The injury was fully healed now, but still caused him pain and had left him with a limp that he expected would be with him the rest of his life. "His medicine is strong, and is of great value to us. When my leg was broken and would not heal, Turndale alone was able to heal me."

"He is a good man, then, even though he is a white man?"

"He is a good healer, and he is loyal to his adopted people and not his own ... but I do not know if he is a good man."

"Why do you say that?"

Ulagu took another bite of roasted venison. "The women tell a story ... they say his woman—he calls her Flower—bore him a daughter, and that he killed the baby because he wanted a son. I know that it is true she was carrying a child, because I saw her that way at the time Turndale was healing me. They say his woman did not want him to kill her child, but that he did. It is a hard man who could do such a thing over his woman's tears. Turndale says the child died at birth, that he did not kill it."

"What does his woman say?"

"Nothing. She speaks very seldom, and says little about herself or her life. She is the most sorrowful woman I have ever known."

Tecumseh said, "You speak as if you pity her."

"She is a sad creature. Her spirit has fled from her, but her life goes on. The women say that Turndale has used his medicines to make her like she is. But whether this is true, I cannot say."

Tecumseh finished his meal and sat the remains of it at his feet. "There are many ways to steal the life of another, without herbs or strange medicines. To be taken from among one's own and forced to live in a new way, without choice, without hope ... that is enough to destroy the spirit of anyone."

Ulagu thought about those words, and realized later that there was more in them than mere comment upon the subject at hand. Tecumseh had been speaking not only of the fate that had befallen Turndale's woman, but also of the potential fate of all the native people, should the white men continue to prevail and force alien ways upon them. The meaning of most men's words rode on the surface of their talk, like water spiders on a pond. Tecumseh's talk was far deeper, and rewarding to those who searched beneath its surface. Every time Ulagu had done this, he had become wiser, and more inspired.

Ulagu was convinced anew that Tecumseh was a man worth watching and listening to. His company had already caused Ulagu to see that only through unity and brotherhood could the natives of the western wilderness hope to keep themselves from being overrun by the white encroachers. It would be fascinating to see what fate held in store for Tecumseh. While men such as Tecumseh lived, Ulagu could yet hope for the future of his people.

Emaline Killefer sat alone at the hearth in Tom Turndale's cabin and stared into the flames, exploring the familiar but frightening numbness inside her mind and wishing she could cry. But tears would not come. She had lost the ability even to grieve for herself.

Even the memory of the beautiful girl-child she had borne, only to lose, could no longer make her weep. How ironic it was that, after so long dreading the idea of bearing any child fathered by Thomas Turndale, she had felt such a burst of love for the squalling infant that had emerged from her body. Even though the girl had been partly the product of a hated man, Emaline had adored her, if only for the brief few minutes that Turndale had allowed her to hold the baby.

Afterward, he had taken the infant from her breast, declaring that she needed a washing. Emaline had watched him carry the child out of the cabin, and waited for him to bring her back. An hour had passed, then two. By the time Turndale returned—alone—Emaline had already accepted what in fact was true: her child would never return to her at all. Turndale told her the baby had died in his arms, that he had tried to save its life but couldn't, that he was sorry.

Emaline knew the truth. The child had been a girl, not the son Turndale wanted. So he had killed her.

She hated him for it. More precisely, she felt the ghost of an emotion that would have been hatred had she not lost so much of her ability to experience, for any long period, the normal feelings of human life. Now she mostly felt a cavernous inner emptiness that remained with her even in sleep.

And fear . . . she still could feel fear. Mostly fear of losing what tiny fragment remained of Emaline Killefer. Every day, she watched a little more of her true self dissolve and be absorbed into the person of Flower. She was continually more certain that once the absorption was complete, it would never be reversed.

That was what she feared. Emaline as Emaline was mostly gone now. Sometimes it was actually hard to remember her life before captivity, even when she tried.

She tried now. Squeezing her eyes tightly closed, she searched her memories until she came upon a scene from her childhood. She pictured the interior of the little North Carolina cabin in which she had been born and raised for the first years of her life. She saw her mother, laboring over the pot at the fire, cooking a stew of venison and vegetables. She was singing ... what was the song? Emaline dug deeper, and found it.

An old hymn, sung to a Scottish tune. Eyes still closed, Emaline began whispering the words to herself.

"Within the Lord we find our refuge,
  A lasting fortress, our God of might
  Whose glory shines among his people,
  The ransomed sinners in whom he delights ..."

The firelight warmed her face. She pulled her knees up against her breasts and wrapped her arms around her legs. *My name is not Flower, my name is Emaline Killefer* ...

"... Who in his mercy have found their portion,
  Whose darkest stains have been washed pure,
  Whose lines have fallen in pleasant places,
  Whose lot by free grace has been secured ...".

Emaline smiled. For the first time in longer than she could remember, she felt a spark of the defiance that had marked her first months with Turndale, the assertion of who she truly was against the person Turndale wanted to make her. *My name is not Flower, my name is Emaline . . . I am not his slave, I am not his wife . . .*

"... Oh, Holy Father, why do you love us?
What merits man to know thy grace?
Only the merit unearned yet given
When thou wert born with human face . . ."

And then the cabin door opened and Thomas Turndale stepped inside, and it all went flying away, slipping from her grasp and vanishing into the void. She lowered her brow against her raised knees, heard the door close, felt him walk up to her.

"Flower, my dear Flower." His voice had the soft quality he used at times when he tried to be affectionate.

My name is not Flower, my name is . . .

"I've missed you, Flower. I'm in need of your company. Look, I've brought us food."

He touched her shoulder. She wanted to cringe, but dared not. *My name is not Flower . . .*

"Stand up, Flower. I want to hold you."

My name is not . . .

She stood, her back still toward him. He put his arms around her and kissed her neck. His whiskers scratched her cheek, and his breath was a sickening mix of the essence of rotten teeth and the cedar twigs and dried teaberry leaves he chewed in a effort to cover the decay stench so she wouldn't be repelled by him. His notion of a kindness, she supposed. It didn't work.

My name is . . .

"Come with me, Flower, over here . . ."

He led her to the place they slept. He smiled; the smile was hungry, dreadful to her. It made her want to run, but there was no place to run. No escape. There was never an escape.

When the familiar ordeal was done, she lay awake late into the night, staring into the darkness above, listening to Tom Turndale snoring contentedly at her side. She struggled to remember the words of the hymn she had soothed herself with earlier, but they were gone now, and she could not find them.

Gone, like the old life they were a part of. Gone, like Emaline Killefer.

She had to face the truth now. No matter how she despised it, no matter how she denied it, she was not the person she had been. Tom Turndale had claimed her, and her name was no longer Emaline Killefer. Her name was Flower, and surely would be for as long as fate forced her life to go on.

Dover Hice looked at his wife in perplexed amazement. "I don't understand, Nell—I thought this news would please you!"

Nell, sitting on the edge of their bed with her head slumped and her face hidden by her hair, made no response. Hice rubbed his hand across his beard and frowned, a man honestly confused by his young wife's present manner.

"It's the Tennessee country I'm talking about, Nell. Did you not understand that? I know you've longed for your old home."

She looked up at him. Her eyes were free of tears, but her expression showed clearly that her emotions were stirred. "Yes, it's the Tennessee country, but not my part of it! You're going to take me even farther from my family than I am already!"

Hice paused. His expression of confusion gave way slightly to a harder look. He chuckled in mirthless exasperation. "Your *family*, you say . . . your family is here in this room, Nell. *I'm* your family!"

She lowered her face again. "No. Never."

Hice did not speak for several moments. When at last he did, his voice was different than before. Firmer, authoritative, stentorian in tone if not volume. He had pulled away from her, thrown up a barrier she had come to know well. "I regret you feel as you do," he said. "But you are my wife, and I am your husband, and you must do as I say. We will be leaving this place, boarding flatboats on the Holston River and traveling to the place that will become our new home." He paused. His voice softened again. "*Our* new home, Nell. It can be that way, if only you will let it be."

Nell looked up at him, making no effort to hide her distaste. "If *I* will let it be, you say? It's not me who has made it impossible for us to live as a man and wife should, Dover. It isn't me who has been cruel and unloving."

"Unloving? Nell, how can you say such a thing? I do love you, dearly. And I've never been cruel."

"No? What about this, then?" She lifted her arm, revealing a dark bruise that encircled it, the result of Hice having roughly gripped her arm during an argument two days before.

"I didn't intend to hurt you—" He lifted his eyes, threw up his hands. "God help me, woman, sometimes you can force a man to be harsh with you, what with your stubborn ways!"

Nell lay down and turned her back toward him.

Hice glared at her. "Very well. Be the child you are, if

you must. It's my duty to head this household—and so I will do, with or without your support."

He took his coat from a peg on the wall and began to put it on. Nell sat up, watching. "Where are you going?"

"Away. Out. I'll be back later."

"You're going to that—that bad place by the river!"

"What 'place' do you mean?"

"You know what I mean, Dover! You're going to that house of—of . . ."

"Harlots, my dear? Trollops? Bawds? Strumpets? Can your pure lips not voice such words?"

"I despise you!"

"Yes, yes. I know you do. You make me see it more clearly day by day." His eyes flashed; anger overcame him. "By heaven, you force me to such things as this! If you were the kind of wife a man requires, then . . . but to the devil with it, and with you! I'm tired of the struggle, Nell. Damned tired! I ought to leave you to that barn boy your father forced upon me."

He stopped then, waiting, as if to see how she would respond to that final barb. If Nell had anything to say, she kept it to herself.

Hice swore and departed, slamming the door shut behind him.

Word went out to the household the next afternoon from a very dissipated-looking, weary Dover Hice: He was selling his current house and lands and would move his household by flatboat to new lands south of the Cumberland River. Hice was a veteran officer of the Revolutionary War, and in payment for his service, he had been granted a certificate redeemable in western lands. Within the past year he had filed the certificate in the Hillsborough, North Carolina, land office, and taken claim on a rich tract in the south Cumberland region. There he and his would soon make their home and seek larger fortunes than Carolina had been able to afford.

The news surprised everyone, and left Owen unsettled. When the Hices moved, would he go along? Was he part of the "household," or merely a hired appendage Hice would at last rid himself of? He didn't dare ask Hice, and was reluctant to ask Nell, even if he found the opportunity.

Time passed, and his question remained unasked and unanswered—strictly speaking, at least. Owen finally concluded that he *was* to remain with the family, because Dover Hice never informed him to the contrary, and because he was given the main responsibility for guiding the physical preparations for the journey.

Owen had to work even harder than usual. Hice sold his stock to a buyer twenty-two miles to the east. Owen, helped by the slave Jubal, drove the cattle the full distance, then returned home to begin dismantling furniture, packing up Hice's goods, gathering and storing traveling food, taking inventory of tools, guns, smithing equipment, and so on.

Hice was a pack rat; he seemingly had never thrown anything away. Now he had no choice, with a flatboat journey impending. Through correspondence with Alexander Carney, Hice purchased two sizable flatboats that would await the voyagers at the boatyard near the Long Island of the Holston. Culling almost all nonessential items was necessary, and most of the work involved fell to Owen.

The plan was for the larger of the flatboats to convey most of the goods, plus three horses Hice insisted on keeping. Jubal and a second slave, Timothy, would man this boat, presumably with Owen, and Hice and Nell would travel with two hired boatman in the smaller boat.

Owen thought it ironic that the voyage would take them past the Chickamauga towns—the very place Tom Turndale was believed to have taken Emaline more than three years ago. He dreaded that portion of the passing, not only for its danger, but also because of the grief its associations with Emaline would rouse in him.

Time passed, labor continued, and at length the household of Dover Hice was ready to begin the overland trek to the Holston for the beginning of the voyage. The day before the departure, when all the goods were packed, the wagons loaded, and the house was an empty shell in which Dover Hice and Nell spent their last night at home on a pallet spread across the floor, Owen crawled into his loft and lay down, so exhausted by the day's work that he looked forward to sleep with a desire approaching passion.

Hardly had he settled down, however, before he heard someone enter the barn and begin climbing the loft ladder. He sat up. "Who's there?"

"It's me, Jubal." Owen left his room and crawled toward the edge of the loft, over which Jubal's face now appeared, barely visible in the darkness. Jubal climbed up and wiped at his trousers, dusting off the straw fragments he had accumulated on the way up.

"What is it, Jubal?"

"Just wanted to talk to you, Owen, if I could."

It wasn't unusual for the slave and Owen to talk frequently. The two labored together most of every day. Their friendship had developed naturally, and was comfortable enough that Jubal, who was two years older than Owen, usually referred to Owen by his first name, with no "Mister" prefixing it. Owen was "Mister Owen" only

when others were within earshot. Jubal couldn't afford to
have it get back to Dover Hice that one of his slaves was
talking too familiarly with a white. Hice wouldn't put up
with such a thing as that, even if the white in point was
the despised "barn boy" Owen Killefer.

"Go ahead and talk, then."

"I heard Mr. Hice and Mrs. Hice talking loud at each
other in their house tonight—they was mad, real mad at
each other."

"Why?"

" 'Cause of you."

"Me?"

"Yes. Mr. Hice, he don't want you to stay on once we
get to the new place. Says he wants rid of you."

So now Owen had his answer: Hice would use his labors in the moving process, then send him off. Knowing
Hice, he should have guessed as much.

Owen frowned. "Well, I'd been wondering about what
would happen to me."

"There's more, Owen. Mrs. Hice, she don't want him
to send you off. Said he'd regret it if he did. She wants
you to stay on."

Owen felt a warm, ruddy flush spread across his face.

"Mrs. Hice, she likes you awful much, Owen."

"She never acted like she liked me before she was
married."

"You ought to be careful of Mr. Hice. He don't like the
way she is around you. I heard him tell her he thinks she
loves you instead of him. You ought to be mighty careful."

"I've not done anything to Dover Hice. I do good
work for him."

"He don't want you around, Owen. You watch out for
him. If he can't make you leave, he might do worse to

you, and try to make it look like it was just something that happened, you know."

"You're saying he'd kill me?"

"Yes. I believe he might. You should've heard him fussing and squalling about you. I thought he'd bust, he was so riled!"

"Let him bust. I'd like to see it." Owen laughed coldly.

Jubal didn't laugh. "I ain't just talking, Owen. You can't tell what he might up and do. If I was you, I'd get away while I could."

"You fret too much, Jubal."

Jubal shook his head with such violence that Owen was surprised. "You didn't hear him going on about you like I did! He hates you, Owen! He'd kill you, no lying!"

Owen sobered. Perhaps this wasn't something he should dismiss. "I'm obliged for you telling me," he said. "I'll be careful."

"You ought to leave now, Owen. You ought to."

Owen looked out the loft window toward the Hice house. "No," he said. "I can't leave."

"Why not?"

"I just can't."

Silence. Jubal chewed his lip, glanced around as if he feared the night itself could hear and betray him. "Well, *I'm* leaving."

He had said it so low that Owen didn't quite catch it. "You're what?"

"I'm leaving. I'm going to run off from the boats about the Five Lower Towns and become an Indian."

Owen's mouth dropped open. He laughed aloud. "Become an Indian? You? You think you can just up and join the Chickamaugas like they was a bunch of Methodists or something?"

Jubal turned and went back to the ladder. Owen saw how deeply his laughter had offended him.

"Wait, Jubal. I didn't mean to—"

Jubal climbed down and stalked off.

Owen scrambled to the edge of the loft. "Jubal!"

The slave kept walking. Owen watched him go out of sight, then returned to his bed. An hour later he was still awake. Physically tired as he was, Jubal's talk had set his mind to scurrying. He stirred and rolled for a long time, thinking mostly about Nell, until sleep finally, reluctantly, took him in.

Mary Carney grew sick on a Sunday and was dead by Thursday. No advance warnings of declining health, no signs or premonitions. Only swift illness, mounting pain in her chest, and death.

When she died, what little remained of Colonel Charles Carney at his best died as well. The rough-hewn old aristocrat was literally struck off his feet. He took to his bed as soon as she was gone, and had to be held up by Alexander Carney to see his wife's burial.

Joshua Colter was not at the burial. He was off with his rangers in response to reports of Indian presence in the lower portion of the county. Two days after Mary Carney was laid away, Joshua and Darcy went to pay their respects to Charles Carney, only to find him away from home. Titus was there and told them that the colonel was gone, with Alexander, to the Long Island of the Holston, there to meet Dover Hice, Nell, and their household entourage, who were on the verge of voyaging to the Cumberland area to resettle on grant land Hice held there.

"They've chosen a dangerous time for a river journey," Joshua said. "I hope all goes well with them." Then as an afterthought: "Do you know if Owen Killefer is going with them?"

205

"As far as I know, Mr. Colter, he is."

The Colters returned home, talking about the Carneys and the Hice family journey. "I wonder if Hice knows what a prospect he faces, running past the Chickamauga towns?" Joshua said, recalling the vivid, terrifying stories Cooper's wife had told of her own participation in the big flatboat flotilla to the Cumberland country in the early weeks of 1780. "It's running a gauntlet, nothing less, especially for only two flatboats."

"I shudder to think of young Nell being out there," Darcy said.

" 'Young Nell' is a grown woman, married and settled," Joshua said. "But I feel the same worries you do. For Nell, and for Owen, if he is with them. Of course, Owen's pretty much a man by now, not the boy we knew."

Two weeks passed before Joshua saw any of the Carneys. Once again he had been out with his rangers, this time patrolling the countryside south of Jonesborough, all the way to the base of the mountains, where the Nolichucky spilled out of a wide gap between high ridges. In Jonesborough the rangers dispersed and headed back toward their various homes. Joshua Colter was the one exception. Something very rare had occurred: He had become sick. While he was still in the mountains, his stomach had begun to burn and ache, and by the end of the venture he didn't even feel up to the final stretch of travel home.

He could have checked into an inn, but chose instead to make his bed in the forest near town. In an inn one never knew whether he would have a bed alone or be crowded up behind some snoring, unwashed stranger with cold feet and stinking breath and lice. Even without that disincentive, an inn certainly was no place for a man who was fighting off the urge to heave up half his insides.

After a wretched first half of the night, during which his internal systems operated by their own set of abnormal and discomforting rules, Joshua finally went to sleep, and by morning felt much better. A little weak and hollow for nature's rough purgings, perhaps, but better. He rolled up his blankets, saddled his horse, and rode out of the woods onto the road. It was a beautiful spring morning.

It crossed Joshua's mind that this would be a handy occasion to see Alexander Carney, express his sorrow at Mary Carney's death, and learn how the Hice family's embarkation down the river had gone. Further, Alexander would surely be kind enough to offer a hungry friend some sort of breakfast better than the jerky and dry biscuit Joshua carried in his bag.

Alexander Carney had been married as a very young man, but his wife had died, with her infant, in childbirth. Since then Carney had lived either alone or with his parents. Upon entering the practice of law in Jonesborough, Carney had built himself a two-room cabin near town, closer in than his father's dwelling. He lived in one room of his log home and kept office in the other.

Joshua found Alexander outside, tying a rope collar around the neck of a big half-mastiff, half-hound dog. The beast growled menacingly at Joshua as he rode up. Joshua's horse flared its nostrils and looked at the dog sidewise, its eyes big with fear.

"Well, hello and good morning, Joshua!" Alexander said. "Come down and pay a visit."

"If I'd been an Indian, I'd have had your scalp by now, Alex," Joshua said. He waved toward the dog. "I'm afraid to get down. Afraid that thing'll eat my leg off. It puts me in mind of them Indian-hunting dogs Cooper says they raise over in the Cumberland settlements."

"This is the same mix. Meet Xerxes! He is a fright to look at, no question. But his former owner tells me he's a gentle beast."

"Where'd you get him?"

"In payment of a fee. I thought it a good exchange; I'd been wanting a dog. They make for a good manly kind of company, don't you think?"

"Hold that rope while I get down—I ain't willing to take anybody's word that a thing like that is gentle."

The dog snarled but did not snap as Joshua slid out of the saddle. Carney led the brute away and tied him to a tree on the side of his cabin while Joshua left his horse to crop the new grass within the paling fence around the yard of the office half of Carney's cabin.

Carney invited Joshua for breakfast, though he had already completed his own, and Joshua accepted. The fare was bread, mush, and cold pork. Basic food, but good.

"You look a mite peaked today, Joshua."

"Rough night. A storm in my belly, as my old Cherokee friends used to put it."

"I hope the problem has passed."

Joshua shot a wry look at his friend. "A right apt choice of words, Alexander."

The lawyer laughed and blushed. Joshua grinned upon seeing a grown man actually embarrassed by so mild a crudity. Alexander Carney was one of the most innocent men he had ever met, almost childishly so. Some thought him odd for that. Joshua found it refreshing.

Joshua finished his meal and wiped his sleeve over his beard. "Good victuals, Alex. Very welcome."

"Thank you."

"Well, I come mostly to tell you I'm very sorry about

your mother's death. She was a wondrous fine woman, and will be missed."

"Indeed she will. Thank you for your sympathy."

"How is your father?"

Alexander grew solemn. "Not good. Not good at all. He's worse by far than before, worse by tenfold."

Silence a moment, then Joshua said, "Come on, Alex. Let's take that dog of yours out and see how it runs."

The day was yet cool and pleasant, though the clarity of the sky and the brilliance of the inclining sun bore promise of a foretaste of the approaching summer season. Now that he had eaten, Joshua felt his usual healthful self. Contrary to his usual habit, he had left his rifle back at Alexander's house. He picked up a long stick from the roadside and used it as a walking staff. Alexander initially led his new dog on a rope lead, but out the road a ways loosened it and let it run free. The hulking beast raced on ahead, stopping frequently to sniff this or that distraction on the roadside, or to mark its territory in typical canine fashion.

Conversation was fine and easy; the men soon had walked farther than either had intended. Joshua inquired about the Hice voyage. Had it begun as planned?

"Indeed, indeed. I'm fresh back from seeing them off. It was a good visit, though too brief, and of course sad. Nell in particular seemed unhappy."

"Because of your mother's death?"

Alexander was slow to answer. "Yes . . . I suppose that was all it was."

"Tell me, is Owen Killefer still with the Hices?"

"Aye. And off to the west on the second of their flat-boats. He's grown much taller, but he's still very slight in girth. He said to send his greetings."

"It's a queer thing, in a way, him leaving Charles Carney and going to work for Hice. You'd halfway think he's still smit with Nell." Joshua watched Alexander from the corner of his eye, wanting to see what kind of response that comment would draw.

Alexander nodded curtly and said, "Yes. It would look that way." Alexander cleared his throat uncomfortably.

At length their conversation turned to the subject of Parnell Tulley, who remained at large. After the death of Aaron Killefer, Tulley had vanished. Saul Greentree was gone too; many believed they had left the area together.

"You can take some comfort in the fact that Tulley never fulfilled his threat against you," Joshua said.

"Ah, but he did try, didn't he! It still makes me feel ill to think of him actually trying to hire Aaron Killefer to kill me."

"Well, Killefer denied there was any truth to that. Likely as not the whole thing was cooked up when they were drunk, and never amounted to nothing anyway."

"Maybe. With Tulley you never know. I worked with him enough to know he isn't your common bird, Joshua. What was heavy on his mind one day, clean eating him alive, was gone the next, with something else taking its place. The only constant thing about the man was that he always seemed angry, always seemed ready to settle some score or another with somebody else."

"You talk about him like he's dead and gone."

"I do, don't I! I suppose it's because I hope that my own associations with him are in fact dead and gone. God willing, I'll never lay eyes on him again."

The dog had run far ahead, going out of view when the road topped a low rise. Unexpectedly, a wild canine cacophony began on the far side of that rise, interspersed with the angry shouts and curses of a man. Joshua and Alexander exchanged a glance, then took off at a run.

They reached the top of the rise just in time to hear a shot, which was followed by a resounding series of clearly pain-caused yelps amid the clamor of other dogs.

Alexander Carney stopped, took in what was happening, slammed the heels of his hands against his brow and yelled, "Xerxes! Good Lord, my dog is shot!" Incredulous, he looked up at the young man who sat astride a big, very fine-looking horse, which was threatening to buck or run because of the lively canine activity around its hooves. The shaggy-haired, ruggedly-featured horseman had plenty to compete for his attention at the moment: a restless mount, a snarling pack of dogs, and two pedestrians facing him with angry looks on their faces.

There was no question that the horseman was responsible for shooting Xerxes. A flintlock pistol, twin of another thrust into a holster on the front of his saddle, still smoked in his hand.

Xerxes, bleeding and pitiful, struggled up the hill to its master, the pack dogs snarling at its heels all the way. Joshua lifted his walking stick and jammed the end of it directly between the eyes of one of the canine aggressors; it yelped and ran back toward the horseman, who had just succeeded in calming his horse. Meanwhile, Joshua gave the identical treatment to two other dogs, then waved the stick and shouted, frightening off the remaining beasts.

Xerxes collapsed at Alexander's feet, looked up sorrowfully, whimpering, then went glass-eyed. Blood and drool dripped off its tongue, which lolled sideways. With a shudder the big dog died.

"He's killed!" Alexander said disbelievingly. "My dog is killed!"

"Sir!" The voice was stern and loud. It came from the horseman. "You there, with the stick! You bludgeon another of my dogs, and I'll give you the same treatment that mastiff got!"

Joshua was seldom taken by surprise by anything, but he was now. The horseman had thrust his empty pistol back into its holster and drawn his second, loaded one, in its place. It was leveled on Joshua's chest. Joshua could hardly believe it: He was being threatened with shooting, all because he had tried to beat off a pack of dogs tormenting a fatally wounded animal.

"You'd shoot me over a bunch of curs?" Joshua said.

"Indeed, sir. As surely as heaven and hell! These 'curs' are fox hounds, the best you'll find between here and the ocean. I'll not see them bludgeoned any more than I would have seen them torn apart by that mastiff yonder."

"That mastiff won't tear apart nothing now—you've killed it."

"When I shoot, I shoot to kill. Keep that in mind."

Joshua eyed the defiant horseman up and down. He had never seen the man before. If he had, he would have remembered him. Not because he was handsome—his nose was a little too long, his lips too thin, his forehead scarred and too high for handsomeness—yet he was distinctive and memorable, especially in his present classically statuesque horseback pose: spine militarily straight; long, swept-back hair blowing in the breeze; expression haughty; pistol arm extended and unshaking.

"I believe you really would shoot me, by gum!" Joshua said.

"Yes, sir, I would."

The fox hounds had gathered back around the horse of their master, snarling and baring their teeth. Joshua could only stand there, holding his walking stick and feeling both anger and amazement. After a few moments, embarrassment joined those other two emotions. This upstart was surely scarcely more than half his age, and here he was, making one of the Overmountain country's most celebrated frontiersmen look like a fool! Joshua was glad there were no witnesses around other than Alexander.

Alexander Carney was usually a timid soul, sometimes almost to the point of cowardice. Not now. The slaughter of his dog had transformed him. With Xerxes's blood fresh on his hands, he ran up, sending the fox hounds into a renewed frenzy. The horseman grew even haughtier, if that was possible, and aimed his pistol at Alexander instead of Joshua.

"Halt, sir, or I'll shoot you down!"

Alexander Carney was far too mad to halt. "Scoundrel!" he shouted, charging right through the dogs to the horse, groping for its rider.

"Alex!" Joshua shouted, stunned at his companion's uncharacteristic rashness. He had never seen anything this brash out of Alexander Carney before; even when he had come to the aid of Owen Killefer the day Parnell Tulley attacked him in Jonesborough, Alexander had seemed just as scared as he was angry. Joshua caught his breath, expecting the horseman to fire his pistol right into Alexander's heart.

Instead the rider seemed taken aback by the attack. "Halt!" he yelled, aiming the pistol skyward. "Halt, I say!"

Alexander Carney grabbed the horseman around the waist and was about to drag him from the saddle when the pistol came down and clubbed Alexander above the ear. He grunted and pulled away. The dogs went after his legs, barking and tearing at his knee breeches and stockings.

Joshua lunged forward, swinging his stick around and aiming the end of it at the horseman's chest. Distracted, the man didn't even see it coming. The long staff caught him in the diaphragm and shoved him off the saddle. He fell backward, and as he did, groped behind him for the ground. Landing on his rump, the pistol, still in his grip, went off. One of his fox hounds yelped in pain, jerked spasmodically, and fell over dead.

That brought the encounter to a halt. In a few moments even the dogs settled down, going over to sniff curiously at their dead companion. The rider looked incredulously at his dead dog, then at the smoking pistol in his hand. "I'm flogged if I haven't killed my own fox hound!" he exclaimed.

"Aye aye, and that proves there's a just fate at work sometimes in this world!" Alexander said. He was still mad, so mad he was breathless. But he didn't seem to be on the attack anymore.

Joshua tossed down his walking staff and approached the unseated rider. "I hate I had to probe you so hard, but I couldn't let you shoot my friend."

The other nodded. Laying his pistol on the ground, he rubbed gingerly at his middle, wincing. "By the eternal, sir, you wield a devil of a stick!"

"And you show a bloody lot of brass and spit, shooting the dogs of other folks, threatening lives over nothing . . . who are you?"

The young man stood, rubbed his middle again, and swept back his long hair. "My name is Jackson, Andrew Jackson. Native of the Waxhaws, and freshly come from Morgantown to begin the practice of law in this district."

"You're an attorney?"

"Aye, yes."

Joshua threw back his head and laughed, causing Jackson to stare at him in bewilderment. "Mr. Jackson, may I introduce you to one of your colleagues of the bar." He waved toward the still-fuming Alexander. "This is Alexander Carney, attorney. I expect you two will be seeing much of each other."

Jackson and Carney stared at each other. Their unfriendly encounter had been no good introduction for men who shared the same profession, and soon would be working in the same court of law. Joshua saw that there remained ice to be cleared.

"Gentlemen, I'm no learned arguer like you both are, but it seems to me the wisest thing to do is look at what's happened here and have a laugh over it, if we can. Alex, you've lost a dog, and Mr. Jackson here has kindly saved you the trouble of having to even things up on your own, by shooting one of his own in return. Now, I know he didn't mean to do it, but it's done, and it's a dog's life for a dog's life, so all's square. Mr. Jackson, my name is Joshua Colter. I'm going to extend my hand to you and put aside any hard feelings for you aiming a pistol at me. Welcome to Washington County."

Jackson, ruffled but trying not to show it, shook the hand with some reluctance. Joshua turned to Alexander. "Alex, you want to do the same? Might as well make peace—you'll be seeing much of each other, after all. May as well get along."

Alexander Carney, still staring into Andrew Jackson's face, shook his head. "No. I'll be thrashed before I'll shake hands with a man who would kill another's dog just for being on the road."

"Your dog attacked one of mine, sir, and would have killed it had I not intervened."

"That is your word."

"Are you implying my word isn't a word of honor? Because if so—"

"That's enough, enough," Joshua said. "Alexander, back

away. Shut your mouth before you say something you'll have to pay for." Joshua was surprised at his friend. He had known Alexander in states of good humor, of sorrow, of fear. Never before had he been around him when his temper had boiled, however. This was a side of the man he wouldn't have expected to find.

Alexander Carney pivoted and walked back to his slain dog. He picked up the heavy body, slung it over his shoulder, and began carrying it back the way he and Joshua had come. Joshua and Jackson watched.

"Perhaps I should offer to let him lay the dog across my packhorse back yonder," Jackson said.

"I suggest, Mr. Jackson, that you'd best avoid making any offers at all until his temper has had time to cool."

"Yes. You're right, I'm sure." Jackson looked Joshua over. "Joshua Colter! I've heard of you, sir."

"Have you?"

"I have. It's an honor to meet you."

"Do you usually greet folks with a pistol in your hand?"

"No, sir. Not usually." Jackson retrieved his dropped pistol, then went farther back down the road and picked up a tricorn hat that must have fallen off when the dogs first began tangling. "Mr. Colter, I'll gladly offer you my place in the saddle, if you would like, to make up for any inconvenience I have caused you. I can walk the rest of the distance."

"No, thank you. I'll walk on ahead and catch up with my friend Carney. I hope you'll be kind enough to wait for a time before you continue on—it might not do for you to catch up to Alexander just now. Troublesome, you know."

"Aye. I'll bury my dead hound yonder in the trees,

then go on." Jackson thrust out his hand. "Mr. Colter, I trust I'll be seeing you again."

"Likely so, Mr. Jackson." They shook hands and parted, Joshua loping on ahead to catch up to Alexander Carney.

He thought about the bizarre meeting just concluded. This Andrew Jackson, whoever he was, certainly had a haughty way about him. Joshua knew the type. Such were always in trouble—and that seemed a poor state for a man who planned on making his living getting others out of their own troubles. But that was Jackson's worry, not his.

He caught up with his companion, and together they walked in silence back to Jonesborough, Alexander bearing the dead animal and refusing to let Joshua help him, even though he panted for breath and the dog's blood dripping down his back was ruining his clothes.

Joshua next saw Andrew Jackson at the Pinnock Inn on an evening in mid-May. He gestured for Jackson to join him at his table. Cooper was there too; Joshua introduced the pair and told Jackson to feel free to address both of them familiarly.

"Thank you, Joshua," Jackson said. "And please call me Andrew."

After cups were filled, Cooper said, with his usual undiplomatic forthrightness, "I hear you and Alexander Carney had a rough little go-'round the other day, Andrew."

Jackson cleared his throat. "Aye. But we seem to have made our peace now. He was very congratulatory to me a few days ago when I was licensed to the Western District bar. Even smiled as he shook my hand. But I'm afraid the man dislikes me. He tries to hide it, but can't."

"That's the way with Alexander," Cooper said. "You can always tell how he feels."

"A bad state for an attorney," Jackson commented.

"Where are you living, Andrew?" Joshua asked.

"About two miles west of town. The mayor's house."

"Christopher Taylor's place? A fine home."

"I'm comfortable there. Of course, my stay here will not be overly long."

"I didn't know that."

"Yes—I'm bound for the Cumberland, whenever traveling arrangements can be made."

"That could be a long time, the way Indian matters are this year."

"I realize that. I'll be practicing in Jonesborough and around the area until it's safer to travel."

"Why not simply stay here for good? This is a growing country. Lots of work for a man of the law."

"I've been appointed state's attorney for the Superior Court of the Western District, under Judge McNairy," Jackson replied. "I must go where his court is centered."

"I see. Well, in the meantime, I hope you'll enjoy your time among us."

"I intend to."

Joshua grinned. "I could tell that as soon as I laid eyes on you. Any man who comes in riding what looks to be a racing horse, leading a pack of fox hounds, is a man who enjoys his diversions."

"Aye, you've got me pegged on that one, Joshua."

Cooper lifted his cup. "Here's to you, and to your future in the west, Andrew Jackson."

"Hear, hear," Joshua said, raising his own cup.

They drank, and talked some more, and before long it

was late, and Joshua invited Jackson to come spend the
night with the Colters and return to Jonesborough the
next day. Jackson declined; he had early business to at-
tend to in the morning and didn't mind the ride by night.

Joshua said his farewell to Jackson and watched his departure. "You know, Cooper, there's something about that
young man that I like. He's got a spirit to him. He's a
man worth keeping an eye on, or I've missed my mark
badly."

13

May brought Salem Pinnock one of the most startling and consequential pieces of news he was ever to record in his journal. Because of its shocking nature, this particular story spread far more rapidly than most, and stirred more anger toward the Indians than any other event in the past several years.

It started on a quiet May morning in the French Broad country, when a farmer named Archibald Sloan looked up from his work to see a lone Indian standing on the opposite side of a rail fence, calmly taking aim at him down the barrel of his rifle. The rifle was propped across the top fence rail.

Sloan's own rifle was out of reach. Sloan was at the Indian's mercy, with no defense except talk. Stirring up his bluster, he grinned at the Indian and said, "You don't want to shoot me, do you?"

The Indian held his pose awhile longer while Sloan continued, with remarkable willpower, to grin placidly. Eventually the rifle came down, the Indian laughed and turned away. Sloan breathed a sigh of relief and watched him go, and noticed only then that a group of several other mounted Indians was on top of the hill. The lone Indian joined them and they rode out of sight.

On that same day, one John Kirk and his son, John Kirk Junior, were away from their little Nine Mile Creek farmstead on the south side of the Little River. The Kirk men had gone off to the mill, something they might not have done had they known the Indian band was in the area. Then again, such knowledge might have made no difference. Such bands were common in that vicinity, for the Kirks had settled in the heart of the Cherokee country, within ten miles of Chota itself. From time to time they gave food to some of the Cherokee men who wandered in from the Overhill towns. Such kindnesses were certainly prudent, given the fact that the Kirks were on forbidden land, and by the terms of the Hopewell Treaty at least, subject to the mercy, or lack thereof, of their Indian neighbors.

John Kirk's wife was busy at her daily chores when she, like Sloan, found herself confronted by a lone Indian who had seemingly come from nowhere. She was initially startled, then relieved. This was the Cherokee called Slim Tom, a frequent visitor to the Kirk home. Many times Mrs. Kirk had fed him and shown him hospitality.

Slim Tom greeted the woman and asked, as usual, for food. Mrs. Kirk promptly began gathering a meal, which she sat before the Indian. As he ate, his eyes scanned the scene. He inquired about the men of the family. Not home, he was told. They'll be back later.

Slim Tom finished his food and said good-bye. He rode across the hill and out of sight, and there joined his companions. The men are gone, he told them. Now is a good time.

Together they turned their horses back across the rise between them and the Kirk cabin, riding as a group into the yard, where the curious children, accustomed to Indians, surrounded them.

When the Kirk men came home that afternoon, they found the children in the yard, killed by tomahawk blows that had come so swiftly and so unexpectedly that some of the Kirk young ones still wore the smiles with which they had greeted the Indians who had slain them.

Mrs. Kirk was dead as well. Her bloodied body lay alongside those of her children.

Response to the Kirk massacre was swift and wide-ranging. The massacre confirmed in the minds of most the long-standing rumor that the Indians as a whole, from the Overhill Cherokees through the war-hungry Chickamaugas, were ready to unite for a major thrust against the white settlements.

Indian agent Joseph Martin, who also was brigadier general over the militia under the authority of North Carolina, was caught in the midst of sweeping cries for military response. Martin was under higher authority and mixed allegiances; he was not free to act against the Indians without orders from the Carolina governor, and these he lacked. Salem Pinnock, no supporter of Martin because of the latter's pro-Carolina stance in the Franklin issue, wrote in his journal: "Poor General Martin! While he awaits the approval of his dear Carolina governor, he can only stand aside and watch the people flock to the side of Nolichucky Jack Sevier, who stands ready and able to do the needed work."

Indeed, John Sevier was in an ideal position to respond to the Indian threat. No longer did he hold official title as Franklin's governor, and certainly he felt no need of the authorization of North Carolina, with whom he remained at odds. Sevier sent the word out for volunteers to rally at a particular station in preparation for a quick and stinging military response.

Joshua Colter, at Sevier's specific request, would again remain on his own home front with his rangers to help guard against any attacks on the Nolichucky settlements. But Cooper Haverly was eager to serve again under Sevier, so Joshua excused him from ranger service. Cooper set off at once, leaving Hannah and all his other loved ones to wonder again if he would ever return.

At the military rendezvous in the region between the Little River and Nine Mile Creek, Sevier put James Hubbert and Henry Conway in second command, and set off at once toward the Cherokee towns. His force consisted of a hundred and fifty men.

Cooper felt fairly at ease. He was growing accustomed to this sort of warfare, and was optimistic that this would be a successful venture, if only because Sevier seemed particularly determined that the Kirk massacre was one for which the Indians would pay dearly. Certainly Cooper could think of no commander under whom he would rather ride than Nolichucky Jack Sevier, whom the Indians sometimes called "Little John," but whom they feared like the wind of death.

Owen Killefer knew nothing of the Kirk slayings or marching armies. He was in an isolated world, the world of a river flatboat. His only companions during most of the daylight hours were the two slaves, Jubal and Timothy, plus the three horses of Dover Hice. The beasts had been troublesome for the first portion of the journey, milling about, bumping each other, edgy at the unfamiliar feeling of standing on a surface that moved. By now the horses were used to flatboat travel and held still.

Owen and his black companions had been operating the rudder and oars, steering the flatboat as the current pushed it along. It was difficult labor, requiring much attention.

Its difficulties aside, Owen found flatboat travel held many charms. The creaking of the oar poles, the wash of the water against the boat, the movement and groaning of the sleepers, the sounds peculiar to a big river when heard from midstream rather than the bank—these were delightful discoveries to him, things until now not part of his experience as a young man of soil and forest.

Whenever his labors allowed him time to look around, he examined the countryside on both sides of the wide river. But even more than that, he watched Nell on the flatboat ahead. He couldn't help it. Whenever she was in view, no other natural wonders could hope to compete successfully for his attention.

Sometimes his gaze would flick over to Dover Hice. Sight of the man brought a mixture of conflicting emotions. He disliked Hice for the obvious reasons. On the other hand, he had to admit that Hice was doing his share of the labor, and seemed concerned for the safety of all on his flatboats. Frequently he would call back to Owen and company, warning of sawyers or shoals ahead. Sometimes he would call back merely to inquire if all was well, and to express his pleasure when the answer was yes.

Despite this, Owen had an odd feeling about Hice. He couldn't forget what Jubal had told him. Hice's overtures of concern for his safety came across as a little too sincere to be authentic. Owen simply couldn't believe that Hice had gone from despising him to caring deeply about his welfare. Probably he's just worried about the horses we're carrying, he thought.

Owen didn't dwell on those thoughts very much. He was too busy. Further, the closer the flatboats came to the Chickamauga towns down the river, the more thoughts of Emaline intruded into Owen's mind. He dreaded the passage through Chickamauga country not only for its inherent danger, but because of how it would surely put him in mind of Emaline.

The river was an unfamiliar route for all on the Hice voyage. No one knew precisely when to expect to reach the Chickamauga country. "It would make little difference anyway," Hice said. "I'm told that redskins will move their towns, name and all, at the drop of a hat. So no one can ever really say exactly where you'll find them."

They passed the night on the north shore as the starry sky filled with clouds and the threat of coming storms hung heavy over the treetops. Dover Hice paced back and forth, seeming unusually tense. Owen watched him until the man's visible nervousness rubbed off on him. Nell sat by the fire, listening to the distant thunder. Owen wished he could join her. He slept restlessly that night, and dreamed sometimes about Emaline, sometimes about Nell.

"Hold it back, Jubal! Hold it back!"

Jubal strained at the rudder, fighting the wild force of the storm-buffeted river. Lightning fired down from the sky and splintered a tree on the south bank, and hail pounded the boats like great fists of stone, driving into the backs of the horses and making them trumpet and mill dangerously on the boat. The river rushed madly along, overflowing with water and pushing the flatboat ever closer to the south bank.

"I can't hold it!" Jubal shouted, his voice mostly swept away by the wind. "We're going toward the cane!"

Owen swore aloud and laid to his pole, trying to divert the clumsy craft. He might as well have been pushing with a stalk of straw. The great pole fought him, pitting the river's force against his muscles and winning. The wind dragged his hat from his head and exposed his pate for a painful battering by the hail. It felt like a score of strong men rapping their knuckles as hard as they could on his skull.

"The horses!" Timothy yelled from the opposite side of the boat. "The horses!"

Owen turned just in time to see two of the horses lose their footing on the edge of the boat and topple into the river. The third horse, panicked, reared and whinnied. Timothy left his oar and went for it. The horse turned away from him, then kicked, catching him with its hind hooves in the chest and knocking him off the boat. Jubal yelled Timothy's name, dropped the rudder grip and ran to the place he had fallen. He yelled for Timothy again and again, but no one answered. Owen searched the troubled water for a sight of Timothy's bobbing head but saw nothing.

"He couldn't swim, not even a lick," Jubal said. Owen couldn't see his face, but from Jubal's voice could tell he was crying. Owen realized he was crying too.

He looked ahead, through the driving rain and hail, for some sign of the lead flatboat. He saw nothing but gray murk and churning water. The storm, which had caught them in mid-river, had driven them apart. The last he had seen of the Hice flatboat, Nell had been scrambling into the peaked shelter to escape the beginning of the hailstorm, and Dover Hice was cursing and yelling orders to his boatmen, and shouting things that Owen couldn't make out back to the second flatboat.

The third horse went into the water then, and began kicking toward the shore. A new freshet caught the craft and swirled it around. They were very close to the southern shore and a vast, wind-whipped canebrake that stretched back toward the forest.

Owen dropped to his knees, clinging to the oar support. He prayed aloud, begging mercy for himself and Jubal, begging to be spared death in the river which already, as best he could tell, had claimed Timothy and perhaps one or two of the horses. He prayed for Nell too, having no idea of how the lead flatboat was faring.

The storm heightened to its zenith as the flatboat crunched against rocks near the shoreline. The boat shivered, groaned, turned on the rocks like a bug impaled on a pin, then came to a rest. Water washed over the sides and sent bundles and casks into the river and out of sight downstream.

"Got to get off, before she breaks up," Owen yelled at Jubal. The slave looked at him uncomprehendingly, and Owen yelled it again, louder. This time Jubal nodded and began scrambling on hands and knees toward Owen's side of the boat.

They linked arms for safety as they abandoned the boat. The water was chest deep and rising. Try as they might, they could hold no footing in it. The current swept them away and apart like two twigs, turning them, putting them under for seconds at a time, then bringing them back up far down the river from where they had gone under. Owen struggled to keep from inhaling water. Nothing he did could keep big swallows of it from going down his throat, carrying occasional shreds of leaves or floating insects with it. His stomach rebelled and heaved;

he feared that even if the river didn't get him first, he would drown in his own retchings.

He struck hard against something dark and heavy. Groping out, his arms closed around a slime-slickened branch. He had washed into the grasping limbs of a big sycamore that had fallen into the river. Tightening his grip, he swung his legs around and managed to wrap them around a submerged limb. There he stayed, as the storm continued, then lessened. Owen retched up more water as the hail gave way to rain, and the rain to a fine sprinkle. The river, bolstered by the runoff currents from the surrounding mountains, rose ever higher. Owen struggled up atop the deadfall and made his way along it to the shore.

By the time he managed to climb onto the bank and into the woods, he was covered with mud and grit. His wet clothing stuck to him like an outer layer of filthy skin. He had never felt so tired.

He wandered to a knoll nearby and found an overhang of stone to shelter him. Crawling under it, he lay down to rest and wait for the last meager raindrops to cease. Water dripped from the stone and splattered against the sodden ground in front of his face. Plop, plop, plop . . . the effect was hypnotically lulling. Owen curled up into a shivering ball, closed his eyes, and fell into an exhausted slumber.

The storm had been as widespread as it was fierce. Many miles from where Owen lay shivering, the Overhill-bound army of John Sevier was also shaking off the effects of the weather. Grumbling was abundant, but not particularly serious. These were frontiersmen, accustomed to the unpredictabilities of nature, and their chief worry was whether they had managed to keep their powder dry.

The storm had introduced a mild chill into the air, and Cooper Haverly huddled into as small a human package as he could make himself, enjoying the body warmth of the horse he straddled. As the army advanced, the breeze slowly dried clothing and flesh, and soon Cooper and his fellows were relatively comfortable again.

They were met unexpectedly by Joseph Martin, who gave Sevier news that his advance was known to the Overhill Indians. Martin said that he himself had been at Chota when news came of an impending attack by the whites. After moving off his Negroes and livestock, Martin had come looking for the advancing army in hopes of averting the attack.

Martin had an interesting story to tell. He had been among the Cherokees for about two months now, doing what he could to maintain peace. He had first come to the lower Holston to investigate reported plans for anti-Indian violence. Upon reaching the settlements there, he found that a recent raid had killed a white man and boy, further raising the war fever. Martin urged calm, and took a delegation of whites to the Cherokee towns, where all were convinced that it was the Chickamaugas, not the Overhill warriors, who were guilty. The white visitors went home, but Martin remained behind in hopes his presence among the Indians would maintain the peace.

Then came the Kirk killings. Two groups of whites formed, even before Sevier came into action, and rode toward the Overhill towns. Martin met and talked back one of the groups. He wasn't so successful with the second. It burned one Indian town and killed an old woman. Two Cherokee children were wounded as well.

Martin found himself in a dangerous position. The

Cherokees suspected him of treachery in his failure to stop both groups, and held him prisoner. Not knowing whether he was to live or die, Martin talked and argued until at last he was freed, but only after being told he was lucky no warriors had died when the town was burned. If any had, Martin would have been killed in recompense.

Martin begged Sevier to turn back and avoid further bloodshed. An attack now would only harden the attitudes of the Cherokees. It was a time for diplomacy, not violence.

Cooper watched Sevier's reaction closely. It was quickly evident that Sevier had no intent of backing down, particularly at the behest of an anti-Franklinite and military rival such as Martin. Cooper was glad; though he knew that Joshua held kindly views toward Martin, by and large Cooper saw the man in the same sort of light Sevier did. He wasn't likely to forgive Martin for his uncooperativeness with the Franklin cause. Further, Cooper believed that this time the Indians sorely needed a lesson.

They marched ahead, leaving the bitterly disappointed Joseph Martin behind. Near the Indian towns, they were met by Old Tassel and Abraham, who told them they were of peaceful intent and would not go to war. If the chiefs hoped this news would dissuade Sevier, they were quickly proven wrong. The militiamen went on.

Reaching Chota, they found the town abandoned—no great surprise, given what Martin had told them. Without a pause they went on to the Hiwassee River and Hiwassee town. Spies crept toward the town, saw it was occupied and evidently unaware of the threat approaching it.

Dividing his force into three wings, Sevier launched

an onslaught. The spies had been correct; these Cherokees were not expecting attack. They fought back franti-
cally, and several of them died. The rest fled into the
hills.

Cooper had been assigned to the right wing of the
force, under James Hubbert. He fired his rifle several
times, but killed no one. Hubbert himself did kill an
Indian he saw running toward the river, and was disappointed to discover afterward it was a woman.

The most prominent Cherokee to die was Fool Warrior, who was among several Indians shot while they
attempted to swim the Hiwassee River. Fool Warrior was
brought down by a ball as he climbed the opposite bank,
and Cooper watched as one of the militiamen quickly
took his scalp as prize.

After returning to their initial rendezvous point, the
avenging whites proceeded the next day up the Little
River to Tallassee town, driving out the inhabitants, killing several of them.

Cooper was tired by now, physically, mentally, spiritu-
ally. This was an ugly business; unlike many around him
here, he found nothing to enjoy in it. But he would do
his part, for his idea of duty, and his belief in John Sevier.

The militia left the smoldering cabins of Tallassee behind, and turned their mounts toward the riverside town
of Chilhowee, the town of Slim Tom.

Owen huddled in the dark little winter house, struggling to accept the truth: He was a prisoner of the Chickamaugas. His life was in the balance; he might be spared,
or he might be killed at any moment. Swiftly, if he was
fortunate; by slow torture if he wasn't.

He was ashamed of how easily he had been found and

captured. After awakening under the rock overhang, he had risen and headed back down to the river, where he stood gazing downstream, looking for any sign of the lead flatboat. He saw nothing but the swollen river gushing toward the west, bearing forest trash of all kinds swept into it by the storm. It appeared the lead flatboat had probably made it through the storm. He hoped so, for Nell's sake.

He had turned his attention to the stretch of river directly before him, hoping to find Jubal or Timothy, if they had survived.

Jubal he did not find; Timothy he did. But not as he had hoped. Timothy's body was lodged against the same dead tree that had kept Owen from being swept farther downriver. The sight of the pitiful corpse brought tears to Owen's eyes. He turned away, and stared straight into the muzzle of a rifle held by an Indian who looked quite satisfied to have given him the drop.

There were five other Indian men there too—and also Jubal, sitting on his knees, hands tied behind him, a mortally frightened expression on his face. He was a prisoner of a stocky, one-eyed Indian who stood proudly beside him with one hand gripping his dark curls. Owen wondered if Jubal was about to be scalped before his eyes, but this didn't happen, even though the one-eyed Indian never loosened his grip on Jubal's hair.

The discovery of Owen brought great excitement to the Indians. They talked among themselves in their own language. Owen understood none of the words, but realized in a few moments that they were surely talking over whether to kill him or make him captive.

Knowing that his very life was being debated filled him with a terror beyond anything he had ever known. His knees quaked, sweat broke out on his face, and suddenly, humiliatingly, a warm dampness spread down his legs as he lost control of his bladder. The Indians saw it, laughed—and it seemed to settle their decision.

The Indian who held the rifle put it down, drew out his tomahawk and strode over to Owen. Putting his hand on Owen's shoulder, he pushed him to his knees, lifted the tomahawk high—then, unexpectedly, seemed to change his mind. The Indian turned and spoke to his fellows, then made Owen look at him. He pointed at his own chest.

"You—*ahu'tsi*. Prisoner."

Owen, whose heart was still skipping beats in his terror, was heartened to realize that this man knew at least a little English. He pointed to himself. "Killefer."

The Indian said, "Kill-uh-far. Killuh-far."

"Yes. Killefer."

They took him and Jubal away, up to a trail and then to a town, where he and Jubal were greeted with loud shouts of triumphant derision. The people of the town swarmed to see this human booty. Some made as if to strike the prisoners, but no one did. At the moment, Owen was glad to be in the custody of his captor; otherwise he would surely be beaten by the mob.

This was his first sight of an Indian village. In some respects it didn't appear that much different than a white settlement. The cabins were much the same as those white men built. The most obvious difference was the presence of conical winter houses, built into the ground and covered with earth, nearby each cabin. He knew nothing of these and assumed they were storage cellars until he was shoved inside one of them and the door closed and barred behind him.

Light shone through the open smoke hole above, and revealed that this place was made not to hold goods, but people. He sat down on a bearskin pallet, drew his knees up against his chest and waited for whatever was going to happen next.

He was dozing the next time the door swung open. He sat up rapidly, drawing in his breath. His captor, name still unknown to Owen, entered; then a second Indian, muscled and handsome and with keen eyes that implied a sharp intelligence and strong self-assurance. This new-comer squatted in the low-roofed winter house, looked unswervingly at Owen while Owen's captor spoke to him in Cherokee.

"You are the boy named Killefer?" the second Indian said.

Owen was surprised by the clarity and ease of the man's English. "Yes."

"You will come with me."

Owen wanted to ask where they were going, and why, but was afraid to do so. For all he knew, he was being taken out for killing.

The men left the little house, and Owen crawled out after them. It was afternoon, and his eyes burned and smarted as they adjusted to the brighter exterior light.

The second Indian pointed. "Go that way," he said. "That is where I live. You will live there too. You have been given to me by Wolf Who Leaps, whose life I saved in battle. My name is Ulagu."

"You know my language—" Owen cut off, realizing that speaking without invitation might sound impudent. But Ulagu answered readily.

"There was a white man who was once a fellow war-rior with me against the Americans. His name was Brecht. I taught him our tongue, he taught me yours."

Immediately Ulagu turned and began striding away.

Owen fell in behind him. He noticed Ulagu's bad limp, his scarred thigh.

Owen didn't much like the idea of being property that could be passed back and forth like a handful of cash or stack of pelts. Still, it was better than being tomahawked or burned to death for the pleasure of the village.

He strode behind Ulagu, feeling the stares and hateful frowns of the people around him, people utterly alien to him and all he had known. A disturbing thought came: Might this captivity be a punishment meted out in recompense for his failure to come after Emaline in her own distress? To a boy raised on superstition, it made an awful kind of sense.

He lowered his head as a band of naked Indian children appeared and began taunting him. One little boy waggled his genitals at him and then urinated in his direction, bringing howls of laughter from his companions. Another pelted him with a rock, and roared in delight as Owen grasped at his temple, where it had struck him hard enough to break the skin.

Owen hurried to keep pace with Ulagu, dabbing at the blood dripping down the side of his face and wondering if he would come out of this captivity alive. He hoped this wasn't a punishment of fate after all. If the cosmos were seeking to even the balance for his failure to rescue Emaline, then he would have to die.

That would be no more than justice, he supposed. But that did nothing to make the prospect of death easier to bear. For all the trouble life had brought him, Owen Killefer discovered right then, it was still worth living, and he wanted to keep on living for a long time to come.

14

This, thought Cooper Haverly, is a bad time for Sevier to be leaving.

He watched John Sevier riding away from the militia's riverside camp across from the Cherokee town of Chilhowee. Cooper wished Sevier would not go at such a tense time as this, when the potential for trouble hung like a smell in the air. It was difficult for Cooper to resist the impulse to run after his superior and urge him to stay. To do so, however, would certainly anger Sevier, who had already put up today, none too happily, with rebellious and recalcitrant men.

The beginning of this troubling scenario had come earlier in the day, when some of the militiamen began taking potshots at one of the Cherokee houses in the town across the river. The word was out that this house belonged to chief Old Abraham, the same Old Abraham who had tried to avert this campaign at its outset. This made it a tempting target for tired and irritable militiamen who held the chief in contempt. Cooper had taken no part in this harassment, partly because it struck him as childish, and mostly because it obviously irritated Sevier as much as it was intended to irritate Old Abraham.

After enduring the peppering of his house for some time, Old Abraham had finally appeared across the river, waving a flag of truce and showing by motions that he wished to cross the river and come to the militiamen's camp. Cooper alerted Sevier, and Sevier, to Cooper's surprise, went to the riverside and waved for the Indian to come over as he wished.

While Old Abraham's canoe was in transit across the water, one of Sevier's men, John McMahen, made an idle comment. "It seems to me," he said, "that yonder Indian will surely die quick."

Cooper interpreted McMahen's comment as a reasonable warning, given the tension and weariness of the militia at the moment. Sevier, however, obviously took it as a defiant threat, and turned on McMahen, scolding him severely. Pointing at the approaching Abraham, who was accompanied by a second Indian, Sevier had said, "Those men are throwing themselves on our mercy. Surely no one here would be so cruel as to kill anyone who has done that."

Cooper had not felt so sure about that. Many in this militia cared nothing for diplomatic immunities, or even basic decency, where Indians were involved. A chance to kill a well-known chief would be enticing. He glanced toward one man in particular, who was staring coldly at the approaching Indians. Only that morning had Cooper learned who this was: John Kirk Junior, one of the few surviving members of the family who had been massacred by Slim Tom and his companions.

Sevier stepped down to the riverside and greeted Old Abraham as he came out of his canoe. The two leaders shook hands and talked solemnly, too quietly for Cooper to hear. Old Abraham, though maintaining an air of stoicism, looked very nervous. After a few minutes of conversation, the chief and his companion reentered the canoe and began paddling back toward the town.

A murmur ran through the militia. What was happening here? Why was Sevier sending away Old Abraham after inviting him to come?

Sevier turned and advanced to one of his officers, who stood nearby Cooper. "Major Craig, Abraham has informed me that Old Tassel and certain others are in yonder town. I have promised them safety if they will come to our camp and place themselves in our custody. He has gone to fetch them. I will talk with them later." Sevier pointed at an empty Indian cabin that stood on the militia's side of the river. "When they return, place them in that house, and keep a close guard. I'll not see harm done our visitors."

Soon the Indians came as promised, six altogether, including Old Tassel, and passed through a gauntlet of staring militiamen. Cooper watched Kirk push his way to the front of the crowd, and saw such open hatred in the man's expression that it sent a shiver down his backbone.

Major Craig escorted the Cherokees into the cabin and closed the door. Turning, he scanned the faces of the militiamen, and ordered several to join him at guard. Cooper was one of them.

Sevier approached Craig. "Stand a close guard and see no harm comes to them," he ordered again. "I must be away from camp for a time, and I'll come here straightaway upon my return."

And thus the present situation had come about, leaving Cooper standing guard against his own fellows and feeling dismayed at Sevier's departure. Craig was clearly as unhappy as Cooper was about this. Sevier's presence was needed as a restraint on what had all the makings for a massacre.

"Why is he leaving, Major?" Cooper asked Craig as Sevier went out of sight.

"He didn't say," Craig replied tersely. Cooper glanced at the major's hands. Craig was gripping the stock of his rifle so tightly that his knuckles were white, and he was visibly shaking.

When Sevier was well away from camp, the assembled militiamen moved in closer. Cooper studied the line of expressionless faces. It was an odd sensation, feeling threatened by men who up until now had been his brothers-in-arms.

"Move away," Craig ordered the onlookers. "There's no need for any of you to be shifting about here."

Silently the group withdrew, but not far. They milled about in silence. Craig licked his lips and continued to tremble.

One of the Cherokees inside the cabin coughed. It was the first sound Cooper had heard from any of the captives. Craning his neck, he peered through the window. The Indians had seated themselves on the floor. None were speaking. Old Abraham's dark eyes looked back at Cooper's. Cooper could not endure their keen and knowing gaze. He looked away and resumed his previous posture.

A guard on the opposite side of Craig shook his head. "I can't do this," he said. "I'll not stand against my own kind for the sake of a gaggle of heathen redskins."

"You'll hold your post, or answer to John Sevier for it," Craig said.

The balky guard said no more. But neither did he desert his position. He was shaking even more badly than Craig.

"I think we should send someone after Sevier," Cooper said.

"Stand your post, and keep quiet. I'll handle this," Craig barked. But he seemed to be thinking about the suggestion.

The situation held without change for several minutes, until a man emerged from the crowd of militiamen. Rifle in hand, he came up to Craig and made a show of cocking the weapon. "Stand aside, Craig, or I'll make daylight shine through you," he said.

"I've been ordered to protect these Indians, and I'll do so," Craig replied.

The man stared at him coldly, smiled coldly, then withdrew. A few moments later he came back, with several others, including Kirk. "We've been talking amongst ourselves, Major. There's something needs doing here, and it will take more than you to stop it. I'll make you a bargain. You go after Sevier, and I'll see that no harm comes to the redskins while you're gone—if you ain't gone too long, that is."

Craig licked his lips again. He glanced over at Cooper. "There's nothing else to be done," he said. "We need Sevier here. You come with me to get him."

Cooper, meanwhile, had changed his opinion about leaving. The offer just made was as obvious a ruse as he had seen. "Major, I don't think it's wise to—"

"That's an order, not a request." Craig lowered his voice to a whisper. "We've got to get Sevier back here. They'll not stand down against us alone. I want you with me as witness to my part in trying to restrain this situation."

Cooper felt torn between duties. At last he nodded. "Very well, Major. If we're to go, let's go quickly."

They rode out together in the direction Sevier had gone. Cooper wondered with dread how Sevier would react when they found him. He dreaded much more what they would find when they returned to the camp.

Owen Killefer squirmed and tried to adjust to his new mode of dress. Upon arrival at Ulagu's cabin, he had been stripped of his old ragged clothing and dressed in a shirt held together by a brooch and a foot-wide breech-cloth, the middle of which draped up over his groin with the ends hanging front and rear to his knees, held up by a rope sash.

Ulagu's mate was a young woman who stared at Owen with almond-shaped eyes widely set in a broad face. Ulagu told Owen her name, Sadayi, and had him repeat it.

Sadayi reached out and felt Owen's hair, which was long and shaggy. She spoke to Ulagu, who drew out his knife and handed it to her. Owen blanched. Had Ulagu brought him here for his woman to kill in sport? Later he would think back on that thought and laugh at it, but in his present ignorance about his captors, the fear seemed perfectly sane. In half a moment, however, as Sadayi turned him and pushed him to a seated position on the floor, he realized that if he was to be killed, they surely wouldn't have bothered to change his clothing.

What the Indian woman had in mind was a proper haircut. Sadayi began hacking away his hair with the knife, cutting out big handfuls, until Owen's head looked like a gleaned field of stubble, then shaving off the re-mainder with the edge of the blade until nothing re-mained but one long scalp lock at the crown of his head. Sadayi was not a very gentle barber, and left Owen's scalp bleeding at several places. So scared was he of committing some unwitting social offense that he dared not even reach up to staunch the blood, which tricked down around his ears and onto his neck.

Sadayi stepped back and examined her work, then spoke to Ulagu, who translated—unnecessarily, for Owen had understood the gist of her talk because of his earlier informal lessons: "She says your head is very white and ugly, but that some time in the sun will make it red."

Owen screwed up his courage to ask a question. "What will become of me?"

"You will work in the fields. You will help me, when I need you, and Sadayi most of all. She is my wife, and I want her life to be happy. You will do whatever she asks."

"Yes," Owen said, agreeing as if he had a choice.

"You will not run away," Ulagu said. "If you try, I will have to cripple you like the Negro that was found with you."

Owen's stomach tightened like a fist. Jubal's captor had maimed him? He felt sick. He remembered Jubal's earlier big talk of joining the Indians. It was all pitiful and ironic now.

"I won't run," Owen said in a subdued tone.

"You must work very hard. You are my property and I can kill you at any time. No one will care."

"I will work hard."

Ulagu turned and walked out of the cabin, leaving Owen alone with Sadayi, feeling bewildered. What should he do now?

Sadayi went about her own business without talking to him further. He slipped over to the corner, sat down on the floor and watched her. After a minute of that she scolded him—for staring, as best he could interpret—and pointed at the door. He went outside and sat down in the shade of a nearby tree, hoping no more children would come around and plague him.

He was jolted by a kick and jerked up with a canine-sounding *woof!* He looked up and saw Ulagu glaring down at him, and realized he had been asleep, probably for an hour or so, judging from the sun's position.

He stood, hoping that by falling asleep he hadn't violated some rule that would bring him punishment. Ulagu said, "Time for you to hoe corn."

Ulagu led Owen to a nearby field and put a long hoe into his hands. Still groggy, and now also very hungry, Owen began grubbing at the dirt. Ulagu watched him a few moments, then came up and yanked the hoe away. "This is how," he said, hoeing with far more vigor than Owen had displayed. He shoved the hoe back into Owen's hands and walked away.

Owen worked the rest of the day, and returned to the cabin only when Ulagu called him in. His stomach was an aching void. Sadayi put before him a bowl of some sort of gruel and a big lump of cornmeal bread. He ate quickly and wished for more, but was offered nothing else. He didn't dare ask.

Cooper had never seen John Sevier so angry. His own feelings were more on the line of feeling sick to his stomach. What had happened while he and Major Craig were gone from the camp was atrocious.

The story varied in details, depending upon who told it; Cooper was sure some of those already interrogated were lying to protect themselves or their friends. But the upshot was the same: After Cooper and Craig rode away, John Kirk Junior entered the cabin where the Indians were held, and tomahawked the six helpless Indians to death. None resisted. They submitted to the fatal blows with a dignity that made their murderer seem all the more vicious by contrast.

Kirk had been the actual wielder of the death weapon, but the guilt was shared by virtually the entire militia. No one had attempted to stop Kirk; in fact, a group had gathered around him and encouraged him to do what he had, and to stop anyone from interfering.

Sevier was a human storm cloud, moving among the men, upbraiding them for killing prisoners who had given themselves up in good faith to a promise of mercy. "This is a scandal upon a Christian nation!" Sevier roared. "This kind of conduct will surely bring a curse upon the nation that practices it!"

Cooper watched the guilty militiamen as Sevier rampaged among them. If any felt sorrow, it didn't show. The situation had the makings for outright revolt. Cooper had always admired the individualism of men of the frontier, their unwillingness to be lorded over—but today the negative aspect of that character was showing itself. The same men who normally would give their own lives for John Sevier now were standing in defiance of him. Some muttered beneath their breaths that he was an "Indian lover" who might need a harsh lesson himself.

Kirk was daring enough to talk back openly to his superior. He didn't regret what he had done, he declared. It was but eye-for-eye justice for the massacre of his kin, and Sevier himself would have done no differently had his family been slaughtered. It obviously made no difference to Kirk that the Indians he had killed were among the most cooperative and peace-oriented in all the Cherokee nation, had pledged their own peaceful intentions at the outset of this very campaign, and had not had any hand at all in the massacre of the Kirk family.

Angry words flew back and forth, and the situation became even more volatile when Sevier brought in for questioning a half-breed named Murphy, one of the signers of the Dumplin Creek Treaty and a frequent interpreter in meetings between the whites and Indians. Some of the militiamen, angered at Sevier's attitude toward them, were ready to move in and kill Murphy as well, and one or two even dared suggest the same fate for Sevier. Only with the greatest effort, bordering on plain begging, did Sevier save the man's life.

Cooper pondered the tragic situation as he lay on his blankets that night. It required no great prophetic skills to anticipate the results of this ruined campaign. Rather than quell Indian troubles, it would worsen them, for every able warrior among the Cherokees would rise to join themselves in anger to the warlike Chickamaugas. Much blood would flow as they took vengeance.

And John Sevier would probably pay a high personal price. At the beginning of this campaign, it seemed that Sevier's status, injured by the debacle of Franklin, was fast repairing itself. By scourging the Cherokees, Sevier was making himself a hero to the border people who lived in constant fear for their families and themselves.

The massacre of Old Tassel, Old Abraham, and the other four Indians was bound to erase all that. The incident would be fodder for the cannon of John Sevier's opponents. His ill-timed absence from the camp would undoubtedly lead to eager speculations of supposed complicity on his part.

Cooper wondered if Sevier would punish the perpetrators beyond giving them a scolding. So far he had given no indication he would. Cooper puzzled over this until he remembered that this entire campaign was taking place with no authorization beyond John Sevier and the will of the frontier people themselves. Any actions of

Sevier or his volunteer militia lay on the shoulders of no legislature, no state, no recognized authority. They lay on the shoulders of Sevier alone, and their weight was heavy.

It was, without question, a time of mixed fortunes for Nolichucky Jack Sevier. He was fiercely loved by some, fiercely despised by others. Cooper knew human nature well enough to know that both camps would find something on which to feed their own views in this bloody campaign.

The passing of time would prove Cooper's anticipations to be on the mark. The Sevier campaign and particularly the murder of the captive Cherokees infuriated the native people of the frontier, who rose almost as one in response.

Band after band of Indians—Cherokee, Chickamauga, and Creek—attacked farmsteads, stations, and settlements throughout the summer. Even those white settlers who had been on the frontier long enough to see many Indian uprisings could not recall a more trying and bloody time than the mid-year of 1788. Old Tassel's kinsmen, including his brother, Doublehead, led the campaign of revenge for his brutal slaying.

The white settlers in the lower settlements, stung hardest by the raids, could respond only with flight or retaliation, and both were employed. Throughout the summer, the narrow mountain trails were filled with people, sometimes riding and as many times on foot, fleeing to the farther settlements, or taking refuge in cramped stockades closer at hand. It was a troubled time, and suffering was great.

Meanwhile, John Sevier took much condemnation for

the actions of himself and his men. The Continental Congress officially condemned the murders of the Indian captives, and the North Carolina governor went so far as to issue a warrant for Sevier's arrest, a warrant that was delayed when Judge David Campbell, an old associate of Sevier's, declined to process it. The warrant would go on to another judge, but only after long delay.

And in the meantime, it would be war—one of the most far-ranging and violent wars the Tennessee country's frontier people, both white and red, had ever fought with each other.

Owen Killefer, though in the heart of the Chickamauga country, actually saw very little of the redoubled Indian activity that resulted from the murder of the Cherokee chief. When word reached the Chickamaugas of the killing of the Cherokees, and when formerly peace-oriented Cherokee men began arriving in great numbers to cast their lot with Dragging Canoe, Owen stayed very close to Ulagu's residence out of fear for his own safety.

The more Owen grew accustomed to his captivity, the more odd it all seemed. Ulagu was fearsome in appearance and manner and never actually said anything to him to indicate he was anything more than a "walking scalp," as Indians perceived their captives. Still, Ulagu's actions indicated some concern for his safety, increasing as days went by. He warned Owen about avoiding Creeks in the town, because the Creeks did not follow the Cherokee law, were hostile to any whites, and might kill him if he was caught out alone. And never, he warned, should Owen stare at any Indian. Such a thing always angered them.

So Owen mostly stayed close to the cabin, even though

he had no physical restraints upon him and was free to come and go as he chose. He worked hard, both to make the time pass more quickly and to stay in the good favor of his keepers. He filled out his knowledge of the Cherokee language he had learned from Joshua Colter and Francis McCarthy, so Sadayi could communicate with him, and he soon could converse clumsily but sufficiently, which impressed Sadayi. As soon as his vocabulary allowed it, he began complimenting Sadayi in every way he could, deliberately showing her great respect and devotion, hoping to work his way into her good graces.

This plan went quite well. Sadayi responded to his behavior with kindness in turn, giving him more to eat than she had initially, talking to him as she worked in order to bolster his command of the language, and in general treating him less like a captive and more like an adopted son—or at least like a pet. Owen knew he had won her over. Whenever she went to town, she took him with her, keeping him close to her and warding off any children who dared to harass him. Owen was with Sadayi far more than with Ulagu, who became active in the renewed war and was often away, raiding with the Shawnee named Tecumseh or with other war parties.

Whenever he was out in public with Sadayi, Owen looked about for Jubal. He saw him only once, limping naked through the center of Black Water Town behind his one-eyed captor, carrying a large heap of firewood while the town's children mocked him. Jubal did not see Owen, and Owen was glad. Jubal would have been humiliated for his friend to see him in such a pitiful state. He was far worse off here, among the very people he had hoped to affiliate himself with, than he had been when he was the property of Dover Hice. Hice, at least, had never maimed him physically, and never set him up for public mockery.

Owen thought very often about Nell, and hoped she was safe and well. Not knowing what had happened to her was distressing. He kept his ears open for any talk of another grounded flatboat and white victims who might have been found farther along the river; he heard of none. This gradually encouraged him to believe that the Hice flatboat had made it through the Chickamauga country safely. For Nell's sake he prayed that this was true.

Owen's status continued to improve. Soon he felt comfortable with his captors, and dared to believe that Ulagu actually liked him.

Still, life in these circumstances was hard. Owen had to work almost continually, and without much covering to protect his skin from the sun. His back and shaved scalp became blistered, raw, oozing, then finally developed a sort of thick callus that endured the sun's rays better. He found that spreading grease from Sadayi's cook pots onto his skin also gave it some limited protection, along with the chance to sneak mouthfuls of the grease, which he did at every opportunity in order to drive off his nearly continual hunger. Indians, he had discovered, lived on far less sustenance than did most whites, yet didn't seem to feel any added hunger.

Owen's constitution wasn't made for such deprivation. He had always been spare of frame. Now, under the stress of his labors and more meager diet, he grew even thinner, grease consumption notwithstanding. When he rolled over in his sleep at night, the ground pressed hard against his ribs, which seemed to lie just below his skin, with little flesh protecting them. Owen wondered if he would literally waste away.

He said little about himself to his captors, and what he did say was mostly false. Why he chose not to be honest was not clear even to his own mind; the best he could say was that it gave him some meager sense of control, and lessened his worries that some slip of his own tongue might somehow endanger him. He made up family, friends, acquaintances, and once, when Sadayi told him that the scar on her husband's thigh resulted from a leg breakage brought about by a rifle ball fired by Colter, the coin-wearing unaka warrior known and grudgingly admired by almost all the Indians, Owen gave her no reaction to reveal that he knew Joshua Colter quite well.

Nor did he ask many questions, even though he often burned with curiosity. Sadayi did not like it when he sought information. Though she was obviously fond of him, he was a white, and not to be told too much.

Even without asking questions, Owen quickly learned much of the Indians' way of life. He even picked up on the town gossip from Sadayi, and discovered that the personal affairs and concerns of Indians were not much different than those of whites. He kept his ears pricked for any mention of Tom Turndale, but no one ever spoke of him. He was secretly glad. To learn of Turndale might mean learning what happened to Emaline. He wasn't sure he really wanted to know. To know she had suffered would only make him suffer in turn.

He was startled the day he went into Black Water Town with Sadayi and, while going home again, saw a white man. This man would have looked startling anywhere. He was short, mop-haired, broad of face and belly, clad in an overly long, robelike hunting shirt, a breechcloth, and moccasins. His fingers were remarkably short, as were his arms, and oddest of all, his voice was high and womanish. He was squatted before a little hut, talking to a group of Indians who were looking through a stack of knives, beads, pelts, rifle horns, blankets, and the like.

Owen stopped and stared at the man, taken with the novelty of seeing another of his race. Clearly this was no captive; he must be a trader. And a bold one indeed, staying in the Chickamauga towns in such a time of trouble.

Sadayi noticed Owen watching the white man, and in Cherokee said, "He is a trader, come with a partner to sell his goods and live among the Real People."

"What is his name?"

"I have heard him called Greentree. His voice is like a woman's, they say, because his stones were cut off when he was young."

Owen was stunned. He had heard of this Greentree at the time of Aaron Killefer's murder. The Carney's slave, Titus, had told him that the three-fingered Indian who had been with Parnell Tulley in the Killefer cabin was a partner to a whiskey-making eunuch and sometime-trader to the Indians named Saul Greentree.

Owen was just turning away when a second white man came out of the little house behind Greentree. Owen could not hide his reaction. He gasped aloud; his mouth dropped open and he took three steps backward.

"What is wrong with you?" Sadayi asked. "Are you sick?"

Owen couldn't find his voice at once. He continued to gape, then turned away suddenly. "I am not sick," he said.

"You were like a man seeing a spirit."

"No, no, I am fine," Owen said.

They went home together. Sadayi didn't seem worried now that Owen was ill; she chattered all the way back about mundane matters. Owen pretended to listen, and hoped his face didn't look as pallid as he felt. He had been very shaken to see the man who had come out of the trader's hut.

It had been Parnell Tulley, scarred palm and all.

After the murders of Old Tassel and his fellows, John Sevier led his army to the stockade of Houston's Station, destroying the Cherokee town of Toquo along the way. The force was attenuated by now, many having left to see to the protection of their own homes and communities. Cooper Haverly was among those who remained.

Already it was evident that major troubles were brewing in the heat of John Kirk Junior's vengeful murders. The frontier army encountered much sign indicating that sizable bands of Indians were beginning to converge in the region—an ominous signal indeed, and indicative of how quickly word of the killing of the Cherokee chiefs was spreading among the natives.

Once ensconced at Houston's fort, John Sevier and James Hubbert, his second-in-command, issued a general proclamation to be carried to as many settlements as possible. It urged the citizenry to be on guard, estimated that as many as five hundred Indians were gathering in the immediate vicinity, and urged that "every good man that can be spared will voluntarily turn out and repair to this place with the utmost expedition, in order to tarry for a few days in the neighborhood and repel the enemy if possible. We intend awaiting at this place some days with the few men now with us, as we cannot reconcile it to our feelings to leave a people who appear to be in such great distress."

Houston's fort was commanded by Captains John Fain and Thomas Stewart, appointed to their posts by Brigadier General Martin. With Sevier's permission, Cooper put himself under their authority, and agreed to stay at Houston's for a time, even after Sevier himself left the station, called by duties elsewhere.

Cooper's volunteerism was welcomed by the station garrison; any able man was sorely needed. Cooper was happy to give his aid. He had only one complaint, which he kept to himself: remaining at Houston's meant spending more time in the company of John Kirk Junior, who in Cooper's opinion was more to blame than anyone else for the present distress of the settlements.

Tom Turndale guided his horse onto the main trail and began the last mile of his homeward journey. He and Flower had been away from his cabin for many weeks, visiting an Indian friend in Crowtown who had called for him to come and use his skills to heal the aging mother of the family. Turndale had done his best, but even his purges and remedies could do nothing to stop the inevitable result of aging. The old woman had died, much to Turndale's displeasure. His feelings did not result from sympathy, for he was a man who knew very little of compassion. He simply didn't like to fail.

But one failure was not enough to erase Turndale's present contentment with life. He had recently won a great personal victory that had taken a long time to achieve, but which now seemed complete. After more than three years of struggle, he had at last won the submission of his woman. He could rest easily. Flower was his. He had battled her will and won.

He stopped and turned in the saddle to look behind him. "Flower, why are you so slow?"

She rode into view as he spoke. He smiled at her, and she smiled back. It was an empty smile, to be sure, but a smile, and that was what mattered.

"Nearly home, Flower. Tonight we'll feast and celebrate our return."

She rode to his side, looking around in silence. Turndale studied her face, studying her expression to see if this homecoming brought her any pleasure. If so, he could not detect it. Flower's face was ever a blank tablet, unreadable even by him, who had lived with her for so long. He wished she were not so indecipherable—but no matter. He had realized long ago he would never win her affection, and no longer sought it. Affection he could live without. What he wanted was her dependency, her unquestioning subjection to him.

"Come, my dear Flower. Let's go on home."

She smiled again, nodding. Turndale clicked his tongue and set his horse to jaunting down the trail toward the cabin. He continued to watch Flower from the corner of his eye. She was a far different young woman than the terrified, often defiant creature he had dragged across the wilderness from the borders of the Nolichucky settlements. He recalled her initial struggles against him, struggles of body and mind. She had presented quite a challenge; sometimes it had almost daunted him.

He knew that he had won at last on the day, about two weeks before, when she finally yielded to him the thing she had held on to long after she had yielded all else: her Christian name. Emaline—Emaline Killefer. He liked the ring of it, though it was a name that would no longer be used.

He had taken her shoulders in his hands, forced her to look into his face, and said, "You are no longer Emaline Killefer. Emaline Killefer is dead."

"Yes," she replied. "Emaline is dead."

"Your name now is Flower."

"Yes."

"Say it."

"Flower."

"Say it all!"

"Emaline is dead . . . my name is Flower."

"And you are mine, forever."

"I am yours forever."

"You will forget everything that ever was before you were with me. It is all dead and gone. I am your husband now, and you are my woman."

"You are my husband. I am your woman."

"And there is no Emaline."

"There is no Emaline."

From then on all had been as Turndale had wanted. Before, he had caught her from time to time lost in reveries that he knew were her escapes to her former existence. He had heard her singing songs from her childhood. But all that had ceased now. He was sure that, in Flower's mind, the person she had formerly been was now killed.

Thomas Turndale was very familiar with the process of mentally destroying one's own past. He had done the same thing himself when he deserted the British army and took up a new life among the people most of his fellow soldiers had viewed as less-than-human savages. His military peers had despised the American natives, even though they had been handy tools with which to fight the

rebellious colonists. The very savagery of Indian warfare
had been abundantly useful to the so-called civilized
people who were sent to subject the Americans.

Tom Turndale had never been a willing soldier. He had
joined himself to the British army only as a means of escaping his home country, and almost certain imprisonment or execution. As a boy growing up orphaned on the
hard streets of London, he had turned to crime as the
only realistic source of livelihood available to him. But to
him that type of life had been more than mere expedi-
ency. He found he relished the power it gave him over
others. As a child he had first robbed, picking pockets in
the beginning, and finally breaking into houses. Soon he
had added murder to his repertoire, his first victim being
a man whose bag he had snatched from a horse-drawn
cab as it pulled to a stop outside a house of prostitution
on a back street of London. The man had chased him
into an alley, and found the end of his existence at the
point of young Tom Turndale's knife.

After an initial burst of repulsion that made him sick to
his stomach, Turndale had found he rather liked the feel
of having killed another human being, especially one who
wore fine clothing and lived a rich life a street orphan
could never hope to enjoy. Before he was an adult,
Turndale killed two other people, one a man, the other a
woman. The latter murder had gotten him arrested; lack
of evidence had gotten him free again.

It was this narrow escape, which chilled him with the
twin prospects of Newgate and the noose, that caused
Turndale to turn to the military. He volunteered for service in the colonies and wound up as part of the British
force that was sent across the mountains to recruit and
bolster loyalists to the crown during the colonial rebellion. This service brought him into contact with the

Cherokees, then with their warlike offshoot, the Chickamaugas. Turndale found the Indian way of life appealing.
It was a life far removed from the world he had known,
which was full of laws and law enforcers, jails and gal-
lows. He loved the wilderness, where a man could be
himself and do as he would, with no one to disturb his
freedom.

A wounding and consequential illness that left him
near death became Tom Turndale's point of departure
into a new existence. An old Cherokee man saved him
from dying by the use of ancient treatments and herbal
remedies, and as soon as he was well, Turndale deserted
and took up with the old man, who taught him first his
language, then the lore of the forest. In this way Turndale
had learned that he had a talent other than back-alley
crime. He had the ability to heal, and that made him useful to the people he wished to affiliate himself with. His
skill with healing herbs and natural remedies, along with
his eager willingness to cast aside his native heritage,
proved to be his inroad into the life he now knew. He
joined first the Cherokees, then their seceders the Chickamaugas, took a Cherokee woman as a mate, and settled
into a life that pleased him far more than anything Euro-
pean or American white civilization had to offer.

Only one thing had he missed: He pined for a mate of
his own race. Now, with the death of his first mate and
the capture and subjection of Flower, Tom Turndale had
all he had ever desired.

He was a happy man, and sure that nothing could
come into his life that would disturb that happiness.

He and Flower reached the cabin. Turndale entered it
and found its contents unmolested. He went outside and
began building a cook fire while Flower hobbled the

horses and turned them into the pasture, now overgrown with flowering weeds because of their absence.

While Flower was returning to the cabin, a rider came down the trail. Turndale stood from his fire-building and greeted the man, a Creek who lived in Running Water Town.

Turndale and the man talked as Flower, moving in her usual listless, lifeless manner, took over the fire-making and went into the cabin to make cornmeal cakes for baking and to skin some squirrels Turndale had shot along the way home. The visitor, as Turndale had anticipated as soon as he saw him, sought his aid for his sick wife. Turndale was not pleased to be disturbed so soon after coming home, but knew better than to let his feelings show. Yes, he said, I will come, as soon as I have eaten. He invited the newcomer to join the meal; the invitation was quickly accepted.

Afterward, Turndale gathered his goods and took the younger and stronger of his horses. "I'll return tomorrow," he told his mate. "You stay at the cabin until I'm back."

She nodded. He mounted and rode away, leaving her standing alone, a solitary figure surrounded by a vast wilderness.

The berry field was a wide expanse of snarled briar tendrils, laden with a few lingering red berries as hard as pebbles, and ripe fruit in clusters of blackish-blue. June bugs and mosquitoes circled and buzzed, and an occasional black snake slithered out of the tangle into the nearby forest, driven away by the approach of the berry picker.

Owen backhanded the sweat-dew from his forehead

and arched his back, cramped from having too long held a clumsy posture as he mined a particularly berry-rich enclave. He was covered with briar scratches, some of them deep enough to bleed. His stained fingers were speckled with the broken-off tips of blackberry vine thorns, and insect bites had raised little hillocks all over him. He gave no heed to any of these irritations. When he had been growing up in Carolina, going blackberry picking had meant covering up with heavy clothing to protect against thorns and insects. Now, among the Chickamaugas, he delved into the thickest seas of briars wearing only a loincloth and moccasins. Without any conscious thought about it, he was adapting the Indian attitude toward discomfort: Since it was sometimes unavoidable, why worry about it? Ignore it and go on.

He did go on, advancing deeper into the thickets and piling his gleanings ever higher into the basket he carried. He hoped to impress Sadayi with the quantity and quality of the berries he would bring back to her, to be eaten as they were, or added to the batters of the various breads Sadayi baked.

Despite the heat and irritation that went with it, Owen always enjoyed berry picking. It was the kind of job that could be done equally well with the mind running free and loose, or on a narrow track, concentrating upon a particular concern or problem. The latter was the case for Owen on this day; the matter he was concerned about was his sighting of Parnell Tulley in Black Water Town.

Initially, Owen had been deeply frightened by the realization of Tulley's presence. The more he thought about it, however, he began to find a strange comfort in this turn of events. Maybe he hadn't been thrown into the hands of the Chickamaugas as punishment for his failure to rescue Emaline. Maybe it had happened so he could even the balance with Tulley.

Owen, with his superstitious, almost fatalistic bent, never considered that Tulley and he had ended up in the same place by mere chance. The hand of fate, or perhaps the hand of God, had brought them together for a reason. And what other reason could it be except for him to avenge the death of his father? He mulled the possibility there among the berries and briars.

He finished his picking and took the berries back to Sadayi's house—and under the Cherokee and Chickamauga system, her house it literally was, because women were the owners of property. Sadayi examined the berries and lavished much praise on Owen. He grinned. It was more evident every day that Sadayi perceived him very positively. He was even beginning to wonder if perhaps Sadayi and Ulagu might make him an adopted son before long.

The next day he returned to the berry field again. He was squatted in the midst of it, resting from his work and scratching the neck of a dog that had followed him into the field, when he heard voices at the edge of the woods about a hundred feet away. He stood slowly, rising just far enough to look over the top of the thicket. His heart raced. He saw the speakers, a man and a woman, mutually embraced. The man was Parnell Tulley.

Owen ducked back out of sight. Tulley! Had the man seen him, in town or in the fields, and come to find and kill him? As his initial burst of panic passed, Owen realized that was highly unlikely. Tulley was with a woman, one Owen recognized, now that he thought about it. She was the widow of a recently deceased man of Black Water Town. Judging from their embrace, it was evident that she and Tulley had come here for a sexual tryst, probably thinking that no one was about.

Owen listened to what little he could hear until he felt certain he had been right. Their sounds and words were those of rising passion. Owen decided that right now, while Tulley and his partner were distracted, was a good time to make an exit before his presence was detected.

He would have succeeded if not for the dog. As Owen crept out of the adjacent side of the briar thicket, the dog spotted a rabbit, began barking loudly, and veered around the side of the thicket, chasing its prey right past Tulley and his woman. Owen froze in place. Then, to his dismay, Tulley's now-bare form rose. Tulley swore at the dog that had startled him, and was about to descend out of view again when his eyes happened to sweep across the top of the berry thicket. He saw Owen; the pair locked gazes across the expanse of briars.

Owen stood as still as a statue, staring at Tulley until his wits returned and he wheeled and walked away. Tulley did not call after him. Owen risked one backward glance. Tulley was no longer in view; probably he had turned his attention back to his lover on the ground.

Tulley hadn't recognized him, Owen told himself. He'd changed a lot since Tulley saw him last—he was thinner, dressed like an Indian, and his hair was cut off.

By the time he retired that night, Owen had convinced himself that this really was true. Was there any reason Tulley should have known him, considering how drastically he had been transformed by his experiences?

Still, he wanted reassurance. So the next day, he went back to the place he had seen Tulley, planning to examine whatever tracks the man had left and determine whether Tulley might have followed him or looked for him after their encounter. What tracks he found didn't give any indication Tulley had done so, as Owen had both anticipated and hoped. He was kneeling on the ground, examining the evidence with a sense of relief and satisfaction, when he stood and saw Tulley standing at the edge of the woods, near the end of a path that was an alternative way to the main road to Black Water Town. It was on the far end of this path that Tulley's widowed lover lived.

"Well, I'm buggered if it ain't young Killefer after all!" Tulley said. "I thought my eyes was making a fool of me yesterday, but it truly is you!"

Owen knew there was no point in denial, and no point in running. "Aye, it's me."

"A captive, are you?"

"Aye."

Tulley laughed in unrestrained delight. "A captive! A sorry little captive of the savages! Hah!"

Owen's rage rose. "That's right—and among the savages there's no one to fuss when I slice your throat."

Tulley twisted his face into an extreme expression of feigned terror. "Oh, he's going to slice my throat! Lord have mercy on me! Save me from this savage boy!" He laughed again.

"I'm not a boy, not anymore."

"Well, you still look it to me! Hell, you're no bigger around than a ramrod! I reckon the redskins ain't been feeding you good, eh? How'd you come to be captive here anyhow?"

Owen had no desire to share banter with the killer of his father. He looked into Tulley's ugly face and fury surged. "I hate you—I'll see you dead, murderer!"

Tulley lifted his upper lip just as if he were a snarling animal. "You think you can threaten me?"

"It's no threat, Tulley. I saw you murder my father. I'll have your life in return for his."

Tulley laughed again. Reaching behind him, he drew a pistol that had been tucked under his belt at the back. Owen recognized it as the same pistol he had tried to steal from Tulley's saddle pack in Jonesborough back in 1785. "I ought to scatter the meat of your head right here and now," Tulley said.

"I'm adopted into the family of a warrior now," Owen said, exaggerating his status for the sake of protection. "If you kill me, there will be blood vengeance."

Tulley frowned. "You're lying."

"I'm not lying."

Tulley's thick tongue swabbed over his lips. He lowered the pistol. "I'll find my chance yet. If it comes to it, I'll make it look like one of the Creeks done it."

Owen's thoughts flashed back to his father's dying words, and a question that had tormented him for too long now. Forcing down his anger and fear, he spoke more calmly to Tulley. "There's something I want you to tell me. I want you to tell me it ain't true that my father agreed to kill Alexander Carney for you in exchange for money."

"Huh! I heard some rubbish talk about that . . . I don't recall no such a thing. He was drunk. So was I. Hell, what does that matter now? I got no time to waste tossing words with a young squat."

It struck Owen that Tulley was right. The past and its questions didn't really matter. What mattered was that Parnell Tulley had killed his father, and now fate was offering the orphaned son the only chance that would probably ever come to see justice done in that matter. As long as he was among the Chickamaugas, Tulley certainly would not be called to account for any crimes he had committed among the whites.

"I'd keep an eye out, if I was you, boy," Tulley said.

"This is a bad time to be a prisoner among the Chicka-maugas."

"I told you I'm no prisoner. I'm adopted."

"So you say. I don't believe it."

"It's you who ought to worry," Owen said. "There's war on against the settlements. You're naught but a trader, and there'll be some mad warrior who'll take your scalp—unless I take it first."

"I'm safe here," Tulley said with a smirk. "I'm with Saul Greentree. The Injuns love him—he's started making liquor for them. Me, I repair their guns and such. They won't harm us. Besides, I got me a woman now. She'll give me warning if any trouble begins."

"She'll not be enough to save you from me."

Tulley laughed again, but there was less authenticity in it. "I'm weary of you, boy. You keep fly-buzzing my ear, and I'll swat you flat."

He wheeled and began striding back up the path. He was glancing back over his shoulder to hurl one more insult and warning when he discovered that Owen had already hurled something his way: a fist-sized stone. It caught Tulley on the upper cheek, scraping off the top layer of skin between beard and eye.

Tulley cursed and drew out his pistol. Owen darted away just as he fired. The ball plowed into the dirt just behind Owen's feet.

Owen didn't pause or look back. He ran as hard as he could toward Ulagu's cabin and headed straight inside when he got there. Sadayi was not present at the moment, and Ulagu had been away on raids for the past few days. Owen went to the door and watched the path, looking for Tulley, but Tulley never appeared.

Owen mentally replayed the picture of the stone smashing Tulley's face. He told himself he was happy he had thrown it, but at the same time he knew Tulley would only be all the more determined to get rid of him because of it.

Owen decided right then that he really would have to kill Parnell Tulley. Not only for the sake of his father's murder and justice that would otherwise never come, but also for the sake of his own safety.

His brash talk and fleet feet had saved him from Tulley's harm today, but the man would certainly be looking for other chances. It wouldn't be all that difficult for him to find them.

It seemed to Owen that there were no limits to the complications and troubles life was willing to throw at him.

Cooper Haverly wasn't at all comfortable with the idea of taking time out for picking apples when the purpose for this reconnoiter was to look for sign of impending Indian attack.

The thirty-one member force had left Houston's Station upon receipt of intelligence that a major attack against the fort was being planned. Captain Thomas Stewart had sent out a force of scouts to explore up and down the river and see if any hint of coming attack could be found. The leader of the reconnoiterers was Captain John Fain.

The examination so far had proven encouraging. There was no clear evidence of any major Indian presence. And after fording the river near Settico, they found the town entirely abandoned. Encouraged, the men moved among the empty houses, looking for any sign of ambush and finding none.

"Look at that orchard yonder," one man near Cooper

said. "Captain Fain, it seems a shame to go back to hungry families empty-handed when there's trees full of good fruit waiting for picking."

Fain rubbed his chin, looked around one more time, then agreed. "Gather what you can," he directed. "Then prepare to return to the station."

Cooper's stomach growled like a deprived animal. Fain was right, he decided. There was no evidence of Indian presence here. A few good apples in the stomach and plenty more to take home was a fine notion. He moved into the orchard with the others, dismounted, leaned his rifle against a tree and began gathering apples from the ground and picking them from the trees.

The Indians didn't show themselves until the men were thoroughly dispersed throughout the orchard. They appeared in great numbers around the edges of the orchard, raising rifles and sending up a horrific war cry that sent ice down Cooper's back. He wheeled, looking all around. The orchard was surrounded. His eyes swept to the river. Indians were there too, cutting them off from the ford.

There was no escape.

The trapped men scrambled for their rifles as the Indians fired their first volley. Several men went down. Cooper reached the tree where he had leaned his rifle, and grabbed for it with his right hand—and had the remarkable experience of feeling a strange, pinching sensation at the base of his little finger, and seeing the finger go flying off his hand like a snapped-off stick. Blood gushed out and splattered the ground. Cooper didn't even pull back his wounded member; he grabbed his rifle. Blood poured from the place his finger had been shot away from and stained the stock.

He raised his rifle and fired at an Indian—his target

was randomly selected; he could have picked any number. As it was, it didn't matter, because he missed. More rifle balls whizzed past him and grazed the earth at his feet. No time to reload. He had to run for the river and hope that by some miracle he could swim to safety.

Others evidently had the same thought. In a wave, the encircled men headed for the water. A few made for the ford, not having yet noticed that the Indians held it. The others, including Cooper, headed for the deeper portions.

As he ran, Cooper saw several of his fellows falling all around. Six, seven, eight bodies within his view alone. What fools they all had been, allowing themselves to be surrounded! Cooper swore at his own part in the collective mistake as he splashed headlong into the water.

He swam as hard as he could, his injured hand numb and leaving pink streaks in the water with each motion. His body jostled against another man, who swore at him, then grunted as a rifle ball slammed into the back of his skull. He went limp. The water became a darker shade of pink.

Behind him Cooper heard the triumphant scalping cries of the Indians as they took trophies from the dead bodies. Rifle balls continued to slap into the water all around him. A man climbing out on the north bank screamed and fell back into the water, where he churned on his back like a partially submerged, belly-up bug until a second rifle ball ended his life.

Cooper reached the bank, scrambled up it and ran. He wondered what had become of his rifle, lost somewhere in the wild scramble. His right hand was bleeding badly. He noticed that in climbing up the bank he had gathered a handful of mud in his left hand, and this he began packing about the base area of the severed finger, trying to staunch the blood flow.

Ahead was a huge, overturned tree. A great mound of clay dirt and fractured sedimentary rock clung to its displaced root mound, behind which grew new saplings, weeds, and ivy. Cooper looked behind him, saw no Indians close at hand. He debated: run or hide? In half a moment, for that was all he had, he made the decision for the latter.

He thrust himself behind the root mass and lay flat amid the weeds. He tried not to breathe loudly, though there was hardly any air left in him and he longed to gasp in great lungfuls.

Through the weeds and brush he saw a man run, then throw up his arms as a rifle ball pierced him in midspine. An Indian was upon the man at once, tomahawking him, then expertly peeling the scalp. The Indian went on, taking the scalp with him, leaving the dead and pitiful corpse for Cooper to stare at.

He lay there until the noise of carnage ended and the Indians returned. No one detected him; they passed back to the river and forded. Only then did Cooper dare to leave his hiding place.

He made his way north, aiming for Houston's Station and praying that no lingering Indians were about to spot him. His right hand was beginning to hurt now.

Abundant sign on the ground around him showed him how far the Indians had chased their quarry. For a full five miles Cooper found their tracks. Then it was dark, and he found a hidden place to sleep for the night.

He was up at dawn the next morning, continuing toward the fort. Along the way he heard a sound of movement in the brush, and a groan. At first he thought it was an Indian, and he hid himself, but further groaning convinced him it was more likely this was one of his own number, wounded and struggling to make it to the station.

Investigation proved this true. Cooper rounded the brush and knelt before the wounded man. The bleary-eyed face that looked back at his own was that of John Kirk Junior.

"I see you made it through, Kirk. You hurt bad?"

"Aye, I am."

"Me, I came out short one finger, but no more than that . . . excepting the ten years of life I was scared out of." Cooper sighed. "Well, we'd best be getting on to the station. They'll be sure to attack, now that they know our number is so reduced. How many died, anyway?"

Kirk didn't know. Cooper helped him to his feet, and together they made the last distance to Houston's Station, where they were welcomed with joy that immediately gave way to grief and fear.

Of the thirty-one who had left under Captain Fain, sixteen had not survived. Three more had been wounded. It was a terrible massacre, and left the station in for a certain siege, with far too few defenders to make a good stand.

16

Tom Turndale came to the part of the trail that broadened away to nothing, and he edged against flat rocks inclining down toward the river. He whistled as he walked, and paused to skip a stone across the river's surface before heading down the rocky bank to the place he had hidden his fish traps the evening before.

The feeling of good humor and satisfaction he had known since his return home hadn't faded. Turndale felt good about himself, about life, about Flower. Especially about Flower. She had been sick at her stomach this morning, as she had the past three mornings. He suspected she was pregnant again—with any luck, pregnant with a boy-child, not a girl, as she had borne him the last time. Ridding himself of the unwanted baby had been an unpleasant task, and he didn't want to do it again, and be faced with making Flower believe one more time that her offspring had died naturally. She had accepted it the first time—or so she said. She would not accept it a second.

But no matter. Turndale felt instinctively that she was carrying a son this time. A son he could teach the skills and lore of forest and herbs, and leave to carry on his life and name after he was gone.

Turndale reached the riverside and checked his traps. He frowned—they were empty! Surely it couldn't be that no fish at all had swum into them since the prior night. He looked for breaks in the traps and found none.

Well, he decided, someone must have stolen the catch. Swearing, he looked around on the ground. Sure enough, there were tracks. Barefoot tracks of two—no, three— boys, and quite fresh.

Placing the traps back in the water and hefting up his rifle, Turndale began following the tracks, which led him along the riverside for some distance until they turned up the bank and into the woods. Turndale swore. On the leafy forest floor it would be difficult to track the thieves. Difficult or not, he was mad enough to try.

He put his foot onto the upslope toward the forest and was about to go on when he stopped. Something tugged at the corner of his vision. He turned back toward the river, squinted into the water near the bank, and went down to it, kneeling, looking more closely.

"A rifle!" he said aloud. He plunged his hand into the water and closed his hand around it. Weeds and mud had partially covered the weapon, making it hard to pull up, but after a few moments of tugging, Turndale got it free.

He held up the dripping, vegetation-draped flintlock rifle, turning it, pouring the water out of the long and rusting barrel. "Now, how did you get here?" Turndale muttered. He tried to work the flintlock and found it too rusted and bound up to move.

"Well, if I had found you three or four months ago, I might have been able to make some use of you," he said. "As it is now, you're naught but rubbish."

He glanced back up the slope, thinking of going on in

search of the fish thieves. But the distraction of finding the rifle had given his temper time to cool. It didn't seem worth it to exert a lot of effort just over a handful of stolen fish. Perhaps he should merely find a new place to set his traps.

Turndale looked over the sodden gun one more time. It wasn't worth keeping, but it surely was interesting. How had it been lost? He pondered it, then remembered having heard some mention of a flatboat being banked in a storm during the time he and Flower were away. A couple of prisoners had been taken, or so he had been told. Possible the rifle had been washed off that flatboat. He looked up the river. Sure enough, the flatboat's wreckage was still there, lodged against the bank.

Turndale idly ran his hand down the stock. His fingers picked out something unusual—nicks or notches of some sort. He turned the gun, scraped more of the muck off the stock—and gaped in astonishment.

A name was crudely engraved on the stock in big block letters: OWEN KILLEFER.

Turndale sank to his haunches. Killefer—the original surname of his Flower. Might this Owen Killefer be her kinsman? The name "Owen" meant nothing to him.

The Englishman turned his thoughts back to the night he had taken his knife to Flower's family, back to before the slaughter, when her father and mother had given him food. What had been the father's name? Not Owen, but something a little like it. Aaron . . . that was it. Aaron Killefer. So this rifle could not be his. Besides, he had cut the man badly. Surely he had died.

But Flower's brother . . . he hadn't been hardly hurt at all. Turndale recalled how he had gone off feeling ambivalent about leaving alive the young witness to his crime.

The only reason he'd done so was that he had feared Flower would escape while he chased the boy down. Had he ever heard the boy's name? If so, he couldn't remember it now.

He wished he could ask Flower about it, but he dared not. He had forced her former life and people out of her mind only after long struggle; he couldn't dare bring up the subject and plant in her thoughts old weeds he had grubbed out by the roots.

Turndale ran his fingers over the carved letters. This surely was an intriguing mystery. Disturbing too. Especially when he considered the report that two from the grounded flatboat had been taken captive. By whom he didn't know. He recalled having heard that one of the captives was a Negro, which of course eliminated him as any kinsman of Flower. But that other one . . . the more Turndale thought about it, the more disturbing it became.

"I'll bloody well keep you for now, after all," Turndale said, as if the rifle could hear him. "You're too curious a thing to be thrown back to the river."

He began the trek home, the rifle dripping beside his tracks until it was mostly dry. When he came in sight of his cabin, he diverted into the canebrake and hid the rifle amid the stalks. He certainly didn't want Flower to see it.

She met him at the door, smiling her hollow smile and asking why he had no fish. He told her his catch had been stolen from the trap and that he had followed the thief's tracks a ways but had lost the trail. After that he was unusually quiet, brooding in the corner of the cabin and feeling a disturbing sensation, a sense of impending trouble, a feeling that the secure and satisfying place his world had been lately might not be as secure as he had thought.

* * *

Alexander Carney put his hand over his chin and pretended to be scratching his cheek when in fact he was stifling a smile. What he had thought would be a typical afternoon in the Jonesborough courthouse, watching the trial of a nondescript lawsuit, had turned into the most enjoyable show he had seen in years. Alexander had no part in the case at trial. He had come merely to watch Waightsell Avery, premiere attorney of the frontier, in action.

Colonel Avery was well-known on both sides of the mountains in court and legislative circles. Connecticut-born, Princeton-educated, he had studied law in Maryland, taken up legal practice in North Carolina, and organized the first court in Washington County. His career had been interesting and colorful, and had thrived despite setbacks such as the burning of his law office in Charlotte by the troops of Lord Cornwallis. No other attorney within hundreds of miles was more respected and more sought-after by clients.

Whenever he had opportunity, Alexander watched Avery work in court, taking note of all he did and said, even the way he moved and spoke. He always benefited from such observations, but not until today's case, which had the veteran Avery squaring off against the neophyte Andrew Jackson, had Alexander seen Avery perform so entertainingly.

Half the fun was that it was Andrew Jackson suffering under Avery's barbed taunts. Alexander had tried sincerely to change his attitude about Jackson and like the man. All he had managed so far was to learn to better hide his dislike. He was friendly to Jackson, conversant with him, jovial when Jackson made a joke —but the truth was that Andrew Jackson had a way of getting under his skin and making him want to lay the back of his hand across his jaw.

Alexander couldn't say just what it was about Jackson that so riled him. It was mostly subtle things, minor in themselves, but intensely irritating. Jackson's mannerisms. His cockiness. His perception of himself as the center of the world, and his seeming assumption that all others did, or at least should, perceive the same. His professional condescension—as if *he*, a fledgling at the bar, was more of a barrister than Alexander, who had several years of experience behind him. And, of course, there remained the fact that Jackson had killed Xerxes the dog. Alexander hadn't fully put that offense behind even yet.

Alexander watched Jackson bristle under another legal ruffling administered by the confident Avery, and tried to restrain himself from chuckling aloud. Jackson glared at Avery, who held an open legal volume in his hand, flourishing it like a preacher waving his Bible.

Alexander knew that volume: *Bacon's Abridgement of Law*. Avery cared for this reference book with devotion, keeping it wrapped in a piece of buckskin and carrying it with him in his green lawyer's pouch wherever he went. When he traveled, *Bacon's Abridgement* was always in his saddlebag. It was his favorite legal reference, and he referred to it repeatedly in any case he handled.

" ... and that, Your Honor, is Bacon's reply to this most curious style of argument being advanced by my opponent," Avery said. "And 'curious' is the word for it. There is no valid precedent for this court to hold as the opposing counsel would have it hold. Bacon is quite clear on this." He cast a glance toward Jackson. "Any attorney worthy of the name would be aware of that."

Alexander lifted his brows, surprised to hear his mentor making such a deep stab at Jackson. Avery had been getting more and more personal in his comments on Jackson all through the trial.

Alexander's gaze shot over to Jackson; the insulted young lawyer had a wild, angry fire in his eye. The court fell very silent.

"I beg your pardon, sir?" Jackson said.

Avery cleared his throat. "I merely commented, counsel, that an attorney of sufficient experience and knowledge to be trying this case should be aware of the inherent weaknesses of the argument you have attempted, and would not disservice his client by attempting such."

Jackson's face grew red. Abruptly, he took two firm steps toward Avery, and spoke with teeth gritted. "Sir, I may not know as much law as is contained in your dear *Bacon's Abridgement*, but I know enough not to take illegal fees!"

Across the courtroom a collective gasp arose. Jackson had just made one of the most serious professional charges one attorney could make against another. Jackson opened his mouth to speak further, but by now Avery had risen up tall and kingly, looking down his nose at the presumptuous whelp before him. He cut off Jackson in a voice that was a low rumble—a deity insulted, speaking in thunder. "Sir, do you mean to suggest I have taken fees illegally?"

"I do, sir," Jackson said. "Now, hear me out. It is a fact that—"

Avery thrust out a long finger at the young lawyer. "It's false as hell!" he shouted, forfeiting his usual dignity. "False as hell!"

Alexander Carney came to his feet with everyone else in the courtroom. Jackson fell silent, his face growing red with fury. The judge rapped his gavel and demanded order, then in obvious frustration, declared the trial of the case would continue the next day, and put the court in recess. Jackson, meanwhile, crossed the room to a table against the wall, ripped a blank leaf from a legal volume there, took up a quill and bottle of ink, and wrote a note on the paper as the entire court watched. Deliberately, slowly, he blew the note dry, read it through silently, folded it, walked over and handed it to Avery. He then bowed to Avery, turned on his heel, and walked out of the courtroom.

Alexander was mystified. He stepped out after Jackson, watching him stride down the street, arms swinging.

Waightsell Avery appeared in the door behind him. "Mr. Avery, what has happened here?" Alexander asked.

"I seem to have been challenged to a duel!" Avery said, handing Alexander the note Jackson had given him.

Alexander opened it and read it:

Sir:

When a man's feelings and character are injured he ought to seek a speedy redress. My character you have injured; and further you have insulted me in the presence of a court and a large audience. I therefore call upon you as a gentleman to give me satisfaction for the same and further call upon you to give me an answer immediately without equivocation and I hope you can do without dinner until the business is done, for it is consistent with the character of a gentleman when he injures a man to make a speedy reparation; therefore I hope you will not fail in meeting me this day.

From your obt st
Andrew Jackson

PS This evening after court adjourns

"Colonel Avery, I hope you will feel no compunction to answer such a challenge," Alexander said, handing back the note.

"I'm bound, Mr. Carney. In fact, sir, I'll be in need of a second—will you do me the honor?"

Alexander hadn't expected this. "Sir, I object on principle to dueling."

Avery smiled. "I agree in heart. But the custom of the day sometimes must rule, eh? Come now, agree to be my second, and deliver my reply to Mr. Jackson."

He handed Alexander a folded note. Reluctantly, his heart heavy, Alexander nodded. "Very well, sir. I'll do it, if you wish. But I do object to dueling."

"Perhaps Mr. Jackson can yet be talked out of his plan," Avery said. "I have no desire to hurt him. You are his friend, are you not? You have influence with him?"

"In truth, I find his company hard to abide for long. But professionally at least, yes, I suppose I am his friend."

"Then go and argue the case for peace," Avery said. "Be off with you, and bring me back word of what he says."

Alexander found Jackson standing in the midst of the avenue, talking intensely to a very weary-looking Joshua Colter. Alexander could tell from Joshua's obvious exhaustion, and the manner in which his horse, standing behind him with its leads in Joshua's hands, was saddled and packed, that Joshua had just come in from the forest. He and his rangers had been quite busy lately in light of the Indian threat, patrolling the lower portions of the county.

Jackson turned when Alexander approached. "Ah—a

witness!" he said. "Alexander, I was telling Joshua about the insult I suffered from that scoundrel, and my intention to get satisfaction."

Alexander handed the note to Jackson without a word. Jackson opened the note and read it. His eyes brightened. "He's agreed. Good!"

"Yes," Alexander said. "He's asked me to be his second."

"You've taken his side, then!"

"I've taken no side. I don't believe in duels, nor the concept of so-called 'honor' behind them. We are civilized men; such violent matters are barbarous."

"Wrong, my dear Carney. The barbarians slaughter each other without procedure and decorum. Far from being barbarous, the duel is the civilized way to redress wrongs." Jackson turned to Joshua. "Joshua, it had crossed my mind to ask Alexander here, as a witness to the events that led up to this, to be my second, but he's been taken already by my opponent. Therefore I turn to you. Will you be my second this evening?"

Joshua looked like a trapped creature. "Andrew, I'm tired, hungry, and eager to see my people. And I've got no use for duels."

"I would hope you would have been honored to be asked," Jackson replied in a tone that implied he might feel insulted.

Alexander said, "Accept, Joshua. Perhaps you and I together can talk sense into our respective combatants."

Joshua scuffed his toe in the dirt, then sighed. "Very well. What the devil. I'll do it."

"Good man, Colter," Jackson said. "Good man."

Alexander said, "Mr. Jackson, that argument in court is not worth the death of any man. Would you really kill

Waightsell Avery merely because he defended himself against your charge?"

"Had the colonel held his peace a moment longer, he would have heard me explain my charge concerning his fees," Jackson replied. "He had accused me of lack of knowledge of the law. I was seeking to show that, in fact, I have a more current understanding than he does. Mr. Avery, you see, has been unaware of the latest statutes fixing legal fees, and has charged in excess of them. I know for a fact that the man accepted two pounds for a case, not knowing the assembly has limited such fees to a lower amount. I had no intention of implying he is corrupt, only that he is wrong to pride himself on his legal knowledge when he is actually ignorant of some important facts." Jackson paused. His face reddened. "And he dared to insult my knowledge of law! Bah!" He spat onto the ground.

Ignoring the burst of temper, Alexander said, "Then this is a smaller matter than it first appeared, and all the less worth drawing blood over. A misunderstanding. I'll explain this to Colonel Avery, and with any luck we'll avoid a tragedy tonight."

"And I'll be able to get to my supper before midnight, besides," Joshua mumbled. "C'mon, horse. Let's get you stabled. It appears we're going to be town dwellers for a time."

The pistols were Andrew Jackson's. The location was a large hill south of town. It was evening.

Jackson straightened his back, twisted from side to side, then rolled his shoulders as he flexed his fingers. Joshua Colter watched and wondered if the man was even nervous. He didn't seem so; merely intense, like a runner about to start on a footrace and concentrating on his goal. Joshua didn't much like that; it struck him as a bad sign that Jackson was still taking this duel very seriously.

Colonel Avery and Alexander Carney came striding up. Avery went through none of Jackson's physical gyrations. He seemed as cool as a winter day, as dignified as ever. With a haughty expression he evaluated his foe, then straightened his collar and cracked his knuckles.

Alexander approached. "Mr. Jackson, Colonel Avery finds the pistols in good order, and is ready to begin."

"I'm ready now," Jackson replied, giving one final roll of his shoulders.

Alexander and Joshua paced off the distance and set marks at either end. The combatants took their places, eyeing each other with expressions so knightly that Joshua might have laughed had he not felt so tired and disgusted.

"Gentlemen, are you ready?" Alexander boomed.

"Aye," both said together.

"Then, gentlemen—*fire!*"

Jackson and Avery both extended their pistols . . . then lifted them together toward the sky, and looking each other in the eye, fired in unison, sending pistol balls hurtling toward the dusky heavens.

Joshua let out a long sigh of relief. Reason had prevailed.

Jackson and Avery advanced toward each other, hands extended. They shook, and even managed a vague smile. The pragmatic Joshua wondered why it had been necessary to go through the form of a duel when the whole thing could have been laughed off and forgotten and two good pistol balls saved at a time when the people in the farther settlements were desperate for ammunition with which to protect their homes and stockades.

"Colonel Avery, I'm pleased we did each other no harm," Jackson was saying as Joshua reached the pair. "And I have a gift for you to mark this occasion."

"A gift?"

"Yes . . . one moment, please."

Jackson trotted back to his mark and picked up a buckskin packet, which he brought back and handed to Avery. "Colonel, I knew that if I had mortally wounded you, but death had been slow to come, the greatest comfort you could enjoy in your final moments would be to have your precious *Bacon* in hand."

Avery opened the packet, and out rolled a large chunk of cured bacon. It plopped onto the ground at Avery's feet. He looked down at it in surprise that turned to anger.

"I say, this is an outrage, another insult—"

His words were cut off by roars of laughter from Joshua and Alexander. Avery reached down, picked up the bacon, and in a few moments was laughing too. He and Jackson again shook hands, and as a group, the men headed down the hill toward the town.

17

No one had to tell Owen
Killefer that something new was in the air, something
big, something unusual. Ulagu returned from raiding,
keen and eager, and told Owen that it would be more essential than ever that he remain close to the cabin for a
time. There were many Indians coming to the Chickamauga towns, more than could be counted.

Owen was more than glad to have reason to stay close
to home, given the threat of Parnell Tulley. Yet this massive rendezvous of Indians concerned him. There could
be only one reason for such a congregating, and that was
to wage battle on a far larger scale than usual.

Ulagu was close-mouthed about what was going on,
but Sadayi was more open with Owen in private. "There
will be a great fight with the unakas," she said. "An army
of unakas is gathering, and the Real People are going to
destroy it. That is why you must stay close to the cabin
now—blood is hot against the white men, and it is dangerous for you to be seen."

Owen nodded. Then a thought arose: "Sadayi, what
about the white traders in Black Water Town?"

"They are hiding in their house and afraid to come
out. Some want to see them killed, and others want to

spare them so they can keep on bringing wares and repair the guns if they are damaged in the fight."

"Which side will win?"

"They will be killed, I think, unless they leave soon,
but they are not able to do that."

Sadayi left the cabin then to go fetch water, and as
Owen thought over what she had said, he laughed aloud.
Old Tulley, so confident that his status was secure among
the Chickamaugas, now was forced to huddle in Greentree's store cabin, in danger of his life the longer he remained, yet unable to leave because of the danger of
doing so! The only thing spoiling the delightful irony of
that situation for Owen was the fact he was in substantially the same position himself.

Parnell Tulley stood in the middle of the little cabin,
gnawing his tongue as he did when he was frightened,
and looked for Saul Greentree as if the man somehow
could be hiding within such a small unobstructed space.
He couldn't believe that Greentree had gone—gone!—
and left him here alone in the midst of such danger.
Earlier Tulley had left the cabin—a dangerous thing in
itself—to go see if his woman-friend would provide him
and his partner some means of escape. He found her
playing hostess to an Indian man Tulley hadn't seen before. When Tulley showed his face, she had thrown a
rock at him, driving him away.

That had left Tulley with a decision to make. Should
he continue his flight alone, going to the river and
looking for a canoe, perhaps, or some other means of
escape—or should he return to the cabin and Greentree?
He finally had decided on the latter, not because it was

more honorable, but because in the cabin was a pistol, the only weapon left between the traders.

The Indians had taken the traders' weapons some days ago, saying they were needed for war. Tulley had managed to retain his saddle pistol by hiding it, along with some powder and ball, beneath one of the bottom logs of the cabin. If he was to escape, he would need that pistol. And so he had come back.

Now, Tulley knelt by the cabin wall and found that the place he had hidden the pistol was dug out and empty. He stood, cursing Saul Greentree's name. The bloody old eunuch had betrayed him! Tulley remembered now that it had been Greentree who had first suggested to him to go to his lover and see what help she could give. Clearly that had been a ruse to get him out of the cabin so Greentree could take the pistol and make a break for freedom on his own, leaving him unarmed and isolated.

Tulley decided then he would have to escape. The haven he and Greentree had sought among the Indians was no longer a haven, but a place of danger. Tulley knew that major warfare was looming; it was this that had changed his and Greentree's perceived good standing with their Indian hosts. Warfare would mean deaths, and deaths would call for revenge, and Parnell Tulley's life would be forfeit.

Tulley went to the door and looked out. The town was busy, far more traffic than usual passing among the cluster of houses. Tulley saw nothing to indicate his cabin was being watched—and he had, after all, left it once today without incident. He decided that now was as good a time as any. Trying to look as casual and inconspicuous as possible, he stepped out.

Tulley hadn't gone fifteen feet, however, before a gruff-looking Indian stepped into his path and ordered him

back into the cabin. Tulley's knees quaked and his throat
went dry. He turned and went back into the cabin, where
he sank to his knees and trembled like a terrified rabbit.

Now he desperately desired to get out, though he obviously couldn't do so in the usual way. He went to the
rear of the cabin and felt along the base of the bottom log
until he found the place where the dirt was softest. He
began scooping it out with his hands, then with a loose
board. The rear of the cabin faced into a grove of woods.
If he could succeed in digging a hole large enough for
his substantial form, if he could do it without being seen,
if he could slide out of the hole without making any
noise—then he would have at least a chance of saving
himself.

He dug as hard and fast as he could, until at last he
saw a ray of daylight come under the base log. After that
he dug more carefully, fearful of breaking farther through
while it was still day; someone might see him. The cabin
was tight, close, hot. He lay on his side while he worked.
Sweat dripped so profusely from him that it drenched his
shirt and turned the dirt under him to a thin layer of
mud that clung to his large body.

Saul Greentree sank to the forest floor behind a vast
oak and panted for breath. A fat man with very flat feet
that were prone to hurt even if he did no more than
stand on them too long at a time, he was unaccustomed
to walking very far, and today it was taking its toll on
him. His heart strained as if it were trying to push mud
through his veins instead of blood.

He reached down and felt the pistol, making sure it
was still there. Looking back through the woods, he wondered how far he had come from Black Water Town. It

felt to him like he had come many miles, though he suspected that in fact he had not come more than two or three. Despair and fear overcame him. He wished he could grow wings and fly.

Greentree was no woodsman. He was soft, heavy, loving of ease and comfort. Up until the mounting of the current Indian campaign, he had felt secure and safe in Black Water Town, where the Indians coveted his trade goods. The abruptness of the change in their attitude had jolted him. He had become sincerely afraid for his own safety, so afraid that today he had fled. Believing that one man had a better chance of fleeing undetected than did two, he had taken the hidden pistol and gone off without Tulley, who, as far as he was concerned, could use his Indian lover as his own means of escape. Or for that matter, Tulley could die. Greentree didn't care. For a long time he had secretly resented Tulley for his contribution to the death of Three Fingers, anyway. Three Fingers had been a close and devoted friend, and Greentree badly missed him. Tulley had certainly proven no worthy substitute.

After his heart slowed a little and his breath came easier, Greentree stood and continued walking. He wished he was able to run and cover more ground; he wished also that he could take to the open road, but that would be far too dangerous. So he was moving well back in the woods, trying to follow the route of the road to his north.

Greentree went on for another half hour, but his progress was even slower than before because of fatigue, and because he had encountered a heavily overgrown area of forest, filled with brambles and ivy. He groped his way through it like a buffalo, heaving and puffing and feeling like his heart would burst.

And then he stopped. He had heard something ahead,

in the thicket. An animal? Probably ... yet something
about its movement through the brush caused Greentree
to believe it was human. He sank to the ground and
pulled out the pistol.

A couple of moments later he heard a voice, very def-
initely human, cursing the briars in nearly whispered
tones—and in English. Greentree's first thought was that
he had stumbled upon Tulley. But the voice wasn't
Tulley's. It sounded like a young man, specifically, a
young black.

The person came into view. It *was* a black man, maybe
twenty years old or slightly younger. He was dressed in
ragged clothing that looked like the castoffs of an Indian,
and he carried a rifle. Greentree wondered if the fellow
was out hunting—and then a sound from the direction of
the road caused the black man to duck fearfully, and
Greentree realized that he too must be on the run.

Greentree remembered the tale he had heard in Black
Water Town about the two young men, one black and one
white, who had been made captives after their flatboat
was damaged by a storm. Tulley had recently brought in
the remarkable information that the white captive was
Aaron Killefer's son, Owen, who Tulley said had shot
Three Fingers right before Aaron Killefer had stabbed
him to death. Tulley had said he planned to kill Owen
Killefer on the sneak, but right after that, the great rendezvous for the coming Indian campaign had begun, and
Tulley had lost his safe status and, therefore, his best
opportunities to get to young Killefer.

Greentree watched the black man carefully. He recognized him now—this was the black captive from the flatboat. Greentree had seen him in town several times, in
the company of a one-eyed Indian who was his captor. In
fact, the rifle this apparent escapee was carrying looked

like a weapon that Tulley had recently repaired for the one-eyed Indian. It was easy to put the pieces together: This captive had wearied of his hopeless state, had stolen his master's rifle and begun a dash for freedom.

Greentree eyed the rifle and coveted it. But how could he obtain it? The easiest way would be to shoot the fellow with his pistol and just take the rifle. The danger of that was that the gunshot, or the victim's howl of pain, might attract attention.

So Greentree did nothing. In a moment or two the young black man pushed on, angling more toward the river. Greentree waited until he was well ahead, then followed. It came to mind that maybe this fellow had planned his escape far ahead, and hidden himself a boat. If so, Greentree thought, he would be glad to take it for himself.

He moved forward, following the other and trying to be as quiet as he could. But here his lack of woodsman's skills, together with his massive form, worked against him. Try as he would, Greentree couldn't help but make noise, and after only a minute or so of progress, he stumbled over a vine root and fell noisily into a clump of sumac.

"Who's there?" The young black man had wheeled and leveled his rifle from the waist. His dark eyes darted from side to side, looking for the origin of the racket.

"Easy, young man, easy," Greentree said in his delicate, womanish voice as he pushed himself heavily to his feet. His eyes flickered down; the pistol had dropped from his belt to the ground. He moved his right foot to hide it.

The other looked back at him, squinting into a frown. "I know you—you're a trader for the Indians."

"That's right. My name is Greentree. And you are . . ."

"Never mind my name. What you doing, following me?"

"I want to help you."

"What do you mean, help me?"

"You're running off, aren't you? So am I. We can go together."

"Why you running?"

"It's a dangerous time for a white man to be among the Chickamauga."

"Where's your partner?"

"Mr. Tulley? Oh, he's waiting ahead, at the river. He was to secure a boat for us to float away in."

"Boat?"

"That's right. Do you have a boat waiting too?"

"No."

That told Greentree what he needed to know. He glanced down at his foot. "My moccasin is loose," he said, and knelt as if to fix it. Instead he picked up the pistol, coughed to cover the sound of cocking it, then went to work unnecessarily retying the leg thong of his moccasin. Meanwhile, the other let the rifle lower slowly, then stood it on its butt plate.

"If you would like, you can go away with Mr. Tulley and me," Greentree said as he fiddled with the thong. "Three of us together could certainly make it through the wilderness safely, don't you think?"

"You'd let me go with you? In the boat?"

"Indeed! And in return, I'll tell you what you can do for me. I have a case of gout that gives me much pain. If you'd let me borrow that rifle to lean on while I walk, it would ease me considerably."

"No. This rifle stays with me."

Greentree sighed. "I was afraid you'd say that." Then he stood, sweeping up the pistol and aiming it at the other man's chest. "The simple truth is, I have no boat. Further, I must insist that you give that rifle to me."

Dark eyes blinked; confusion and fear showed on the young man's face. For a couple of moments he hesitated, then he lifted up the rifle as if to hand it to Greentree, but instead leveled it quickly, cocking it in the same motion, and fired it into the fat man's chest, driving him back against a tree behind him. The pistol went off harmlessly in Greentree's hand, then fell from his pudgy fingers to the ground.

Saul Greentree blubbered, touched his punctured chest, and slid like a great round sack of flesh to his haunches. A trace of blood appeared at the corner of his mouth, and he fell forward onto his face, dying with a great shudder and expulsion of breath.

Jubal looked down at the obese corpse and drew in a long, hissing breath. *I've killed a man—killed a man!*

Kneeling, he examined Greentree's body more closely, and fear struck him. He had killed a white man—for that he would hang! Then he remembered where he was, and that here there was no white man's law that would call him for retribution. Perhaps under the Indian law there would be a price to pay—but what did that matter? He was already a captive attempting escape. If he was caught, punishment would be certain, probably death. What further penalty could this killing possibly add to that? He had made a mortal gamble even before this happened.

He looked around, up toward the road, wondering if the sound of the shot might have drawn attention. He was glad the fat man hadn't yelled. After a minute or so Jubal decided that even if the shot had been heard, it would probably be taken for that of a hunter. He stood, reloaded the rifle clumsily, because he was little accustomed to using firearms, and then took the pistol Greentree had used. "You won't be needing it no more," he muttered. Rolling the body over, he found the powder and ball Greentree had hidden under his baggy shirt, and after reloading the pistol, tucked them away on his own person. Feeling better for the extra armament, he advanced again, limping along on the foot his captor had broken to keep him from running. He twisted his lip defiantly. Bah! He would run now if he had no feet at all! Better that than to continue in this hell.

The thicket gave way to more open forest, making travel easier but also more dangerous. Jubal wondered whether it was best to keep under cover, or to travel in the open under the pretense of hunting. The latter would do him no good if he was seen by someone who knew him, but a stranger might assume he was a trusted captive or an adoptee and let him go unmolested. As it turned out, he alternated between both kinds of travel, and it made no difference anyway, because he saw no one and no one saw him.

He stopped when through the trees he saw the outline of a cabin built on a path back from the road. He looked at it, watching for signs of movement outside it. Advancing a little farther, he saw that on the far side of the cabin and stretching somewhat behind it was a vast canebrake. To the near side of the cabin was an arborlike shelter, beneath which hung long strands of drying plants and herbs. A big mortar made from a hollowed stump sat beneath them, with a carved wooden pestle in it. Sleeping beside the mortar in the shade was a plump, ancient-looking dog.

The dog was worrisome; Jubal expected that if it detected him, it would bark and expose him. He edged sideways, hoping to quietly get out of its way, and in the process stepped on a stick that broke loudly. The old dog lifted its head and cocked its ears, looking into the woods. Jubal froze in place.

The dog saw him nevertheless, but it did not bark. It didn't even rise, but merely wagged its tail and bobbed its head. Jubal relaxed. This was a friendly beast, a pet and not a watchdog. He could probably walk right up to it without it making a noise.

Jubal moved to the left and looked into the canebrake. He saw a pathway leading through it, starting about the rear of the cabin and heading southward. A path to the river? It looked likely, and he decided to try it.

The dog was still watching him, and as he glanced back at it he had an idea. He was hungry already, and had no food. Even if he safely reached the river, even if he managed to find a boat of some kind, it would be a day or so before he would get far enough through the Indian country to risk hunting for food. But the docile old dog could be a source of meat. If only he could get it without stirring any noise, carry it deep into the canebrake and there club it to death, he could tote it along with him and eat on it a day or two. Raw, if it wasn't safe to cook. He was that determined to escape.

Jubal had always been fond of dogs and hadn't ever perceived them as a food source until his time among the Indians. He had heard of dogs bred by Indians just for eating; this old cur was not one of those, just a weary old mongrel. Still, it would have to do.

Jubal crept over to the dog with the greatest stealth, scratched behind its ears gently to reassure it, then slipped his arm beneath it. Carefully he began to lift it—

and it yelped in pain. Surprised, Jubal dropped it, and it yelped again.

Something moved inside the cabin. Jubal panicked. He turned and started to run, and tripped over the butt of his own rifle. He lost the Flintlock pistol, but did not notice it. By the time he scrambled up again, a person had emerged from the cabin and come around to the side. It was a young woman, with stringy, dirty-blond hair—and white skin. Jubal hadn't expected that. But her race wasn't what stopped him in his tracks and made him stare. It was her face. She was the very image, in female incarnation, of Owen Killefer.

Jubal's mind immediately fetched up a memory from North Carolina, something he had overheard Nell Hice telling a neighbor woman over their teacups one day. "Poor Owen," she had said. "He's suffered so much loss in his life. Most of his family was murdered by a man called 'Mad Tom' Turndale when he was fifteen, and his older sister was taken away by this man, to the Chickamauga towns, they say. She's dead now, surely. Her name was Emaline—isn't that a lovely name: Emaline? What a sad thing for poor Owen! He seldom talks of his sister, but I know the memory of her hurts him."

Jubal had brought up the subject with Owen sometime later, and from him heard the entire story. Owen had even told him that once he had set out, while still a childish-minded boy, to fetch back his sister on his own. But now, he had said, he knew she had to be dead.

The young woman looked at Jubal with an expression of fear—*animal* fear, it seemed to him, because there was something wild and strange in her eyes—and he knew at once that Emaline Killefer wasn't dead at all, and that it was she who stood before him.

She spoke to him in Cherokee, asking who he was and

why he had come and what he had done to the dog, and warning him in the next breath that her husband would soon be there, and would kill him if he hurt his dog.

Jubal didn't answer her questions. Looking her in the face, he said, "Emaline? Emaline Killefer?"

She stunned him with the radical change in her expression. It was as if he had lifted his rifle and shot her. The fear that had been on her face became terror, or perhaps intense amazement, and she backed away. Slowly she sank to her haunches, staring wildly at him, and then she leaped up again and ran away, around the front of the cabin and into the canebrake.

She felt as if lightning had jolted her. This black-skinned stranger had called her name, a name she had put so far behind her that she had almost forgotten it. And his calling of it, so unexplainable, so unexpected, had torn a huge hole through the wall she had built in her mind, separating the life that had been from the life that was. The person who was Flower was suddenly overwhelmed with a flood of memories from the days she had been Emaline Killefer. They burned her like the sun burns the eyes of a person who had emerged too quickly from a dark cave.

The great lie that was her existence now strained under the sudden burden of truth, and broke.

My name is not Flower. My name is Emaline Killefer!

She heard him at the edge of the canebrake, and squatted like a beast amid the tall, swaying stalks.

"Emaline Killefer? That is you, ain't it! Come out—I won't hurt you!"

Who was this stranger? How had he come here, and how did he know her? She wished he would go away . . .

no. How could she wish that, until the mystery was solved? She was scared, but intensely curious. She had to know.

He was speaking English, and it sounded odd. Turndale seldom spoke their mutual native tongue to her, and didn't allow her to speak it to him—it was one of his means of keeping the past at bay and making it dead in her mind.

"Emaline? Miz Killefer? Answer me!"

No, no, I cannot answer! Cannot! But she longed to answer, ached to answer. By simply speaking her true name, this man had already brought about a change inside her that felt nothing less than miraculous. In one wrenching jerk she had been pulled from the dark to the light. She couldn't let the dark overtake her again.

She opened her mouth, and when she spoke, found that her English was like a strange tongue, and she could only speak it haltingly. "Who . . . are you?"

"My name is Jubal. Are you Emaline?"

"Yes," she said in a low voice. Then, in a loud, emotional burst of intense joy, "Yes! I am Emaline!"

"I won't hurt you. I'm your friend." She heard him enter the canebrake. "I know your brother."

"Know my . . . Owen? You know Owen?" She came out of hiding. He saw her through the cane and came toward her. They looked each other in the face.

"Yes. You look so much like him. It's how I knew you."

"Owen is alive?" Emaline began to feel dizzy; this was too much to take in at once.

"Yes. He is alive. And he's here."

"Here?"

"Yes—not *right* here. Among the Chickamaugas, I mean. Me and him, we were stranded when our flatboat washed against the shore on the river, back in the spring.

We was took captive. Me, I won't be captive no more. I'm escaping."

"Owen is alive . . ." She sat down hard, like her knees had been kicked out from behind, and slid to the side, struggling not to faint. Her stomach gnarled and hurt; she felt nauseous.

"Are you well, Miz Killefer?"

"Sick . . . I feel sick. I'll be fine." How odd it felt to be talking in English again! This whole encounter was beginning to feel increasingly dreamlike.

"Where is the man who keeps you?"

"Gone off hunting."

Jubal rubbed his chin, looked around, seemed uncertain, then said: "I reckon you'd best come with me, Miz Killefer, if you want to get away from him."

"Come with you?"

"Yes, ma'am. Don't you want to be free? Come fast, before he gets back."

"Come with you . . ."

"Yes. I'll keep you safe, I promise."

The notion of leaving was so novel, so far from anything she had thought about for the longest time, that Emaline was having trouble fitting it into her mind. She looked at Jubal quizzically.

"Why do you care what happens to me?"

"Because of Owen. He was a friend to me, the only white man what ever treated me good. He'd want to see you free. He come after you once, not long after you was took. He didn't get far. Now he believes you're dead."

Emaline sat up, feeling frantic. "Owen is near—oh, God, you've got to take me to him!"

"I can't, ma'am. I can't. He's in the house of a warrior. We can't go back there. We've got to get away." Jubal paused. "I wish I could take you to him, so you could be with each other. But I can't. Best I can do for Owen is to get you free—but there's no time for talking. We got to get to the river. Does this man of yours keep a boat there?"

"Yes. A canoe, tied up and hidden."

"You know where?"

"Yes."

"Come with me, Miz Killefer. Let's you and me get free of this place together. Owen would want that. We'll take food from your cabin. Come on now. Come on." His voice was gentle. He held out his hand toward her.

She took it in hers. "Yes," she said. "I'll go."

Thomas Turndale knelt beside his herb mortar and picked up the flintlock pistol that lay there. A new mystery this was, added to the one that already had him puzzled, and afraid. Flower was gone. He had searched for her, called her name, tried to find her track. All in vain. She was nowhere to be found.

"Flower?" he called again into the dusk. His voice filtered into the canebrake and was lost. "Flower? Where are you?"

No sound came back but the cawing of a crow somewhere in the cane. Turndale looked again at the pistol in his hand. His lip began to tremble, and to his own surprise a tear ran down his cheek.

She can't be gone. Can't be!

He looked up. In the dimming sky carrion birds circled above the nearby forest. Turndale's stomach turned over inside him as he realized the possible implication: a pistol, a missing young woman, birds circling above the trees . . .

"Flower! Flower!" He darted out from beneath the arbor and into the forest. "Flower, are you here? Are you hurt?"

He found the body within five minutes. Not Flower, but a man, a very fat and thoroughly dead man. Turndale looked at the face. This was the trader from Black Water Town, the eunuch named Greentree. Who had killed him? Might Flower have done it under some threat from him? Was this Greentree's pistol? Turndale checked and found it was loaded. With what weapon, then, had Greentree been killed?

Turndale could make no sense of this at all. All he knew was that Flower was gone, there was a dead man in the forest, and something fundamental was badly amiss. Abandoning the body of Greentree—though thinking in the back of his mind that this corpse might somehow cause him trouble and wrongful blame—he returned to the house and searched again for sign of his woman.

This time he found some tracks, remnants of tracks, actually, for it appeared that someone had brushed the earth with a branch and simply failed to cover these. One of the track fragments was small, but might have been left by Flower's heel. The other was more complete. The track of a man . . .

Owen Killefer! Turndale remembered the rifle he had found and hidden in the cane. The thought made him rage. Surely this Killefer had something to do with this! Perhaps it was he who had killed Greentree for some reason, and he who had taken away Flower.

The old dog came sniffing around Turndale's feet. He kicked it away with a curse. It hobbled off at the closest thing to a run it could achieve, and hid in the canebrake.

Thomas Turndale went into a rage then, ripping down his drying herbs, turning over his mortar, tearing the shutter off his window, knocking over one of the arbor supports and bringing the roof crashing down. Then something came to mind, and he stopped in his tracks, turned, and began running along the long path to the river. He made the entire distance, nearly two miles, with only one brief pause for rest. By the time he reached the water, it was totally dark.

He went to the place where he kept his canoe and found it was gone. He ran into the river itself, until the water was as high as his waist, and cupped his hands around his mouth.

He shouted her name down the dark waterway as loud as he could, time and time again. No one shouted back.

She was gone.

Parnell Tulley scraped out one last scoop of earth and tossed the board aside. The opening was big enough now, he believed, for him to squeeze through. He lay down, peering under the log. It was fully night, and he saw no sign of human presence behind the cabin.

Throughout the afternoon the men of Black Water Town had plagued him—playfully, to be sure, but with an edge on the fun that scared him. A couple of times the same man who had ordered him back into his cabin had come bursting inside, tomahawk uplifted, and let out a scalping cry. Both times Tulley had yelled in fright, bringing great mirth to his antagonist, who laughed in his face and then withdrew.

Tulley took a breath and let it out slowly. Sucking in his big belly and trying to make himself as small as possible, he pushed into the space under the log and wriggled toward freedom. The fit was horribly tight, and at one point he was so squeezed that he couldn't breathe and began to panic. Pushing so hard that it felt he would tear the hide from his body, he managed to get past that point, and from there on it was easier. A few more twists and wiggles and he was free.

He sat up behind the cabin, panted for breath, then smeared his sweaty face to make it dark with mud, so that he would be less visible in the night. He stood and gingerly moved into the forest, keeping under cover and putting, as quickly as possible, as much distance between himself and the town as he could.

He would make for the river, going a long, looping route that would take him past the towns and deep into the wilderness. When he reached the river, he wanted to be well away from any populated place. After that . . . after that, he didn't know what he would do. Get away, somehow. Find safety and civilization before the entire wilderness became the killing field of the vengeful Chickamaugas, Cherokees, and Creeks, who were ready to work with a greater unity than they had known before.

18

It took all Owen Killefer's effort to hide the great burst of astonishment Sadayi's just-spoken words had generated inside him. She had made the comment in the most casual and offhand way, yet the information it contained made it feel like the world had suddenly spun out from under his feet.

Sadayi had been speaking of a woman aquaintance in Crowtown who had died three weeks earlier. Sadayi had heard of her death only the prior day. It was too bad, Sadayi commented, that Tom Turndale, the white healer, had not used his medicines on her. Otherwise she might have lived.

This was the first mention of Turndale that Owen had heard within this household since his captivity had begun. That lack of mention, and of any sighting of him, had caused Owen to suspect that Turndale was either dead or gone away from the Chickamauga towns, or that maybe he had never lived here at all, contrary to what Joshua Colter had said back in the settlements. Yet now, with one casual statement, Sadayi had shattered that illusion like thin ice.

Owen leaned back against the frame of the door and steadied himself, swallowed to moisten a throat that had abruptly gone dry, and did his best to keep his voice from quaking. "This Turndale," he asked in his still slightly halting Cherokee, "does he have a mate?"

Sadayi looked puzzled at the odd question. "Yes. A white woman, younger than he is . . ."

Alive! Emaline is alive!

". . . but I haven't seen her much. She stays mostly at his cabin. She is a sad-looking lady. Ulagu says it as if Tom Turndale stole her soul. He is a strange man, this Turndale, and frightening to me, even though it was he whose medicine kept Ulagu alive when his leg was hurt and trying to kill him."

Owen's head was beginning to swim. The news Sadayi was unwittingly giving him was so stunning that he sought even more comfirmation. "Turndale's woman . . . what color is her hair?"

"The color of corn silk. Why do you ask about her?"

"And her face . . ."

"Her face is . . ." And here Sadayi, looking at him, paused as if something startling had swept across her mind. ". . . much like yours. Very much like it. I hadn't noticed it before." She stared at him like he had suddenly become strange, frowned, turned away her head. "Unakas, they all look much alike to me," she said flatly, with a sniff, as if that settled it. But her frown didn't leave, and she continued to look at him from the corner of her eye.

He knew now there was no mistake. The woman Sadayi had described could only be Emaline, not dead after all, but still living as Turndale's captive.

He wanted to cry, but couldn't let himself do it. It seemed essential, for reasons he could not explicate, that Sadayi develop no suspicions. And so, with an effort of will that strained him to the limit, he kept his expression blank and his eyes dry. Yet all the while, the wrenching new fact he had learned turned over and over in his mind, every turn revealing a new aspect. His mind cascaded with wild thought.

Oh, Emaline, all these years you've been here, and all declared you dead and gone. Father, Joshua Colter, Cooper Haverly ... me. In my mind I buried your corpse, Emaline. I didn't know. Please forgive me—I didn't know. And then, another turn, another facet revealing itself for consideration: *Would she know me now? Is she the same as she was? They say that captives change, that sometimes they come to love their captors more than their own people.*

"Go away from me now," Sadayi said abruptly. "Gather wood for the fire, and be careful that no one hurts you."

He nodded and walked out of the cabin, whistling an old song and trying so hard to act nonchalant that he failed badly and knew it. Even without glancing back, he knew Sadayi was watching him, and wondering. She was a keen woman, particularly when it came to observing people, and he had roused questions in her.

He was glad she had sent him away, and into the forest in particular. There he could be alone, and think. How badly he needed time to think right now! And to decide what to do, now that he knew the truth.

When Owen came back out of the woods with an armload of wood that, atypically, had taken him an hour to gather, he knew what he would do. Thinking about it made him feel almost as scared as he had been at that moment at the outset of his captivity when it appeared he was about to be tomahawked to death. But beneath the fear he had a sense of peace. At long last, after more than three years, he would have the chance to do what he had longed to do in the days before everyone around him convinced him that Emaline was surely dead.

Now he knew the reason for his captivity, if reason there was. It wasn't to bring justice to bear on Parnell Tulley. Somehow that seemed unimportant now. It wasn't even to punish him for his past failures. Fate had brought him here to rescue his sister, the very thing he had longed to do from the beginning.

Ulagu was home that night, talking of war. Information had come to the Chickamaugas that a great white army was gathering to smite the Indians, and the great Indian rendezvous now going on was to meet that challenge. Ulagu, distracted by his subject and eating heartily because soon it would be time for the traditional fast before war-making, paid little attention to Owen, who sat against the wall of the cabin, staring into the corner and seeming to listen to Ulagu, when in fact his thoughts were his own. But Sadayi watched Owen intently. Whenever he raised his own eyes, hers were looking back at him.

Later that night he broke his usual rule again, and asked Sadayi another question: Where was the cabin of Tom Turndale? She looked at him in that same odd way she had earlier in the day, told him in general terms where the cabin stood, and asked why he wished to know.

"My stomach hurts me," he said. "If you will allow me, I'll go in the morning to see if he can give me a cure."

"You may go," she said, but only after a long pause.

He lay down on his bed, convinced that Sadayi somehow understood more than he would have thought possible. At the very least she obviously sensed there was something in this situation beyond what had been said, even if she didn't fully apprehend what it was.

He didn't wait until the morning to go; such had never been his plan. As soon as the others were asleep, he rose and dressed himself, and crept toward the door. He was almost out when Sadayi appeared in the darkness behind him, looking at him. He stopped, looked back. The darkness hid her face. He said nothing, nor did she. When he turned and left, she did not call after him or try to stop him in any way.

Owen knew as he left that, however this night turned out, he was unlikely to ever set foot in the cabin of Ulagu and Sadayi again. And Sadayi, he believed, sensed the same thing, even though she could not possibly know exactly what he was doing, or why.

One word, and she could have awakened Ulagu and stopped him from going. She hadn't spoken. In her deliberate silence, she had given him two gifts, both of which he found very touching: her trust, and his freedom.

Cooper Haverly couldn't sleep. There was nothing new in that: He hadn't had a good night's sleep in many days. During the Houston's Station siege in the wake of the Settico orchard massacre, everyone had been too busy fighting for their lives to even consider resting. And even when that ordeal began to lighten, Cooper had suffered so much pain from his missing little finger that he hadn't rested well. Oddly and aggravatingly, the pain wasn't at the place where the finger had been shot from his hand, but in the fingertip, a fingertip no longer there. Cooper's impulse was to press the aching digit against his side. That, of course, was impossible—there *was* no digit. At length the phantom pain lessened, which was good, but only to give way to an eternally unscratchable itch, which was as bad, maybe worse, than the pain had been.

What kept Cooper awake tonight, however, was excitement. He was riding with Sevier again—that was reason enough to be excited, especially after the ordeal at Houston's Station—but even better than that, he was bound for home.

He looked forward to home, wife, and family. He had been too long gone. Sadly, his time among them probably would be short. Sevier was talking about an expedition against the Chickamaugas, and the preliminary motions toward that would occur as soon as they were home again.

After stirring about restlessly on his bedroll for too long, Cooper rose and filled a pipe. He lit it with a twig from the nearly dead cook fire, and sat puffing, enjoying the weed in the hollowed-out corncob bowl. The corncob pipe was a replacement for the good churchwarden pipe he had brought with him at the outset of the expedition against the Cherokees. Somewhere along the way he had lost it. In the orchard at Settico, he suspected.

Thinking of that set his mind on a more grim turn, and he puffed at the reed pipe stem deeply and furiously. He had come close to death several times in his past, but never had he felt its proximity as he had in that orchard. The rifle ball that had taken his finger from him might as easily have passed through his head or his heart. It was enough to make a man think hard about the things that matter in his life.

Someone approached from the side, making him start. It was John Sevier.

"Colonel, I thought you was asleep."

Sevier squatted and sat down on the earth near Cooper. "No, no. Been talking to an Indian."

"Indian? Here at camp?"

"A scout of mine. He tells me there's some fierce big movement among the Chickamaugas. Hundreds of warriors coming together, getting ready for the 'big fight' against the unakas."

"But you haven't got war plans laid yet, do you, Colonel?"

"No, and there's the thing that rubs me. Apparently intelligence is out among the Indians that the 'big fight' is going to be led by Joseph Martin. *The general.*" He said the title very deliberately, and Cooper knew the significance of that emphasis. At one time North Carolina had offered Sevier the brigadier general post that Martin now held, and Sevier had turned it down in order to lead the state of Franklin. The subject remained a touchy one for the man, whom North Carolina considered and treated as an outlaw.

"Martin!" Cooper exclaimed. "Pshaw! Joe Martin has the contempt of half the population. He's a deuced Carolina lover, and too much in the Indian camp to boot, I don't care what my brother says. Martin will never gain the loyalty of his men the way you can, John . . . pardon me, Colonel, or Governor . . ."

He never had been really sure how Sevier preferred to be addressed.

"John is fine with me, Cooper. There's times a man prefers to be just his plain self, without titles and duties and such. Leading can be a heavy mantle on the shoulders."

"Well, maybe so, but when there's Indian fighting to be done, I'd rather see the mantle on your shoulders than on Joe Martin's."

"I doubt I'll be a part of General Joe's campaign at all. Don't expect to be invited, not after me turning him down when he was trying to talk us out of punishing the Overhills."

Cooper's pipe had gone out. He relit it. "Well," he said between draws, "if it's Joseph Martin leading, Cooper Haverly won't be following. I'll sit this campaign out. Even without Martin, it bodes bad enough that the Indians are expecting the attack. No sir. I'll not be going on this one." He pulled the pipe from his teeth and made a face. "This pipe bites the tongue too much."

"What if Joshua Colter goes along with Martin? Would you go then?"

Cooper hadn't thought about that. "Well—I hope he won't." He puffed thoughtfully. "Then again, he thinks higher of Joseph Martin than I do."

Sevier stood abruptly. He kicked at the dirt impatiently. "By the eternal, Cooper, I wish I had a good jug of whiskey at hand and the circumstances to allow me to drain it dry. I do indeed." He walked away without another word.

And left Cooper surprised. John Sevier had never been a man prone to try to brighten his dark times with alcohol. He took an occasional drink, like almost all frontiersmen, from farmers to preachers, but Cooper had never seen him drunk. It bothered him to hear Sevier talking in a longing way about liquor. It was like noticing a threatening crack in the base stone of a long-worshiped idol that had always seemed stable before.

Caution made Owen move more slowly than he would have liked. The road was no more than a wide trail, hard to see in the darkness. The forest rose on both sides, indistinct except for the places where late-burning cook fires sent light between the nearer vertical lines of tree trunks. Owen was unarmed, and moving along a path that he had never taken in all his time here. Occasionally he would encounter others on the trail, coming back toward Black Water Town after some overextended visit in an outlying cabin, or perhaps a late hunt, but the darkness, Owen's Indian style of dress, and the tanning effect of months in the sun, made him unrecognizable as a white in these poor visual conditions. No one stopped him or asked where he was going.

Just what he was going to do when he reached Tom Turndale's cabin was an open question. He was weaponless, not sure what he would find, not sure even what he should do, much less could do. What if Emaline, after all this time, had shifted from captive to willing mate? He scolded himself for thinking that way. Emaline would never do such a thing. Not her.

The farther he went out the road, the more uncertain Owen became that he would know Turndale's cabin when he saw it. He was worrying over this when he saw a figure approaching up the trail. It was a man, no, a boy. Owen stopped and waited for him to grow nearer.

"Where is Tom Turndale's cabin?" he asked.

"There," the boy said, pointing back in the direction he had come from. "His house is south of the road, against the canebrake."

Owen gave his thanks and went on. A burst of nervousness struck him, hard, and made him feel inwardly cold. In the next few minutes he expected to look into two faces he hadn't seen since a snowy night early in 1785, one the face of a loved one, the other the face of the killer of his mother, grandfather, and uncle.

Tom Turndale turned up the crockery vessel and let the last drop of the potato beer it had contained drop onto his tongue. He hadn't imbibed all that much of the homemade brew, but it had been enough to make him quite drunk, because he was sensitive to alcohol. It wasn't common for him to drink to the point of intoxication. But it also wasn't common for him to feel the level of despair and loss that he felt tonight.

The absence of Flower hung heavy around him, a palpable, lingering emptiness that devastated him. It had never been like this before, not with anyone else. In London there had been a girl, a street prostitute, with whom he had become infatuated. Her death by one of the several loathsome illnesses that plagued women of her trade had saddened him, but within a week he had forgotten her. Then there had been his Cherokee wife who had lived with him in the Overhill Towns, and then here in this very cabin until her own death from a weak heart. Her passing had left him in grief for a month. But not deep grief, not devastating.

His grief over Flower was different. He hadn't realized how deep his affection for her had been until now, when she was gone. The prospect of life without her seemed hollow beyond all telling.

Turndale paced the cabin like a caged puma, then went to the fireside, above which the pistol he had found outside hung by the trigger guard on a peg stuck into the log wall. He took the pistol down, played around with it. It was loaded. From nowhere an impulse raced through him—to put the pistol against his own head, cock it, squeeze the trigger, and enter into a blessed oblivion in which he would know and feel nothing.

Horrified at that unexpected urge, he quickly hung the pistol back on the peg and retreated to the far side of the cabin. He had just played through the idea of killing himself! Never before had even the ghost of such a notion found a home inside his head.

Turndale's turbulent emotions made another sudden change. He became angry. Why should *he* consider death because of the great loss he had suffered, when in fact the person responsible was whoever had led Flower away? He remembered the rifle he had found, the one with the name "Killefer" carved into it. At the moment he couldn't recall the initial name on the gun; the potato beer had sullied his mind. If this whoever-he-was Killefer was one of the captives from the grounded flatboat, and if he was in fact Emaline's kin, he might be the one who had taken her away.

Turndale could think of no more likely candidate.

Or might Flower have gone away on her own? He hadn't thought much about this possibility, because he didn't like to think of her willingly turning against him, and because it didn't fit with the fact she had made no earlier escape tries in more than three years of captivity, despite abundant opportunity to do so.

But then he remembered that she was pregnant again. She might have fled to keep him from destroying this child like he had the first.

He declined, by sheer will, to take that possibility seriously. It would make him responsible for her absence, and that wasn't something he was willing to accept. No, Flower hadn't fled. She had been lured away, kidnapped, or maybe killed.

What was the first name on that rifle stock? Turndale's inability to remember aggravated him. He left the cabin and walked back into the canebrake in the cool night air. Though it was dark, he was familiar with this terrain, and went right to the place he had hidden the rifle. It was still there. Retrieving it, he took it back to the cabin. With Emaline gone, there was no reason to hide it now.

He came back around the cabin and stopped. He had an odd feeling, a sense of something different. Looking around, he saw nothing to surprise him. Still frowning cautiously, he turned to enter the cabin.

Standing in the open door, looking out at him and silhouetted by the dim background cabin light, was a lean, young Indian man. He took it as an Indian because of the dress, and because he would expect to find no other type of person in the middle of the Chickamauga country. Another person come wanting my medicines, he thought.

"Who are you?" he asked in Cherokee.

The voice that came back to him spoke in English. "You are Turndale?"

He stepped back, surprised and frightened. "Who are you? What do you want with me?"

"Where is she?"

Something approaching understanding began to dawn in Turndale's mind, but as of yet not brightly enough to illuminate what was happening.

"Who are you looking for?"

"For Emaline Killefer. My sister."

Turndale almost dropped the rifle in his surprise. "Killefer!"

"That's right. Owen Killefer. Son of Doanie Killefer, who you murdered. Nephew of Nash Winston, who you murdered too. Grandson of Joseph Killefer—killed by your hand. Son of Aaron Killefer, who turned to liquor and met his end as a sorry drunkard because of what you did to his family. And brother of Emaline Killefer, who you took away and have kept captive for more than three years now. Where is she, Turndale? Where is she?"

Turndale looked intently at the backlit figure. The shadow across his face kept him from seeing the features, but he knew even so that this truly was Flower's natural brother. Something in the voice and the stance reflected the young woman who had grown so familiar and beloved.

"I had it figured that you were here," Turndale said. "The rifle told me." He cast the rusted-out weapon onto the ground at Owen's feet. Without lowering his gaze from Turndale, Owen knelt and picked it up. His fingers ran over the carved letters of his own name. "The river?"

"Aye."

Owen cast the rifle aside. "Where is she?"

Turndale said, "She's gone."

Silence for a moment. "I don't believe you. I was told she still lived here. What have you done with her?"

"Nothing. But she's gone. Run away. I had thought it was you who had taken her."

"No. No. And you're lying. I know you're lying!"

"No lie. She's gone. I don't know where. My canoe is missing. She must have taken it down the river." Turndale's eyes swept up and down the silhouetted form. No knife, no tomahawk, no other weapon that he could see. Maybe he had something hidden behind him, but he doubted it. Captives were seldom allowed to keep weapons of their own.

"You're lying, Turndale. And it won't work. I'll not be run off by falsehoods! I've come to fetch Emaline to safety. God knows it should have happened long before now."

Turndale, his cunning mind beginning to overcome its surprise and seek the advantage, laughed. "You, a wormy little captive of the Chickamaugas, believe you could 'fetch' her to 'safety'? Bloody hell! Where would you take her in this wilderness?"

"No more talk, Turndale. You bring her out, and give her to me. And then I'll—" He went silent.

"Don't choke off your words, worm. I know what you were going to say." Turndale stepped forward one pace. "You were going to say that you'll kill me."

"There'll be no justice brought on you otherwise, with you hidden away among the Indians."

Another pace forward. Owen backstepped in response, back into the cabin. Some light came onto his face now, and Turndale saw his features. Indeed this was Flower's kin; he bore the mark of her looks in his face. A face, Turndale noted with satisfaction, that also betrayed a rising fear.

"I should have killed you at the same time I killed the others," Turndale said, drawing a knife from a sheath at his side. "I remember you—you rabbit-scampered too fast for me to bother chasing down. Too bad—I would have been as pleasured by killing you as much as by the others. Well, worm, I'll take that pleasure now!"

He lunged forward with a yell, sweeping up the knife and aiming it at Owen's midsection. Owen jerked to the side, and Turndale went past him. Spinning, he came at him again. Owen lurched toward the wall. Turndale stabbed, missed, dug the point of the knife into the logs. It took him a moment to wrench it out again and turn. When he did, he was looking down the muzzle of the pistol he had found outside by the herb mortar. Owen had yanked it off the peg.

"Where is she, Turndale?"

"Gone, dead and gone, worm! I killed her!" Turndale threw the lie like a dagger, threw it hard so it would stab.

The pistol in Owen's hand trembled and wavered.

Turndale laughed. He had unnerved the young man, as he had intended. He lunged with the knife, sure he could move more quickly than his stunned opponent could react. But Owen was better than that. The trigger snapped, the flint descended, the pan powder flashed, and half a moment later the charge deep in the muzzle exploded and sent the pistol ball hurtling out, into the forehead of Mad Tom Turndale and through his brain. He fell against Owen, dropped the knife, and died open-eyed before his body could slump to the ground.

Owen Killefer looked down at Turndale's body and gasped for breath. It would barely come; it was as if some giant hand was squeezed around his middle. He knew it was only panic, and after a few moments it subsided and his lungs took in air. Then he looked at the pistol in his hand, and panic gave way entirely to a sense of amazement.

Owen's belief in destiny was confirmed anew. On the butt of the pistol were the initials P.T. This was Parnell Tulley's pistol, the very one Owen had seen jutting out of Tulley's saddlebag that day in Jonesborough when he had seen that vivid mental picture of himself shooting down Tom Turndale with this very firearm.

He dropped the pistol as if it were too hot to hold, overwhelmed with awe. How had this pistol, of all the pistols in the world, come to be in Turndale's house? It was too astounding to believe, and yet the evidence was there, right before him. There truly was such a thing as the hand of providence. Owen could find no other explanation.

He looked at Turndale's dead form, at the pool of deep red spreading around his head, and felt sick. Then he remembered Turndale's last words, and abruptly sobbed aloud. Emaline was dead! He had come too late to save her. He had killed Tom Turndale, but what did that really matter? His family was gone now, every one of them. None were left but him. If fate was real, it was also cruel.

He left the cabin, went into the canebrake and cried like a small child. When the tears were out of him, he returned to the cabin, took up the pistol, a rifle and gear he found in a corner, and food from the shelves at the far corner. He left at once, hiking as fast as he could through the canebrake in the direction of the river. The odds of successful escape seemed stacked against him, but he was so sorrowful right now, thinking of the lost Emaline, that he hardly cared if he succeeded or not.

Many were the speculations that circulated through Black Water Town and the surrounding Chickamauga country concerning the bloody, mysterious events that centered around the house of Thomas Turndale. The puzzle had several pieces, and no one was able to fit them all together very well.

There were the dead men: Saul Greentree, the trader, whose stinking corpse was found in the woods not far from Turndale's cabin, and Turndale himself, shot through the head in his own dwelling, which itself showed evidence that someone had fought or raged violently around it, ripping down the arbor, scattering Turndale's herbs, and so on. And there was that rusted rifle found there, with white men's writing carved into the stock. Where had it come from? Did it hold a clue to the mystery of what had happened?

Then there were the missing ones to be considered: Flower, Turndale's sad young mate, whose hollow eyes

had shown the emptiness of her soul to anyone who
bothered to look. And the two captives from the flatboat,
also missing. The black-skinned one, maimed and humiliated by his captor, had gotten the best of it in the end
by actually running away and not getting caught—a wonderful joke on his harsh captor, many thought. And the
white captive, claimed by Ulagu—he was gone as well,
as was the trader and gunsmith named Tulley, who had
been Greentree's partner. A search was made and none
of the four were found.

Some thought that the three escaped ones must have
killed Greentree and Turndale, possibly for their weapons, and fled together. Others said that perhaps the
young woman Flower had killed Turndale on her own
and fled independently, maybe in revenge for Turndale's
rumored murder of her girl-child months before. Others
came up with even more theories, linking up the various
puzzle pieces in vastly different ways. And others, particularly Sadayi, seemed determined not to speculate aloud
on the mystery at all. She would not talk of it even to
Ulagu. In the end it seemed clear that no one knew what
had happened, and it would probably remain that way
perpetually.

But one minor piece of further information, nothing
that really answered any of the big questions, did come
in regarding one of the missing ones. A band of raiders
skirmished with three whites caught fleeing through the
forests—traders from some of the various Chickamauga
towns, they were, who had come together in common
flight from the towns as the impending war thrust against
the unakas heated up. One of the traders had been killed.
A second had been tomahawked severely, but apparently
not fatally, and had rolled off a bluff into some thick

brush in which he was not found. The third got away without harm, hiding somewhere in the forest.

The tomahawked man who had gone over the drop, two of the warriors from Black Water Town said, had been Parnell Tulley. They had searched for him and the unhurt survivor for a quarter of a day, but had not found either, and finally gave up because it seemed too much trouble to continue. There would be plenty of opportunities soon to collect white scalps that would come much easier than those, and which would be far better trophies than the scalps of mere traders. They would be scalps of warring men, taken in battle. It was the intention of the Chickamaugas to gather them in abundance and stretch them on their winter houses for all to see.

RALLY IN THE
CANEBRAKE

19

Darcy Colter smiled as she rode beside her husband, and occasionally let her hand slip secretly to touch her belly. She was almost sure now that she was pregnant, a secret she still kept, but which she planned to share with Joshua whenever they were alone and the time was right. Perhaps tonight, when they would be camped at Greasy Cove. It all depended on whether the children and the others who would be all around granted them any privacy.

Certainly she could not tell Joshua at the moment, not in a crowd like this—and especially not with Alexander Carney continually chattering in Joshua's opposite ear. Darcy, Joshua, and their children Will and Hester, were part of a group of Andrew Jackson's neighbors, professional peers, and friends who were on their way to the home of Colonel Robert Love, a leading citizen of the Greasy Cove settlement south of Jonesborough. Love's home lay just ahead, so close now that Darcy could smell the earthy, delicious smoke of the barbecue pits already laden and simmering with venison, beef, and pork. The well-trampled road revealed that many people had already preceded their own group; these were the closer neighbors of Love. The group of which the Colters were part had come much farther, riding down by way of Jonesborough, trailing behind Andrew Jackson, who was proudly mounted astride his big racing horse like a king at the head of his army. No one minded Jackson taking the lead today, not even Alexander Carney. Today, after all, was Jackson's day.

When Jackson's group came in sight of Love's homestead, they sent up a great cheer, which was echoed at once by those already gathered around the barbecue pits and at the semicircular racetrack Love had built on a flat portion of his Nolichucky River land. Love, like Jackson, was a devoted lover of horse racing. He enjoyed the reputation of owning the fastest horse in the region, a horse so far unbeaten and reputedly unbeatable. It was Andrew Jackson's intention to change all that today.

The day's planned race and celebration had come about in the spontaneous manner most frontier festivities developed. Jackson was fiercely proud of his racing horse, and had talked it up considerably in Jonesborough, Greasy Cove, Greene Courthouse, and all the other communities into which his professional travels took him. It was only a matter of time before word of the talkative upstart reached Love, and the revered colonel quickly accepted when Jackson challenged him to a race. News of the race spread. By the time a date was settled upon, the Overmountain people, wearied by fears of constant Indian raids, news of more and more killings and scalpings, and repeated military excursions into the besieged lower Holston country, had turned what had initially been a private challenge into a big public spectacle and excuse for much-needed revelry and relaxation.

Darcy looked forward to the festivities as a chance to talk to friends not often seen. She regretted that Hannah Haverly hadn't come along, but Hannah had good reason.

Cooper had recently returned home from warfare in the farther settlements, and he and Hannah were enjoying their reunion. Darcy was glad for them both, especially for Hannah; she knew how deeply Hannah worried every time her husband rode off to fight.

Darcy would have enjoyed the ride to Love's farm even more if not for one unpleasant fact that Alexander Carney just wouldn't quit talking about. But he seemed compelled to do so, and had been for about ten minutes now.

A three-month-old letter to Colonel Charles Carney from his daughter Nell had recently arrived from the Cumberland settlements after delay caused by distance and the ongoing Indian trouble. The only good news it contained was that the Hices had arrived safely at their destination. The rest of its information was terribly sad. The second Hice flatboat, bearing two slaves, three horses, many household goods, and Owen Killefer, had been lost in a violent river storm in the Chickamauga country. None of the boat's occupants had turned up, and it appeared very likely now that they were dead, probably killed by drowning, and if not, by exposure or Indians.

It begrieved Darcy to think of poor Owen Killefer dying in such a way. She and Joshua had frequently discussed the sad life the young man had lived, so fraught with loss. And the saddest part of all to Darcy was the fact that Owen had so obviously loved the unattainable Nell. She pictured him on that second flatboat, poling, steering, looking up to the first boat and the woman he loved, now married to another—and she pictured the storm, swirling the boats apart, and Owen dying in the water while his beloved was swept farther and farther away down the river. The mental scene was so vivid in her imagination that it had sufficed several times to bring a tear to her eye.

Today, despite Alexander Carney's talk, she was doing her best not to think about it. She was in no mood for tears. Neither was Joshua, she could see. But he was too polite to tell Alexander to let the sorrowful subject drop.

But Alexander did let it drop at last, out of necessity. The travelers dismounted and turned their horses into the care of awaiting slaves—all but Jackson. He trusted no one but himself to see to the welfare of his precious mount. The man was a bigger fool for a good horse than even Charles Carney had been before his mind failed him.

Unhappiness was soon forgotten in the bustle of greetings and conversation that followed their arrival. Jackson, whose jockey had fallen ill and would not ride today, rested his horse and made ready to make the race himself. Love, expansive and beaming, came over and complimented Jackson's horse, tempering the comments with good-humored doubts about the horse's ability to beat his own. Jackson went along with the joke, but his manner told all that he didn't take the matter lightly at all.

The crowd gathered at the track, Jackson's supporters on one side and Love's on the other. Judges were stationed on each side of the course. Love's jockey was a small-framed black boy very accustomed to his job; his face showed quiet confidence. Jackson, looking much larger in his saddle, showed more than confidence. Pomposity, it seemed to Darcy. A look that would seem more appropriate if the race were already won. Then she realized that in Jackson's mind, the race probably already *was* won. The notion of losing probably never crossed Andrew Jackson's mind.

The race itself was exciting, and caused Darcy to hop

and clap like a little girl. Jackson and Love's jockey rode
with heads low and backsides high, their faces lined with
intensity and concentration. The horses raced with ease,
streaking along the curving track, the pounding of their
hooves so fast it made an almost unbroken sound. The
horses ran neck and neck as the end of the course neared
. . . it appeared either could take the victory, or both
might tie . . . and then, abruptly, the jockey astride Love's
horse bent a little lower, urged a new burst of speed out
of his animal, and dashed across the finish line in a clear
victory over his opponent. Love's supporters cheered and
tossed hats skyward, while Jackson's friends groaned in
disappointment.

Alexander Carney, one of the judges at the finish line,
moved toward Jackson, politely applauding for both win-
ner and loser. He smiled in condolence at Jackson as the
red-faced loser dismounted. "Well, my friend, it was a
good race, even if—"

"Step aside, Carney, and let a man pass!"

Jackson shoved Alexander Carney aside and with an
angry glare stormed up to Colonel Love, who watched
the approach with one brow lifted. The crowd, which
had been cheering and laughing in good nature, quickly
fell silent. It was evident that Andrew Jackson was not
going to be a good loser.

Alexander looked astounded as he listened to Jackson
launch into a tirade against Love that was far out of measure for the offense committed—if winning a horse race
fair and square could be called an "offense."

Joshua came to his side. "Lord have mercy, what a
show!" he said. "This beats the race itself." He spoke as
if to make light of what was happening, but was watching
with concern. Love, like Jackson, was hot-tempered. He

might not endure Jackson's unjustified insults for long without issuing a challenge.

Jackson continued his harangue for an absurdly long time, insulting Love's horse, his track, his jockey, his family, his business dealings. He accused him of being a "land pirate," referring to the large Love family land holdings in the region. It was at this point that Joshua and others who had come with Jackson, Alexander Carney included, began to move forward.

When Jackson was done, Love's face was red from brow to chin. Hardly was Jackson's last word out before Love fired back acid of his own, ending with a description of Jackson as a "damned long, gangling, sorrel-topped soap stick."

By now Love's own family members and supporters had moved in as well, and pulled him back from Jackson, who was lunging forward just as Joshua got to him. Alexander Carney grabbed Jackson's opposite shoulder and, with Joshua on the other side, pulled him back, where he was surrounded by others and cut off from Love.

"I believe it's time for tempers to calm. It was just a race, no more," Joshua said.

"That's right," Alexander interjected.

Jackson jerked free of Joshua's grasp and with that free hand pushed Carney away. "Get your hands off me, dog!"

"'There's no call for talk like that," Joshua said. "Alexander is doing naught but saving you from your own temper. Colonel Love isn't a man to take an insult."

Alexander's temper, easily stirred by Jackson, was stirred now. "For that matter, neither am I," he said. "I don't appreciate being called a dog."

Jackson, cut off from his prior target of fury, now turned his wrath on Alexander Carney. "You don't like it, do you? Then up your fists and show your feelings like a man!"

Alexander was obviously stunned by the unexpected challenge, and said nothing.

Jackson laughed in contempt. "What are you, Carney? A woman? You haven't the manhood to fight!" And with that Jackson shoved Alexander again.

Alexander grew livid. He balled his fists and stepped forward. Jackson's eyes met his head-on. Carney's jaw twitched. The fire in Jackson's eyes flared . . . and that in Carney's died. He seemed to wilt. Jackson came a stride closer.

"You don't like me, do you, Carney? You never have, whatever pretenses you've made."

Alexander answered softly. "I don't like your ways, Mr. Jackson. Your attitudes, your arrogance and condescension. Your seeming belief that your personal honor and pride are more all-fired important than anything else at any given time."

"A man's honor is of utmost importance—perhaps you don't share that view, Carney."

"My idea of what makes a man does not match yours—that is clear enough."

"Are you seeking to insult me, Carney?"

Joshua Colter cut in. "This is bloody foolishness. Enough of it!"

Jackson was too hot to be cooled. Jackson ignored Joshua. "Clarify yourself, Carney! Are you casting insult on my manhood?"

"It's you, sir, who have already cast insult on mine."

"I challenge you, sir. Fisticuffs. If you wish to prove your manhood, do it in a manly way!"

Alexander's reply was so soft it could hardly be heard. "I'll not fight you."

A murmur ran through the watching crowd. To be insulted and challenged, yet to refuse to respond, was unheard of. A man who refused a challenge ran against convention and risked public ridicule.

"You refuse to honor my challenge?"

"I choose to honor myself. I'm not a man of physical strength. I know you would defeat me, Mr. Jackson. There's no proof required, and no honor gained by submitting myself to a beating that gains nothing."

"You stand against the very standard, sir!"

"I don't accept your standard."

Another murmur, louder. Jackson smiled slowly, looking down his nose at Carney with unveiled contempt. "You waste my time, coward," he said, and turned away, walking back to his horse, which he mounted and rode away on without saying anything more to anyone.

The people watched Jackson leave, then every eye turned to Alexander Carney, a man whose status had just changed dramatically. He had refused a direct challenge, and left a charge of cowardice unanswered.

Joshua called Alexander aside. "You must realize that what has happened here won't quickly be forgotten," he said.

"And do you look down on me for it, Joshua?"

Joshua didn't answer immediately. "No," he finally said. "I know the kind of man you are. I believe you did what you did today because you were following your own lights as best you could. But let me tell you, Alexander: even before today, some have whispered you are a—a . . ."

"A coward? Is that what you don't want to say?" Alexander took a deep breath. "I understand that, Joshua. I'm ready to take any consequences of acting upon my own conscience." He paused, then smiled sadly. "Perhaps there are those who will see that it requires more manhood to stand on an unpopular principle than to do otherwise."

The celebration didn't last long after that. Jackson's temperamental display and Alexander Carney's perceived show of cowardice threw water on the fires of festivity. After eating of the abundant roasted meat, most of the participants departed early, heading toward their homes. Only those who had come the farthest remained to camp for the night, the Colters included. Alexander Carney was to have stayed with them, but he didn't. He rode toward home alone, saying he wouldn't mind the solitude and the late ride.

The Colters found him the next morning, lying beaten at the roadside with his clothing torn. Several men from the race had jumped him, beaten him, and mocked him as a coward. He had tried to fight back, but there were five of them against him and he hadn't had a chance.

"Tell me who they are, and by heaven, I'll even the balance for you!" Joshua declared.

But Alexander refused to reveal their names. There was no point in it, he said. Doing so would just get someone else hurt. Just best to let it die.

They took him home and did what they could for him. Carney closed the door behind him and crawled into bed, and three days passed before he showed himself in public again.

Joshua rejoiced at the news of Darcy's pregnancy, but the time for sharing happiness was cut short. As had been rumored for weeks now, Brigadier General Martin was indeed mounting a campaign against the Chickamaugas. Joshua was asked to participate, and agreed. Cooper received no invitation this time, and declared he was glad. He wouldn't have gone anyway, he declared, not with "General Joe" at command. Give him John Sevier, or give him the rocking chair and fireside.

The officers of the campaign were called into council at Jonesborough, where Colonel Robert Love, still fuming mad at Andrew Jackson, was placed in charge of Washington County. Other officers of note were placed in charge of soldiers from the various other counties and regions, and Colonel Alexander Outlaw was given the commissary post, partly because he was a longtime associate and supporter of John Sevier, and his inclusion, it was hoped, would help smooth matters over with those unhappy with Sevier's exclusion from this campaign.

The actual assembly of troops took place at White's Fort, standing near the place the French Broad and Holston rivers joined. This was the station of James White, a leading citizen of Scottish ancestry who had come in 1786 from North Carolina to claim land given to him by North Carolina for payment of his services during the Revolution. Joshua thought White's house was one of the most appealing frontier homes he had ever seen, barring the "mansion" of the prominent Carter clan on the Old Fields of the Watauga, and the fine house Joshua's late adoptive brother Gabriel had owned until the Cherokees burned it down in the prior decade. White's house was one and a half stories tall, and twenty-by-thirty paces big. Because of its location, it had become an important stopping point for river travelers, and White had built a stockade around his home to provide greater security for himself and his frequent visitors.

White's Fort was a bustling, crowded place as some five hundred armed men milled about, preparing themselves, their weapons, and their gear for battle. As soon as all was ready, the march began at rapid pace.

Their course took them to Hiwassee by way of an ancient war path over which innumerable native feet had trodden for years beyond recall. By the close of the third day, the army had reached the Hiwassee River mouth, where they found evidence of many canoes having been launched by Indians. Hoping to surprise the Indians at Lookout Mountain, the weary soldiers tramped on through the night, covering twenty miles by darkness, and did not stop even when the next day came and Lookout Mountain loomed in view.

An Indian town stood at the base of the mountain; it was found deserted and mostly burned, with fires still smoldering. Only four Indians were seen, and one of these, a captive mulatto-turned-Chickamauga, was killed. There the army finally took rest and camped for the night. But for some the exertion was not yet over. A proposal came from one of the captains that a volunteer force go ahead across the mountain to secure the pass there, and go on to the town of Tuskegee, where the Indians were thought to be keeping their horses.

Joshua Colter was not among those who went on. He, along with many other of the more experienced soldiers present, did not think the plan was wise and did not volunteer. His caution proved to be wise. The force that advanced onward was ambushed along the rocky Indian trail where it mounted the bench of the mountain. Their opponents were mostly unseen, being hidden in the large and abundant boulders all about.

The ambushed men fled on horseback, riding in a mad panic back toward safety. Below in Martin's camp, the men came to their feet at the first sounds of distant gunfire and ran for their own horses to head up to give assistance. By the time they were ready to ride out, however, the first of the returning ambush victims came in, so frightened they could hardly speak to tell what had happened.

The night was spent at guard, watching the darkness, listening to the ominous thrumming of Chickamauga drums and occasional rifle blasts, fired as signals from one Indian band to another. Out there in the mountains the Indians were gathering, developing whatever scheme they had to deal with the unakas who had come against them. Joshua knew Indian fighting well, and had been in many a dangerous spot, and tonight he was as nervous as the most tender neophyte.

Joshua was among the scouts sent into the mountains with Captain John Beard at first light. His eyes shifted back and forth, up and down, as they progressed, knowing ambush was likely but not knowing when and where it would come.

In fact, it came at the same spot it had the night before. Indian riflemen rose over the boulders to aim fire at the scouts, then dropped down again, fully covered and out of harm's way. Beard's advance force, like the one before it, had no option but to flee. They did so, losing not a man, though Beard's horse was wounded beneath him.

Meanwhile, in the camp below, General Martin had ordered an advance of the full body of troops. They could hear the crackle of ambuscade gunfire ahead, up in the rocks. At the mountain base the soldiers left their horses and began climbing up the narrow trail on foot. When it became so steep and narrow that they were forced into single file, they left the trail itself and moved closer to the base of the cliff beside them, struggling over the rugged terrain in hopes of avoiding the ambush that travel on the open trail would certainly have invited. They crawled like ants among the boulders.

In the meantime, Joshua and Beard's other men were continuing their retreat. Joshua at last found himself near the main body of the troops that had come up from the camp. He searched for Martin, hoping to advise him of the futility of continuing in this manner. Before he found him, however, a new Chickamauga fusillade opened up from a different direction than the prior ambushes. Joshua dropped to the ground and squeezed down behind a boulder. He heard men scream, saw one fall.

The men began to flee the deadly trap. Joshua leaped up and joined them; today, he believed, was not a good day to die. If he was to die in battle, he intended it would be in a battle that had hope of victory.

Martin attempted to rally his troops, but with little success. Even his officers refused to advance into certain slaughter, and some even accused Martin, who normally advocated for the Indians rather than led militarily against them, of deliberately trying to lead them to defeat. Joshua, who for personal reasons had always held Martin in generally high esteem, spoke up on his behalf. It made little difference. The campaign was finished. The battle, such as it had been, was a total loss.

And three good men had died, all of them captains. Five others had been wounded.

They took the three bodies back to the abandoned Indian town below the mountain and buried them under the council house. There, it was hoped, the corpses would not be found and subjected to the usual indignities. Then, defeated, sorrowful, and angry, the frontier soldiers mounted their horses and began the long ride home, leaving the Chickamaugas in the mountains in possession of an undeniable, heady victory.

*   *   *

Ulagu looked at the three bodies that had been found under the council house. Two he did not know, but one looked familiar. He knelt to study the face, blue now in its death pallor, and then stood. He turned to Dragging Canoe, who had already offered his opinion on the identity of the corpse in question.

"Yes, I believe you are right," he said. "It is John Sevier."

Already great whoops of delight were resounding through the assembled Chickamaugas, who were all but delirious at their success in repelling Joseph Martin's force. The victory had given great confidence to them all. If this was the best the unakas could do, what could stop the Chickamaugas from driving them out at last? Especially now that Tsan-usdi—"Little John" Sevier—was dead?

They bore the three corpses back to Running Water Town and there celebrated over them, particularly over the one that had been identified as John Sevier. For a day and night warriors danced around that corpse, thrilled with their success, happy that at last the great scourge of the native people was dead.

But Ulagu had his doubts, and they were growing. He had seen Sevier a few times in his life, and indeed the corpse's face had looked like Sevier's. Yet he couldn't shake the idea that Sevier was not really dead. Had not earlier reports said that Sevier was not even to be part of this campaign?

Perhaps it was as Sadayi had often said: so many unakas look so much alike. Ulagu joined the festivities celebrating the supposed death of Sevier, but by the time it was done he was still without confidence that the great enemy at last had fallen.

Soon, he was sure, the Chickamaugas would know one way or another. In the afterswell of victory, it was time to strike anew. The Indians gathered, hundreds upon hundreds of them, and began their advance toward the white settlements. There they would divide and strike like many snakes—and whether Nolichucky Jack Sevier was dead or alive, the fangs of the Chickamaugas would sink deeper than ever this time. Of this Ulagu had no uncertainty at all.

20

Warm nights were past. The forest was cool and breezy now that the sun had gone down. Cooper Haverly tucked in his hunting shirt a little tighter as he stood beside John Sevier on a stony hillside and looked across the dark forest toward a distant flickering light.

"It's a cabin, possibly a stockade," Cooper said to his chief commander, who despite the Chickamauga conviction to the contrary, was thoroughly alive, having not been part of Martin's campaign. It was Captain Joseph Bullard whose corpse had been mistaken for Sevier's. Bullard and Sevier had often been confused because of a close facial similarity.

"Do you know what station lies in that direction?" Sevier asked.

Cooper thought about it for a moment. "Samuel Sherrill's, isn't it—good Lord! That's your wife's people!"

"Aye," Sevier said solemnly.

"A night march will get us there. We can go to their aid."

Sevier nodded. "So we will, Cooper. Spread the word among the men, and prepare yourself."

There were some forty of them there on the mountain

called Unicoi, good frontiersmen to the last, and devoted
to Sevier, who had emerged from his Nolichucky home
in the aftermath of Martin's great defeat and gone off to
do the job most now said should have been his to begin
with. The force was far smaller than the one Martin had
fielded the month before, but because of its very com-
pactness and the quality of its members, could react
quickly and pursue aggressively, and that fit the needs of
the border at the moment. The massive Indian force that
had held off Martin had broken up into many small
bands, each striking on their own all across the border,
stinging stations, cabins, and farmsteads like a swarm of
angry bees. Sevier's group, like most he led, was com-
prised of volunteers such as Cooper Haverly. Joshua Colter would have been there too, had not a fierce fever laid
him low directly after his return from the Martin campaign.

Sevier's force reacted quickly to the order for a march,
and gathered up their gear in hardly more than the time
required to order it. They traveled in near silence, moving invisibly in the dark forest, keeping the flickering
light in the distance as their guiding star. Everyone knew
what the fire meant: Indians had struck again. How badly
remained to be seen.

Travel by night was difficult, especially through territory in which hostiles clearly were present. The men
passed near the burning structure Cooper and Sevier had
spotted. It was a cabin, now a pile of hot cinders. They
went on toward Sherrill's Station. By the time they
reached it, the sun was edging up over the eastern
slopes. The scene it illuminated was shocking.

Sherrill's fort was under siege, and by coincidence of
timing, Sevier's force had arrived at almost the precise
moment of the attack. Cooper looked from hiding at the

massive body of warriors assaulting the station. Scores upon scores of them, well over a hundred, maybe twice that number. The fort's defenders had quite a challenge on their hands—but they at least had the advantage of a protective wall. Cooper and comrades had no protection but their rifles and momentary invisibility afforded by the forest.

Sevier pulled his men back a ways into the woods and gathered them around him. "Men, we cannot let that station suffer without doing all we can to help it. I don't need to tell you the danger we will draw upon ourselves once we expose our presence. I propose that we charge into the very midst of the Indians, firing and yelling for all we're worth. If we can drive them back, we can reinforce the station and perhaps discourage any further attack."

"It'll be mighty dangerous," one of the men said.

"Mortally so. Even so, I intend to make the effort or die. Who is willing to go with me?"

Not a man backed down. Sevier smiled, nodded. "At the signal, then, and may God go with us."

Cooper remembered for the rest of his days the combination of exhilaration and mortal terror he felt as he and his companions ran from the forest, throwing back at the thoroughly surprised Indians their own war cry. Cooper dropped to his knee, raised his rifle and fired at a warrior. He missed, but the warrior ran as hard as he could back in the direction he had come. He looked very scared.

Cooper ran for the closest cover, a tree, and reloaded as quickly as possible. Meanwhile, his fellows continued yelling and firing, making quite a ruckus and managing to sound like a group three times the size they were.

Cooper finished reloading, let out another wild yell, and searched for another target.

It went on like this for a few minutes, until finally they were at the stockade gate. The defenders inside the fort, cheered and as surprised as the Indians by Sevier's arrival, opened the gate and let the reinforcements inside.

The people of Sherrill's Station sent up a loud cheer. Several of Cooper's companions hoisted Sevier onto their shoulders and carried the smiling man into the heart of the fort, where the besieged people swarmed around and hurrahed his name. Cooper grinned at the show.

From the rifle platform came a shout: "They're leaving! The bloody redskins are going away!"

Cooper laughed aloud. What a success Sevier's ploy had been! Obviously the attackers had been bewildered by such a speedy arrival of enforcements. And they had probably believed the group to be much larger than it actually was.

Caught up in the joy of victory, Cooper lifted his rifle skyward and whooped at the top of his lungs, dancing in a circle as he did so. Abruptly he stopped, staring.

Looking back at him from the rifle platform was a familiar face. It was far more weathered and lean than the last time he had seen it, but he knew it well. He froze in place, rifle still uplifted, and gaped in astonishment, then slowly lowered the gun and walked to the base of the platform. The one atop it, grinning now, knelt and thrust out his hand.

"Owen . . . is it really you?"

"It's me. Good to see you, Cooper."

Owen Killefer's voice was deeper than it had been. Though his frame was thinner than ever, it showed the hard lines of muscles beneath his darkened skin. Owen's hair was short but shaggy, and irregularly shaped; at his crown one long lock hung, Indian-style. His eyes had a clear, mature sharpness. All in all, he had the look of a young man who had gone through an ordeal and come out the harder, more weathered for it.

"Lord, Owen, we thought you was dead!"

"Not me. Still kicking."

"There was a letter from Nell Hice, saying your flatboat had been lost and you had almost surely been killed—"

Owen's eyes sparked. "Nell is alive?"

"Yes, yes. She and her husband made it safe and sound to the Cumberland."

"Thank God!"

"But the flatboat—"

"There was a storm, a crash. I was captured by the Chickamaugas."

"Captured! How did you get free?"

"It's a story that'll take some time to tell. Come up here with me and I'll tell it to you. And there's things I want to know from you too."

Cooper climbed onto the platform, and for the next hour listened as Owen Killefer told the story of his captivity, of his discovery that Emaline had in fact remained alive for years after her kidnapping, of his encounters with Parnell Tulley, and his relatively comfortable existence with Ulagu and Sadayi. He spared no details, even admitting to killing Tom Turndale. And he sadly told how, right before his own death, Turndale had boasted of killing Emaline, a claim Owen believed was probably true.

He told too of his harrowing escape, of traveling by night through the forests, struggling to avoid being caught by the Indians or killed as a perceived Indian by any whites he might encounter. At last he had come upon a farmstead that was being deserted by a very frightened family on its way to Sherrill's Station, and had convinced them he was not an Indian just in time to avoid being shot. They had let him join them, and reached the fort, where Owen had been welcomed with that special enthusiasm reserved by frontier people for those who had suffered Indian captivity and come out of it alive.

Owen was as eager to learn as he was to talk. He asked for news of those he knew, particularly for every detail Cooper might know of Nell's letter to the Carneys.

"When this is done, come back with me," Cooper said. "You've got land there, and people who know and care for you. And Lord knows there's nothing to hold you here."

Owen thought about it, and nodded. "I believe I will," he said. "Whenever this is over."

Unlike most around him, Ulagu felt no surprise when he learned that it was none other than John Sevier who had come to the rescue of Sherrill's Station. The news simply confirmed his prior doubts about the identity of the corpse dug up from beneath the Lookout Mountain town council house.

"Don't be sorrowful because Sevier is alive," he counseled his fellows. "It simply means there is a chance for glory for the man who finally does kill him."

And that chance could easily come. On the heels of his dramatic arrival at Sherrill's Station, Sevier had moved to enlarge his force and march against the middle and valley towns of the Cherokees, where most of the richest Indian crops were grown. To destroy those crops seemed the surest and speediest way to force an Indian withdrawal.

Ulagu was with the half-breed John Watts when they observed Sevier's force crossing the mountains toward the towns, and present when the large Indian force attempted to ambush a small group that splintered off from Sevier's main body to return to their homes. The ambush failed because Sevier's group heard its shots and came back to join the fight. Ulagu was astonished to see, among Sevier's group, a lean young man who looked for all the world like Owen Killefer. He was unable to get a close enough look to be sure.

Though he didn't want to admit it to himself, Ulagu was sorry that his young captive had fled. In the relatively brief time he had known Owen, Ulagu had grown fond of him. This was even more true of Sadayi, who had grieved for Owen after he vanished. Ulagu had easily seen through her efforts to hide her sorrow. She had shown no inclination to talk about the matter, and had not brought it up. He was a practical and warlike man, and frowned upon soft sentiments . . . especially those he found, against his will, inside himself.

Cooper became Owen's constant companion and trainer during the fast-moving expedition against the middle and valley towns. Owen had taken part in no such military exercises before. But he did well, and was gratified to observe that Cooper was impressed with his skills and speed of learning.

At the seemingly abandoned town of Ustally, a band of scouts under Major James Hubbert discovered several Indian men hiding in apparent hope of ambush. They killed most of them, and captured one of the younger ones. The force moved on, leaving the town in flames behind them.

At the mouth of the Valley River, the Sevier family came close to suffering great loss when an Indian ambush almost succeeded in doing in John Sevier's sons, Valentine, Joseph, and John Sevier Junior. The army drove off the ambushers, but in anger one of the frontiersmen present killed the Cherokee youth captured at Ustally. With his tomahawk still wet with fresh blood, he stood over the dead boy and explained his rationale for the murder. Nits, he said, make lice. Owen personally heard that comment, and was chilled by it. He realized how easily the Chickamaugas who had held him might have taken the same coldly practical attitude toward him and killed him upon capture.

The army continued its sweep, going on to Cootacloohee, where it destroyed twenty acres of corn before a rainy night set in. The next morning the destruction continued, but word came that a large body of Indians had been spotted in the woods nearby. Investigation revealed frightening evidence that a large band of Indians had actually passed the army's encampment in the night.

The army headed toward the Hiwassee River crossing, which they found filled with debris and over its banks because of the recent rain. Sevier was faced with a decision. Should the army attempt such a treacherous crossing? Might ambush be planned?

The answer came in the form of a rifle shot, fired by a hidden Indian at Sevier himself. The colonel turned his mount, called for retreat.

Some, such as James Hubbert, protested the ordered retreat, but that sentiment was far from unanimous. The evidence so far indicated a massive Indian force, too big to be safely engaged, and the failed attempt to kill Sevier showed how close at least some of the Indians were. The frontiersmen retreated swiftly. Darkness fell as the troops crossed the Unicoi Pass.

On the far side of the pass, as the army began looking for a suitable camp ground, Owen pawed around on himself and told Cooper he had unwittingly left behind his knife and needed to return back up the pass to get it. He knew right where he had left it—lying atop a log at the top of the pass, where he had paused to probe a splinter out of his heel.

"No, Owen. It's too dangerous. They're almost close enough to smell."

But Owen wouldn't listen. The knife was a good one, given to him by a man at Sherrill's Station, and he was loathe to lose it. He scampered back toward the pass, vanishing into the dark. Cooper hung back, peering into the dark after him, then turned and moved on ahead to the encampment.

Sometime later Owen paused near the top of the rise and looked back across Tellico Plains. Flaring lights across the flats revealed the campfires of the army. Owen paused, wondering if he should have listened to Cooper and stayed behind. Back at the camp there was light and warmth and the company of armed men. Here he was alone, and in danger, had any of the Indians scouted ahead of their main body. It wasn't really worth the risk simply to retrieve a knife, he decided. He turned to go back.

Then he stopped. What the devil—he was almost to the top of the rise. He might as well go on. It should take him only another five minutes or so to retrieve the knife, and then he would return to the camp as fast as he could travel.

*　　*　　*

Ulagu crept up the dark slope of the pass, feeling shame like a weight upon his shoulders. Earlier in the day he had made a humiliating mistake, and costly. It was his rifle that had fired the too-early shot at John Sevier, betraying the ambush that had been set for the frontiersmen at the river ford. A full five hundred Indians had hidden themselves strategically and surely would have devastated the unaka army—if only he hadn't been overeager to be the man who brought down Sevier.

He was determined now to make up for his error. He had left the main body of Indians far behind and was scouting ahead, hoping to perform some recompensing act to atone for his mistake—maybe even by killing John Sevier in his own camp, if such a daring thing was possible! If it was, it could only be done with the greatest stealth and skill, and only by a man alone.

Ulagu paused, taking deep breaths through his nose to keep from breathing too loudly and betraying his presence to any sentinel the unakas might have posted atop the dark pass. As he held still, he listened, then cocked his head, held his breath altogether, and listened more closely still.

Someone *was* up there . . . more than one? He crouched, putting his ear to the earth and feeling the faint vibrations the movement of the unseen person above caused. As best he could tell, it was one man only. Ulagu smiled and stood. The unakas *had* posted a guard, and that guard would now spill his blood around his knife.

Ulagu laid his rifle aside, knowing he could move better and sting more swiftly without being cumbered by it. Silently, with the experience of scores of battles, skirmishes, and raids behind him, he advanced up the slope. So skilled was his movement that only the keenest of ears would have any chance of detecting him. The closer he came to the top of the rise, the more slowly and carefully he proceeded. By the time he reached it, his knife was drawn and he was as tightly coiled as a panther ready to spring.

There he was—a lone unaka, bending over and picking up something. Watching carefully, Ulagu surmised from the man's motion—it was too dark to see anything but broad movements—that the retrieved item was probably a knife, because the man seemed to be sheathing it. He also had a rifle in hand. He turned his back to Ulagu and began walking back down the slope in the other direction.

Ulagu advanced, swift as a snake. The gap between him and the lone figure closed. His knife rose, the man turned, only now detecting the danger upon him—and something inexplicably caused Ulagu to hesitate. Hardly half a second did he falter, but falter he did, and as a result the man dodged to the side and avoided the blade. The rifle swung up. Ulagu, astounded that for the second time in a day he had made a major blunder, could do nothing but grasp out at the rifle muzzle in hopes of turning it away. By sheer luck he succeeded, pushing the rifle aside as the unaka pulled the trigger. The pan flashed, but nothing else happened. The rifle had misfired.

Ulagu had kept his grip on the gun and now yanked it hard, pulling it from the grasp of its possessor and flinging it aside. His knife flashed out, but in the darkness missed its target. The unaka backed away, and a faint slicing sound in the air informed Ulagu that his opponent had drawn his own knife again and had slashed with it.

The Chickamauga backed away two steps, bending into a crouch and looking for the best way to approach his foe, whose figure was barely visible. Then an odd thing happened. Ulagu felt another moment of hesitation, an unaccountable something that nagged at his mind and roused uncertainty. What was wrong with him? Never before had anything like this occurred.

The man closed in, and a sharp sting in his upper left arm made Ulagu draw in his breath. He probed out with his own blade, missed again. The unaka surprised him, kicking out with a moccasined foot that found Ulagu's belly and knocked him off balance. More clumsily than was typical of him, Ulagu staggered backward. He struggled to right himself, at the same time hearing odd sounds from the throat of his opponent. Fear sounds, unwitting vocalizations, the sounds of a man driven by pure panic.

And again that unexplainable impulse gripped Ulagu, confusing him. He realized it was something in those sounds, no, in the voice that had made them . . . familiar, somehow—and it was suddenly too late to ponder the mystery further, because Ulagu's heel bumped against an unseen log behind him and he fell, face toward the black sky.

The unaka was atop him at once, blade rising, falling, rising again, the unaka making those odd and panicked sounds with each thrust. And it was only in the last moment before life fled his body that Ulagu realized what had caused him to hesitate, and who it was who had killed him.

The army was camped that night at Tellico Plains, where Sevier had erected rough fortifications when they had marched through before, going the other direction. Cooper roasted his share of a beef that had been slaughtered and distributed to the troops, and kept his eye out for Owen, who he now feared would never return.

But he did return, about an hour later. Sitting down wordlessly at the fireside, he stared into the blaze, forearms across his upraised knees and chin on his hands.

"Did you find your knife?"

"Yes."

"Any trouble? You were a long time coming back."

Owen held his silence a few moments before he answered. "Yes, there was some trouble."

"Indians?"

"One Indian."

"Did he see you?"

Owen was slow to answer. "Yes."

"Lord a'mighty, Owen! What happened?"

"I killed him. With my knife."

Cooper took a deep breath. "Well, I'm mighty glad it was you killed him, and not the other way around."

Owen looked up at Cooper. "I dragged his body down the near side of the pass and struck fire to some of my powder. I wanted to see his face."

"Why?"

"I don't know . . . something about him . . . it was just something I had to do."

"It was dangerous. The fire could have brought others down on you."

"Well, it didn't." Owen snapped the words. Silence followed. "The light showed his face. It—" He stopped.

Cooper asked, "Did you know him, Owen?"

Owen looked down at his feet. "No," he said. "Just another Indian. That's all."

He went to his bedroll and lay down, back to the fire and Cooper.

*   *   *

Owen had finally drifted off to a troubled sleep when shots awakened him. He sat up, groping for his rifle.

The Indians were shooting into the camp from a nearby ridge, guiding their shots by the light of the fires. Owen rolled away from the campfire as Cooper rose and scattered the burning wood with his foot, reducing the light and making the target more imprecise. Across the camp others were doing the same.

John Sevier appeared, striding to the front of the camp and shouting at the hidden Indians with defiance, seemingly unafraid of their gunfire.

"Listen to me!" Sevier yelled. "I've burned your towns to satisfy the crimes you have done against my people. Now I am ready to return home, if you will not further molest my men. I am sorry it was necessary to harm your towns and bring trouble to your women and children, but you have provoked it, you have brought it on yourself. Now hear me: If you don't stop firing on my men, I will return to your nation and destroy every town in it!"

A pause, then a cry from the darkness: "Will you?"

"Yes!" Sevier bellowed back. "I'm damned if I won't!"

More silence. The air hung heavy with it. It remained unbroken the rest of the night, and by the next morning the army knew the Indians were gone, driven off by the losses their people had suffered, and by the sheer grit and brashness of Nolichucky Jack Sevier.

The fever had passed, leaving Joshua Colter weak but relieved of the sweats and aches and bad dreams sickness had brought. He had never been prone to illness in his life, and it disturbed him that he had been sick twice this very year. It was a sign of age, and he took no pleasure in it.

But he did take pleasure in the extra time with Darcy that sickness had given him. Now that the illness itself was past, he felt well enough to enjoy her company and conversation. Darcy was to him the most beautiful and delightful of women. Never mind that her face was plain by most men's standards, and one of her hands was withered and small. Such things mattered not at all. Joshua had the only Darcy Fiske Colter there was anywhere, and that made him as gifted as any king across any distant ocean.

Joshua was out chopping wood the day that Cooper Haverly rode through the stockade gate with an oddly familiar stranger at his side. The stranger remained a stranger only a minute. Joshua stared, recognition dawned, and he dropped his axe and ran forward.

"Owen? Owen Killefer? Is that you?"

"Aye," Owen said, grinning. "It's me. How are you faring, Captain Colter?"

Darcy appeared at the door, wiping her hands on a rag and gaping in astonishment as she realized who the new arrival was. She tossed the rag aside as she ran out to greet him, and to welcome Cooper home.

From the door of Cooper's cabin a screech of delight wafted skyward as Hannah Haverly came darting out to reunite with her husband. As they embraced, she caught sight of Owen, let out a fearful-sounding yell and jumped back. "An Indian!" she declared.

Cooper laughed and pulled her back to him. "No, not an Indian, nor even a ghost, though you might think so. It's Owen Killefer, and he's got a story to tell that will peel your hide."

"I don't want stories right now—I want you," Hannah declared.

They built a big bonfire in the center of the family stockade that night, and roasted pork on spits. Smokes and sparks rose into the dark sky. Food was good, the company better. Even Owen Killefer, whose life had been so disrupted for so long, felt like he was home.

And though he wasn't a praying man by habit, Owen prayed that night, giving thanks for his freedom and life, and for his friends. Then he prayed for other people and situations . . . mostly for Nell. He prayed for the soul of Emaline, who he believed slain. And last of all he prayed for Sadayi, widowed by his hand, to his sorrow.

21

Nell Hice felt very small and
alone as she stood in the autumn wind, a shawl across
her shoulders, her hair pulled up beneath an undeco-
rated cap of the style brought to the frontier by German
settler women. Before her was a grave, days old, marked
with a stone upon which was carved the name of Dover
Hice.

Now that the first shock of her husband's sudden
death was fading, Nell was able to see the irony in it.
Dover had successfully made a treacherous river voyage
in times of Indian trouble, had endured a terrific storm
that robbed him of slaves, an employee, horses, and
abundant goods. He had taken his claim and erected a
small but well-built cabin. And then, with all those overcome trials freshly behind him, he had awoken one night,
complaining in a panic of pain in his chest and an inability to draw his breath deeply. He had arisen, walked
across to the fireplace, leaned his hand on the mantelpiece, and collapsed with a groan. He was dead before
Nell could reach him. What storms and dangers hadn't
achieved, a faulty heart had.

Nell was honest enough with herself not to pretend
she grieved for her husband in the usual manner. She

rarely even lingered by his grave, as she was today. She had gotten out her grieving over Dover Hice while he was still alive—grief over the fact that the Dover Hice of reality was far from the Dover Hice she had perceived before marriage. What she missed, now that he was dead, was not particularly the man himself, but the security he had provided, the support of having a mate and partner.

Her true grief was reserved for Owen Killefer, who she was sure had died on the river or, worse, at the hands of Indians. Nell was widowed and isolated, living far from family and friends on a frontier increasingly ravaged by Indians. She was grateful for the comfort of having a stockade nearby; it was recently built by neighbors and stood so close to Nell's cabin that when the leaves were off the trees, she could see its log palisades pointing their sharpened tops toward the clouds. She had fled to the safety of that stockade twice since coming here—once with Dover, the second time alone.

Now she faced a decision. What should she do in light of Dover's passing? Her indecision over this so far had kept her from even writing to her family to tell them of his death. As far as the Carneys knew, nothing in Nell's marital situation had changed.

A noise behind her made her turn, and for a moment she was frightened, misinterpreting the sight presented to her. Indians! Then the approaching group drew closer, and she saw they weren't Indians at all, though two of them, a young black man on foot, limping badly, and a mounted woman, white-skinned and approximately Nell's age, were dressed in Indian manner. The third and last of the group was an old man with a rifle cradled over his arm. His white beard was long and bushy and hung to the middle of his chest; his smallish head was covered with a furry Canadian cap with a tuft at the crown. The tuft was his only condescension to ornamentation. His clothing was buckskin, very old and worn, lacking beads or fringes. The old man was vaguely familiar, but it was to the black-skinned man that Nell's eyes were most drawn. As he came nearer, she suddenly understood why he intrigued her.

"Jubal?" she said, putting her hand to the base of her throat like she always did when astonished. "Jubal—is that you?"

"Yes'm, it is me," he said. "Hello, Miz Nell."

Jubal—alive! How could it be? How had he survived the destruction of the flatboat? Who were these people with him, and how had they found her?

"Jubal? Heaven be praised—I believed you were dead!"

"I was a prisoner of the Chickamaugas, Mrs. Hice. But I got free of them, and brung her out with me." He gestured up at the young white woman, who was looking down at Nell with an expression that combined caution and intense interest. Nell looked up into the tanned, dirty face, and felt unnerved. The girl bore a resemblance to someone she knew—and with a start she realized the someone was Owen Killefer.

Then it came to her: If Jubal was still alive, might Owen be alive as well? And confusion, hope, joy, and astonishment mixed and left her speechless.

"Howdy there, my lady," the white-bearded man said, tipping up his fur hat. In her excitement, Nell had all but overlooked him, so his voice startled her. "Do you remember me? I'm Asher Felton. I come to see your husband a month ago, looking for work."

Nell did remember. That was why Felton looked familiar. The old hunter and trapper, who supposedly had a cabin somewhere, but who spent most of his time roaming the wild country, living off the land and residing in caves and crude forest shelters, had sought employment with Dover, who had turned him down quite gruffly and sent him on his way. After Felton had gone, Dover had summarily declared him unfit for trust; he had "heard some bad talk about him."

"Yes ... I remember you, Mr. Felton." She looked around the group, waved her hands helplessly and said, "I'm bewildered."

"We have somewhat to talk about, indeed we do," Felton said. He glanced around Nell to look at Dover Hice's grave. "So, Mr. Hice *did* die. I had heard it, but didn't know for certain. Mighty sorry, my lady."

Even though Nell wondered how sincere that condolence was, given the way Hice had treated Felton, she nodded her appreciation for the sympathetic comment. Then she invited the group over to the cabin porch, eager to hear what they had to tell her, and full of newborn hope that Owen Killefer might still be among the living.

John Sevier rode into Jonesborough on a crisp October day, uncharacteristically drunk. Alexander Carney was walking down the street, shoulders slumped and spirits low, his mind sunk into a mire of depression, when Sevier guided his horse over and demanded, "You, Carney! Where is the meeting of the militia officers being held!"

Alexander replied, "It's over, Colonel. They've already dismissed."

To that Sevier replied with some fierce swearing, and rode on down the street with the spirit of abandonment brought on by liquor. Alexander watched him listlessly, noting that Sevier obviously was upset about something or another, but not caring at all what it was. He had his own problems to mull over.

Since his humiliation by Andrew Jackson at the Greasy Cove horse race, Alexander had noticed a great and negative difference in the way people treated him. He was whispered about, ignored, sometimes actually taunted from the doors of taverns or the shadows of alleyways. This morning he had left the house and happened to glance up at the shingle that hung on a post at the gate: ALEXANDER E. CARNEY, ATTORNEY-AT-LAW. He had painted it neatly with his own hand. In the night, someone had vandalized the title with big, boyish letters. ALEXANDER E. CARNEY, COWARD. That was how it now read. Alexander had ripped the shingle off its pole and flung it into the yard with an oath.

He tried not to resent Andrew Jackson for what had happened, but it was hard. And it made it harder, oddly, to have learned only the day before that Jackson was ready to journey on to Nashville, as the town at Fort Nashborough was now called. It seemed that Jackson had been able to find a place in a large body of travelers bound for the Cumberland—and with the current Indian strife, only a large traveling group had any reasonable hope of being safe on such an extended wilderness trek. Alexander was intensely irritated by the thought of Jackson trailing off to the Cumberland, there, most likely, forgetting the hurt he had doled out to a fellow barrister. But Alexander could never forget it. Nor would the people of his area. By making him look a coward, Jackson had wounded Alexander Carney's reputation in a fundamental way.

Yet this was not the total of Alexander Carney's worries. His father Charles was an even greater concern.

The old colonel's physical and mental decline had done nothing but escalate. Colonel Carney was a very unstable man, prone to abrupt swings of mood, agitation, and very deep confusion over his place and circumstances. There were no more "good" days for the old gentleman, as there had been before Mary Carney's death. Colonel Carney's decline obviously was not going to reverse itself, and it gave Alexander no comfort to recall that the colonel's own father had gone through an identical deterioration in the winter of his own life. Such things, he had heard, were sometimes inherited. Such might be his own future.

Alexander was struggling against an unwanted conclusion. His father needed care beyond that which his slave Titus could provide. With Nell far away, only he himself could fill that gap. It was increasingly obvious that circumstances would soon force him to leave his own house and move back into his father's home. He didn't want to do it; he enjoyed living independently. But duty was duty. Besides, with people now going so far as to mock his reputation on his very shingle, maybe it wouldn't be so hard to leave his present quarters.

Deep in contemplation of these matters, Alexander turned and began pacing down the other side of the street, watching his toes scuff the dirt before them. A noise ahead caused him to look up. There was John Sevier, arguing loudly with Major David Craig, one of the participants in the day's meeting of militia officers. Alexander had no involvement in that meeting, which had concerned discussion of a possible second strike against the Chickamaugas in the wake of Joseph Martin's failure. Participating had been Martin himself, along with Colonel Love of Greasy Cove, and Colonel John Tipton, Sevier's old antagonist. Sevier himself had not been invited to take part, and that, Alexander gathered from what he could make out of Sevier's slurred shouts, was what had Sevier angry.

Others came and pulled Sevier away from Craig. As they hustled him away, trying to calm him, Alexander recalled something he had overheard outside the courthouse earlier in the day. He had not heard enough to fully understand it, but it had to do with a North Carolina arrest warrant for Colonel Sevier, issued earlier in the year, now being in the hands of John Tipton. The men talking of it had laughed about the matter, so Alexander had dismissed it as a joke. Now he wondered if there might be something to it. Perhaps Sevier's anger had something to do with the warrant.

Later in the day, Alexander witnessed a second loud display from Sevier, who came pounding on the door of merchant David Deaderick, demanding liquor. Deaderick came to the door, he and the colonel exchanged words, and Sevier went to his horse, mounted, and rode off in a huff.

Alexander walked up to Deaderick, one of the few men around town who hadn't ostracized him because of his reputed cowardice. "The colonel is in quite a state tonight, eh?"

"Hello, Alex. Aye, he is. He's off now, and mad as blazes. He's an angry man."

"Over what?"

"Oh, over Franklin's decline, over the jibes his enemies constantly throw at him, over military affairs, General Martin, John Tipton— over the whole deuced world, you might say. He believes he has been slighted by being excluded from the militia meeting today. He's off now to Jacob Brown's old place to spend the night. I say Godspeed to him. With him in such a state, I've no need for him around here."

Alexander took a deep breath. "Well, Colonel Sevier has my sympathy. There are problems enough for all of us in this world, are there not, David? Good evening to you."

"Good evening, Alex. Enjoy your walk."

Joshua opened the door of his cabin and jumped back as Cooper Haverly bolted through, followed by Mark Travis. Owen Killefer, living for the present with the Colters, stood as the men entered.

"Joshua, Owen, get your rifles," Cooper said. "John Sevier's been arrested."

"By bloody old Tipton hisself!" Travis added.

"Arrested—on what grounds?"

"A North Carolina warrant, given out earlier in the year but slowed up somehow or another. Well, it's wound its way around to Tipton's hands. Sevier came into Jonesborough yesterday afternoon, stirred up some trouble, then rode out and spent the night at Jacob Brown's widow's place. Tipton got word of where he was and rode out there, got there early this morning and took Sevier prisoner."

"He's in Tipton's custody? Fires of hell—Tipton will kill him!"

"It was Colonel Love he directly surrendered to," Travis said. "Love joined himself to Tipton, but he holds Colonel Sevier in high regard. I hope he'll keep him safe. I understand that he was trying to persuade Tipton to take the chains off Sevier . . ."

"Tipton had *chained* him?"

"Indeed—and would have hanged him on the spot if cooler heads hadn't stopped it."

"Where will they take Sevier?"

"Morganton, I'm told. In the meantime, Colonel Love is remaining here to talk to Kate Sevier and see if some sort of money or sustenance can't be sent to her husband."

Joshua ran his hand through his hair. "Well, we can't let Sevier be eat up by wolves. He needs more than sustenance—he needs rescue. We'll have to go after him."

"There's already plans afoot, Joshua," Cooper said. He grinned. "Glad you want to be a part of them."

Joshua slapped Cooper's shoulder and grinned back. "Go saddle my horse, brother. I'll fetch my rifle and fixings. Owen, you want to come too?"

"Wouldn't want to miss it."

"Good. Gentlemen, let's move with all due haste."

The forted station called Gillespie's stood on the Holston in the Little River region. It was a small outpost, sparsely occupied, and the few male defenders inside it knew the odds of holding out successfully were slim. Still, they were determined. Outside, about two hundred warriors under John Watts, who had so recently quailed before the obstinate John Sevier on the Tellico Plains, were hungry for a more successful fight. John Watts was determined too.

The battle began as the sun edged up. On the rifle platforms, the men fired cautiously, because their ammunition was as limited as their numbers. The women and children reloaded the rifles, each time using as light a charge as they dared to stretch their dwindling powder.

And for a time the defense seemed to be going well. Some dared hope that John Watts's warriors would at last tire and give up the attack.

It wasn't to be. Soon the ammunition was all but gone, and as it petered away, so did hope. The Indians, a mix of Cherokees and Creeks, saw their opportunity and rushed the station, boosting themselves over the walls, scrambling across the roofs, dropping into the midst of the unarmed people. Screams arose from women and children who watched their fathers and brothers slaughtered before their eyes. Then the women began to fall victim, some being taken prisoner, others killed outright. One woman, pulled back and forth between two warriors, was knifed to death by one of them when he grew too exasperated with the tug-of-war. When it was done, about thirty women and children were prisoners, and corpses lay all about.

With the bodies still inside, the fort was set afire, and in the ruins, John Watts and three other chiefs left a note to John Sevier and Joseph Martin, accusing the whites of having prompted the attack by their refusal to abandon the region, and strongly implying that Sevier was responsible for the murder of Old Tassel.

The massacre at Gillespie's sickened the embattled residents of other Holston-region stations, not only because of the horror of it in itself, but because it represented one more success for the Indians, one more motivation for them to strike again and then again.

The group was small, consisting of Sevier's brother, Joseph; his son, John Sevier Junior; Cooper Haverly, Joshua Colter, Mark Travis, Nathaniel Evans, Owen Killefer, and a handful of others. They crossed the mountains, following the narrow and often winding roads into Burke County. They didn't know just what circumstance they would find Sevier in, but Joseph Sevier didn't seem too worried. "We'll go to Kate's brother Uriah," he said. "I expect he's already familiar with the situation and has interceded."

It was as anticipated. Uriah Sherrill informed them that brothers Charles and Joseph McDowell, two of North Carolina's most revered sons and Sevier's old partners in war-making against the British, had come to him shortly after Sevier was brought in to Morganton. Already they had taken Sevier in under their own charge to keep him from imprisonment, and had asked Sherrill to pay Sevier's trial bond. Sherrill had agreed without hesitation. Sevier was, after all, his brother-in-law.

But Sevier, though now free on bond, was not at Uriah Sherrill's house. He was with the McDowell brothers, and if Uriah's guess was good, could be found in Morganton the next day, most likely sharing old stories with his North Carolina comrades.

"It looks like this rescue might not turn out to be much of a rescue at all," Joshua said that night as he stretched out his blankets on the floor at Sherrill's house. "Old John's likely having the time of his life. He might not even want to go home."

"Don't count on that," Cooper replied. "There's danger for him here. You heard about the shooting. Carolina is no safe place for the governor of Franklin."

The shooting Cooper was referring to was a remarkable story Sherrill had told them earlier in the day. He in turn had heard the story from the McDowells, who had heard it from Sevier himself. It seemed to Joshua to be one more illustration of Sevier's seemingly superhuman ability to escape danger.

The people who had actually taken Sevier across the mountains under guard had been Jacob Tipton, John Tipton's brother, one Tom Gorley, and a third man named George French. Colonel Love had been part of the escort only as far as Greasy Cove, where he had successfully talked the others out of requiring Sevier to wear chains all the way across the mountains.

During the journey to Morganton, Gorley and French had conspired to make Sevier attempt an escape, all for the chance to have an excuse to shoot him dead. Gorley had come to Sevier on the sly, telling him he'd best flee because French intended to kill him at first chance. See that horse there? Gorley had said. Take it and run—it's your only hope.

Sevier, having already narrowly escaped being hanged by John Tipton when he was arrested at the Jacob Brown house, believed Gorley and at first opportunity leaped on the horse and tried to run. Immediately Gorley's treachery became evident. He had lamed the horse to make Sevier easy to catch. French pursued, caught Sevier, and fired a pistol at him almost point-blank. The powder flashed in the pan, scorching Sevier's face, but the main charge missed fire and Sevier's life was saved.

Gorley's and French's lives too, it turned out. After the incident, Jacob Tipton declared that had his companions killed Sevier, he would have killed them. Despite his brotherhood to Sevier's most bitter enemy, Jacob Tipton was not a malicious, hate-mongering, grudge-bearing man. Sevier was to be protected, not harmed. Had the others succeeded in their scheme, he declared, he would have put bullets through their heads for it.

"I doubt Sevier is in danger now, not with Joe McDowell guarding him," Joshua said to Cooper. "I expect we'll find him having a fine old time. Owen, I hope you ain't disappointed at this adventure turning out so tame."

Owen shook his head. "I've had adventures enough to last me for nigh most my life." He lowered his voice. "The only thing about this I don't like is that it reminds me that there was one other rescue I tried to make that came too late to do any good."

Joshua slapped Owen's shoulder. "You tried. It wasn't your fault Turndale did what he did. Put it behind you, Owen. Put it behind and go on."

They rode into Morganton the next morning. Court was out of session, and the Burke County sheriff was not even in town. The group plodded down the center of the street on their horses, drawing interested glances from onlookers. One man stepped up to Joseph Sevier and said, "If you're looking for 'Chucky Jack, try yonder place." He pointed to a tavern.

"Thank you, sir. But I must ask you why you believe I've come for Sevier."

"Why, I can see the look of him in your face. Brother? I thought so. Yes sir, you're men from over-the-mountain—I can see it in your ways and bearing."

John Sevier's back was to the door when his "rescuers" came in, so it was Joseph McDowell who first saw them. He stood, grinning and extending his hand, as Sevier turned and did the same. "Here so soon, brother?" Sevier said to his sibling. "I'd have hoped it would take you longer—me and the major here have been having a good talk over old times."

Hands were shook all around, introductions made where required, and the powder burn on Sevier's face was examined and commented upon. The men sat down together, pulling tables against each other, ordering food and drink and entering into as pleasant a time of comradery as any had known in a good while. At one point Joshua looked over at Cooper and said, "I think the danger has past, eh, brother?"

"Reckon it has."

Joseph Sevier stood. "John, we've come to fetch you home. Your horse is outside."

"I'm under sheriff's orders not to leave."

"Does that have aught to do with anything?"

"Not a bit of it." John Sevier stood, putting out his hand to Joseph McDowell. "Major, it's been a pleasure to share your company."

"And yours, Colonel. We'll hope to meet again under better circumstances."

They rode out of Morganton in the clear light of day, making no pretenses and expecting no pursuit. The people here knew John Sevier, who had fought alongside so many of their men at King's Mountain and ridden so frequently against the Indians of their state; no one desired to see him harmed. Sevier and company made their ride home in the highest of spirits, with Sevier talking of hosting a celebration as soon as they arrived.

Joshua edged his horse over to Owen's. "We ought to get John arrested more often," he said. "It's done more to lift his spirits than anything that's come down the way in a durn long time."

When John Sevier promised a celebration, it was a pledge to prick the ears of the most somnolent. Jubilees at Mount Pleasant, as John and "Bonnie Kate" Sevier called their Nolichucky River home, were generally days long, featuring dancing, shooting, racing, roasting, eating, storytelling, betting, and most of all, excellent company and conversation.

Upon his return from North Carolina, Sevier launched a party that he pledged would last a week if it lasted a day. Cabins all over the countryside emptied as people made their way to Mount Pleasant, and the Colter and Haverly families were among the throngs.

With Owen Killefer at his side, Joshua Colter stood with cup in hand and a smile on his face, tapping his foot to the tune of "The White Cockade," played by a fiddler named Black who had wandered onto the scene and been invited to stay. Not a bad fiddler, in Joshua's estimation, though he had always enjoyed Callum McSwain's jigs more than any other fiddle music he had heard.

Joshua looked across the colorful sight of the swinging and bobbing dancers, at men talking big talk and comparing rifles, at others eyeing some of Sevier's horses. A few Indians wandered about; Sevier had a habit of bringing home Indian prisoners from his campaigns and keeping them on the grounds of his home, where they were treated well and usually made into friends of the family. It was an odd thing, the "Cherokee scourge" taking on Indian friends like that. Odd, but good. More friendships might just mean less fighting.

His smile faded as he noticed two men sitting off to the side of it all, looking out of place, and in one case, unhappy. The unhappy one was Alexander Carney, a man who these days lived alone in the midst of his own people, shamed by the stigma of cowardice. The other man was Charles Carney, and although he was not unhappy at all, the sight of him was even more saddening than that of his moping son. Carney had a broad grin on his face and was talking expansively, waving his hand in the air—and no one was listening. He was exhorting incoherently to the treetops, unaware he had no audience.

It was hard to watch a good man decline; it reminded

Joshua of seeing Alphus Colter, his adoptive father, in his own last years, when his mind was slipping. In Alphus's case, however, the problem had been deep, intense brooding spells that no one could break through. Colonel Carney was not like that at all. He was talkative, vocal, but in a reality apart from that everyone else lived in. His state was worse by the week. Joshua had learned only an hour or so before that Alexander Carney had the day prior moved back into his father's house to see to his care. The old man couldn't be counted on to have the competence any more not to hurt himself.

Joshua glanced over and caught his own son and a couple of his young friends snickering at Colonel Carney from the other side of the fence. Joshua caught Will's eye and flashed him a look that took the smile right off the boy's face. Looking chagrined, Will crept away. Joshua fought back his anger. He despised seeing folks laughed at for things they can't help. But, Joshua reminded himself, Will was only a boy. All too soon he would learn to see the sadness in what now struck him only as funny.

About an hour later, when Joshua was engrossed in conversation with a couple of John Sevier's sons, and Owen was off by the bonfire enjoying the attention of two attractive young women who found his tale of Indian captive romantic and thrilling, Darcy came to her husband and grasped his shoulder. "Joshua, there's trouble with Alexander—over in the trees yonder."

Joshua immediately went to the indicated area, followed by several others who had overheard. He found Alexander Carney on the ground, grimacing and gripping his stomach, while a couple of rough-looking frontiersmen taunted and toed him. "Up from there, town boy! What's it take to make you fight? You got no stones on you, is that it?"

"What's going on here?"

The man turned quickly at the sound of Joshua's voice. "Colter . . ." Before he could hold it back, an expression of fear crossed his face. Everyone knew that Joshua Colter was a friend of the Carney family, just as everyone knew that Joshua Colter was not a man one wanted to offend. "Nothing, Colter. Nothing but a little funning."

"Don't look like funning to me. Looks like you're kicking my friend while he's down."

"Corn shucks!" the second man said. "We're just trying to get him to show himself a man, that's all. We're just provoking him some, nothing more."

"You're provoking *me*," Joshua said. "You'd best move on."

Joshua knew lots of people held a fierce respect for him, but he was surprised to see how wide the eyes of both men grew, and how rapidly they scrambled backward. What had he said or done that was all that frightening? The crack of a rifle just behind him immediately let him know it wasn't him that had scared them. He wheeled.

Charles Carney held a smoking flintlock rifle in his wavering hands. He had picked it up unnoticed and brought it in as a tool to rescue Alexander. "Off with you, you two bloody redskins!" he yelled. "You leave my little boy be!"

Lord have mercy, Joshua thought. He's thinking of them as Indians, and of Alexander as a child.

"Colonel Carney, calm yourself. Everything is fine," Joshua said. "Alexander ain't hurt. Just let me have the rifle."

Charles Carney crunched his bushy brows together. "Sir, do I know you? What are you, the Indian agent?"

Alexander was on his feet now, looking deeply embarrassed. "Thank you, Joshua," he said. "I'll take care of him from here on out."

"Are you well, Alexander?"

"I'm well. Thank you for your help. I'll take Father home now."

Joshua sadly watched the Carneys walk away, Colonel Carney still babbling about Indians. Darcy came to Joshua and slipped her arm around his. They watched wordlessly as the Carney men mounted and rode away together down the road until they were swallowed by the darkness. Joshua and Darcy returned to the celebration, but the festive spirit had been drained from both of them, and for the rest of the evening they stayed together, apart from the others, and talked quietly between themselves.

One night later, Colonel Charles Carney rose at midnight and walked, mumbling and grumbling and naked, through his house. He looked into the little room in which Alexander now lived, and saw the bed empty.

"So they've returned," he said aloud in the darkness. "Bloody savages think they can return on me and harm my own!" He went back to his own room, looking for his rifle. It was missing. Alexander had quietly hidden the colonel's rifle immediately after returning from the celebration at Sevier's. In Charles Carney's mind, however, the rifle had been taken by the Indians, whom he vividly imagined were even now creeping about the cabin.

"Take a man's rifle, will you! I'm damned if I'll stand for it . . ."

He went back to Alexander's room and, behind the door, found his son's long rifle. Alexander Carney had seldom used the weapon, but kept it loaded and in fine condition, with powder and ammunition close by it.

"I'll kill them, one and all," the senile old man said in a hoarse voice. His mind blended past times and present, old circumstances and current. "Steal Belshazzar, will they! Murder young Owen's father, and capture my son? No, no! Not without hearing from me they won't!"

Titus, who enjoyed a privilege seldom given to slaves—a bed in the loft of the house—descended the ladder, wearing only his trousers. "Colonel Carney, sir? Is something wrong?"

The old man spun, knocking the rifle barrel against the door and almost losing his grip on the gun. He pulled it back and free, and swung it up at his slave. "Savage!" he shouted as loudly as he could, and fired.

Titus fell back, his heart pierced by his own master's rifle ball, and died instantly. Colonel Carney looked down at the body in the darkness. "May God have mercy on your soul, Cherokee heathen! You'll hurt me and mine no longer!" He looked around. "Alexander! Where are you, boy?"

No answer came back. The past clawed out to further tighten its claim on Colonel Carney's perceptions. In his thoughts Alexander was a small boy again. "Down by the creek, I'll wager. How many times have I told him not to play there after dark? The bloody Indians have probably killed and scalped him by now. If they have, I'll yank his ear till he howls!"

He turned and shouted back toward his bed, "Wait for me, Mary! I'm off to fetch Alex, and will be back. Have supper waiting, if you please!"

The old man paused at the door and took his coat from its peg. He slipped it on and closed it around his naked white body, hefted up the spent rifle and walked into the darkness, leaving the door standing open behind him.

The sight of the front door standing ajar brought Alexander Carney to a halt. Unable to sleep, he had gone out for a midnight stroll, bearing his griefs with him. When he had left, his father was snoring loudly, sleeping that deep sleep from which it was usually hard to rouse him. Alexander had even climbed to the loft to ask Titus to rise if he heard the Colonel do so, just to be sure all was well. Titus had agreed and Alexander had left, taking his walking stick and the dogs.

The cool air had been refreshing, the night comforting. His burden had lightened. It was a happy thing to be on the road when no others were up and about, enjoying utter solitude, without responsibility, burdens, shame. When Alexander turned and headed back toward his house, he felt more rested than when he had begun.

Then came the sight of the open door, and the memory that he had closed it securely when he left. For a moment a dozen possibilities, all of them frightening, raced through his head. "Father . . ." He ran to the cabin.

"Father! Father? Where are you?"

No answer from the interior darkness. He ran toward his father's room, tripped and sprawled over something warm, heavy, fleshy. He sat up. "Oh no, Father . . ."

He felt the body, and realized it wasn't his father, but Titus. No breath, no pulse. He was dead! When Alexander pulled his hand away from Titus's chest, he felt a warm, thick liquid on his fingers and knew it was blood.

His first thought was that someone had entered the cabin in his absence and killed Titus and his father. Oh God, might it have been some of the ones who had tormented him lately, come to harm him but harming others instead? Alexander went to the fire, poked up the ashes, and lit a candle from a hot coal. Cupping his trembling hand to shield the flame, he explored the house, desperately looking for Charles Carney's body.

There was no body to be found. His father was gone.

Puzzled and feeling an agonizing burning in the pit of his stomach, Alexander stood in the center of the cabin, trying to figure out what might have happened. He went back to his room, gingerly stepping over the body on the floor. He looked behind his door. His rifle and ammunition were not there.

Alexander didn't at all like the direction his thoughts were taking. He was beginning to believe no one had trespassed in this house at all. His mind went back to the celebration at Sevier's house, his father firing off that rifle at those men, yelling about Indians . . .

I should have never left the house tonight. It's my fault. Father has killed Titus and left, and it's my fault.

Alexander, blinking back tears, left the cabin and went out to the road. He looked in both directions, wondering which way his father might have gone. He hadn't encountered his father on his walk, so most likely the old man had headed the other way, toward town.

Alexander drew in a deep breath and set off at a lope down the road toward the little log town.

Salem Pinnock sat down the mug in front of Joshua Colter and sadly shook his head as he nestled his heavy body into the chair opposite. ". . . and the rest you've probably heard. Alexander found the colonel by the roadside just outside of town, shot near to death and bleeding badly. He passed away cradled in his arms."

"And the rifle missing from the house was not there," Joshua said. "It must have taken by whoever it was who shot the colonel."

"Yes, and there's the strangest part, don't you think?"

"The rifle being taken? Not strange as I see it. Robbery was probably the reason the colonel was shot."

"Ah, you haven't heard it all, have you? Has no one told you what the colonel said at the last, just before he died?"

"No."

Pinnock leaned forward. "He said that the man who shot him had someone with him. Parnell Tulley."

Joshua stared at Pinnock for a moment, then gave one mirthless chuckle. "You've picked a queer time to make a jest, Salem."

"No jest, no jest. That's what Colonel Carney said. Alexander told me that himself. While he lay dying, the colonel told Alexander how he had come upon Tulley and the other man in the darkness, recognized Tulley in the moonlight, and declared he would take him into his custody. Colonel Carney leveled his rifle on Tulley, but when he pulled the trigger, the gun was empty. The man with Tulley pulled out a pistol and shot the colonel with it. That's the very tale he himself told Alexander with his last breaths."

Joshua shook his head. "Well, it's as fool a bit of babble as the old fellow ever came up with. Owen Killefer says Tulley has been among the Chickamaugas as a trader—he saw him with his own eyes, and spoke to him, even busted his head with a rock one time. And even if Tulley got away from the Indian towns, he sure as blazes wouldn't come back here, where he's killed one man already and is sought by the law. I'm telling you, it was one of the colonel's wild notions."

Pinnock firmly shook his head. "I don't believe that, Joshua. The evidence of truth is all there. Colonel Carney's story was full of detail. It was clear and consistent. I believe his sensibilities returned to him at the end. I know such a thing can happen. My own mother babbled and raved for two weeks before her own death, and the last three hours of her life she was as clear of mind as when she was a young girl."

Joshua drained off his mug, stood and shook his head. "Maybe so, Salem, but I don't accept it in the colonel's case. I don't believe even Parnell Tulley would be fool enough to come back to parts where he's had such troubles in the past."

"This is still a wild country, Joshua. A man can hide himself easily, even among the settlements. And in times of Indian troubles, what better place to be?"

Joshua hadn't thought about it that way. It made a certain sense. He shrugged. "Maybe you're right. But I hope not. We don't need such as Tulley around. Well, good day to you, Salem, I'm off for home. If you should see Alexander by chance, give him my sorrows at the death of his father, and tell him I'll be by to pay my respects in person the next time I'm about Jonesborough."

"I shall, though I doubt I'll see him. Alexander mostly hides away these days, ever since that unfortunate matter with Mr. Jackson."

"Aye. That he does," Joshua replied. "Good day to you."

"Good day, Joshua. Come again soon."

Joshua rode home slowly, thinking over the sad story of Colonel Carney's death. Parnell Tulley, back in the Nolichucky settlements? Would he really be brazen enough to return? Surely not. Then again . . .

Joshua reluctantly decided he should mention the rumor to Owen. Perhaps that would be disturbing the young man over a mere dying delusion of Colonel Carney. But if the rumor held even a chance of being true, Owen had a right to know about it.

* * *

Owen Killefer dismounted and stood for a full minute beside his big Chickasaw horse, looking at the overgrown pathway that led toward his father's old house. His feelings were stirred by this place. Memories came back; it was remarkable how few of them were at all pleasant. And the gloom of the cloudy late afternoon did nothing to brighten any of them.

I needn't be here, he thought. No reason for me to stir up dead sorrow.

But since his return to the Overmountain settlements, there was very little that didn't stir up sorrow. The fact was, his sorrows really weren't dead at all. The tragedy of his kin's murders, the capture and subsequent death—as he believed—of Emaline, and the tragedy of his father's sad latter days and passing, his unrequited love of Nell . . . all these pains were still alive to Owen Killefer. The death of Tom Turndale had done nothing to allay them.

He looked down the brambly path again. *What the devil,* he thought. *I might as well have a look at my own property.* Taking up the leads of his horse, he began walking down the path toward the house.

Since Aaron Killefer's death, no one had lived in the cabin. The land itself was, technically, Owen's, though he had done nothing with his inheritance. Alexander Carney had at the beginning tried to get him to sell it, but he hadn't done so. He simply hadn't wanted to deal with the matter. At that time, he had cared little for money; his mind had been full of grief and Nell Carney, with little room left for other concerns. But now he was a man rather than a boy, and he had accepted the fact that Nell could not be his. Yes, he decided, he would go ahead and sell the land. God knew he had no desire to live on it. He'd get rid of the place and move off elsewhere. Maybe into Virginia, where he had a distant relative. Or perhaps

Kentucky, a place that had always attracted him. Yes, Kentucky. That was the place.

The Killefer cabin was in great disrepair; it was remarkable how quickly an unoccupied house would decline. Owen walked through the weedy yard, examining the gaping holes in the chinking, the dangling shutters, the rotten door. Looking through a window, he recalled the night he had looked through that same opening to see Parnell Tulley and Three Fingers facing off with his father on the last night of Aaron Killefer's life. He shuddered.

Now he regretted having come down here. He turned and mounted his horse, riding up the trail back toward the road, feeling unsettled. Into his mind flashed the afternoon's conversation with Joshua Colter, who had told him of a rumor that Parnell Tulley was back in the area and had in fact been with the unknown party who killed poor old Colonel Carney. Joshua had indicated he strongly doubted the tale. Owen did too. He didn't believe Tulley would have been able to get away from the Chickamauga towns. It was remarkable enough that he himself had.

Owen returned to the Colter house, where he had been staying since his return from the west. He'd been sleeping in the loft of the cabin, sharing the space with young Will Colter, an active boy nearing twelve years of age. Since his captivity among the Chickamaugas, Owen had grown to giant proportions in Will's eyes. He stood in awe of Owen and bragged to his friends about sharing sleeping quarters with him. Owen found it slightly funny, slightly bothersome, and even a little sad, because thoughts of his captivity now almost always roused anew the pain of having failed to help Emaline before Turndale killed her.

Tonight Will came into the house very late. Owen, already asleep, was awakened by Darcy Colter's scolding voice as she gave her son torment for his lateness. "I was sure you were skinned alive by the Indians," she said. "You ain't too big to turn over my knee, and by my stars, I'm going to do it!"

Owen listened to the sound of mother's hand smacking son's backside, and winced sympathetically. When Will came climbing up to the loft, Owen rose on one elbow.

"Sorry you was whupped."

"Pshaw! Mother can't whup worth a damn."

"She hears you cussing, she'll do it again."

Will scrambled over toward Owen, not seeming at all disturbed at having been punished. He came up close, whispering.

"Owen, me and Jimmy Travis seen somebody tonight, and you'll never suppose who!"

"Tell me, then."

"Parnell Tulley!"

Owen felt a chill that went down to his toes. "Tulley? You sure about that?"

"Yes! We seen him clear as springwater, riding along up the mountain path toward Saul Greentree's old place. We hid, I'll tell you! I'm scared of old Tulley."

"He was alone?"

"No. Had somebody with him."

"That would have been Saul Greentree, I suppose. Lord a'mighty! They really did get away from the Chickamauga towns!"

"It wasn't Greentree. I've seen Greentree before. This was somebody I ain't ever laid eyes on."

Owen frowned. "Look, Will, you could have been wrong. I don't believe Tulley is really about. Did he look the same?"

"Well, not exactly."

"See there? It wasn't him."

"It was him, I tell you! But now he's got a big scar on his head. Big old ugly place, right here, like he'd been hit and had the skin laid open." Will rubbed across the side of his brow. "He had an odd look about him too. I can't put it in words. He was quiet, and just looking straight ahead."

"Well, I don't know that you ain't mistook somebody else for him," Owen said. "Tulley never had no scar before."

"It was him, I'm telling you!"

"If you think you saw Tulley, you ought to tell your pap."

"No! He don't allow me along that path. Says there's too many troublesome folk who travel that way. He'd whup me good if he knew—and his whuppings hurt like hell blaze! They ain't like mother's. You won't tell him, will you?"

"I won't tell. Go to sleep. That's what I'm going to do."

And he did, but only after long thought. Could it really be? He still couldn't swallow the notion. Will had to be wrong.

But the next day Owen was still filled with questions. He called Will aside and quizzed him again; the boy remained as confident as ever that he had seen Parnell Tulley.

By evening Owen knew he had to investigate for himself. He thought he had made peace with the idea of forgetting about Tulley, but the thought of Tulley being this close, of roaming with impunity the very territory in which he had committed his offenses, stirred Owen's blood. Besides, there was the matter of Colonel Carney's death to be considered too. If Tulley and his partner were responsible, they needed to be caught and brought in.

In mid-afternoon Owen went to the barn outside the Colter family stockade, where Cooper Haverly was feeding a monstrous hog that was being fattened for slaughter as soon as the weather grew cold.

He took Cooper into his confidence, telling him what Will had said. "Will you go with me to the old Greentree place, and let me see for myself if it's really Tulley?" he asked. "Or tell me how to get there, and I'll go alone, if you'd like."

"Go alone? No. I'll go with you, this very night. That would be the time to see them on the sneak. By gum, I hope it is Tulley! I'd like to be the man to bring that scoundrel in."

Cooper's excuse to Hannah that evening was that he was taking Owen to Pinnock's inn to see Matthew Barton, who had often been kind to Owen in the past and now was ailing. No, nothing serious, but he was wanting to see Owen, Cooper claimed. It was a total lie; if Barton was sick, Cooper didn't know about it. Hannah accepted the story, however, and Cooper and Owen rode out together, taking their rifles with them. They made sure they left when Joshua was not about, because Owen was determined not to break his pledge of confidence to young Will.

The path up to Greentree's place was nearly as overgrown as that to the old Killefer cabin had been. Since Greentree's departure to become an Indian trader, no one except occasional hunters had had any reason to travel this way, the lure of Greentree's whiskey being removed. Still, the way was sufficiently clear to make both Owen and Cooper believe that someone indeed had been coming and going recently.

Owen felt intensely nervous the closer they came to the top of the ridge. At last Cooper signaled for them to stop, and they dismounted, tying their horses and taking their rifles in hand. Owen followed Cooper as they crept the rest of the way in silence.

There was light at the top, outside the Greentree cabin. A fire, burning in the same spot Greentree and Three Fingers had burned their bonfires back in the days they infested this particular spot. "There's somebody there, sure enough," Cooper said. "We'll see if it might be Tulley."

"I doubt it is."

"You never can tell till you look. Come on, and keep it quiet."

Joshua Colter, his face atypically ashen, galloped to a stop in front of the Pinnock Inn and leaped out of the saddle in a smooth, fluid motion. He had left behind the young boy sent to bring him the news and fetch him to the inn. He was at the door and pushing his way through before Salem Pinnock could even put a hand to the latch. It was about an hour before dawn, and very dark.

"Where is Cooper?"

"Upstairs."

"How bad?"

"Bad . . . but he'll live, Joshua. I'm nigh certain of it."

But Joshua was already pounding his way up to the second story before Pinnock even finished his sentence. Owen Killefer faced him there, eyes wide with the horror of what had happened atop Greentree's ridge. Joshua looked into the young but weathered face for a second, then shoved Owen aside and went into the room.

Cooper was bloody, his chest caked with gore, his face of an unusual, deathly hue. His chest barely moved when he struggled in his feeble breaths.

Matthew Barton was at the far side of the bed. "I dug the ball out of him," he said. "He'll live, I think."

"He has to live. I'll not lose him, I'll not!" Joshua's voice choked; tears came against his will. "God above, I'll not stand for losing him!"

He knelt beside Cooper, putting his hand on the wounded man's shoulder. Owen leaned against the frame of the door, looking weak. Joshua stood, went to him, gestured for him to join him below. In the empty tavern Joshua paced restlessly. "How did it happen?"

"It's a long story."

"Tell it." Joshua continued his pacing, rubbing the back of his neck, tugging at the Roman coin on its thong, sweeping his hands across his hair.

Owen took a deep, trembling breath. He spoke softly. "I had heard a tale that Parnell Tulley and another man had been seen camped at the old Saul Greentree place. Cooper and me went to see if it was true. It was Tulley, all right, and a stranger. The stranger saw us, got the jump on me, and made Cooper drop his rifle.

"He thought we were sheriffs or constables or some such, come to arrest him. He started denying right off that he had killed 'that old man'—and us not having accused him of it, so we knew right off that he surely was the one who had killed the colonel. He said he had come here after running from Crowtown down in the Chickamauga country, where he was a trader among the Indians. He said he was a good man, and kind, and had even taken this other old Indian trader under his wing after he got tomahawked while fleeing from the Chickamauga towns himself—and he pointed over at Tulley, who was sitting and staring and hanging his mouth open like his mind was gone. He was staring right at me, but if he knew me, you couldn't tell it. I reckon it was because of the tomahawking.

"This other fellow, he wouldn't say his name, and kept on declaring he was innocent of anything, that he was just a wayfarer coming through on his way to Virginia, and that the only reason he was in the region was that once he had lived here for a few months. He kept talking, talking, and the more he talked the more worked up he got.

"Cooper and me, we kept looking at each other, because you could tell that something was about to happen, the way this fellow was raging on. All at once Cooper scrambled for his rifle, which the fellow had leaned against a tree close by. Tulley just sat, staring at us like a fool. Cooper got his rifle, but the talking fellow drew out a pistol from behind him and shot Cooper before he could get the rifle level. He took the ball in the lower part of his chest—but he still was able to get off a shot. Killed the man, stone dead. I got Cooper onto his horse and brought him here. It was the closest place, and I knew Mr. Pinnock could help more than anybody else."

"Where is Tulley?"

"Still on the ridge, I reckon, probably sitting by the corpse and staring like he did all through."

Pinnock had just descended and joined them. "Joshua, where is Hannah?"

"I wouldn't let her come, not without knowing what she would find."

Pinnock cocked his ear. "I hear someone coming in outside right now."

"It's Hannah, most likely. And Darcy. I knew they

would come on as soon as I was gone. I don't blame them."

It was as Joshua suspected. The women entered and ascended without words to the upper level. Joshua went with them. Hannah struggled to keep the tears from her eyes as she resolutely declared that Cooper would be fine. Darcy didn't do so well; she stood in the corner, crying despite all her efforts not to.

"Where are the children?" Joshua asked her.

"Will is watching them. Yes, alone. Don't fault me for it. I had to come with her."

"I know."

Joshua again descended to the tavern, rejoining Pinnock and Owen. He went to the mantelpiece and stood gazing into the glowing coals of the nearly dead fire. Owen said, "Joshua, I'm sorry. Mighty sorry. If I hadn't asked Cooper to go to that ridge with me, none of this would have happened."

"It ain't your fault. Cooper is his own man, and he's never run from any kind of danger. If he went, he did it because he wanted to. Don't fret. Salem says he'll live. So does Matthew."

"What do you think? I recall what you said when it was my father lying up in that room. You looked at him and said there was life yet in his face, and that he would make it through. What about Cooper's face? Is there life in it?"

Joshua had no answer.

Pinnock said, "Joshua, there's something that yet must be done. Parnell Tulley must be fetched down from that ridge."

Joshua nodded. "I'll go. I don't think I can bear to linger about here."

"I'll go with you," Owen said.

"Very well—and along the way we'll roust up Lige McKee. His house is near, and he'll be glad to help. Any chance Tulley will be dangerous?"

"Not that I can see. The man's been rendered foolish."

One more time Joshua went to the upper level and to Cooper's bedside. Owen followed, watching. Joshua bent over and looked closely into Cooper's face for almost a minute. When he straightened, he went to Darcy and quietly told her of what he and Owen were going to do. A quick kiss, a final glance at Cooper, and he departed, Owen at his heels.

Outside, as they mounted under the thin light of a new dawn, Owen asked: "What did you see? Is there life in his face?"

Joshua paused before answering. "This is one time I honestly can't say, Owen. He's hurt bad. It's in hands bigger than ours, and all we can do is leave it there. Now let's be off, and see if Tulley is still where you left him."

23

Parnell Tulley was not where Owen had left him, but he wasn't far away. He had wandered to the edge of the clearing, now mostly overgrown, around the cabin and lean-to, and now was sitting on a stump, looking across the forest by the light of morning.

"Tulley?" Joshua said as he approached from behind, rifle ready in case Tulley should turn out to be more lucid, and dangerous, than they anticipated. Tulley did not respond to his voice. Joshua said the name again, and this time Tulley turned and looked at him. The big scar across his brow was starkly visible. It had the look of a scar healed not that long ago.

"Tulley, it's Joshua Colter here. Do you remember me?"

No answer. No sign Tulley comprehended him. Joshua lowered his rifle a little.

"Tulley—can you talk to me?"

Still no answer. Tulley looked away from Joshua and back across the misty autumn forest.

"I'm not sure he even understands you," Owen said.

"I don't believe he does."

They left him sitting there, and went back to examine the body of the man who had been Tulley's companion.

Joshua rolled him over and looked at the pale face. "Well, I'll be! This here is Gideon Bailey. He was at one time part of Greentree's gaggle. I recall when he was in these parts before, there was lots of trouble from him. Look here." Joshua reached down and peeled off a leather glove that covered the base of Bailey's right hand. The glove's fingers had been cut off so that Bailey's digits came through. When the glove was off, Joshua turned the palm up to reveal a branded letter T in the center of it. "See there? He always did wear this glove, never taking it off. I figured he had been branded some time or another. He was the same breed of man as Tulley. Typical of traders; many of them are thieves, or scarcely more."

"Well," Owen said, "there's one thing about him you can't fault. He must have had some bit of mercy in his heart, to take care of Tulley in the shape he's in now."

Joshua nodded. "That's true. As much as I have to despise him for shooting Cooper, I have to agree with you." He drew in a long breath. "Well, we'll drape him over one of them horses yonder"—he pointed at the two hobbled horses, evidently property of Tulley and Bailey, that grazed nearby—"and take him in for burying. As for Tulley, I'd say he's able to ride." He looked at the solitary form of the former troublemaker, still sitting on his stump. "Hard to despise him, in that shape, even when I think of all the bad he's done."

"I know," Owen said. "It makes me feel half guilty. I feel I ought to hate him. If not for him and Three Fingers, my father would yet be living." He paused. "But I can't hate . . . that." He waved toward the pitiful man.

"Come on. Let's get it done. Now that I'm away from Cooper, I'm eager to get back to him again."

*   *   *

Owen watched Joshua as he sat at Cooper's bedside. He felt responsible, having been the one who led Cooper into the deadly situation. What worried Owen most was that he knew this was not the first time in his life that Cooper had been seriously injured. Some years before, Joshua had told Owen, he had been gravely hurt in a battle against a combined band of Chickamaugas and Tory "outliers." Cooper had survived that time. But could a man twice brush the edge of death and return to the living? Owen hoped so.

Over the next week and a half it was obvious several times that Cooper was declining, but each time breath and heartbeat continued, until one day Joshua declared he could now see that indefinable look of life he had been watching for.

A day after that, Cooper was taken home to rest in more familiar environs. He had been unconscious most of the time, and only half conscious whenever he had stirred. Now, however, he was able to look around, even to converse weakly. Owen was as joyous and grateful as anyone. He wouldn't have to bear the guilt of having led Cooper to his death after all.

Owen decided to take his leave of the Nolichucky settlements when it was clear that Cooper would live. The fall was ending now; the trees were bare, and what meager breath of summer warmth had lingered through the waning of the season vanished into the cold emptiness of winter.

Joshua Colter stood in the stockade gate as Owen prepared to ride out.

"Where will you go, Owen?"

"Kentucky, I think. I've always wanted to see that country."

"What about your land here? It's still your property, and you've not dealt with it. It's a good farm. If that old cabin holds too many bad memories, I could help you put up a new one."

"No," Owen replied. "I've given Alexander Carney attorney power to sell it for me. I'll come back and meet with him sometime later to see how he did with it. So I'll be back around. Some of these days."

"I'm glad to hear it. Godspeed to you. Listen: When you get to Kentucky, there's good folks about Logan's Station. Callum McSwain for one, and Israel Coffman. He's a preacher, blinded since the King's Mountain fight. A fine man and a good friend. Look them up and show them this." Joshua took the thong holding the Roman coin from around his neck, reached up and slipped it over Owen's head. The coin glinted dully against his hunting shirt. "They'll know you're a friend of mine when they see that."

"You're giving this to me?"

"For now."

"Why?"

"Two reasons. The first is I want you to know I think highly of you, and that you've got a friend in the Tennessee country if ever you need one. The second is that someday I want to pass that coin on to my son."

"Then why are you giving it to me?"

"Because for me to pass it on, you'll have to bring it back to me. You said you'd come back again. That's my way of making sure you keep that promise."

Owen grinned. Joshua's act both amused him and made him feel honored. "I'm obliged. I'll wear it with pride."

"You do that. And look up Coffman and McSwain in Kentucky. Will you do it?"

"I'll do it."

"Good-bye, Owen."

"Good-bye, Joshua Colter."

Joshua Colter had always held Salem Pinnock in high esteem, but never higher than now, since Parnell Tulley had come back onto the scene in his present state. He was a pitiful figure, silent and seemingly cut off from the world. Sometimes he would react to noises, to the calling of his name or the opening of a door. Other times he would be unreachable.

The man had no family, and no friends who would claim themselves as friends now. Those who had consorted and gambled and laughed and drank with him before now could not be found. They had been blue-sky companions, not friends. It was Pinnock, who had hardly known Tulley, and who never would have claimed friendship with him, who turned out to be his best friend in time of trouble.

Pinnock took Tulley in, giving him a bed and food, caring for him much as he would care for a small child—which was very much what Tulley had become. The selflessness of the innkeeper was remarkable. Even the Reverend Samuel Doak, Pinnock's philosophical opposite, was touched by Pinnock's action, and commented upon it from the pulpit, citing it as an example of "sinners exceeding the righteousness of saints," and shaming the latter in so doing.

Then he spoke words that struck one member of his congregation in particular. "It is the essential part of true manhood not to be self-serving, but selfless, and the essential part of selflessness not to be prideful, but humble. It is to seek mercy rather than vengeance, and to forgive even as we have been forgiven: without reservation, without payment, without limit."

Joshua and his family were present in the church the day Doak preached that sermon. When the congregation rose to leave, Joshua noticed that Alexander Carney remained on his bench after all others had left. When the Colters began their ride homeward, Alexander was still talking intensely with Doak, a thoughtful frown on his face.

Three days later Joshua had the pleasure of taking Cooper on his first trip to the inn since his wounding. When they arrived, Joshua noticed that the stool upon which Tulley usually sat in the corner was empty.

"Where's Tulley, Salem?"

"Gone to his new home."

"New home? Where?"

"Beyond Jonesborough. Colonel Carney's old house."

"What? Are you saying—"

"Indeed. Alexander Carney came to me two days ago, telling me he wished to take over Tulley's care. I hardly knew what to make of it; I wondered if he was drunk or looking for some means of getting Tulley away so he could do him harm. After all, Tulley has certainly been involved in enough grief for the Carney family. But he persuaded me he meant it. I gathered that a sermon by our good friend the Reverend Doak had something to do with it. And Andrew Jackson too."

"Jackson? How so?"

"Because of the humiliation that Jackson brought to him. He forced Alexander to ponder what it meant to suffer, and what it meant to be an honorable man. His conclusion was that man is man in the best sense of the word when he puts his pride aside and seeks the welfare of others. And that way, for him, would be to care for Parnell Tulley, a man who by all rights he should despise."

"I'll be jiggered!"

"Aye, it's astounding, is it not? Alexander Carney is quite a man after all, eh? He's proven himself better than most, and Jackson's challenges and the so-called 'honor' of battle look rather pale in that light. By heaven, I'm no religious man in Sam Doak's sense of the word, but I know goodness when I see it, and I know honor, and I know courage. There'll be no man who'll dare to again mock the manliness or dignity of Alexander Carney in my presence, not if he wants to warm his backside at my fireplace or drink his fill of my liquor!"

Joshua grinned. "Salem, you've grown red from your chin all the way up your pate, just like the Reverend Doak when he's going at it hard. Before you know it, you'll be off missionarying to the Indians or something."

"I doubt it, my friend, I doubt it. I'm yet a long way from your brand of religion. But my hat is off to Alex, and if God indeed does give blessings, as you churchgoing folk believe, then I hope he'll give a double share to Alexander Carney."

As the year ended, John Sevier was involved in a desperate, hopeless enterprise: trying to breathe new life into the corpse of Franklin. What feeble pulse of the "new state" remained by now beat only in the lower counties, where the Indian dangers were greatest, where recent diplomatic overtures from North Carolina had threatened to turn the settlers unguarded into the hands of the Indians, and where Sevier's supporters were

therefore the most stalwart. Hard feelings remained between Carolina officialdom and John Sevier; the state
had recently voted to forgive all Franklinites who swore
allegiance to Carolina. The Colters, and even Cooper
Haverly, had joined the great majority of Overmountain
settlers in taking that oath.

But Sevier and his deepest core of followers even yet
held out hope for Franklin. Sevier was purportedly going
so far as to correspond with Spanish authorities in hopes
of securing loans to bolster his would-be state. Joshua
Colter heard those rumors and shook his head. Sevier
was determined; he had to give him that. But concerning
Franklin, perhaps he was also a little blind.

But one aspect of Sevier's efforts was of the most practical importance. Sevier held the post, under the feeble
authority of the new state's remnants, of leader of the
Franklin Council of Safety, bypassing Joseph Martin's authority as North Carolina brigadier general. Joshua had
no quarrel with this; John Sevier's leadership was badly
needed, because of a most unusual and chilling situation
developing in a hidden valley at Greasy Cove.

The word came first from the scouts who roamed the
rugged ridges where the Nolichucky spilled out of the
mountains. It spread through the informal militia chan-
nels to Sevier, and then Sevier's orders spread back
again: In early January, those ready to defend their
homes should muster at Buffalo Creek, which spilled
through a deep mountain valley about ten miles south
southeast of Jonesborough.

Joshua Colter, though technically no longer a Franklinite, rode to the muster site nonetheless, because he knew
what was prompting this call to arms. The recent successes of the Cherokees, Chickamaugas, and Creeks at
places such as Gillespie's had led the Indians to adopt a

new tactic. Normally, war-making was not a winter activity; the Indians would retire to their towns and await better weather before resuming battle. This year was different. Sevier's scouts reported a large Indian presence in the mountains around Greasy Cove. There was no evidence of the usual winter withdrawal.

The implication was clear. The recent Indian successes had made them change their usual practice. From the remote mountain valleys they would strike the settlements throughout the winter, then withdraw. By springtime many unaka scalps would be taken, many lives wiped out. The settlements would be weak and ready for an even more severe springtime thrashing.

On the snowy and bitterly cold ninth day of January, when the muster was complete, scouts came in with more specific news. John Watts, Kitegisky, and Bloody Fellow had been spotted among a large body of Indians camped in quickly erected huts at Flint Creek. Their movements and armament indicated they planned an attack, probably upon Sevier's encampment.

The rest of the day was spent by Sevier in close consultation with his officers. Meanwhile, the soldiers themselves made ready for battle, and then began the actual march toward the Indian encampment.

The next morning, as cold as the day before, saw the army still in motion. Lines of smoke rising to the sky from Indian campfires about a mile away guided the troops as they moved in phantom silence through the frozen forest. Joshua found one aspect of this advance particularly interesting. Among the armament being carried was a handful of "grasshopper guns," small swivel weapons fired on a tripod. Never before had he seen such guns being brought to play in Indian fighting.

A body of troops were sent to take the pass out of the

valley, the only means of escape for the Indians camped along the creek. At the same time, Sevier formed the rest of his troops into a line extending right and left.

Then the men settled in to wait. It had been agreed that a grasshopper gun would be fired as soon as the pass was secured; this would herald the beginning of the battle. Joshua's fingers played over the lock of his rifle as he awaited the boom. When it came, he started despite the fact he had been anticipating the sound, then immediately felt a surge of energy. His breath quickened.

The boom of the swivel gun brought the Indians out of their shelters. Immediately the riflemen hidden behind the trees edging the valley opened fire. Indians fell in great numbers.

The situation was much like the Settico orchard battle that had cost Cooper Haverly a finger, except this time the Indians were the ones trapped like bugs in the bottom of a bottle. In desperation they began fighting back, and actually succeeded in killing the operators of the swivel guns. And the weather helped them too. Marching through heavy snow at night had dampened much of the ammunition of the attacking army, causing much misfiring. At length Sevier, frustrated by the ammunition problems and now lacking the aid of the swivel guns, ordered his men to charge with knives, swords, and tomahawks. A hundred horsemen raced down to the foe, swords swinging and drawing blood, and behind them came the tomahawk men, among them Joshua Colter. Then came the remnants of the force that had blocked the pass, coming in to aid their fellows.

Throughout the rest of the fight, Joshua was much reminded of the Point Pleasant battle in which he had participated as a younger man. It too had been a substantially hand-to-hand fight, the bloodiest, most

painful, most personal kind of warfare. He took no pleasure in it beyond the wild and animal kind of pleasure
that comes from survival in the very face of hungry
death. And survive he did, at the expense of several enemies' lives.

It was substantially over by the time half an hour had
passed. Joshua stopped, his panting breath steaming in
the bitter air, and looked around at the bloodstained
snow. He could hardly recall a scene of more widespread
gore.

Well over a hundred Indians lay unmoving, their bodies melting the snow around them as the heat lingering
from life cooled in death. Long trails of blood and foot-
prints showed the track of wounded Indians who had
fled into the surrounding hills—and from the look of
matters, it appeared that almost all who had fled had
done so with injuries.

The rest were made prisoners, stripped of their weapons and left to stand glum and helpless, looking around
at the results of their own bitter defeat, while the whites
celebrated the fact that only five of their number had
died, with a mere sixteen wounded.

It was one of the most thorough victories John Sevier
had ever won, and almost certainly the bloodiest.

For a time after the battle, Joshua remained with
Sevier's force back at their muster camp on Buffalo
Creek. The Indian prisoners were kept there too, including a chief of some prominence, named Cotetoy,
along with the daughter of another chief, Little Turkey.
Sevier's plan was to take these home with him, where
they would be kept as captives but treated as guests, and

used to barter for other white prisoners whenever the opportunity arose.

At length Joshua was excused from duty and sent home. Word of the battle's success and the names of the killed and wounded had already been sent by messengers back to the settlements, so there was no pressing need for Joshua to hurry home to allay worries of his kin for his welfare. He hurried anyway. He was eager for his home and family, and besides that, it was still horrifically cold.

Darcy had a most odd expression on her face when she welcomed Joshua at the stockade. For a moment he was afraid she was ill, or very sad. Had someone died in his absence? Then she smiled, and he knew it could not be that. Her expression, he realized, was that of a person who was in great awe. A person who had seen a vision, or a ghost, or a miracle.

"Darcy, what is it?"

"Joshua, Nell Hice has come home. Three days ago it was. She came in with a group of travelers who had come from the west by way of the Kentucky road. And Joshua . . . one of those with her is Emaline Killefer. Alive and well, and very much with child."

Joshua drank in the astounding story related by Darcy, based on what Nell had told earlier. After the death of Dover Hice and the seeming miraculous return of Emaline and Jubal, Nell had decided it was time to go back home. She had then written and dispatched a letter to her family, informing them of her husband's death, Emaline's return, and her plans to come home with her companions at first opportunity, but the letter had never arrived. This was no surprise, given the Indian wars and the lack of a real postal system—but it did leave Nell's return unheralded, and therefore amazing when it came about.

"The child Emaline carries is Turndale's," Darcy said. "She escaped him with the help of one of the slaves who was captured with Owen off the flatboat. Remember Owen telling us about him? His name is Jubal. He came home with Nell too. It was him who got Emaline Killefer away from Turndale. They took a canoe, went far down the river, and were found by an old trapper. This trapper had met Dover Hice sometime before, and took Jubal and Emaline to the Hice cabin. But by this time Dover Hice was dead and Nell was thinking already of returning home. She gave the trapper some livestock in payment, took Emaline and Jubal in. They began looking for an eastbound escort, and finally found one. And now they're home again, right in the coldest part of winter, and it's surely the greatest miracle that's ever been!"

Joshua had to agree. He would have never dreamed that Emaline Killefer could survive her ordeal. He had assumed almost since the outset that she was probably dead.

Then it struck him. Emaline, safe and among her own people again . . . Nell, unmarried and home once more— and Owen was gone.

Even miracles, it appeared, could take a cruel twist.

Owen Killefer's journey to Kentucky was a deliberately slow one. He didn't much mind the cold; he was woodsman enough to live comfortably in winter weather. There wasn't any particular goal awaiting him at the end of his road, whatever road that might be. So he traveled steadily but without haste up the wilderness trail that led through the Cumberland Gap and into the wilds of Kentucky. It was a time of reflection and rest, and of seeking to accept the world as it was, not as he wished it would be.

He searched out Israel Coffman without difficulty; the blinded clergyman was well-known. Once he made himself and his friendship with Joshua Colter known, Owen found himself received with such warmth he hardly knew how to take it. Coffman took Owen into his home for a stay of several days, during which time he told his life story in detail. Coffman and his family made for a receptive audience. The tenderhearted preacher actually wept when Owen related how Turndale claimed to have murdered Emaline.

From Coffman's, Owen went a few miles farther to the home of Callum McSwain, and there found a welcome equally warm. The Roman coin around his neck served as a symbolic key to the hospitality of the McSwains, who were just as interested in Owen and his story as the Coffmans had been.

A few days after joining the McSwains, a band of five hunters, bound for hunting grounds along the Kentucky River, came by the McSwain cabin. McSwain had been host to this group once before and welcomed them now. Owen listened to the newcomers tell of their plans, and found inspiration in them. There was talk, questions, and when the hunters rode out again, Owen Killefer went with them.

"Be wary," McSwain warned. "There are bandits in the wilds about the river. Watch out for them."

The hunters rode on. Before they went out of sight, Owen halted his horse, turned, and waved broadly at Callum McSwain, then rode into the forest and out of sight.

*   *   *

Emaline Killefer's baby came the seventeenth day of February, the same day that John Sevier himself rode into Greeneville, strode into the courthouse and swore allegiance to North Carolina, leading to widespread speculation among those who witnessed it that surely, far below their feet, hell had just frozen over. The last shadow of Franklin was gone now; there would be no more pretense otherwise. Nolichucky Jack had fought the good fight, but now even he knew the fight was over.

Emaline's baby was born in Joshua and Darcy Colter's cabin; she had moved there, by general agreement, when her birthing time drew near, so Darcy could be ready at hand to assist, and because the crowding presence of silent Parnell Tulley made it inconvenient for her to remain within the Carney house. Further, Tulley was now ailing with a lung disease, and Nell feared Emaline might catch it, to the detriment of her child.

The infant was a girl, and when Emaline saw that, she cried hard, knowing that had the child been born in Tom Turndale's house, she would have died as her sister had died before her. For the first time since her rescue, Emaline was able to truly know, with her heart and will as well as her intellect, that she was free. And she owed it all to Jubal, and loved him for it.

He loved her too. From the moment he had taken her away from her captivity, he had felt intensely devoted to her. It was a new feeling for him. Never before had he known what it was to have the fundamental welfare of another human being in his hands—two humans, in fact, one born, the other awaiting birth. It had made him feel important in a way he had never felt before. And it made him feel toward Emaline in ways he knew were hopeless, doomed. Her skin was white, his was black, and that alone was enough to put an impassable void between them. What he dreamed of, when he dared let himself, could never be.

But if he could not have her for his own, he could do good things for her, help her in every way he could, give her what she wanted. He knew what she wanted most right now: to see her brother Owen. Both he and Emaline had left the Chickamauga towns not knowing that Owen was making his own escape. And now Owen, gone off to Kentucky, had no idea that the sister he had wished for so long was, as it were, resurrected from the dead. Jubal wanted to go find Owen and fetch him back, for Owen's sake, but mostly for Emaline's.

At the same time, Joshua was having similar thoughts on his own. It made him grin to picture how Owen's face would look as he learned that his sister was alive and safe, and that the woman he loved was home and widowed and openly thrilled to have learned that Dover Hice's former "barn boy" was neither dead nor captive, but alive and free.

Joshua talked the matter over with Darcy in private. Her own pregnancy was moving along now; the baby was anticipated sometime in late spring. Joshua intended to be home when it was born. If he was to go retrieve Owen, the time to do so was now.

Darcy touched his face tenderly. "Go, husband. Go and find him and bring him back. It's the only right thing."

"I could write a letter, send it in care of Israel or Callum, and give it to somebody going up that way so they could drop it off . . ." Joshua wished there were a postal route established. Such a thing was talked about, but it would be about three years before a regular mail courier would be carrying mail along the dangerous route into Kentucky, riding between the Holston and the town of Danville.

Darcy shook her head. "You could never know if the letter was even delivered, or whether Owen was even still there to receive it. He might not linger long in Kentucky, if he doesn't take to it. You've talked a long time of wanting to visit Israel and all our old friends. Now you've got good reason to do it. And take Jubal with you. He has talked of wishing he could go and bring back Owen, and he'll provide you company and protection."

Joshua smiled. "Very well, my dear lady. I'll go, and if Owen is there to be found, find him I will. And whatever happens, I'll be back in plenty of good time to see our own little one born into this world."

With Jubal at his side, Joshua Colter rode out of the little stockade and headed past the Pinnock Inn, up through the rolling countryside toward Kentucky. They hadn't traveled ten miles before Joshua quietly told Jubal to veer left into a ravine just large enough to hide them while giving them view of the narrow road on which they had been traveling.

"Why we doing this, Mr. Colter?"

"We're being followed."

A rider appeared within a minute. Jubal craned his neck, looking through the entwined branches at him.

"Why, that's—"

"Cooper Haverly," Joshua finished. "My own dear brother."

Joshua urged his horse up out of the ravine. Cooper jerked and looked alarmed, then relieved, when he saw who had so rapidly emerged.

"Cooper, why are you following us?"

Cooper grinned sheepishly. "I couldn't stand it, you heading into Kentucky without me. So I'm coming too."

"You up to it?"

"A body heals, you know."

Joshua twitched his brows. "Well, if you're bound on coming, come you will. Glad to have you along, Cooper."

They passed the great Long Island of the Holston and bore west into Carter's Valley. The valley, like most of the region, was steadily filling with new cabins and farmsteads, a process under way in this vicinity since the early 1770s. In the early 1780s one Thomas Amis had built himself a house of stone, a store, gristmill, and sawmill, settling in to stay. And now there was a town in the valley too, about three years old and called Rogersville after an Irishman named Joseph Rogers who had come to work for Thomas Amis at his store and ultimately married one of his daughters. In Carter's Valley, Joshua was put in mind of his neighbor John Crockett, whose boy David was now an active child of two. John Crockett's parents had died in an Indian raid in this very valley years before and lay buried in Rogersville.

They crossed Clinch Mountain, the Clinch River and the Powell, and reached Cumberland Gap. Beyond the gap Joshua struggled with emotion. In these hills his adoptive father Alphus Colter lay buried in a little forest cavern near the spot he had died while hunting with Joshua in 1783.

They went through the Yellow Creek valley, to the ford of the Cumberland River, and into the tangled mountains beyond. Many days and miles had fallen away behind them now, and for Joshua the travel was good. He was glad Cooper had joined them. The travel reminded him of past hunting trips and of the long exploratory jaunts he had undertaken in more youthful days.

They traveled until the trail divided, one branch reaching north toward the settlement established by Daniel Boone on the Kentucky River, the other extending more northeasterly toward Logan's Fort, and beyond that,

Harrodsburg. They traveled swiftly now, despite being tired. They were close to their destination, and the first stop would be the home of Israel Coffman.

Joshua's reunion with Coffman, the now-blind preacher who had become his friend and mentor many years before in the days he had been among the first to bear Christianity across the mountains, was as happy as Joshua had expected. Coffman, looking older and far more settled now than in his younger days of sight, embraced Joshua with a far more crushing strength than appearances would have suggested possible. Joshua was greeted with more restraint, but equal sincerity, by Coffman's wife, Virginia, and by their adopted son Judah, full-blooded Cherokee by birth. Joshua was astounded to see what a fine-looking young man Judah had turned out to be—and how closely he was beginning to resemble his late father, John Hawk.

They talked together of families and friendships, and Coffman was so eager to learn of the welfare of his many old Tennessee country acquaintants that more than an hour passed before Joshua could tell the preacher he had come hoping to locate Owen Killefer. Coffman brightened immediately. "Killefer! Yes, a fine young fellow. He did come, wearing your coin, they tell me, and talking of you. He told a remarkable tale—the loss of his family, captivity among the Chickamaugas, coming so close to finding his poor lost sister, only to learn she was murdered by her captor—"

"That's why I've come after him," Joshua cut in. "She wasn't murdered—it was a lie told to Owen by the scoundrel she had escaped from. And as I speak, she's at my own house, waiting for her brother to be found and brought back to her."

"God be praised! What a glorious thing!"

"Aye aye—and you say Owen is about?" Joshua seldom got excited, but now he couldn't help it.

"Indeed he is. But he left here many days ago, heading to Callum McSwain's."

"I don't know where Callum lives."

"Judah can guide you there. You will return to me before you go home again?"

"I will. It's good to see you, Israel. Mighty good."

"A gift from our Father above, Joshua. Now, let's see if we can roust up Judah."

The McSwain house stood some six miles from the Coffman cabin. Joshua rode into the yard at the heels of Judah's horse, and grinned when he saw Ayasta McSwain come to the door of the large cabin and squint at the newcomers. The squint spread to a wide-open stare as she realized who had come calling. Her young daughter Walini, who shared white and Indian heritage, gazed shyly from a nearby window, ducking behind the shutter when anyone glanced her way.

As happy as Ayasta was to see Joshua Colter and Cooper Haverly, whom she had known well in the Tennessee country, her greeting was reserved and dignified. Joshua had expected that. Ayasta had always been quiet, even stoic. There was no hiding the happy sparkle in her eyes, however. Joshua was glad to see it. It was visible evidence that her life was good and her home was happy.

Ayasta was much interested in Cooper, whom she had tended back to health after battle injuries earlier in the decade. Was he well? Did he have pain? How did he lose his finger? He told her of his more recent wounding, and that any pain he had was a result of it, not his prior one. He told her he remained deeply grateful to her for what she had done for him.

When Joshua told Ayasta whom he sought, she said, "He has already gone, toward the north with a band of hunters."

Joshua felt a sinking sensation. "Gone . . . how long?"

"Several days now."

"Maybe I can catch up with him, if you know where he was going. Callum might help me. Where is he?"

"Callum is gone as well, for two days. Some of the militia were called out. There are bandits to the north, killing and robbing along the river. The militia is searching to find them. And one of the militiamen came back by this morning; he had been hurt and was sent home. He told me that yesterday they found the bodies of men killed by the bandits."

Cooper said, "I'm loath to ask it, but might the travelers have been the group Owen had joined?"

Ayasta didn't know. Joshua's expression became grim. It would be devastating to come this near to finding Owen, bearing news for him that would turn his life around, only to have him killed when he was almost within reach.

Callum McSwain did not return that day. Ayasta let the visitors spread their blankets on the floor to make their beds. The next morning they were at their hearty breakfast when Callum McSwain, flanked by three other militiamen, rode into the yard. Joshua rose and looked out the window as McSwain caught sight of the extra horses in the stock pen and frowned. He said something to the others with him, dismounted, and carried his rifle toward the house.

"Ayasta?" Even after all his years on the American frontier, McSwain still sounded very Scottish.

"What are you doing, hollering for the woman you see nigh every day, when an old friend who's seldom seen at all has come to call?" Joshua said as he emerged.

The Scotsman looked flabbergasted, then broke into a wide grin. "Joshua Colter, you dolt and scoundrel! Is it you I'm looking at?"

"You don't trust your own eyes?" Joshua went to him, hand extended. "Good to see you, my friend."

"Aye aye, it is! Hang me! Is that Cooper Haverly yonder?"

Cooper replied, "It is, shy one finger from the last time I saw you—but the rest of me is still of one piece, I'm glad to say."

The necessary greetings, and for Jubal, introductions, were quickly made, and then McSwain asked Joshua what business had brought him.

"I've come to fetch Owen Killefer back home again," he said. "There's been something of a miracle to take place, and a sister he thought to be dead is waiting for him."

McSwain said, "The sister who was Indian captive?"

"Aye. He told you about her."

"He did." McSwain fell silent. His smile was gone.

"What is it, Callum?"

Silently the bearded Scot reached under his coat and pulled out a familiar thong. He handed it to Joshua, who closed his hand around the Roman coin it bore.

"The travelers who were attacked?"

"Aye." McSwain sadly shook his shaggy head. "What a sad thing! To have died not knowing that his sister yet lives!"

"And that the young woman he was in love with is now a widow, and eager for his homecoming," Cooper added.

"There is somewhat of the story I don't know, then," McSwain said.

"There is," Joshua said. He looked at the coin in his hand and tears welled in his eyes. "But right now I don't have the heart in me to tell it."

Over cups of a bittersweet tea Ayasta had brewed from a carefully blended mixture of various leaves, stripped bark, and root shavings, they listened to McSwain's story. Even though the tea was delicious, Joshua could hardly taste it, heartsick as he was.

The killers had been bandits, not Indians, all evidence indicated. The bandit problem along the wilderness trails had become fearsomely bad lately, almost as bad as the wartime days in the Tennessee country when outliers such as the late, infamous Elisha Brecht had been a bane to Colter's Rangers. McSwain had made the identification of the four dead bodies that were found; both were of the group of hunters whom Owen had joined at McSwain's own house. The men had been killed for their horses and gear, as best could be determined.

"Four corpses?" Cooper asked. "You said at the beginning there were six, including Owen. What of the other two?"

"Their corpses were there, but far out of reach. There's a cave, you see, a great pit, and the bodies obviously were being dumped when we came nigh and drove the murderers off. The four I identified were piled together at the edge of the hole, but the others were deep in the hole already."

"You could see them? You know one of them was Owen?"

"Well, I know that none of the corpses atop the hole

were him. And yes, I did see the bodies. We lit pine knots and dropped them in the pit, and by that light we saw them."

"The faces?"

"No . . ."

"Then you can't be certain one was Owen."

"But the coin, Joshua, the coin. It was lying at the edge of the hole. It had pulled off the body when it fell, I suppose, or maybe one of the ones doing the dumping yanked it off for a trinket and dropped it when he fled from us."

"Why didn't you bring out the two bodies from the pit?"

"We lacked the rope to reach them. Some others of the militia have volunteered to go back and do the sorry job. I have no doubt, sorry to say, that one of the bodies will be Owen's."

Joshua kept his promise and did visit Israel Coffman again before heading toward home again. Coffman urged a night's rest upon them, saying he desired good company under his own roof, and as it was late, Joshua agreed.

That night, as the others slept, Coffman sat up late by his fireside, talking to Jubal, and mostly listening. He had asked Jubal to tell him of his Indian captivity; he had an interest in such matters, he explained. Jubal talked at length, and Coffman listened in fascination.

The next morning the preacher made a surprising announcement. "I have given Jubal an invitation to remain with me for as long as he would like. Permanently, if he wishes and is able. There are reasons, he says, why he does not wish to return home again."

Joshua knew full well what those reasons were. He had watched Jubal with Emaline, and suspected his feelings toward her were deeper than simple friendship or affection. And for those feelings there could be no possible consummation. But there was a problem with Jubal's desire to stay in Kentucky, and Joshua felt obliged to point it out.

"You're not a free man, Jubal. You're property of Nell Hice."

"No, sir. Not no more. She's give me my freedom. Give it to me while we was coming back from the Cumberland country. I stayed on because it was what I wanted to do, not because I had to. Now I don't want to no more. I want to be here, with the preacher. He's a good man, better than any I've known. I can be of help to him, even when his son is grown and gone."

Joshua walked over and thrust out his hand. "Then may God be with you, Jubal. It's a good household you've come into."

Cooper and Joshua rode out that same morning, just the pair of them, sorrowful at parting so soon from their friends, but unable to bear the thought of leaving alive for any longer than was necessary the false expectations of those back home who awaited, vainly, the return of Owen Killefer.

The Roman coin was back in its old place around Joshua Colter's neck. He had worn it so many years that he had long ago ceased to be physically aware of its presence. It wasn't that way now. Every time he thought of Owen Killefer, the coin seemed heavy and cold against his chest.

They talked little along the southward way. The first day's journey was through beautiful, nippy weather; the second day, rain set in, falling so hard that Joshua and

Cooper gave up travel through the worst of it and took refuge beneath a big overhanging rock. Cooper whistled and whittled on a stick to pass the time. Joshua sat on his haunches, staring into the rain, and twisted the Roman coin between his fingers.

Abruptly he stood—and bumped his head painfully on the overhang. He swore, rubbed his injured skull, and said, "Cooper, we're going back."

"Back? Why?"

"I have to know for certain that the body in that pit is Owen's. I have to see it with my own eyes."

"That's fool talk! They'll have it pulled out and buried before we could even get back up there."

"Then they can dig it up again. I'm going to know for certain it's him."

"Callum found the coin."

"Not on the body. And all he saw was a body in a pit, and that by the light of a pine knot blaze. That don't prove a thing. He didn't see the face."

Cooper frowned. "You're stretching it mighty thin, brother. Who else would it be?"

"I don't know. But I've been sitting here thinking about all that time that you, me, Aaron Killefer, and everybody else were telling Owen that his sister was surely dead and gone, and that he ought to accept the truth and forget about her. Well, the truth didn't turn out to be the truth at all. She was alive the whole time. And I've been remembering back after the battle of Point Pleasant, when everybody was sure that I was killed because there was a body found all sliced up by the Indians, and this here coin on the ground beside it. They brung the coin home and gave it to Alphus and told him I was dead. But I wasn't. It just appeared that way. Now, at the moment it appears that Owen is dead—but we don't know it for certain. I won't go back to Emaline Killefer and Nell Hice and tell them he's gone unless I know, really know, that he is."

Cooper let out a slow, long breath, and scratched his chin. "Well, it's foolishness, most likely—but I been a fool before. Back we'll go, if that's what you want."

They arrived at Callum McSwain's just in time to see the Scotsman hurriedly saddling his horse. He looked at them riding in and frowned. "What the devil . . ."

"We've come back for a look at that corpse in the cave," Joshua said. "I couldn't shake it from my head that it might not be Owen."

"By the saints, my friend, you must have a second sight about you, that's all I can say. I was just mounting to ride out and fetch you back!"

"Why?"

"I've heard more of the dead men in the cave since you left. Neither was Owen! One was one of the hunters, and the other was an old gent, known to those who fetched him out to be one of our local bandits. He must have been killed during the attack and his body tossed in with the others."

Joshua turned and grinned firmly at Cooper. His instincts had been vindicated. "Then Owen may yet be alive," Joshua said.

"Maybe," Cooper said. "But why hasn't he returned, if he is?"

"Perhaps he's hurt, lost—I don't know. We'd best go find out. Callum, you can lead us to the place where the killing happened?"

"Aye, with ease."

"Then let's be off."

"And so we shall, as soon as I tell Ayasta what we're doing. Gor! A man never knows what's to happen, does he!"

They rode. Miles fell away behind them. They entered a land of rugged hills and very dense undergrowth. If not for the narrow trail laboriously sliced through it, they would have had to pick their way, inches at a time, through the nearly impenetrable tangle. After about three miles of this, the flora loosened its grip a little, the forest becoming more open and more easily traversable.

By now it was almost dark, and they had no option but to camp. They made no fire out of caution, ate a cold supper, and slept lightly.

They reached the cavern by mid-morning. No bodies were there now; they had all been taken away and buried. The earth all around was much marked with sign left by the abundant activity that had recently occurred here.

"Well, we're here—and what shall we do now?"

"Look, and think," Joshua said. "If Owen was with the group that was attacked, and if he wasn't killed, then he either ran away or was taken away. I can't figure any reason he'd be taken away; all the others were killed. So he must have run off. Now, the sensible thing to do would have been to come back to your house, Callum, and Owen is a sensible fellow. So the only thing I can figure is, he didn't come back because he wasn't able to."

"Lost?"

"I doubt it. Owen has a nose for the woods."

Cooper said, "Then he must have been too hurt to make it back . . . and if that's true, then he could be dead by now."

"He could be. And if he is, or is nigh to dead—" Joshua stopped talking abruptly, turned and walked down the trail, stopped at the top of a rise and looked around at the trees. Selecting one, he began to climb.

"What the devil is he up to?" Callum McSwain asked Cooper.

"I believe I know," Cooper replied. "Wait and see if I'm right."

Joshua clambered up, higher and higher, until he reached a point allowing him to see across the treetops. Cupping one hand over his eyes as he clung to the tree with the other, he scanned the sky. After a few minutes he began descending.

"Carrion birds?" Cooper asked.

Joshua nodded grimly. "Southeast, maybe a mile."

Now McSwain understood. He fell in behind Joshua and Cooper, who were already cutting southeastward through the woodlands. They were leading their horses; the undergrowth here was too heavy to allow for riding.

They had gone almost a mile when Joshua and Cooper glanced at each other. "Smell it?" Joshua said.

"Aye."

"I fear we're too late," Joshua said.

Before long even McSwain, whose sense of smell was far less keen than that of Joshua and Cooper, could not mistake the stench that the breeze bore through the forest. "Perhaps it's only a dead buck or bear," he said.

"Maybe so," Joshua replied.

And then, minutes later, they reached the thicket from which the smell exuded and above which great birds circled just above treetop level. Joshua steeled himself for what he would find, and pushed his way into the thicket.

It was Owen, lying on his back, his trousers leg sliced open to reveal a wounded leg thoroughly gangrenous below the knee. The thicket was heavy with the stench of dead flesh, misted with the foul smell of the bodily wastes in which Owen lay.

"Oh, God . . ." Cooper said.

Joshua knelt beside Owen, put his hand on his chest. He looked back over his shoulder at the others, who were struggling to keep from retching. "He's alive."

"Alive?" Astonishment overcame repulsion, and they moved closer, gathering around the supine form.

Owen was alive, though barely. His pallor was grayish-white, his eyes three-quarters closed, his dry lips cracked and open. Every shallow breath came slowly and with effort. Joshua leaned close to him.

"Owen? It's Joshua Colter talking to you. We've found you, Owen. We'll help you if we can."

He did not answer, but it seemed to Joshua that Owen's eyelids gave the faintest of flutters and that his breathing became more rapid.

"Your leg is in a bad way, Owen. The flesh is putrid and dead. There's no saving it, if we're to save you."

"Joshua, is there any point in even trying to—"

"Yes, Cooper. There's a point. If we take the leg, we may yet save his life."

Cooper blanched, but nodded sharply. "I'll give what help I can."

"And so shall I," McSwain said.

"There's no time to spare," Joshua said. "Cooper, build a fire. I want to sear my blade—and it will be up to both of you to hold him, because even like he is, I fear he's going to feel it. Find a stout stick for him to bite on."

When it was over, Joshua Colter sat beside the pale, tourniqueted body of Owen Killefer and struggled with his feelings. Taking the leg had been a horrific experience, especially at the beginning of the crude surgery. Owen had writhed and cried out, and then, blessedly, unconsciousness had come. Now Joshua watched in desperate hope for any sign of improvement. By nightfall none had come that he could detect—but life lingered. As long as it did, he would not give up hope.

Cooper built a small fire as the sun set, and cooked a meal. Joshua declined to eat; he had no interests now except the welfare of the young man upon whose body he had so dramatically carved. Had he been right to do it? He was no physician. And if Owen died now, how could he know if his rough surgery had slowed or hastened that death?

Joshua was drained of strength and ached for sleep, but when it tried to take him, he shook it off. He would not rest until he knew what the outcome of this would be. And so he sat, the night dragging on, the morning seeming an eternity away.

Winter passed, and Parnell Tulley died a death as peaceful as his life had been violent. His passing came in the night, while he slept, and when Alexander Carney found him, he actually wept in sorrow. Tulley as he was at the end was far different than Tulley as he had been. He had been a sad, harmless thing at the last, cut off from the world around him and a danger to no one. Any bitterness or fear Alexander had felt toward him was long gone.

At Darcy Colter's invitation, they buried Tulley on Colter land, beneath a shady oak tree. There was no funeral as such, only a gathering of people around the grave, which Alexander dug with his own hand.

"He was a hard and sinful man, Lord," Alexander

prayed aloud when the cloth-wrapped body was in its final place. "We pray, Lord, for whatever mercies may be found for him, and in trembling are reminded that we too will stand before your judgment."

Standing to the side and holding her baby girl, Emaline Killefer watched Alexander and thought, as she had many times in the past weeks, how different a man he was than Tom Turndale. Where Turndale had been evil and selfish, Alexander was gentle and kind, good to others. A better man than Emaline had ever known, even among her own family.

It was spring; the day had begun with soft rain and turned clear and bright. Now it was nearing evening. The baby moved in Emaline's arms and turned its mouth toward her breast. Emaline felt a hand touch her elbow, and turned to find Nell Hice at her side.

"Come, Emaline. There's the most beautiful hill yonder, with the maples atop it. I've wanted to go climb it since the first day I saw it. Let's go now, you and me. You can suckle your little one there while we watch the sun set."

Emaline smiled her agreement, and the young women set off together. Emaline had grown very affectionate toward Nell, who had shown her much kindness. Sometimes at night Emaline would awaken and look around her, thinking for a moment she was again in Tom Turndale's house. Then she would realize the truth, and relief would overwhelm her, sometimes to tears.

Life was good here, despite its uncertainties and dangers. Among the Colters and the Carneys, Emaline was healing, a little more every day, and learning again to be herself. She talked seldom, especially in large groups. Silence had become such a refuge and companion for her in captivity that now she hardly knew how to live again without it. Talking came easiest when she was with Nell. To Nell she could reveal her private thoughts with ease. And Nell herself spoke with equal freedom back to her. This was how Emaline had come to know that Nell loved Owen.

So far, Joshua Colter, Jubal, and Cooper Haverly had not returned from Kentucky. Nor had word come from any other source as to whether their quest to find Owen had been successful. By now Emaline had substantially given up hope. If the searchers had found Owen, surely they would have brought him back already. Something must have gone wrong.

She didn't allow herself to think about it much, but secretly she feared Owen was dead.

The baby suckled at her breast, its mouth warm and wet and tugging. Emaline caressed the little head and loved her daughter with an almost painful intensity. That the baby had grown from Tom Turndale's seed, that she was in the eyes of the law illegitimate, made no difference in how Emaline felt about her. She had learned that from bad things good ones could come, and that when this happened, the bad had no power to overcome the good. Her daughter was her daughter, a person unto herself, a life to be loved regardless of origins.

Emaline drew her baby closer, bent her face down to kiss it. Nell was talking, pointing out the most beautiful aspects of the sunset, but Emaline wasn't really listening. Right now she was simply feeling the life within her, and within her child, and enjoying it. At the moment it seemed that was all she needed.

Nell Hice stood abruptly. "Listen!"

Emaline said, "I don't hear—" then cut off, because now she did hear. A high, thin noise, musical . . . a fiddle.

Emaline rose and went to Nell's side. "Where is it coming from?"

"The forest, I think—yonder! Yes! Hear it now? It's louder . . ."

And with it now, a voice. Not a particularly good one either. A man, singing at the top of his lungs and occasionally hitting the right notes as if by happy accident. Nell's eyes flashed wide. "That's Cooper Haverly's voice!"

Emaline heard it plainly now, the familiar words of a song often sung:

> "Come along, my darling,
> Come and journey far with me
> to a home beyond the mountains
> where the land is broad and free . . ."

"Oh, I can see them!" Nell said, pointing. "Oh, Emaline, they've come back!"

"How many are there?" Emaline asked intensely, shifting her baby in her arms as she reclosed her homespun dress. Cooper's voice rang out even louder, rough as a corn cob, but to the ears that welcomed it, ruggedly beautiful.

> ". . . where we'll raise a home and family,
> in a cabin wide and low,
> and we'll rally in the canebrake
> and shoot the buffalo!"

"I can't tell how many—can't see them all just yet. There's Cooper, singing up a storm, and Joshua Colter, and that must be Jubal . . . no, no, it's a white man—it's him playing the fiddle! It's the Scotsman McSwain

perhaps—I know he plays the fiddle. He must have
turned with them for some reason. I don't see Jubal;
must be—" Nell caught her breath sharply. "Oh, God
above, God be praised, Emaline, it's Owen! It's Owen! I
can see his face from here! It's him, Emaline! Your
brother has come home!"

They ran down the hill together, the babe bouncing in
Emaline's arms. The sun sat on the edge of the mountains now, red as ruby and close enough to touch.

EPILOGUE

Jonesborough, 1800

ndrew Jackson leaned back on the tavern bench and rested his shoulders against the wall, his fingers locked behind his head and his eyes fixed on the crag-faced, gray-haired frontiersman before him. The eleven years that had passed since Jackson last talked to this man had changed both of them. But much was still the same. The frontiersman's eyes were as sharp and clear as ever, despite the crow's-feet wrinkles around them. His form was every bit as lean. But the Roman coin he had always worn no longer hung on its thong around his neck.

Joshua Colter took a sip from his cup, swallowed, and cleared his throat. As always, he was not much used to long talking, and such was what he had just engaged in. Andrew Jackson had been an eager listener; there was much he had not known about the people among whom

424

he had briefly made his livelihood as a lawyer in the pr
vious decade.

"So Alexander Carney married the Killefer girl!" Jackson said reflectively, mulling over what information
Joshua had already given. "Well, I'm happy for him—and
for her. She could have fared much worse for a man."

Joshua Colter gave Jackson a wry look. "Andrew, I'm
surprised to hear you say that. It was Alexander who you
so shamed that day at the Greasy Cove horse race. Do
you recall that? You challenged his manliness and called
him a coward."

Jackson winced. "I was a much younger fellow then,
and too headstrong for my own good. I still am, for that
matter! But I confess to you, Joshua, that I came to regret my words of that day. In reflection I could see what
they must have done to Mr. Carney's standing among his
peers."

"It was no easy time for him, but he made it through.
As for his standing, he earned that back a little at a time,
proving himself a man in his own way. And not a bad
way at that. Through kindness. I don't reckon I've ever
known a man more kind."

"Where is Alexander now?"

"Lexington, Kentucky. He and Emaline have four children now, I believe. Or five? I don't recall. Darcy keeps
up with such more than I do."

"And how is Cooper?"

"Restless. The same as me. Tired of farming, tired of
being crowded, tired of all the good game being long
gone from the forests. I think he's even tired of having
no Indians left to fight."

"He and I would be at odds on that matter," Jackson
replied. "So what does Cooper plan to do? Adjust to the
changes of our times, or go looking for new territory?"

He's been talking some about moving on," Joshua said. He took another drink. "I should say, he and me have been talking."

"What? You would move on to wilder country at your age?"

"I'm a half century old, Andrew. If I ain't got thirty good years left in me at the least, I'll be deuced surprised. I plan to dance a jig with Darcy on my hundredth birthday."

"I don't doubt you'll do it." Jackson stood. "Come now, Joshua. Let's stretch our legs a bit. Too long on the bench, whether in court or tavern, makes my bones grow stiff."

They walked through the town together, talking quietly, until a voice behind them called Joshua's name. They turned and saw a slender man of about thirty coming toward them. He moved fairly swiftly despite the fact that one of his legs was gone and he walked upon a carved wooden substitute. His hair was beginning to thin and there were visible lines around his mouth and eyes, but all in all he retained a youthful look.

"Hello, Owen!" Joshua said. "Come say hello to Andrew Jackson, an old friend of mine."

The two shook hands. "Owen Killefer, I presume? I've just been enjoying hearing your remarkable story," Jackson said. "Quite a pleasure to see you."

"The pleasure's mine, Mr. Jackson. I had heard you were in town, and when I saw you pass with Joshua, I decided to say hello."

"Andrew's an important man now, Owen," Joshua said. "He's . . . Andrew, what's that title you carry around after your name these days?"

"Judge of the Superior Court of Law and Equity. One of three in the state of Tennessee holding that position."

"Yes, indeed. That's mighty outstanding. I'm p
you, Andrew."

With Owen joining them, the men continued t
walk. "You move well on that peg leg," Jackson con
mented to Owen.

"Thank you. I get by. The truth is, I hardly notice it
now, I'm so used to it. Joshua here carved it—did you
know that?"

"Carved off the old leg and whittled him out a
wood one to replace it while we waited around in Kentucky for him to heal up," Joshua said with a grin. "He
wore that same peg the day we arrived home again.
Callum McSwain—you don't know Callum, do you,
Andrew?—he came with us. Fiddled us through the final
stretch, with Cooper singing like a parson. We scarce got
back in time for me to see the birth of my third child.
She came along a week or two after I rode through the
stockade gate."

"Girl or boy?"

"Girl. And since then, two more boys."

"Quite a houseful."

"Aye. But I like it that way. Especially since my oldest,
Will, has took off on his own. He's been gone for seven
years. And I still miss him bad. He wears my coin now,
the one my father gave me for an amulet when I was just
a boy."

"Where is Will?"

Joshua smiled. "Darcy and I received a letter from him
two weeks ago. It was nigh two months old when it
reached us, but I expect his situation is the same. He's
on the Missouri River, on a creek called the Femme
Osage. Living among the kin of old Daniel Boone and his
wife. He wants me to come, maybe settle there with him.
He talked like he'd met a woman he might just marry."

ooked wistful. "I'd surely like to see that country
, Andrew. It's across the big river, you know." His
e began to grow more animated. "And the Indians in
ose parts say that way off in the west, there's mountains that make them around here look like hills. Big
mountains of stone, reaching all the way to the sky.
Wouldn't it be a thing to see! Wouldn't it be a place to
hunt!"

"Do you have children, Owen?" Jackson asked.

"Nell and me, we have four of them. Had a fifth, and
lost that one to fever. But four's aplenty for us. A fine
family."

"I'm sure." Jackson stopped. "Well, we've reached my
quarters, and I'll take my leave. Owen, it's been a pleasure. Joshua, good to have seen you again. Give my best
to Darcy, and God go with you."

"I've come to believe he always has, Andrew."

The dusk brought a chill, and with it one of those rare
moments when the sun makes a last, valiant thrust
through the clouds to reaffirm its kingship of the skies
before night comes inevitably on. A glorious ray burst
from behind the cloud mantle and struck the mountains,
drawing Joshua Colter and Owen Killefer to a halt on
their homeward journey, just so they could watch the unexpected show before it faded.

So much had changed in this land! The Indians were
subdued; the feared Dragging Canoe himself was dead
for these past eight years, not of war but of a failing
heart. John Sevier was no longer the handsome scourge
of Cherokee and Chickamauga, but the first governor of
Tennessee, a state four years old, successor to the terri-

tory that the region had become shortly afte
the Franklin effort.

Owen broke the silence. "Would you really lea
Joshua, and go join Will?"

Joshua smiled. "Maybe. I don't know. Sometimes I
ready, and then I look around me like this, and think o
all the people I've known here, the ones gone on. My
mother, buried where Fort Loudoun stood, and Alphus,
lying up in Kentucky. Little Carpenter, Israel Coffman ... John Hawk. I've known many people worth
knowing here in this place, Owen, you being among
them. Don't know for sure I could leave it now. Not for
good, at least."

"Me, I'll never go, not even for a little while," Owen
said. "I'm happy here. Me, Nell, the children. I've got all
a man could ever want."

"Then cherish it, Owen. Cherish it every day, and give
thanks every night."

They watched the sunset a few moments longer, in silence, then turned their mounts toward home.

AFTERWORD

THE CANEBRAKE MEN is the third in a trilogy of novels set on the frontier that became Tennessee. Like its two predecessors, THE OVERMOUNTAIN MEN and THE BORDER MEN, both published by Bantam Books, this third novel entwines fiction around a framework of fact in what I hope is a compelling and entertaining manner.

Those familiar with Tennessee frontier history will recognize that history itself provides the basic outline for all three novels. Though the central characters such as the Colters, Haverlys, Killefers, and Carneys are fictional, many of the characters with whom they interact actually existed in the roles and contexts presented. Many of the plot events in the three novels actually occurred substantially as described, and with only a few exceptions, the regions, towns, and waterways mentioned actually existed.

Most events in the story involving historical characters

either occurred as depicted or are imaginative[?] preted and expanded from actual events. For exa[?] young and cocky Andrew Jackson did ride [?] Jonesborough on a racing horse, leading a pack of [?] hounds and carrying a brace of pistols. The row with Alexander Carney over the killed dog, however, is a fictional addition. Jackson did practice law in Jonesborough, and did fight a duel with his professional peer, Colonel Waightsell Avery. The related "bacon" joke really happened. So also did the Greasy Cove horse race, in which Jackson lost both the competition and his temper.

Several of the novel's fictional characters were loosely suggested by figures out of history, though they are not simply disguised versions of any historical personages. Some aspects of the fictional Parnell Tulley, for example, were suggested by the historical figure of Russell Bean, son of Tennessee's purported first permanent settler. Russell Bean was as rugged and rough a character as has ever graced any frontier. Branded on the hand for thievery, he is said to have bitten the brand mark from his palm as a show of contempt. This incident inspired inclusion of a similar act by Tulley in THE CANEBRAKE MEN—though I opted to have Tulley use a knife to perform his self-surgery.

The captivity of fictional Owen Killefer was loosely suggested by the historical captivity of one Joseph Brown, who was taken prisoner by the Chickamaugas in 1788 while traveling with his family on a flatboat to claim land on the Duck River. Many details of Owen's life in captivity are based on portions of the Brown story, chronicled by Brown himself in a famous and fascinating captivity narrative that has survived in several versions. The Tom Turndale character also has his inspiration out of the Brown narrative. His character was suggested by the his-

...igure Tom Tunbridge, an Irish deserter from the
...n army who had taken up residence among the In-
...s.

As this trilogy closes, I must thank those who have
made it possible, particularly noting Greg Tobin, Tom
Dupree, Don D'Auria, Tom Beer, and Richard Curtis. A
special word of thanks in relation to THE CANEBRAKE MEN
goes to Cherel Henderson, administrative assistant for
the East Tennessee Historical Society, who generously
shared her detailed research on James Hubbert with me,
and in so doing diverted me from following the tradition
that lays the bulk of the blame (wrongly, her research in-
dicates) for the Old Tassel murder upon Hubbert's shoulders. Most of all, thanks to the readers who have been so
liberal in their compliments for the first two books in this
trilogy.

And, as always, I thank my family for their continuing
love and support. They are the greatest of my many
blessings.

CAMERON JUDD

Greene County, Tennessee
August 29, 1992

Turn the page for a special note from
CAMERON JUDD
about his next novel for Bantam.

A Note to My Readers:

I'm at work on a project that has me quite excited: a novel drawn from the life of one of America's most famous frontiersmen, David "Davy" Crockett. If all goes as planned, it will hit the bookstore shelves in 1994. It's going to be a worthy yarn, I believe, probably the best I've done to date. The working title is *Crockett of Tennessee*.

I wish I could claim credit for coming up with the idea for this Crockett novel on my own, but honesty constrains me. The concept was actually the brainchild of a Bantam Books editor two or three years ago, and as soon as I heard it, I wondered why I hadn't thought of it myself.

Perhaps it was a case of propinquity, of being blinded to the subject's merits simply by being too close to it. There are reminders of Crockett and his kin all around me. Within a ten minute drive from my house is the spot where Crockett was born (not on a mountaintop, as the song says, but beside a river) and where he spent his earliest years, when he was still so small as to have, as he later put it, "no knowledge of the use of breeches," having never "had any nor worn any." North of nearby Greeneville (where Walt Disney's famed Crockett movie had its big screen world premiere, complete with a visit

435

ckskin-clad Fess Parker, back in the 1950s) is the
where David's uncle shot a man in a hunting acci-
t that the boy witnessed and later recorded in his au-
biography. To Greeneville's south is the site of the
Crockett family's grist mill, which was washed away by a
flood in 1794, when David was a boy. Nearby Rogersville
is where David's grandparents were killed by Creek and
Chickamauga raiders, and where a deaf-and-mute uncle
was taken into a long Indian captivity during which he
reputedly labored in a secret silver mine. And to my
west, in Morristown, is the site of a tavern that Crockett's
impoverished father operated, from which a youthful David set out on some remarkable, far-ranging adventures.
There are plenty of other Crockett-related sites scattered
across Tennessee, following the westering path that finally led Crockett to Texas and the Alamo.

With Crockett's legacy so deeply permeating my environs, perhaps it was fated that I would eventually write
about him. Certainly it seems that various circumstances
of my life have shuttled me into a position to make such
a project quite natural. In 1986, when I was still in the
newspaper business in Greeneville, the State of Tennessee scheduled what was to be a massive 200th birthday
celebration of "Davy" Crockett, focusing on his Greene
County birthplace. Our newspaper became involved in
publicity and special publications for the celebration,
working closely with state historical interpreters and
planners. For that summer I was immersed in anything
and everything Crockett. By the time the celebration
ended, I had been Crocketted nearly to death, and would
have hardly cared had I never heard the name again. But
now, with the fatigue long behind and *Crockett of Tennessee* in the works, I am grateful for that "summer of
Crockett," for the resources it opened to me, for the his-

torical authorities I met or became aware of, fo.
all experience of getting to know the "Gentlen.
the Cane" far better than I would have otherwise.

And he is a gentleman worth knowing. Tho.
Crockett legends and tall tales began mixing with fac
even during his lifetime (a process he sometimes helped),
the real David Crockett still shines through. Crockett
was a man invigorated by the strength and high spirits of
the Scots-Irish, but tempered and matured by an influential early contact with gentle Quakers. He knew poverty
and failure firsthand, having watched his own father go
to his grave with little to leave behind but debt. He received almost no formal education, yet became a relatively influential figure in state and national politics,
largely by the clever use of an intuitive wit and charm
that appealed to the common voter. He knew romantic
love, successful and otherwise, and performed his "court-
ing" in an unsophisticated yet formalized frontier style.

He was a natural humorist; his contributions to American humor can be traced in the later writings of Mark
Twain and others. And Crockett was a man who could
stretch or shrink the truth with the best of Twain's characters, yet who could record, with an undefensive honesty unusual for its day, terrible sufferings inflicted upon
Creek Indians by an army of which he himself was a
part. He could brag with one breath and exude humility
with the next.

Crockett is a man of many literary and cinematic incar-
nations, all of which (including Crockett's own accounts
of himself) have mixed fiction with fact in varying de-
grees. To claim my novel will not do the same would be
to contradict the very fact that it is a novel, not a
straightforward history, and to ignore the reality that the
historical record of portions of Crockett's life is scant and

.tain, and must be supplemented by "educated
and cautious imagination. There is not even to-
.eement among genealogists about the names of
.d's brothers and sisters!

Nevertheless, there is much to be known of Crockett
as he was, and of the world in which he lived. In
Crockett of Tennessee, it is my desire to capture as much
of the man and his world as I can, and to present them
in the context of a story that is compelling, dramatic, and
appealing. Where that story deals with historical fact, it
will be as accurate as I can make it; where the facts are
supplemented by probabilities and a novelist's imaginative license, this will be done in a manner historically
plausible and, I fully intend, thoroughly entertaining.

Crockett's tale is a story worth the telling . . . and
worth the reading. I'm having a lot of fun with it, and
when the book reaches your hand, I believe you'll have
fun with it, too.

CAMERON JUDD

Greene County, Tennessee
December 3, 1992